Amy Myers was born ... ... in L... ... literature, she was director of a London publishing company and is now a writer and a freelance editor. She is married to an American, and they live in a Kentish village on the North Downs. She also writes under the name Harriet Hudson.

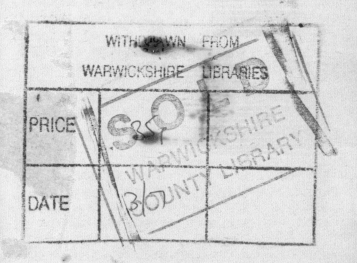

Also by Amy Myers

Murder makes an Entree
Murder at the Masque
Murder at Plum's
Murder in the Limelight
Murder in Pug's Parlour

Writing as Harriet Hudson

The Wooing of the Katie May
The Sun in Glory
When Nightingales Sang
Look for me by Moonlight

Murder Under the Kissing Bough

Amy Myers

HEADLINE

First published in 1992
by HEADLINE BOOK PUBLISHING PLC

First published in paperback in 1993
by HEADLINE BOOK PUBLISHING PLC

10 9 8 7 6 5 4 3 2 1

ISBN 0 7472 4014 0

Printed and bound in Great Britain by
HarperCollins Manufacturing, Glasgow

HEADLINE BOOK PUBLISHING PLC
Headline House
79 Great Titchfield Street
London W1P 7FN

For Natalie
with love

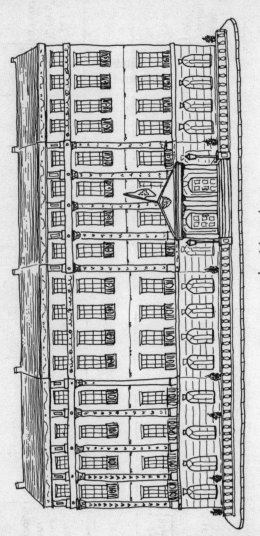

Cranton's Hotel

1st floor hotel plan

Bathroom	Bathroom	Bathroom		Spare	Spare	Spare	Linen room	House-keeping room
Service lift								

| Mr and Mrs Harbottle | Miss Ethel Pembrey | Miss Evelyn Pembrey | Maj Frederick Dalmaine | Miss Gladys Guessings | | Sir John Harnet | Miss Rosanna Pembrey | Marquise Bella de Castillon | Marquis Gaston de Castillon | Col Arthur Carruthers |

2nd floor hotel plan

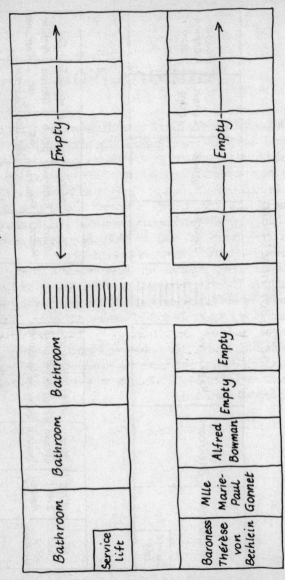

Author's Note

This novel is set at the close of the nineteenth century, and I should therefore explain that although there was debate on the matter, the Victorians greeted the dawn of the new century on 1 January 1901, and not 1900.

In 1900 Portman Square was generally acknowledged one of the handsomest in London, but very little of its original splendid architecture now remains. Cranton's Hotel is fictitious, and in 1900 the original Adam houses were still standing in its place.

I am very grateful for help received from the Auguste Escoffier Foundation at the Musée de l'Art Culinaire at Villeneuve-Loubet, for the expert guidance of my agent Dorothy Lumley, to Adele Wainwright and all departments of Headline Book Publishing, and to the publisher Lionel Leventhal of Greenhill Books, who generously gave me Jac Weller's classic and readable *Wellington at Waterloo* which he has recently reissued.

A.M.

Prologue

It clawed at his face. It fought his every breath. He drew deep, gasping gulps of air, then spluttered as the fog caught at his throat in triumph. Damp and oppressive, the blanket that had woven itself so insidiously round him distorted reality, seeking its final victory over his mind. A London Particular, they called it. Particular what? he thought savagely, ridiculously, his head swimming partly from the medicine he was taking for the perpetual *rhum* that seemed to single him out for a vicious attack each winter, and partly from disorientation in the fog.

Auguste Didier gulped; he was, he assured himself, a practical man. His French logic would come to his aid, and subdue the wild phantoms of imagination that were the heritage of his English mother. He had, he reasoned, set out from Albion Street such a short time ago that he could hardly be far from it now, despite his blundering by error into the old cemetery of St George. Here lay buried Mrs Radcliffe, authoress of the *Mysteries of Udolpho*, whose Gothic horrors it would not be wise to dwell on at the moment. It had taken some time to find his way out again, and relief had made him careless – he had turned a corner, but which? And where was he now? Logic also reminded him that every mortal person and every wise animal was safely at home, and he would do well to follow their example speedily, but the fog seemed to thicken. Curzon Street and London's Mayfair had never seemed more attractive.

1

'I will take basil, and balm, catnep and clivers,' he told himself fervently. 'I will take linseed, liquorice; I will take Monsieur Soyer's *lait de poule*, but never, never again will I take Armstrong's Black Drop medicine for colds.'

Dizzily he clung to a lamp-post, and tried once more to think where he might be. Connaught Place – this was Connaught Place. Of course. Relief flooded over him. This was the site of the Three-legged Mare, the old Tyburn tree where so many had perished in public executions, where bones were still found sometimes during digging work. The atmosphere still seemed foetid, even in this November of 1900, the threshold of the twentieth century. In this thick fog, relieved only by the occasional pool of dim light from a street light, it was all too easy to think of the murderers that had died here. Murder. . .

He shivered. Murder indeed. This was a fog. Murder had not touched his life now for well over a year; his visits to dear Egbert Rose now had little to do with the business of Scotland Yard. They had been free to concentrate on the important matters of life, to discuss the intriguing subject of a cuisine fit for the twentieth century.

Absorbed in this compelling subject he cautiously worked his way along, crossing roads hurriedly as the occasional carriage, its sound deadened in the fog, loomed up as a monstrous shape in the gloom. One came upon him so suddenly he had to run, stumbling, catching his breath with painful difficulty, as he cannoned into iron railings on the opposite side of the road. Clinging to them, he worked his way along in the direction of Grosvenor Square. He should turn to the right surely, down South Audley Street. But there was no right turn. And these railings, they were not those of Mayfair, he realised, fighting an irrational panic welling up inside him. These houses towering up into the fog above him were taller, more uniform. He must still be north of Oxford Street, and once again lost.

He smiled at the irony. He, Auguste Didier, born in the sun of Provence. What was he doing here soaked in the fogs and rains of England? For a moment he could not think what kept him here.

'Custard tansy,' he reminded himself firmly. 'Quince sauce. Marsh-grazed mutton. . .'

But even delights such as these failed to calm him. He stopped, trying to concentrate on a reasoned plan to work out where he was. Where there were railings there must eventually be steps to a door.

He laughed at himself, glad at this evidence that his powers of detection were not deserting him. Then the unpleasant thought occurred to him that unless he found out where he was he might never see Egbert again. Could one die of fog? A nameless master chef found dead on the pavement only yards from his home. Panic began to grip him. He would knock on the nearest door, plead for sanctuary. Nay, demand it. The owner would welcome the famous Auguste Didier. Even Mrs Marshall, who ran a rival cooking school to his, would open her doors to Auguste Didier on a night like this. Rival? Did he say rival? Nonsense. There was no comparison. He, Auguste, ran an establishment to teach true cuisine, the highest perfection of the art of cookery. Mrs Marshall –

He stopped. He knew where he was at last. He could just make out the name over the door as the fog swirled around it. Cranton's Hotel. Though it was a hotel no longer, for its doors had closed for the last time; the rooms that had entertained Lord Byron, Robert Browning and Thomas Carlyle were shabby and dusty, the famous wood panelling left to rot after the last of

3

the Crantons had died some years ago. Now the hotel was but a sad reminder of days that were gone. Someday, he too would have a hotel, he told himself, a hotel whose kitchens would rival those of his old master, Auguste Escoffier, at the new Carlton Hotel.

Heartened, he pulled his Raglan overcoat more closely round his neck, as a swirl of fog left its damp trail on his face and neck. He knew now that he was at the tradesmen's entrance in the mews at the back of the hotel, which fronted Portman Square. He mused on all the tradesmen's entrances he'd known in his life. Would he ever earn the right to go in the front entrance? Firmly he reminded himself of all he had to be grateful for, yet as the fog pressed in upon him, the task was difficult.

'Here? *At Cranton's?* Christmas?'

The voice, a woman's, was hoarse, coming from nowhere, urgent and compelling, yet he could see no one in the fog, deepened by the gloom of late afternoon. A murmur in answer. Another woman. Strange. Out alone at this time of day? And one voice was cultured, the other seemed rough. They could only be a few feet away from him, though the sound was both magnified and distorted by the fog.

He could offer his services in escort. They might travel the better in company.

'*J'arrive!*' he cried out eagerly.

He left the security of the railings and plunged towards where he guessed the two women might be, just as the fog was pierced by a strange sound, a gurgle, a muffled choking. Then nothing. Then another gurgle. Auguste stood for a second transfixed. Someone needed help. Which way to go? What had happened? The noises seemed to have come from all round him, the impression of someone, something passing close.

And then there was nothing but the oppressive fog swirling down again.

He ran blindly for a few yards, tripped and fell. He scrambled to his feet and limped another few yards, fog and fear catching him in their toils within this world of grey. But now the grey was broken by another colour. Red. Red blood oozing over the pavement in front of him. And the huddled body of a woman – no, a girl.

In an unreal world, he knelt down, turning her slightly until sightless eyes gave him the answer to his fear. He hardly needed to feel for a pulse. She was dead. Slowly he stood up and watched a trickle of blood run into the roadway, as the fog closed once more around him.

Chapter One

Torn by conflicting emotions, Auguste dithered at the door to the kitchens. How could he entrust the important matter of the duck forcemeat to a new untried chef? Yet how could he superintend the work without offering the greatest insult one chef could offer another – lack of trust? Perhaps in this case he might plead justification as he did not know Signor Fancelli's work. . .

No. Auguste's hand removed itself reluctantly from the knob of the door as its owner reminded himself that he was both *maître d'hôtel* and host. And Mine Host, he told himself regretfully, did not involve himself in the cooking, however great the temptation. The merest eye on the kitchen and tables would be all that was called for, save that he had reserved for himself the task of final preparation of the boar's head, and moreover intended to head the procession bearing the boar's head in for Christmas luncheon. He deserved it, Auguste told himself defiantly. After all, what was the point of being the host if other people had all the exciting duties?

The kitchen door flew open from the other side and Auguste blushed lest he be thought to be loitering at the door. But Antonio Fancelli did not seem to notice.

'Monsieur Didier, the pudding,' he said accusingly. 'You wished to stir him. You 'ave no come.'

'Ah.' Auguste's chest swelled. Maître Escoffier, after all, would not allow anything important to escape his eagle eye, not even the dreaded but so important plum pudding. The stirring was but a pretext to ensure proper attention had been paid to it. His mind flew back a few years to stirring the Christmas pudding with Maisie, the ritual so beloved of the English in honour of the Three Kings. Dear Maisie. He smiled a little ruefully. How could he have refused her request? And after all, there was no certainty that some villainy was to take place at Cranton's. He carefully refrained from thinking of murder. He had had quite enough of murder. . .

No one had believed him. Not even Inspector Egbert Rose of Scotland Yard.

'But there *was* a body,' Auguste had shouted endlessly, only to be faced with politely disbelieving faces.

Rose was convinced that it had been his imagination. Auguste's 'body' had become quite a joke at the Factory. Twitch, or Sergeant Stitch to give him his correct title (something Rose frequently forgot to do), had seen to that. Twitch was no admirer of Auguste Didier's gifts as a detective and was delighted to see that Frenchie brought down more than a peg, 'a whole clothes line', as he smugly put it. Rose told Auguste as tactfully as possible that he must have been overworking. His men had crawled over every inch of the roads surrounding Cranton's Hotel; there was no body, not a trace of blood.

'Naturally,' Auguste had retorted crossly, 'the murderess had time to get rid of it.'

By the time he had managed to persuade a shopkeeper that he was not a madman and that a telephone call to Scotland Yard was all he required, there would have been time to move twenty bodies.

'How?' Rose asked him bluntly. 'Dead bodies weigh

8

heavy. Your murderess couldn't just heave her over a shoulder and walk off.'

'Perhaps she lives nearby,' countered Auguste defiantly.

'Young ladies don't live alone,' grunted Rose. 'And it might occasion comment if she walked into the family parlour with a corpse.'

'Then someone else moved it,' glared Auguste.

'Why?' asked Rose, kindly enough.

'I do not know,' shouted Auguste. 'This is *your* job.'

'Not without a body it isn't,' said Rose shortly, avoiding Auguste's reproachful look. 'No girl's even been reported missing.'

'Surely this is not unusual in London?' retorted Auguste. 'Even nowadays, many, many girls leave their homes for the streets, and no one notices if they disappear.'

'The aim of the white slavers is to keep the girls alive, not kill 'em off,' observed Rose drily.

Egbert Rose was tired, and he'd wasted more than a week on and off in a fruitless search for Auguste's 'body', a fact Twitch was making great play with at the Factory. It was a week he could ill afford, for there were grave matters on hand that if proved to have substance would far outweigh the disappearance of one girl. Matters that could not be discussed with Auguste.

'You've had a touch of influenza, I expect. Does funny things to you. Makes you see things.' Rose made an effort to break the uncomfortable silence.

'It is true I had some opium-based medicine. But so little that—'

''Allucinations,' proclaimed Twitch happily from the doorway.

'Can blood be a hallucination?' Auguste demanded passionately. There had been a smear of blood on the

9

sleeve of his overcoat, which had left them unimpressed.

'Come from a red herring,' snorted Twitch and sniggered in surprise at having made a joke.

Auguste's eyes travelled to Rose. Rose said nothing, but the corners of his mouth quivered. Auguste departed with what dignity he could muster and had not seen his friend since.

The shock he received two days later was therefore all the more unpleasant. He had called at her request to take tea with dear Maisie, who had vanished both from his arms and from the Galaxy Theatre to marry into the ranks of the aristocracy. Maisie, her plump curves encased in a flowing blue robe that looked a cross between a Lily Langtry jersey dress and a *peignoir*, was as at ease in Eaton Square as in the green room of the Galaxy. He had seen very little of her since her marriage, and the summons came as a most delightful surprise. He suppressed the thought that her husband might be proving inferior to himself in intimate matters, knowing full well that if this was indeed the case Maisie would have no hesitation in making her wishes known. His hopes, if hopes they were, were doomed. Maisie had business, not love, on her mind.

'Cranton's?' Auguste repeated blankly. '*Cranton's?*' wondering whether this were some elaborate conspiracy.

'Nothing wrong with Cranton's that a bit of spit and polish won't put right,' Maisie said cheerfully. 'Now what's wrong? I thought you'd be pleased, but you look as if you've dropped a bad egg into the Christmas pudding.'

'I do not wish to know anything, *anything at all*,' Auguste said vehemently, 'about Cranton's.'

Maisie was taken aback at this unexpected response. But she knew Auguste. 'Very well.' She sighed heavily.

'I'll have to ask someone else. Perhaps Mrs Marshall,' she added thoughtfully. 'Or Nicholas Soyer. He's a descendant of Alexis, isn't he? He's got a good reputation. Perhaps he'd like the job.'

'No!' thundered Auguste, roused by the sound of hated rival names.

They eyed each other for a moment.

'Tell me more about it,' he said resignedly.

'I run a travel business, you know,' said Maisie with some pride. 'I must say, Auguste, this seed cake is not half bad. I pinched the recipe from the Ritz.'

'I am sure its chef would be delighted to hear your recommendation,' announced Auguste through gritted teeth. 'Now, kindly tell me about Cranton's and about *why* you are running a business. Does your husband not provide for you? Ah, Maisie, I warned you—'

'Don't be so old-fashioned, Auguste.' Maisie licked her fingers. 'Now, I couldn't do *that* with George here,' she announced in satisfaction.

'I am honoured,' murmured Auguste.

'George and I have an understanding,' Maisie told him briskly. 'At least, I have an understanding and he accepts it. I've provided the son and heir, and a daughter. Now I'm having a year or two off and doing what I want to do. I have to have a manager, of course, while I do some countessing in between, but I keep an eye on 'im. You know what men are. No attention to detail.'

'Now, Maisie, you know very well—' Auguste stopped as he saw her twinkling at him. Ah, how he remembered that look.

'I provide a sort of Cook's Tours for Coronets,' explained Maisie happily. 'Lady Gincrack's Holidays for Gentlefolk. Like it?'

'Who is this terrible lady?' he asked blankly.

'Me of course. It's a spare title of George's family that isn't used much.'

'I can understand why.'

'But it's splendid for me,' enthused Maisie. 'At this time of year I specialise in folks from the colonies who remember their Christmases and come back to Europe without any ancestral mansions to go to, and in folks left alone here who want to escape from their own families and find another one for a few days. There's quite a few of them. So I've hired Cranton's for a Twelve Days of Christmas party. A grand old English Christmas, wassails and warbling, that sort of thing.'

'*At Cranton's. Christmas.*' That voice floated through his mind.

'*Non,*' he told her firmly. '*Absolument pas.*'

This Christmas he must consider the future of the cooking school. He would not go anywhere that held the slightest whiff of any crime, let alone murder. The nightmare of November was with him still. 'I could not get the staff in time,' he pleaded, unwilling to tell her what had happened, 'train them to produce forcemeat, and puddings to the required standard. And the dinner, and mince pies, *le réveillon* for the new century . . . There would be too much to plan for in the time. Yet,' he was suddenly abstracted, 'we could have, I suppose, all roasted fowl, with lighter desserts. And I have always wished to try punch sauce with plum pudding. The boar's head of course would be borne in by me, as *maître chef.*'

'You haven't changed, Auguste.' Maisie was amused. 'Don't you ever think of anything but food? I don't want you to be the cook.'

'What?' His face blanched. 'Not the chef? Then who? Ah, Maisie, you were not serious about Soyer? You would not wish me to work *under* someone?'

'No, no,' said Maisie patiently. 'I want you to be the

host, the manager, the *maître d'hôtel* for the holiday. I plan to drop in myself from time to time. George is going to Switzerland with his dear Mama, and it's understood that where dear Mama goes, I don't. I'll divide my time between you and the children.'

But Auguste was scarcely listening. 'The host?' All those unattainable dreams of his own hotel, for how could he ever afford to buy his own hotel? Now he was being offered a chance to pretend. . .

'I'd get you a wonderful chef,' promised Maisie gleefully, seeing sudden indecision on his face.

He regarded her doubtfully. 'He must be one who can both cook a baron of beef to perfection as well as the most delicate chanterelles, who loves both the raised pie and the paté de foie gras, the English crayfish and the. . .'

'Yes, yes, I'll make sure,' Maisie said hastily. 'You are free, aren't you?'

Auguste stiffened, his pride under attack. 'As it happens,' he said loftily, 'I am.' His current pupils would leave in a week's time, two weeks before Christmas, and so far he had no new clients. It was tempting – but impossible. 'But I cannot do it,' he announced.

'Why not?' she said indignantly.

'Because of murder,' he blurted out, unable to dissemble any longer.

'You're planning one?' she asked with interest.

'I fear one,' he said darkly. 'I *saw* one.'

She began to laugh. 'If you could see my list of guests, Auguste, you'd know there was nothing to worry about. Stuffy as an embalmed crocodile, this party is. You'll see.'

'No, I will not see,' he said sadly. 'Hard though it is to refuse you anything, dear Maisie, this I cannot do.' He rose to his feet in dignity, then remembered he had not yet tasted that most interesting looking confection, and sat down again.

'What a pity,' Maisie smiled sweetly. 'And the owner of Cranton's is a friend of Princess Tatiana too! How disappointed your Tatiana will be.'

Auguste stiffened. He had no idea Maisie knew Tatiana. Now he had no choice. If the owner of Cranton's was a friend of Tatiana's, then to Cranton's he must go. Otherwise news of his churlishness might reach her ears. Hopeless his love for her might be, but his honour at least must be kept brightly burnished in her eyes. So to Cranton's he must go and forget this nonsense, his wild fancy of murder. After all, Egbert had told him there was no body, so no body existed. It had been his imagination. And as for what he *thought* he had heard, had he not just seen the legend Cranton's Hotel above the doorway? Probably the words, if words there had indeed been, were Bantams at Christmas, phantoms at Christmas, Canton at Christmas – some reference to the Boxer trouble in China, perhaps. Certainly nothing to worry him. . .

Auguste stood on the wide wooden staircase in the grand entrance hall of Cranton's Hotel and sniffed appreciatively; for once not at food but at the smell of beeswax polish. All around him shone the ornate wood panelling, installed earlier that century, when the original Adam houses had been converted for use as a hotel. Their uniform high windows on three storeys surmounted by a smaller row in the attics, presented a majestic front – and rear – to the citizens of London. Old, comfortable furniture invited use, new Sommier Elastique Portatif spring mattresses from Heal's awaited occupants, log fires burned already on the hearths; suddenly Cranton's was alive again.

Ah, what a Christmas they would have. They would

see the century out in style. He had planned menus –
this much Maisie had permitted – such as would grace
the Prince of Wales's own table. His anxiety over the
standard of the chef had been calmed by a surreptitious
visit to his current establishment, devoted to Italian
cuisine. He had been somewhat shamefaced when
Maisie herself arrived with her husband, finding
Auguste the only other diner, engrossed in determining
the quality of a soufflé. He had not met the chef, he
mentioned innocently. Who was it?

The three days Auguste had spent at Cranton's were
a time of great anxiety as well as hard work. As
manager he had naturally taken a personal interest in
the re-equipment of the kitchens. No matter how good
these new gas stoves, they would not replace the taste
of spit-roasted meat. He cast an approving eye at the
new cake mixer and chopping device, the Lovelock
sausage machine and tinplate pudding moulds. How
right Maître Escoffier was to devote time to inventions
to take unnecessary work away. He had himself been
doubtful earlier in his career, seeing routine chores as
part of a chef's work. But *le maître* had proved to him
that to use a fruit cutter or mechanical spit freed the
chef for more important tasks. He recalled the day
when *le maître* had shown him a small cube, which he
had told him had all the strength of a complete stockpot, or a court-bouillon. A miracle indeed if it were
true, he had marvelled. Why, one could produce a
soupe in hours rather than days. It could revolutionise
la cuisine.

Auguste still had doubts about his chef at Cranton's.
He was after all Italian, and Italian food in his view
consisted of spaghetti, macaroni, *les tomates* and no
finesse. Could a goose be entrusted to such a person,
let alone a plum pudding?

He had been somewhat mollified when Signor Fancelli, who had a definite look of independence in his eye, told him he had been brought up in England, when his parents came to work in the kitchens of the Café Royal, and that accordingly he held a true cosmopolitan outlook on cuisine. However, these last three days had shown that he had a distinct leaning towards Parmesan cheese with everything. Indeed, he was as addicted to it as Mrs Marshall was towards her coralline pepper. Fancelli could only be in his late twenties, Auguste told himself tolerantly. There was time for him to learn – but not before Christmas. An eye would have to be kept on him, Auguste thought with pleasure.

All had gone well at first. Fancelli had displayed a proper deference towards him. Fire flashed, however, over the matter of the forcemeat for the goose, after Fancelli had yielded over the wild boar.

'I am the chef, Monsieur Didier,' Fancelli said, his plump, short figure quivering with passion.

'And I am the manager,' pointed out Auguste.

Signor Fancelli folded his arms. 'Duck,' he said tersely.

'Plum,' said Auguste, equally tersely.

'Prune,' conceded Fancelli, as a gesture of compromise.

'*Non*,' said Auguste.

Antonio Fancelli unfolded his arms, removed his apron and donned his pork-pie hat. 'I go,' he announced.

'It is Christmas Eve,' said Auguste, standing his ground. He was well used to recalcitrant staff.

'No plum,' said Fancelli.

'Plum *and* duck,' said Auguste. 'With Armagnac.'

Fancelli stood indecisively for a moment. Then: 'It is so,' he declared reluctantly.

Henceforth Fancelli was allowed to rule his kitchen,

but Auguste was permitted an honorary tour once every two hours, a privilege he had managed not to abuse. Fancelli watched him warily on each occasion, singing snatches of the works of Signor Verdi or Herr Mozart irritatingly well throughout.

At twelve o'clock on Christmas Eve, Auguste pronounced himself ready and summoned his staff together. He beamed at them happily, caught by a sudden headiness at the arrival of Christmas. It was going to be a wonderful time. Here in this cocoon of warmth and welcome, his greatest dream – or nearly his greatest – would flicker into reality.

'*Eh bien, mes enfants*,' he announced. 'Follow me, for the ceremony of the hanging of the kissing bough.' He led the way into the huge drawing room, his staff crowding behind him. Greenery and tinsel adorned every picture, every nook and cranny. A large, decorated Christmas tree stood in one corner, with a present carefully chosen for each one of the fourteen guests, plus one for each member of staff and sundry accompanying maids and valets. Auguste looked at the glittering tree approvingly. It was not the French way of Christmas – imagine this in his native Provence – but for an English Christmas, it was *magnifique*.

Taking the kissing bough from the footman, he climbed the ladder to suspend the bough from the ceiling, to denote the beginning of Christmas. He glanced down at the smiling upturned faces of his staff. This was a proud moment indeed. What a symbol. Two hoops at right-angles made a sphere of holly, mistletoe and other greenery, and from it were suspended small candles, gifts and tinsel, the latter catching the light as the bough twisted and turned in the slight draught from the fire. Mistletoe – that most ancient of mystical plants, the destroyer, the healer and, some said, the peacemaker of quarrels. Perhaps it would heal the

17

breach between himself and Egbert, he thought wistfully.

'The holly and the ivy,' carolled one irrepressible member of staff enthusiastically, while another rushed to the piano, only yesterday tuned by Messrs Steinway after years of disuse.

'For all the trees that are in the wood. . .'

Auguste felt his eyes misting over. Why had he worried? This was Christmas; he could imagine he was running his very own hotel. He could forget the fogs of November in the joys of December. Yes, suddenly, excitingly, he was looking forward to Christmas.

'*Mes amis,*' he beamed, 'now we await only our guests. . .'

Major Frederick Dalmaine of the Queen's Own Royal West Kent Regiment climbed slowly down from the express at London's Paddington railway station, somewhat annoyed that he had actually to seek a porter. Everyone else seemed to have porters gravitating to their side, yet what he thought of as his innate authority appeared to have deserted him. He hoped that his slowness of gait would immediately suggest a wounded combatant of the South African War. It was in fact true, and he had no objection to everyone knowing it.

He was more than somewhat aggrieved. His brother, with whom he normally spent Christmas, was very much elsewhere. (His letter, received on arrival at his Southampton home, still burned a hole in his pocket. What the devil was he to do about that?) His brother being abroad, he had naturally counted on spending the festive season with his sister Evelyn and her family, only to be informed by telegram at Southampton that they were going to Scotland, and that consequently she had arranged for him to spend a real old-fashioned English Christmas at a London hotel. He was going to love every minute, the telegram assured him. Dalmaine had no intention of loving every minute. He had looked forward to being the centre of an admiring circle of small boys and their grown-up counterparts demanding every detail of the relief of Kimberley and Roberts's victorious advance, not to mention his own face to face encounter with Jan Smuts.

Instead he was going to be one of a party of strangers who wouldn't be in the least interested in his leg wound even if Field Marshal Roberts himself dropped in to chat about it. He pursed his lips, and remembered that one of his objects in returning to England before deciding on his future was to seek a wife. At thirty-five it was high time, and quite apart from his war career, he had not been idle in his years in Africa. There had been opportunities for civilians with foresight out there, and he was going to seize them, now his army career seemed over. Even if it meant acting on that letter. . .

'Young ladies who have been launched in Society,' shouted Sir John Harnet, goaded to a loss of control that his colleagues longed to provoke but failed, for his phlegmatic calm was legendary in the Colonial Office, 'do not place jumping beans in a feller's riding boots.'

'Why not?' enquired the Honourable Evelyn Pembrey, an expression of great interest in her blue eyes.

'They are considerate of the feelings of others,' her guardian replied stiltedly, wondering why on earth he had offered to take the job on, and when Clarence and Bertha could reasonably be expected to settle back in England to take responsibility for their offspring. True, twenty-one years ago he had fervently sworn to Bertha he would devote his life to her service despite her obstinate preference for knuckle-headed Clarence as a husband, but there was service and service. And he was beginning to feel that the joys of sponsoring the coming-out season of the Pembrey twins and trying to control the waywardness of a beautiful twenty-year-old were outside the boundary.

'Oh,' offered the Honourable Miss Ethel, stealing a glance at her twin sister. 'In that case,' she continued politely, 'would you like us to remove the live frog from your muffler too?'

A stifled exclamation from Sir John abandoned plans of taking the muffler from the butler. The butler's eyes dilated slightly, his fingers distinctly trembling as he backed hastily from the room and disposed of the livestock in language that formed an odd contrast to that generally heard from his lips above stairs.

'How,' enquired Sir John sternly, 'do you expect to find husbands prepared to take you two hoydens on?'

'I thought they were supposed to find us,' remarked Evelyn innocently. 'It always is so in Ouida's novels.'

Her sister giggled. 'Mrs Toombs says it isn't ladylike to ogle men,' producing the oracle of their long-suffering chaperone.

'It's time you two girls learned you have a responsibility to society once you have been received at court. Childhood is over, and you have to be prepared to play your part as future wives and mothers in this great nation of ours, and forget these rubbishy romances. On the noble tradition of British womanhood a great empire has been built, in which you, too, must play your part now you are Out.'

'I think I'll go back In,' pronounced Evelyn gravely.

'Me, too,' agreed Ethel.

'You can't,' shouted Sir John, forgetting his resolution to impress them with quiet gravity. 'Don't be ridiculous. You've been received by Her Majesty.'

And what an experience that had been. Even though Mrs Toombs had faced the main burden, as the twins' guardian in England he had had to be present to see the ostrich plumes so nearly tickling the Prince of Wales's chin. Not that he seemed to object; he had even danced with Ethel at the Westminsters' ball last week. The honour had not been fully appreciated by its recipient, judging by Ethel's irreverent mentions of princely stomachs and unspritely gait.

Whatever had possessed him to book up for this Christmas in the hotel? Lack of options, he thought glumly. Mrs Toombs firmly excluded Christmas from their arrangement. His sister had flatly refused to have them at Chevenings, after the fiasco of their coming-out ball, so what was he, a bachelor, to do? And even if he'd had second thoughts, it had been made quite clear to him by his superiors that they were all in favour of this particular plan for the festive season, and listening to them he had been forced to agree. So it was Cranton's for Christmas. After all, it was being arranged by a countess. Even if one with somewhat doubtful origins. He could only trust that the excitement of being in London would occupy the girls sufficiently not to terrorise the entire party. He had enough worries at the Colonial Office at the moment without having to act as a blasted prison warder to the Honourable Misses Pembrey. Bertha had a lot to answer for.

'Uncle Grumps!' It was the last straw. Sir John looked up at the golden-haired vision floating down the staircase in blue velvet.

'I thought I told you never to call me that ridiculous name again, Rosanna,' he thundered.

'Oh, Guardian,' Rosanna looked distressed, 'don't be grumpy. It is Christmas, after all.' She smiled winningly, as she made the slightest adjustment to her blue felt hat perched on top of her curls. It was a Christmas for which she had her own plans.

21

Bella settled herself into their first-class compartment on the railway train for London, wearing her practical travelling dress and a decidedly impractical hat. She was determinedly ignoring the possibly rough crossing of the Channel that lay ahead by fixing her thoughts on Christmas at Cranton's. An English Christmas after all these years – how welcome her friend's suggestion of a free holiday at Cranton's had been. Even Gaston had been almost enthusiastic. The estates swallowed a great deal of money.

She stole a glance at her stiffly upright husband, Gaston, Marquis de Castillon. If only he weren't always so stiffly upright, always so conscious of his position both in French society and in France's colonial ministry. She supposed he was very clever at his job, yet his nose was so very high in the air that he didn't notice very much what was going on under his nose at home. She was very fond of him, in a kind of way . . . He was always there, a pillar of respectability. Which was why he had married her, the daughter of a Hungarian baron. If he had since discovered that pedigrees do not ensure conformity, he never revealed it, and Bella led her merry way through Parisian society unhindered.

True, she had been a little surprised by the ease with which Gaston had agreed to this visit, but she supposed that he was enticed by the prospect of a long, free holiday away from work, over which his brow had seemed more than usually furrowed recently.

Colonel Arthur Carruthers, late of the Buffs, was in excellent mood. Or as excellent as he could be in his aggrieved bereavement. He had retired from the army only to find that his wife died almost immediately afterwards. Wives were not supposed to die and leave husbands unattended, and he held it against her memory. Carruthers Hall seemed a large, empty shell without her, and the prospect of a lonely Christmas in the West Country had filled him with gloom. A chance meeting had given him a greatly daring idea. Why not spend a real old-fashioned English Christmas, all too many of which he had missed while serving in such faraway places as Zululand, the Perak jungles and Chitral, where they didn't understand roast turkey. As befitted a man of action, he made up his mind quickly and had the satisfaction of feeling that he was somewhat outwitting the unkind fates. Only now on his way to Cranton's in a hansom did he suddenly have forebodings, as he realised belatedly that something would be expected of him. He would have to hobnob, as he put it, with a load of strangers. Crossly he rapped for the driver to pull up. His luggage having gone in advance, he could walk the rest of the way. Grimly he set out, marching against the winter winds, head held high before adversity, towards Cranton's Hotel.

Miss Gladys Guessings, too, was feeling greatly daring. Tired of the kindly invitations dutifully tendered by nieces and sisters-in-law, she had struck out for independence.

'No thank you, May,' she informed this year's reluctant volunteer. 'I have another engagement.'

May's face brightened. 'Oh, I'm so sorry, Aunt Gladys,' she told her happily. 'Where are you going?'

'To London,' replied Gladys truthfully, without specifying the ignominious fact of its being a hotel. There was a note of reverence in her voice at the pronouncement of 'London', this being a far-off place that had grown in her imagination as a fairy land over the years, despite the evidence of two brief visits to the contrary, and her tone was sufficient to stop May from enquiring further.

This suited Gladys, who was thereby able to fuel speculation that she had a gentleman admirer. Really, how ridiculous, Gladys thought, going pink. The very thought made her feel like a housemaid. Though indeed she might well find congenial masculine company at Cranton's. After all, she was not too old at forty-five to find an elderly widower who required sensible companionship and who would know nothing of her life at Much Wallop. She could begin a new life. Yes, she decided brightly, she would enjoy Christmas at Cranton's.

The elegant carriage hired by Thérèse, Baroness von Bechlein, jolted its way towards Cranton's Hotel. 'Marie-Paul,' Thérèse said to her quiet companion, breaking a long silence, 'this English Christmas party, do you think we shall enjoy it?'

A small smile crossed the lips of Mademoiselle Marie-Paul Gonnet. 'Undoubtedly, madame.'

Thérèse's strong, humorous face held a glint of reassurance. 'I hear this cook is good,' she murmured. 'Auguste Didier.'

'Then we will surely enjoy it,' said Marie-Paul stoutly.

'I have always wanted to spend Christmas in England,' Thérèse said absently.

'What shall you say about your husband?' asked Marie-Paul.

'Absent,' replied Thérèse, after a moment's consideration. 'I think that's best, don't you? At my age, one is permitted an absent husband.'

'Madame is always young,' her companion assured her fervently.

Alfred Bowman relaxed in his private carriage, regarding his stomach with some affection, as it lay peacefully and expectantly under his golden watch chain. His stomach reminded him of the status he had achieved in life, a status honoured by the Prince of Wales himself who wasn't too proud to recognise what industrialists achieved, he'd say that for him. Alfred grinned. Bertie – if these rumours about the Queen's health were true – would be getting ready to jump right into her shoes. Poor devil. Bowman almost had it in him to feel sorry for him.

Alfred Bowman, a self-made man and proud of it: this was the message he liked people to receive. He had worked damned hard and was still doing so. No wife now, children settled. He could please himself what he did. And this Christmas he fully intended to do so. He was a man with a mission in life. Nevertheless, he was going to see that his stomach got the feast it deserved this Christmas. All twelve days of it. Wasn't that how this caper had been advertised? 'The Twelve Days of Christmas at Cranton's Hotel.' All the joys of London at Christmastime – and a first-class cook in charge. He'd heard of Auguste Didier. A frown crossed his face. Heard of him in more ways than one. Never mind, perhaps he'd have his mind on the cooking.

Mr and Mrs Thomas Harbottle sat silently in the hansom as it jolted towards Portman Square.

'Do you think I shall enjoy an English Christmas?' Eva asked, only a trace of Germanic accent remaining in her voice, although they had been married such a brief time. Small, plump and brown-haired, she looked like a little wren in her new brown serge travelling dress and coat, Thomas had told her affectionately. Eva took a serious view of life, which entirely suited Thomas. Bankers, even junior ones, had a duty to be serious.

'We will.' Thomas patted his wife's hand confidently, more confidently than he felt. 'It's our first Christmas

25

together, no matter what happens afterwards.'

'But—'

'Don't worry,' he said more sharply.

He cleared his throat in the uncomfortable silence that suddenly fell. 'I wonder if you are aware,' he said hurriedly, 'that London's only one-legged Mayor took office in 1796.' Thomas, as his bride was about to discover, prided himself on his knowledge of English history.

Eva Harbottle did not reply. She had no interest at all in England's past. It was the present that concerned her.

Among the other guests making their way to Cranton's to complete the party was one who had not been invited. He had his mind on matters other than the purely festive. Daniel Nash, eager reporter, intended taking up temporary abode in one of the unused basement rooms, from which position he could the more easily pursue both his inquiries and, secondly, his romantic aspirations.

Egbert Rose stared out on the Thames from his office window. He was not happy. This was partly because it was almost Christmas, and he had had to face the unwelcome choice of either Edith's assault on Christmas luncheon by producing what originally started life as a turkey or accepting the hospitality of her sister Ermyntrude, whose cooking, if better, was definitely uninspired, and whose children were worse. He sighed. He had always understood that one of the pleasures of life away from home was watching other people's children without the responsibility. This was not always the case, he had found. Watching, perhaps. Being cooped up at close quarters for some time, however, was definitely not an attractive proposition.

'Christmas isn't Christmas without children, Egbert,' Edith had said reproachfully when he tried to voice this reservation.

In this case, no loss, was his private instant reaction, amended to, 'You're right, my love,' for Edith's sake. 'Of course we'll go to Ermyntrude's again.' So tonight would see them jostling their way to Bayswater amid late shoppers and office workers all making determinedly for home, buried in bundles of packages of all sorts and awkward shapes.

'Bah, humbug,' Rose said viciously to himself, thinking that Scrooge might well have had a point after all.

The other reason he was unhappy was because of Auguste Didier. Rose was uneasily conscious that due to various other matters on hand he had not been as sympathetic as he might have been to Auguste's wild plea for help over the matter of a disappearing body. Although he had convinced himself that Auguste had been suffering from an overdose of Armstrong's Black Drops, the memory of his sad and indignant face still made him feel uneasy. However, friends were friends and the Factory was the Factory. Although Auguste had been extremely helpful, to put it at its least, to the Yard on several occasions in the past in clearing up murders, this did not mean that Rose was unable to divide the two in his mind.

On this occasion the policeman in him had definitely won. Even as he had made this plain, he had felt a traitor as he saw Twitch's look of triumph, although he was quite sure he was right. Having thus convinced himself, he once again applied himself to a last look at the lists of those entering the country. Time was running out. . .

Auguste on the other hand was feeling much happier, murder having fled his mind. So this was what it was like to have one's own hotel. A glorious warm feeling of power, of knowledge that the welfare of a group of people was in your hands. Why, this might be better than being a chef alone, even a master chef, for all too often one's finest creations, prepared with love, with anguish, with inspirational artistry, would simply disappear without comment. A timbale with grouse purée, or a capon stuffed with the finest truffles of Kent could go for nothing if a domestic dispute raged between the diners above them.

As a manager, however, one received elegant and charming guests, all bent on enjoyment, one watched tea served in an elegant drawing room, saw the delights of *fanchonettes* and Coburg cake truly appreciated, instead of having to stand over hot ovens, or rush frantically around reproaching recalcitrant assistants. Ah yes, ah yes, this was the life for him.

True, his eye had become a trifle glazed when it fell on the cucumber sandwiches. Had Fancelli no idea of how to present a sandwich? He could see the hint of a crust remaining. However, he restrained himself from comment in the interests of good relations – but with a reservation to watch for detail on his honorary tour before dinner.

He feigned a nonchalance he did not feel as he entered the kitchens one hour before dinner. He treated Fancelli to a charming smile. 'Is all well?' he enquired, apparently offhandedly, his eyes darting suspiciously from beef to *bavarois*, from oysters to ortolans.

Fancelli was not deceived. 'Yis,' he said firmly, guarding his creations like Cerberus his domain, but even his plump body could not conceal the entire range of supper for fourteen guests.

'I see you mince your mirepoix,' began Auguste, attempting to be tactful.

'Yis,' replied Antonio, stiffening warily, prepared for battle.

'Interesting, interesting,' said Auguste hastily. 'And so time-saving,' he could not resist adding.

There might one day be a confrontation between himself and Signor Fancelli, but today was not the day. He reminded himself firmly how fortunate he was. This was the first English Christmas he would see at such close quarters. Normally he would be hard at work like Fancelli in the kitchen; now he could enjoy just a little of the other delights of the festival.

Perhaps he should suggest Fancelli should attend one of his courses? Even if he had been brought up in England, his parents were Italian. There would be much he could learn from French cuisine, with its superior attention to detail and its centuries-old tradition.

'Monsieur Didier?' Auguste jumped, caught in a head-turning contemplation of Fancelli's turtle soup sitting in its Royal Derby tureen on a side table. The great master Carême had laid down that a soup should herald what was to follow it, like a portico a palace. All that could follow this turtle soup would be the lightest of light sole, yet he knew from the menu that the palace to follow this soup was far from fitting such a doorway. By turtle soup he had naturally intended a consommé, he brooded darkly. Perhaps an Italian chef had been a mistake on Maisie's part. They had no instinctive grasp of what was required of an English menu.

'You are French, are you not? I am Hungarian, but my husband is French. I do so *like* French men.' Bella's lovely face, surrounded by her blazing red curls, gazed innocently at Auguste, who was sitting at one end of the table. Fashionable golden tinsel gauze, in an equally fashionable décolleté gown, made her a glittering figure, not to mention a provocative one.

'We are honoured, madame. And from one of such beauty as yours, the compliment is indeed valued.'

There was a giggle, not from Bella but from one of the startlingly identical twins, upon whom Auguste turned a stern eye. They had only been in the hotel thirty minutes before the stag antlers in the entrance hall, despite hanging nearly twenty feet from the ground, were seen to be wearing the latest mode in Paris hats. Authorship of this crime was in no doubt. On their arrival only one sister had greeted Auguste, imperiously demanding personal escort to her room. On his return, the other, identically dressed in dark red gabardine, marched in at the entrance, demanding the same service. Doubting the evidence of his eyes, he had rendered it, returning to the entrance hall to see, as he thought, yet another young Miss Pembrey in dark red gabardine entering from the street, demanding escort. On the fifth such arrival, he paused to collect his thoughts, and then escorted the lady to her room. Five footmen and five maids followed them, each accompanied by a tray of tea.

'I wonder if you are aware,' Thomas Harbottle began, conscious that he had a social duty to address his neighbour, Rosanna Pembrey, 'that Mrs Montague, inaugurator of the famous Blue-Stocking Club, lived in Montague House?'

'I prefer white myself,' answered Rosanna simply, out of her depth since blue stockings were indeed out of her ken.

Harbottle, unable to make anything of this reply, swallowed hastily and addressed Dalmaine. 'I see you are a military man, sir.'

Dalmaine glared, conscious of Rosanna's eye on him. 'The Queen's Own, Royal West Kents, sir.' A pause. 'We're out *there*, you know.'

Harbottle stiffened. This was a subject he did not wish to pursue. 'Indeed? My father is General Harbottle, late of the Fourteenth Foot, the Bedfordshires.'

'Mitchell,' trumpeted Colonel Carruthers, whose slight deafness was remarkably easily cured on subjects of interest.

'I beg your pardon, sir?' Harbottle asked uneasily, wondering if the entire Christmas would consist of such Mad Hatter dinners and tea-parties.

Carruthers glared. 'Part of Mitchell's Fourth Brigade. Waterloo, man, Waterloo.'

'I regret he did not take part in that battle, sir. He was not born until 1840. Waterloo took place in 1815,' Harbottle informed him nervously.

Carruthers did not tolerate fools gladly. 'Think I don't know when Waterloo was? Greatest victory in the history of the British Army.'

Frederick Dalmaine turned to him. 'A battle Wellington was lucky to have won, sir. I have made a study—'

'Lucky?' Carruthers's eyes bulged. '*Lucky, sir?*'

Seeing the look on his face, Maisie hastily intervened. 'You are quite comfortable in your room, I trust, Colonel?'

Reluctantly he turned away from Dalmaine. 'Yes,' he grunted. 'Good idea of yours to reopen Cranton's.'

'We aim to please,' said Maisie meekly, winking at Auguste. Six years of marriage into the aristocracy had done little to soften Maisie's dramatic sense of colour in her dress and she rustled in purple taffeta that did nothing to compliment her to the stranger. To him who had loved her it was a different matter. He felt another stirring of the old passion, and more than a moment's regret that after due consideration he had decided his honour would not allow him to pursue dear Maisie to recapture those moments of bliss he remembered so clearly from their days at the Galaxy Theatre. He firmly ordered his mind not to remember them any more and fixed his attention on his guests. An army gentleman stealing glances at the eldest Miss Pembrey, who was talking to the other army gentleman. The maiden lady listening to a gentleman who bellowed and guffawed a great deal. A young married couple stealing glances at each other. The Baroness was engaged in deep conversation with Sir John and the Marquis de Castillon, her companion sitting quietly by her side. Ah yes, all was well. It was Christmas. This party was already at ease with itself. All would go smoothly, like a large happy family. The future for the twenty-first century looked rosy indeed.

For a moment, a mere second, Auguste relaxed, taking his eagle-eyed attention off the serving of dinner. A girl's startled cry, a clatter, a crash. 'I'm very sorry, ma'am.'

The merest blob of *crème de marrons* adorned the Baroness's face as all eyes turned to the waitress who hastily picked up the spoon she had somehow managed to drop.

Oddly, Auguste's first thought was not of such inexcusable inattention on the part of an incompetent waitress but a sudden feeling of foreboding, together with a sense that the apparent unity here was at best a fragile shell. Why, he wondered, had the girl cried out before she dropped the spoon? And why were her eyes not on the recipient of her carelessness, but on someone else at the table? Sir John? Mr Bowman? Miss Guessings? He pulled his thoughts back. 'A thousand apologies, madame,' he said to the Baroness.

She waved them aside. 'An old woman such as I am is used to applying creams in plenty, Monsieur Didier. What is one more – particularly such a *crème de marrons* as this?'

The moment passed, and all but Auguste resumed their conversations. He knew he should be thinking of what words of upbraiding he should be speaking to the waitress; he should have insisted on all male waiters, not doubling up with mere parlourmaids, but he found it difficult to shake off his sudden fear that the threat of danger had not gone away. The thought of Egbert came into his mind. Egbert and Edith, home together at the cosy house in Highbury. *That* was a happy Christmas, not a party of strangers thrown together by loneliness.

Yet when they were all seated in Cranton's long drawing room, the old gas lights glowing, hissing gently, and the log fire spitting in the centre, he quickly forgot apprehension once more, and looked round complacently at his little flock.

'Ghosts, Mr Didier,' said Rosanna, drawing him in to the group's conversation. 'Have you ever seen one?'

Dalmaine cleared his throat. Now was the time to say something witty, or complimentary, to attract her attention to him. 'I—' was all he managed, as Maisie answered the question for Auguste, laughing. 'He only sees the ghosts of dinners past, present, and particularly future, Miss Pembrey.'

'Maisie – Lady Gincrack –' what a ridiculous name, Auguste thought, and how typical of her husband to own such a title – 'You are not fair. Occasionally,' he explained, hurt, 'I see the ghost of luncheon too.'

'Talking of luncheon,' Colonel Carruthers cleared his throat, 'what have you got for us tomorrow? Turkey?'

'And goose, capons,' said Auguste eagerly. 'And of course the boar.'

'*Alors*, which one of us is that?' asked Thérèse von Bechlein innocently.

'The *sanglier*, Madame la Baronne, for the boar's head procession.'

'We ought to tell ghost stories,' put in Gladys shrilly. 'It *is* Christmas Eve after all.'

'You told me you'd seen a real ghost once, Auguste,' urged Maisie. 'Tell us about it.'

'There is no such thing as a real ghost.' Auguste had no intention of being drawn into recalling *that* story. 'I will tell you instead of another,' he said with sudden inspiration. 'A tale of a maiden long ago.' He looked round as a pleasurable sigh ran through the assembly, a breathless silence only broken by the sound of nut-crackers in action and the spitting of dry wood.

'*Il était une fois*,' he began, 'once upon a time, there took place the wedding feast of the beautiful Ginevra and the handsome Lord Lovell. After the feast, the guests began to play hide and seek in the huge old castle, and after a while it was noticed that the bride had disappeared.'

'Oh,' proclaimed his audience on cue in sombre tones on recognising the familiar tale.

'At first, not overworried, the young nobleman sought his bride, calling softly in tones of love, then more anxiously, then desperately, in all the nooks and crannies and disused rooms of the old castle. The guests joined in, calling her name, "Ginevra, Ginevra," but no trace of the lovely bride could be found. Nor ever was that night. Her father lost his wits, the young husband, heartbroken, went off to battle and did not return for many a year.'

'Ah,' sighed his audience.

'Returning to his homestead at last, he wandered the scene of her disappearance. Coming upon a room of cobwebs, in a disused part of the castle, he found an old carved oaken chest. Curious, he laid his hand upon it, and some impulse made him open it. There inside was a skeleton and rags that once had been a wedding gown. Upon the bony finger was a ring he recognised. 'Twas

34

his own, the one he gave the lovely Ginevra.'

An obedient united gasp of horror.

'Since that day the castle is haunted by the ghost of a lady in white who seeks her bridegroom in vain.'

A silence. Then Bella pronounced, 'How very sad, Mr Didier. Now if my father were here, he could relate many tales of vampires that would leave your English Ginevra looking a very pale spectre.'

'Vampires,' breathed Gladys excitedly, eyes agleam.

'Hunting for ladies with lovely necks such as yours, Miss Guessings,' boomed Alfred Bowman.

'Oh,' Gladys was pink with excitement. Her eyes had fallen first on Colonel Carruthers, but clearly here was metal much more malleable.

'Garlic keeps them away, I've heard,' observed Major Dalmaine, determined to be noticed.

'Maybe that's why Lord Lovell pushed his bride in the chest,' suggested Thomas Harbottle nervously with the same idea. Then as everyone looked at him, added, 'Too much garlic, you know,' weakly, and wished he hadn't spoken.

'Perhaps it was murder?' suggested Thérèse thoughtfully. 'Have you considered that? Perhaps a jealous lover pushed her in. What do you think, Mr Didier?'

Auguste stiffened. Murder was not an option he wished to consider. But before he could reply, the twins glanced at each other and ran to the piano excitedly, one playing the familiar haunting strains of Sir Henry Bishop's rendering of the Bride in the Chest story, 'The Mistletoe Bough', the other standing by her twin's side, one hand on the lace fichu of her ivory satin-clad bosom.

'The mistletoe hung in the drawing room
The holly bush shone on the hotel wall,'

intoned the twin, one eye on her guardian who seemed not to be listening to the change of words, and the other on Auguste who was:

> 'And Mr Didier's retainers were blithe and
>   gay
> And keeping their Christmas holiday.'

Auguste sat rigid. She was a guest. He could say nothing. He was bound to listen, whatever devilry they came up with:

> And Auguste be sure thou'rt the first to trace
> The clue to my secret lurking place. . .
> Oh the mistletoe bough, the mistletoe bough. . .'

Auguste clapped politely, vowing that no portion of his special *soufflé aux violettes* tomorrow would be allowed to pass the lips of either twin.

In the very early hours of Christmas morning, Auguste walked home from the Catholic church on Maida Hill. He was once again tranquil, the air was still around him, hushed as it once had seemed to him in the days of his youth as the angels waited for the birth of the Christchild, and cattle knelt, Maman told him, to greet the holy day. He was transported back to his beloved church of Notre Dame on the hill of Mont Chevalier in his native town of Cannes. He saw again the *santons* round the Provençal crib, so lifelike they almost moved, it seemed to him as a child, as he stood in the candlelight of the church, holding the hands of Maman and Papa. The sound of the old French carol, '*Nous voici dans la ville*', the women taking Mary's part, the men Joseph's. It haunted him still; it spoke of his youth, it spoke of what he was.

Here there was fog in place of the Provençal sun. . .
He loved England, but it was not home and Christmas
was a time for home. Yet a home should have a wife,
and he had none. Tatiana, his princess, was far away,
beyond his reach. He had last seen her so tantalisingly
in Cannes two years ago. And that reminded him that
even in Provence murder could appear.

Murder! Auguste stood stock-still in the middle of
Baker Street. He knew now what troubled him. He had
heard that inefficient waitress's voice before. On the
night of the murder. It was the voice of the murderess.

Chapter Two

Auguste woke up with a start. Immediately a hammer that seemed to have hit the pit of his stomach reminded him that it was Christmas morning, that he had had far too little sleep, and lastly that all his carefully stifled forebodings about sinister happenings at Cranton's were swiftly rising to the surface again, like scum in a stockpot. The events of that November fog had not been a figment of his imagination as everyone, even Egbert, had been at such pains to persuade him. That voice was unmistakable. Or was it? he wondered feverishly. Perhaps it was merely that he had fastened on the voice to give substance to what had indeed been fantasy. Eagerly he seized on this enticing possibility. But conscience whispered sternly in his ear. He swung his legs to the floor, and contemplated what might be going on in the kitchens below him.

Firmly he turned his mind to happier matters as he washed and shaved in the hot water provided for him – there were some pleasures in responsibility, he told himself. It would have been cold had he still been a chef. As he was shiveringly climbing into his combinations, Dr Jaeger-approved, he thought back to the excitement of his childhood, for with an English mother he had been privileged among his friends to hang up a small stocking at the foot of his bed in case Père Noël should happen to call. And call he always did – for eight years anyway. And many the little toys and delights he found in it, and at the bottom a glacéed orange from Monsieur Nègre's establishment in Grasse. How clever Père Noël was to know where to find the very best. But more even than these delights were those of later in the day, when Maman would produce her own candies – sugary almonds, bonbons and toffee. It was as his first almond had entered his mouth as a six-year-old that his first perceptions of the glories of cuisine had struck him. *Maman had made this*. What wondrous worlds lay ahead of him if such glories could be created by human hand. They did indeed. As soon as was possible, he was apprenticed to the famous young cook Auguste Escoffier, and from then on cuisine had been his life's work, pure pleasure – until murder had crept in with beckoning finger, the evil witch in his fairy tale. An evil that had to be erased.

Breakfast was already served in the dining room; devilled kidneys, mushrooms and coddled eggs waited in chafing dishes for the arrival of guests – nothing heavy to dull the appetite, merely to provide a firm basis for the delights to come. Auguste stood at the entrance to the kitchens, endeavouring to control a wistfulness that he was not in sole charge of this entrancing realm. Here in the kitchens it was clear who was in charge – or attempting to be. Antonio Fancelli streaked round his three assistants, an avenging angel in pursuit of misdemeanours. A mixture of smells met Auguste's nostrils, roasting fat, plum puddings already on to steam, the smell of freshly prepared vegetables, of cinnamon, cloves and other spices, the smell of baking – mince pies, no doubt. Geese, turkeys, ducks, capons were busily being stuffed with forcemeat. Jealousy gripped him. All this should be *his*. He should be able to inspect that forcemeat. How could an Italian know about such English matters as mincemeat and forcemeat? And indeed was there not something amiss here? He frowned, and restrained himself from rushing

40

forward as he saw a young cook preparing to unmould a port jelly. No. He was here on a different matter: murder.

'Signor Fancelli,' he began firmly, 'the young lady who helped wait at dinner yesterday evening—'

'No,' answered Fancelli defensively, waving him away as if sensing some kind of danger, 'I no have anything to do with women.'

Looking at his plump, unprepossessing figure, Auguste found this easy to believe; moreover the hierarchy of servants, and the chain of command, were clearly defined. The girl might well come under the jurisdiction of the housekeeper, Mrs Pomfret.

'Have you seen her in the kitchen this morning? Is she on duty for breakfast?'

Fancelli considered, one eye ostentatiously on the turkey even now being borne to an oven; he was clearly longing for an excuse to be free of this turbulent manager and back to what really mattered. In other circumstances Auguste might have sympathised.

'No,' Fancelli said at last, 'I think no.'

'Is she living in the hotel? Did you talk to her at all? She must have been in and out of the kitchens last night.'

Fancelli's dark eyes flashed. 'I not remember. This is not my business,' he cried, his arms lifted despairingly to some far-off god of cuisine in supplication. 'One girl, one man – they are *hands*, Monsieur Didier. You know how it is,' he added cunningly.

Auguste did indeed know how it was. When dressed in black and white, they were simply part of a highly organised procession to supply food to tables, a cog in the performance of an art.

'Is Christmas morning,' Fancelli said rather pathetically, playing on the softening in Auguste's eyes. 'Is much to do.'

It was plain that little more could be gained from remaining here at the moment. Consoling himself that he would be able to return to decorate his beloved boar's head, and double-check that the horrible sight he had just seen was not what he suspected, Auguste set forth in search of Mrs Pomfret.

A thin, severe-looking woman, she was hard at work in the linen room, young girls clad in print dresses scuttling in and out with their consignments, casting satisfyingly nervous glances at the unexpected arrival of the manager in their midst.

He looked around, gratified. 'May I compliment you, madame, on the excellent whiteness of your linen,' then, hastily, in case this might be construed too personally, 'sheets of incomparable glowing white.'

'Reckitts,' Mrs Pomfret informed him tersely, still suspicious of working, however temporarily, for a foreigner.

'And experience, I'm sure, Mrs Pomfret.'

'Thir—twenty years, sir,' she informed him with pride. 'I shouldn't by rights be here, but Lady Gincrack pleaded, and I thought I'd oblige.' She stood belligerently as if expecting attack. 'So if there are any complaints—'

'No, no. Very good of you to come,' Auguste reassured her hastily. 'I merely wished to find the maid who waited at table yesterday, and dropped the puréed chestnut cream.'

'It isn't my fault, Mr Didier, I'm sure. I didn't choose these girls. Lady Gincrack did all that. Or her company did.'

Never, never would Auguste get used to this ridiculous name. Why should not Maisie use her real name? His opinion of Maisie's husband fell even further.

'Yes, yes, I do not wish to upbraid her in any way,' he hastily explained, 'merely to –' feverishly he searched his mind for an excuse – 'speak to her about – about – walking in the boar's head procession.'

Mrs Pomfret pursed her lips. Matters were getting out of control if flibbertigibbety young girls marched in processions giving themselves airs. Mr Didier had taken a fancy to her, that was clear. These Frenchies. She'd have to watch him. A housekeeper was responsible for the morals of the girls under her roof, and Mrs Pomfret was not one to shirk her duty.

'She must be here somewhere, Mr Didier. She started at six. On the fires, of course; then at eight she was doing the teas with Bessie; then servants' breakfast. Then dusting the drawing room, seeing how she's a trained parlour maid, and the library.'

The drawing room. Of course. She would be dusting and tidying before the guests entered for the ceremony of the Christmas tree later that morning, after church.

At first he thought the room was empty. Then he realised it was not. Bella de Castillon peered round from the back of a Chesterfield.

'Oh don't go, Mr Didier,' she told him as he immediately began to back out of the room. There was a certain look in her eye . . . 'Do come in and talk to me.'

Thus commanded, he must obey. It was against his better judgment, as a highly embarrassing episode had occurred after he returned from midnight service the previous evening. Bella had taken advantage of her husband's preoccupation organising the arrival of whisky to demand seasonal greetings under the mistletoe. She was, she informed him, an authority on the sexual power of mistletoe; but he could not help observing she appeared even more interested in his own. Bella was so attractive, he would hardly have objected save that her husband was only temporarily engaged and might at any moment turn round. Further intriguing favours had been suggestively whispered in his ear. Still, seeing these could hardly be proffered at ten in the morning in a public drawing room, Auguste advanced, albeit cautiously.

'I'm looking for a maid,' he blurted out, his usual savoir-faire deserting him.

Bella shrugged. 'You will be disappointed with an old married woman such as me. Maid no longer, I fear.' Laughter bubbled out of her, as Auguste blushed red.

If this was one of the advantages of being on (almost) equal terms with Society, Auguste thought furiously to himself, he was not at all sure he wanted to be. He bowed with what dignity he could muster, and escaped as soon as he could. There was no sign of the girl.

The library, he thought wildly – she must be dusting the library. A murderess, on *his* staff. He felt aggrieved, longing to share his outrage with Maisie, but she would not be here until twelve.

With a curious foreboding, he saw the girl was not in the library either. Had she fled? Had she realised he had heard her voice? Was that why she had dropped the purée? And was that purée of the correct consistency, i.e. the Didier-approved consistency? Thoughts tumbling in his mind, ridiculously, he stood uncertainly in the library wondering where to go next.

'Ah, Didier, I want a word with you.'

Too late for escape. Colonel Carruthers had entered and shut the door firmly behind him.

'Happy Christmas, Colonel.' Auguste mustered a smile, hoping he had not been confused with Major Dalmaine. His knowledge of the details of Waterloo was somewhat sketchy, since as Maman and Papa held opposing views on the subject, they avoided giving their son instruction in the matter.

'Not much of a happy Christmas without kedgeree.'

'Without what?'

'Kedgeree,' Carruthers repeated impatiently.

'We thought it a little heavy to precede Christmas luncheon.'

'I *always* have kedgeree for breakfast,' the Colonel pointed out.

'Tomorrow,' promised Auguste, quickly edging round and out, straight into Miss Guessings who was loitering in the corridor, hoping Mr Bowman might appear on the staircase and head for the library.

'Can I help you?' Auguste asked, startled.

Gladys turned pink. 'I wish to complain,' she blurted out. 'There are no antimacassars on the armchairs in my room. My dear mother would be shocked.'

'I will have a word with the housekeeper,' murmured Auguste, trying to keep a straight face. 'Most reprehensible.' Whom, he refrained from asking, did she expect to entertain in her room who would wear macassar oil?

Not in the library, nor the drawing room. The smoking room perhaps. Auguste darted for the staircase again, only to meet Thérèse von Bechlein and Mademoiselle Gonnet returning from a walk.

'You seem in a hurry, Mr Didier,' Thérèse commented serenely.

He tried to calm himself and smile. 'On Christmas morning, the boar's head awaits me, madame.'

She smiled. 'Ah monsieur, you are the famous chef, *n'est ce pas*? And detective. *Mon mari* the Baron, *m'a informé de votre succès en quatre-vingt-neuf – ah non, plus tard, nonante-et-un, à* Stockbery Towers. *C'était magnifique, monsieur*.'

Auguste bowed politely. Delightful though it was to converse in French, he did not wish to think of past murders when one much more recent was so uncomfortably weighing on his mind, as heavy as an inexpert mincemeat. Fancelli – he must go to see how he fared.

No, first he must find the girl.

In the smoking room a maid was tending the fire. This must be her. He advanced, reminding himself that this was a murderess. 'Mademoiselle—' he broke off as she turned round. That was not the face. Those bovine features had not the same intelligence as shone from the eyes of that girl last night. He swallowed. 'Be sure to empty the ashtrays each half-hour,' he said weakly.

She stared. 'Yessir.'

'Didier,' Alfred Bowman's voice boomed from the recesses of a winged leather armchair. 'There's a cracked bowl in my room.'

Auguste gulped. So this was being a manager. He was irresistibly reminded of the *Punch* joke of the fly in the soup, and succumbed to temptation. 'Hush, sir, they'll all want one,' he said conspiratorially.

'Eh?'

'A joke, sir,' muttered Auguste, defeated by the blank expression.

Geniality returned. Bowman guffawed. After all, jokes were supposed to be his stock in trade. He stood up and slapped Auguste on the back. 'Not serious. Doing a good job here. Quite a decent kidney at breakfast, I'll say that for you.'

'You are most kind,' said Auguste through gritted teeth, taking a definite dislike to bonhomie. 'If you'll excuse me.'

He made a parade of taking out his watch – and was glad he had done so. It was high time he was in the kitchen adorning the boar's head. The girl, murderess or no, would have to wait. Unless she had indeed fled, she would undoubtedly be present for the Christmas tree ceremony, he assured himself uneasily, and he would get to the bottom of the mystery then.

The kitchens were even hotter now, the pace gathering intensity with the heat. With both ovens and

Micklethwaite coal ranges at full tilt, the heat was extreme indeed, and he noted approvingly that Fancelli had given permission for jackets to be removed. As far as he could judge, Fancelli had matters well in hand. Or had he? He looked a little closer. True, there were signs of much activity. John the undercook appeared to have vegetables and roasts under control, and also the underchefs. But Fancelli himself – he on whom success or failure hinged – why was he chopping tomatoes? He was not a vegetable chef. Why were the puddings not yet to be seen? And, yes, his earlier suspicions had been correct, the gravy was going to owe more to Mr Liebig's products than to the giblets. The giblets had been *thrown out*. And this was a chef?

'What,' he demanded of Fancelli, 'is this?' He picked up the tin of gravy powder with disdainful finger and thumb.

'Is Christmas morning,' said Fancelli menacingly, halfway through throwing tomatoes into a stew pan. 'I is too busy.'

'You is not too busy,' hissed Auguste, forgetting his English in his fury. 'And where is the celery sauce?'

'Tomato sauce,' said Fancelli, 'is better.'

Auguste's voice rose, regardless of the interest of the rest of the kitchen. 'We do as the English do, not as the Romans.'

'I am chef,' Fancelli danced up and down.

Auguste counted to three. It was Christmas luncheon. '*I* will do the celery sauce,' he announced. '*You* do the gravy.'

Fancelli slowly nodded, rather to Auguste's surprise. Peace was restored. Or was it a temporary armistice?

Taking off his morning coat, Auguste rapidly donned his chef's overall and speedily dispensed with the trifling matter of celery sauce. After all, the moment was approaching. The moment of the boar's head.

Snapping his fingers at the vegetable peeler to accompany him, he went to the larder where it had rested overnight after glazing. He flung open the door – and there it was. Eyeless, tuskless, noseless, undecorated, but a boar's head to surpass all boar's heads. For three days, the empty head and the meat carefully sculpted from it in fillets had marinated in wine and spices. Such spices! Christmas spices. Mace, cloves, laurel. Then two days ago the head had been filled first with a forcemeat *à la Didier*, then with the boar's meat, interlarded with fillets of partridge, chicken, rabbit, with slivers of rare Kentish truffles between them, and slowly cooked. Yesterday that all-important finish, the glaze, provided by the jelly made from boiling the uneatable pieces such as bones and gristle and ears, was prepared. Now there remained only the finishing touches, for he had entrusted the mustard to John to make. Rather doubtfully, it was true, but he was reasonably confident of his ability.

Auguste popped olives mounted on the whites of boiled eggs for eyes, added tusks of macaroni and almonds, put the traditional apple in its mouth, and carefully decorated it with glaze, lemons and parsley. Half an hour later the task was complete, and he regarded his work with pride. Christmas had truly begun, the season of peace and goodwill to all men.

The aforesaid season did not get off to a good start in the drawing room. Some guests were at church, some had gone for a walk round nearby streets and lanes, some were in the library or the smoking room. Gradually, however, they all began to drift towards the drawing room for twelve o'clock when a punch bowl was expected to make its appearance, and the ceremony of the Christmas tree would commence.

Colonel Carruthers was the first. No damned walks for

him. He had left the smoking room, explaining loudly that in his young day housemaids left a chap alone to smoke, and didn't they have any proper servants in this damn hotel? At Raffles, all you had to do was snap your fingers at the wallahs and they jumped to it. Precious little jumping round here! Now he was ensconced in an armchair, bitterly noting the absence of *The Times*. Christmas was too much of a good thing. This whole damned idea had been a mistake. His view was confirmed when he saw Dalmaine come limping into the hotel. The presence of another army man was not pleasing. Carruthers was used to the authority of being the sole soldier around and a faint scar from an assegai wound could not compete with a gammy leg from the South African War.

Dalmaine was sulky, to say the least. He had offered his escort to the eldest Miss Pembrey for a brief walk round the Portman Square Gardens only to have it promptly refused with no reason given. He had made his way into the library, where he seemed to have a choice of companionship between Miss Gladys Guessings and Mademoiselle Gonnet. He had promptly chosen the latter, but conversation in the gardens had been distinctly limited. Certainly, no maidenly hearts appeared to be set on fire, and he was glad to be back.

'Good morning, sir,' he greeted Carruthers unenthusiastically. He had at once determined Carruthers to be ex-army, somewhat to his displeasure. Colonels were not his favourite army rank. Even retired ones. Mind you, the old fellow did seem to have a proper interest in Waterloo. 'Mind if I join you by the fire?' Dalmaine continued with a self-conscious laugh, after only a grunt in reply. 'The old leg won't hold me up too long.' Carruthers again did not comment, to Dalmaine's disappointment. He tried again. 'Beastly show out there. Glad we're through it now. Good old Roberts, eh?'

Carruthers lowered the *Illustrated London News*, bearing in mind that this young jackanapes had extraordinary ideas about the Great Duke. 'Over? Stuff and nonsense. Only just beginning, you'll see,' and raised it again.

'Sir!' Dalmaine was genuinely shocked and somewhat indignant. He was, after all, *there*, so to speak, and thus knew as much about it as Roberts himself in his view.

Carruthers deliberately laid the magazine aside and glared. 'Why would they have left Kitchener there if they thought it was over?'

'To impress them,' said Dalmaine defiantly. 'If you'd fought with Kitchener at Omdurman, you'd know—'

'Dervishes,' snorted Carruthers dismissively. 'You ought to have faced a few Zulus, young man. Then you'd have known what fighting is. Ever heard of the horns and chest formation? Gad, they understand battle. We held 'em though. Rorke's Drift, Inyezane. . .'

'What about Isandhlwana?' said Dalmaine, then regretted it, as the Colonel blanched at the mention of this unforgivable word. After all, it was a disgrace to the British Army, when all was said and done, and he and the old chap were both part of it.

'You there?' retorted Carruthers.

'No, sir,' replied Dalmaine, wishing he'd never mentioned it. 'I was not. Major Frederick Dalmaine of the Queen's Own Royal West Kents, at your service.'

Carruthers's moment had come. Slowly he heaved himself to his feet and majestically drew himself to full soldierly attention.

'Carruthers of the Buffs, sir. The East Kents. Late of the Third Foot. I tell you, sir, if I'd been warned I'd be breaking bread with one of the Queen's Own, the whole damned cavalry wouldn't have got me to Cranton's for Christmas.'

Major Dalmaine saw his chance and took it. 'I must say, sir, that's a highly unpatriotic statement at a time of national military crisis. We are laying our life's blood down to bring civilisation and peace to Africa—'

'Poppycock, sir. I say poppycock—'

'But I would say, sir,' Sir John Harnet had entered the room followed by his counterpart from the French Colonial Office, the Marquis de Castillon, and saw an opportunity for subtle British propaganda here, 'that Major Dalmaine has truth on his side. Now that the Transvaal has been annexed and Kruger gone off with his tail between his legs, and now that the Ashanti business is over—'

'What Ashanti business?' asked Bella, sweeping in in a delightfully immodest dress for the time of day. All the other ladies had elected to wear ornate day wear, and the sight of Bella's bosom insufficiently covered by lace raised a gamut of emotions from jealousy to shock.

'The Governor had been besieged in Kumasi; this year we had to send troops in and Hodgson decided to go on the offensive, break out of Kumasi, and make for the coast. Small matter – not so much a war as a native skirmish,' said Sir John hastily.

Dalmaine and Carruthers glanced at each other and stiffened. Suddenly they stood shoulder by shoulder at this outrage. How dared one of those Colonial Office johnnies presume to know when a war was a war?

'I doubt, sir, if faced by a hundred screaming Ashantis fully armed with Dane guns and powder and given to human sacrifice, you would term it a native skirmish,' Carruthers commented sarcastically.

'Hear, hear,' supported Dalmaine.

'Human sacrifice?' asked Bella. 'How very exciting.

51

Is it one of Mr Didier's recipes?'

Following the Harbottles, Auguste entered in time to shoot her an indignant glare.

The Marquis, however, as usual ignored or did not recognise his wife's frivolities. Like Sir John, he could see his opportunity.

'*L'affaire de la Chaise d'Or*, my dear. They are talking about the Ashantis and the Golden Stool.'

'It sounds very pretty,' said Bella.

'More than pretty, madame,' said Eva Harbottle indignantly. 'It is very important to the Ashantis. It is to them their symbol of kingship. When the British subdued them four years ago, they captured their king and so the Ashantis hid the Golden Stool, for they recognised no other authority. The Governor decided to look for it, and the Ashantis did not like this, so they besieged Kumasi. I think they were quite right,' she burst out.

Auguste saw her husband take her hand. In comfort? Not quite that. There seemed to be—

'And where's the precious Golden Stool now?' boomed Bowman.

There was a sudden stillness, despite the people crowding in. Eyes turned to Sir John, who said nothing.

The Marquis smiled blandly, thin-lipped. 'You have embarrassed your compatriot, Mr Bowman. There is a rumour, you see, that the Stool's whereabouts are known, that it might even have been stolen.'

'That's enough, de Castillon,' said Sir John coolly.

'Which is awkward for the British Government.' De Castillon seemed unperturbed at British disapprobation. 'The Ashantis are subdued, true, but for how long if the Stool is missing?'

'It doesn't seem right for the British to stay in Africa,' ventured Gladys, waving away a glass of punch. 'Perhaps the Africans should rule themselves, with just a—'

'My dear lady!' exploded Sir John.

'Madam!' said Dalmaine, his gammy leg suddenly gammier as he limped up to her. 'Heroes are risking their lives for Africa.'

'Why?' demanded Eva Harbottle. 'Has Africa requested it of them?'

'You're not English, madam, or you'd know why,' barked Carruthers. 'You Germans don't understand foreign policy.'

'This lady is my wife. We think as one,' put in Thomas Harbottle bravely but unwisely.

'Then, sir, you are no true Englishman,' shouted Carruthers.

'The lady is quite correct,' remarked the Marquis superciliously. 'The British do nothing but harm in their colonies.'

Sir John turned purple. 'How about Martinique, Algeria? You French fancy yourselves around half the world.'

'That is different, monsieur. We regard them as part of France.'

'I don't like the French,' remarked Gladys conversationally.

'Quite right, my dear lady,' said Bowman instantly. 'Poodles to us bulldogs, eh?' Guffaw.

Auguste's hands trembled round his glass.

'Ah bah!' remarked Thérèse von Bechlein huskily. 'A toast. Peace on earth and goodwill to all men!'

The boar's head, in all its glory, decked with rosemary twigs and a garland round its ears, was ready. The procession was forming. First Auguste, then two flute players, then Fancelli and Mrs Pomfret, and the rest of the staff in livery. Flaming torches were carried,

53

Auguste anxiously watching lest one get too near the glaze. The rest of the meal would be served as soon as the head was placed on the sideboards with the other cold meats and fowl. He had inspected the dining room. Polished crystal glass shone, gas lights (for Cranton's would not speedily be equipped with electricity) glowed low and gently hissed, through the windows the pale December sunshine shone into a room decorated with greenery and garlands.

Only one matter marred Auguste's happiness. There was still no sign of the murderess. In the stress of Christmas preparations he had almost managed to persuade himself that Egbert was correct. His imagination had been working far too hard, like he himself. Yet his uneasiness grew. He *must* speak to Maisie, but preoccupied with her guests, there had been no opportunity. The girl must have fled, and he could not get hold of Egbert until tomorrow or the following day at the earliest. He did not relish the thought of telling Egbert his suspicions, but even less did he like the idea of leaving a message with Twitch. 'The body gone and now the murderess too, eh?' he could almost hear him chortle. 'Very unfortunate you are, Mr Didier, very unfortunate.'

The flutes began to pipe. It was time to raise the boar's head and start the candlelit procession. Auguste took a deep breath and began to sing. There had been fierce competition between himself and Fancelli, an argument he only won by pointing out yet once more that he was the manager. The chatter in the dining room was hushed as lights were dimmed and the guests listened to the sound of approaching festivity.

> *The boar's head in hand bear I*
> *With garlands, bays and rosemary. . .*

I pray you all sing merrily
Qui estis in convivio.

The old boar's head carol banished murder from Auguste's mind as he bore his joy and delight high in his arms, leading the garlanded and greenery-waving footmen and other staff up from the kitchens into the dining room.

Ah, what tradition, what centuries of meaning lay behind it. For a moment Auguste almost forgot the side of him that was French in valuing the traditions of England – or rather the Vikings, he thought more realistically. As usual the English had taken a custom from others and made it peculiarly their own. Who could doubt that Father Christmas, the Christmas tree, the yule log were other than purely English now? As the procession neared the dining rooms Auguste could hear the guests who were all now singing.

Caput apri defero
Reddens laudes Domino.

Even Carruthers seemed to be joining in with gusto, napkin already tucked in neck in preparation. The twins, side by side, were singing with almost angelic sweetness and Auguste wondered suspiciously what devilry they might be cooking up. Cooking up – what an insult to the purest of all arts that phrase was. Cook the books – ah, these English. What travesties of language they committed.

And there was Maisie, her buxom figure resplendent in red velvet, and with a child on either side. How fortunate for both their honours that she was not staying in the hotel last night or this night. As if reading his thoughts, she grinned at him, and the years fell away. Six years . . . in which he had cooked countless marvels of cuisine, and solved three more murder cases. Murder . . . the disagreeable thought jolted him back to reality.

'*The finest dish in all the land* . . .' The carol came to a triumphant close as the boar's head was reverently put in pride of place, and Fancelli took his place by it to carve. Auguste longed to do it, could not bear to leave it, and as if sensing his dilemma, Maisie came to lead him away and place him at her side.

'Remember the plum pudding we stirred, Auguste?'

'Ah, you stir more than my puddings, Maisie.'

'Auguste! What a thing to say.'

'Maisie,' he leaned towards her quickly, pausing only momentarily to assess the texture of the walnut and prune forcemeat as he was served a portion, 'a problem presents itself.'

'The guests?' she hissed instantly, defensively.

'*Non, non,*' said Auguste hastily, 'they are quite –' he swallowed, 'delightful.' This forcemeat was not so delightful. It was merely adequate. 'It is the murder that I mentioned to you.'

'The one Inspector Rose said never happened?' She eyed him keenly.

'It happened. And the murderess is here, or rather, not here.'

She laughed. 'I'll take the "not here".' She looked at him curiously. 'You are in earnest, aren't you, my old cock-sparrer?'

Auguste nodded. How incongruous to speak of murder while all around goose, duck, turkey were sending out delicious aromas, their message of comfort and wellbeing. Not to mention the slices of boar's head – his eye went to a plate piled high with slices. Bowman of course. A man who enjoyed his food. 'Last night I recognised the voice I heard that night, Maisie. It was *sans doute* the same voice. The voice of the murderess. It was one of the maids.'

She stared at him. 'Oh come, Auguste. I can't believe it. One of the *maids*?'

'Yes,' he said quietly. 'And she must somehow have recognised me, because she is nowhere to be found. So I want you to tell me, Maisie, all you can about the staff.'

'I would if I could, Auguste. But I didn't interview them. My staff did. And the office is closed till next Monday.'

At that moment the Lady Ellen, Maisie's daughter, caused a diversion by dropping a dollop of John's cream mustard sauce on Maisie's lap, which temporarily concluded discussions.

'This is delicious forcemeat,' announced Gladys distinctly, taking a large and ostentatious sip of orange cup. 'Really, I'm quite glad I came away.'

'I am glad of that too, dear lady.'

'Oh, Mr Bowman, I fear you are a tease,' she giggled.

Auguste looked at the industrialist's portly figure and wondered what made him so attractive in Miss Guessings's eyes. Compared with his own figure – he squinted complacently down. A master chef, and over forty – only a *little* over forty – and still almost as slim as when he had created a *poularde à la Didier* in the kitchens of the Faisan Doré at Cannes. Yet the eighteen-year-old twins treated him as a father figure. What was worse was that he no longer found eighteen-year-old girls objects of great desire. Maturity and mystery were of more interest, like Madame la Marquise with her full, womanly figure and her delightful red hair, and mischievous eyes. He realised he was staring at her and hastily averted his eyes. Too late, for Bella was well aware of his gaze.

'Will you pull the wishbone with me, Monsieur Didier?'

Maisie kicked him amicably under the table.

'Certainly, madame.' He was far from feeling this was a good idea. What, after all, did 1901 hold for him, that he could wish for? Then he remembered something he could indeed request of the wishbone.

'You've won, Mr Didier. What did you wish?'

'That there should be no more murder in my life,' he said lightly. It was not in fact his wish. But that was an impossible one. Tatiana would never be his, even if a hundred genii jumped out of magic lamps to help him.

'But your wish won't come true now, Mr Didier,' said Bella, laughing. 'You've broken the spell by letting us know what you wished. So, there *will* be another murder in your life.'

A sudden silence at the table, as all eyes turned to Auguste.

'Murder?' said Thérèse von Bechlein slowly. 'Not here, I trust, Mr Didier. Not at Christmas.'

Inspector Egbert Rose was thinking longingly of his quiet working life (quiet by comparison with this noisy brood), in a semi-comatose state of Christmas collapse. His and Edith's morning had begun exceptionally early at 4 a.m. with the unexpected arrival of Edith's elder sister's daughter's youngest in the middle of his chest. It appeared that Gertrude wished to show him her mechanical musical pig at the earliest possible opportunity – approximately three minutes after Father Christmas's reindeer had galloped off to their next port of call. Musical was not the word Rose would have chosen of this pig, but Edith had seemed delighted at the honour paid to them. Shortly after that, Edith's younger sister's son arrived. Ten-year-old Augustus had a cast-iron model of a hansom cab, which appeared only to operate on beds and recumbent limbs.

One or two later arrivals ensured that there was no

chance of recapturing that paradise called sleep, and a decidedly morose Egbert but surprisingly cheerful Edith appeared at breakfast only a little after eight. Rose had then tried hard to repair to the study with his brother-in-law, but it appeared that Oswald thought Christmas morning should be spent with the young folks. Edith disappeared into the kitchen with her two sisters, a cook and an overwhelmed tweeny. Gusts of muffled laughter could be heard at intervals.

When the Hornby had clattered round the rails for the twentieth time, fallen off thirty times, and the stations and Great Western Railway personnel had been suitably named, even Oswald had had enough of the young folk and suggested gruffly to his brother-in-law that a Christmas whisky and soda in the study might be in order. It certainly was with Rose.

Once in this masculine haunt, Oswald cleared his throat. 'Much on at present?' he enquired, in the opening gambit of a time-honoured custom. If Rose replied, 'One or two things to be cleared up,' that was the end of the conversation. Matters of serious import were under way. If on the other hand he replied, 'Not a lot, Oswald,' Oswald felt at liberty to enquire further as to the situation regarding the latest scandal or murder. Particularly the latter. Oswald had a morbid interest in murder.

Today, however, there were one or two things to be cleared up. Then in Christmas spirit, Rose threw a sop to his brother-in-law. 'We had a non-murder though. No murder, no body.'

Oswald brightened. 'Sounds interesting.'

'Our friend Auguste. Swears he saw a murder committed in the fog. A young girl. Had to go some way to contact us. Time we got there, no body, no trace, no one reported missing and no bodies turned up. Auguste had been overdoing it. Had a dose of influenza. Took one of these patent remedies with too much opium, if you ask me. Fog can produce funny feelings.'

'Oh.' Oswald drew in his breath with a sigh of satisfaction. He could participate in this. 'Not usually wrong is Auguste,' he pointed out, pulling weightily on his pipe.

'No,' Rose said shortly, uneasily aware that he'd been hoping Oswald would agree he was right in dismissing Auguste's fantasy.

'Could have got rid of the body. In the river.'

'True.' Rose paused. 'The Three Tuns nearby didn't hear anything,' he said defiantly.

'Lot of noise in pubs,' pointed out Oswald.

A long silence while they both contemplated the situation.

'Why didn't he go to the pub right away for help?'

'Says he didn't know it was there. It was just behind him when he reached the place where he says the body was, and he couldn't see it for the fog. It was a Particular all right that night,' Rose added. 'A pea-souper. He was right about that.'

'Oh.' A long pause. 'Could have been an unfortunate,' Oswald offered, trying not to sound over-eager in his detection.

'What?'

'An unfortunate,' Oswald repeated shamefacedly. 'They don't get reported missing. White slavers and all that.'

'White slavers' victims don't get murdered either – leastways, not by women, and Auguste says it was a woman did it.'

'None of your Jack the Rippers then,' said Oswald rather regretfully, remembering Rose's involvement with that case. 'No mutilated bodies left lying around.'

'Time for turkey, you two.' Edith's head popped round the door, flushed red from laughter, the heat of the kitchen, and an unaccustomed glass of sweet sherry.

'Any of your work, my dear?' Rose enquired interestedly.

'Clarice let me make the bread sauce this morning,' Edith answered proudly.

Rose made a mental note to avoid all but a token portion.

If only his present worries were as straightforward as, with hindsight, the case of Jack the Ripper had been. Rose was lucky to be here at all today. One day off, that was all, he'd been told. He'd be back at the Yard this evening, at his desk, hoping that something, anything would turn up to give them a lead. So far not a whiff, and all the usual lines of investigation had proved to be dead ends. Perhaps the tip-off was all a mare's nest, but if so it was a filly they could not afford to ignore.

He had been informed by Inspector Chesnais of the Paris Sûreté that they'd received a tip-off of a planned assassination of the Prince of Wales, and that was followed by an urgent summons to Paris. Chesnais' man had been found dead. In true Sherlock Holmes style, the only clue – if clue it was, and not his laundry bill thought Rose savagely – was a piece of paper in the dead man's hands, the merest scrap where the rest had been torn away in some struggle. And then it had rained, and the ink had run. This famous clue, or non-clue, consisted of a 'P', an 'a' or 'o', and two letters following that could have been 'l' or 'd'.

Even Watson would have little difficulty solving that one at the moment. It had immediate and ominous significance for Rose. On 3 January, Field Marshal Lord Roberts would be arriving at Paddington Station on his triumphant return from South Africa, after his meeting with Her Majesty the Queen at Osborne. At

Paddington Lord Roberts would be greeted by two notable dignitaries, the Duke of Connaught and the Prince of Wales. And, thanks to Chesnais' tip-off, Rose now had every reason to believe that there an attempt would be made to assassinate the heir to the throne.

Albert Edward, Prince of Wales, yawned. At least he wasn't at Osborne, owing to Mama's unaccountable failure to insist on his presence. Perhaps she really wasn't feeling up to the mark, despite all her denials. Obstinate, that's what she was. Here she was at eighty-one, still insisting on behaving as though she had the constitution of a twenty-year-old. Christmas anywhere was much the same, though, even at Sandringham. Children squabbling, women grimacing – and not interesting women either. Only your family, approved guests, and the estate workers lining up for Christmas gifts. Gone were the days when *droits de seigneur* gave the latter ceremony any interest. Anyway, either something had happened to the standard of Norfolk beauty over the centuries, or *droits de seigneur* hadn't been all they were cracked up to be, judging by the lot this morning.

Yes, Christmas was always the same. Too much family, too much to eat. He thought uneasily of the pheasant, turkey and boar he had consumed, and wondered if his cook was really up to it. What would that French fellow, Tatiana's chum, make of Christmas dinner? he wondered. It wouldn't be lying quite as heavily on his stomach as the results of the last hour or two, that was for sure.

A few days' shooting, and then he'd have to get back to London to greet old Roberts. He remembered somewhat uneasily that he'd been told someone was about to assassinate him again. He was getting quite used to it. Poor fellows. Probably they all thought they were doing the world a good turn. Perhaps they were, he concluded gloomily. What kind of a king would he make now? He was nearly sixty. He'd shown good form at foreign affairs (and not only the Folies Bergères), but as to home affairs, Mama gave him less free rein than one of her blasted dogs.

He wondered who could be planning to assassinate him this time. Willie perhaps, His Imperial Majesty the Kaiser Wilhelm II? No, his beloved cousin Willie seemed curiously friendly at the moment. He'd shown Kruger the door when he called a few weeks ago, and any enemy of President Kruger was at present a friend of Britain's. Perhaps it was Kruger himself behind it. That was the most likely. The Boers were getting their own back for Roberts's victories. Perhaps they hoped to wipe both of them out with the same bomb. He wondered if the Yard had thought about *that*. Well, he squared his shoulders, if he was going to go, he might as well have another brandy and soda first.

Alfred Bowman wriggled uncomfortably in tights and livery, wondering whether this was too high a price to pay for having been elected Lord of Misrule of the Christmas evening festivities. He had deliberately purloined the all-important ring from Miss Guessings's portion of plum pudding, this being a time-honoured method of electing the important post. Unfortunately, the plum pudding was taking its revenge and he felt by no means as lithe and enthusiastic about the revelries to come under his command as he had in the sunshine of the December morn. For the first time, he seriously considered the acquisition of a Harness Electropathic Belt.

He had staved off the more energetic games until later, but the younger members of the household had grown weary of Hunt the Slipper, and even the delights of Snapdragon, in plucking raisins and sweetmeats from flaming brandy, had palled, despite the attractions of its taking place in the dark where all manner of liberties might be taken under the mistletoe.

> *'With his blue and lapping tongue*
> *Many of you will be stung,*
> *Snip, Snap! Dragon'*

shouted the twins strumming at the piano. Thérèse von Bechlein pursed her lips and looked at Marie-Paul. Had they, she wondered, been right to attend this Old English Christmas?

Blind Man's Buff had provided more amusement, particularly to Bella who innocently suggested the roles were reversed. Auguste should be the target, the ladies blindfolded and seeking him. Oddly, Bella managed to find him surprisingly easily and the kiss she bestowed was dangerously sweet. Others were less sweet, and one decidedly bristly. Fortunately most contented themselves with the merest peck. All the same, it was not a game that he would wish to repeat, delightful though it had been to feel Maisie's lips on his once more. Less so to hear her muttered: 'And don't you go thinking that's going to happen again, my Young Lochinvar.' Yet as the women took their turns, one by one, he tired of the game, remembering the missing girl with a lurch, and that while their festivities ruled inside, outside there was still a murderess. Suppose she had come to him, blindfolded in a game, pressed her lips to his cheek!

He shivered at the thought and then acknowledged this was ridiculous. In the morning he would telephone Egbert. Meanwhile this was Christmas evening and he had a duty to his guests.

'Hide and seek, oh hide and seek, please,' pleaded

young Lady Ellen, one eye on her mother. Her mother smiled indulgently.

'Yes,' chorused the twins happily, glancing at each other.

'Yes,' breathed Bella, her eyes on Auguste.

'Must we?' said Bowman with a groan.

'Oh yes,' said Gladys firmly, seeing many opportunities ahead. 'And you must play.'

Reluctantly, Auguste led his flock into the entrance hall, where at the twins' insistence they drew lots for the first person to hide.

Thérèse was the first hare for the hunt. Or should have been. In the event, she passed the honour on to her pale-faced companion, with a somewhat cruel: 'You, Marie-Paul, shall be the hare. At my age it is more pleasant to play the hound. Is it not, Mr Didier?'

Outraged at being thus classified in her age bracket – she must be nearly sixty – Auguste replied somewhat stiffly, then obediently shut his eyes at the twins' insistence so that the hare could disappear.

In her dull burgundy-coloured evening gown, Marie-Paul was not easy to find. Having searched the corridors, even the attics in vain – bedrooms and his own small suite at the back of the ground floor were out of bounds – Auguste descended to the cellars. After all, where else would a true daughter of France hide? Except the kitchens – and Fancelli had already expressed his outrage at intrusions into that domain. The only hares that had entered his kitchen were destined for tomorrow's game pies, he assured the intruders grimly.

Auguste crept down the cellar steps, candle in hand. It seemed unlikely that the nervous Mademoiselle Gonnet would have ventured here, but he would be sure. The candle threw mysterious shadows onto walls and wine racks. The smell of cold mustiness assailed him. Nothing here, he thought in relief. Only ghosts. Ghosts of ages past. Perhaps of the early days of these houses, for Cranton's had originally been four houses, one of which was said to have been lived in by a Georgian prince. Perhaps his ghost haunted the cellars still, in search of his favourite claret.

Auguste shivered. He must go. Then he stopped. He was not alone. He could sense something, someone. Where? Who? Surely not that timid, sad Mademoiselle Gonnet? Cautiously he tried to open the door next to the wine cellar. One of the larders, wasn't it? It would not budge. He had this terrible fear that on the other side might be a ghost – or a girl. A murderess. He could do nothing, he must go. He saw one of the twins coming from the opposite direction.

'Oh, Mr Didier, I'm so glad to see you. It's so *creepy*, isn't it? Can I come with you?'

'But of course, my child.' What was he saying? Child? She was an adult woman, an attractive girl – or would be once she had stopped her childish giggles. She was not giggling now.

'I don't like it,' she said nervously as they came up into the entrance hall again. 'All these dark passage-ways and . . . and those *ghost* stories. Let's go back into the drawing room.'

'You are afraid of finding Lord Lovell's bride?' Auguste asked gently enough as he followed her in. Who was he to scoff?

Ethel stopped so abruptly that he cannoned into her. 'Oh,' she said faintly, pointing at the huge oak chest that stood by a window at the side of the room. Near it, high above, hung the kissing bough, candles flickering in the low light, glittering and colourful.

Ethel caught her breath. 'You don't think Mademoiselle Gonnet could have hidden *there*?'

'Surely not,' said Auguste feebly, emotions tearing at him. The lovely Ginevra's body mouldering away, a skeleton . . . Or suppose—His masculine pride took over. 'We will look to make sure, mademoiselle.'

'You *are* brave, Mr Auguste,' Ethel said admiringly, keeping well behind him as he advanced to the chest. He took hold of the rounded convex lid, and tried in vain to keep himself from trembling. It was ridiculous even to look. The Baroness, perhaps, but her companion would never choose this place. He lifted the lid slightly – and dropped it again, suppressing the cry which came to his lips. Inside he had seen a hint, not of burgundy, but of white.

'Mr Didier! What's the matter?' Ethel asked.

He turned to her, face drained of colour. 'Stand back,' he ordered, and flung open the lid. This time the cry could not be repressed.

The woman's hands were folded in prayer across her chest. Her gown was of the purest white, a lace veil lay over her face.

The corpse sat up slowly. 'I am the ghost of young Lovell's bride,' it declared brightly.

'Oh, how could you, Evelyn,' said Ethel delightedly. 'You did give poor Mr Didier a scare.'

Chapter Three

Auguste opened an eye and shut it again quickly. Then duty whispered in one ear, and her sister conscience confiscated the other. It was Boxing Day, they informed him; the exciting Twelve Days of Christmas, for which he had sole responsibility for the enjoyment of fourteen paying guests in his very first hotel, had barely begun. To superintend breakfast should be his sole desire at present. Somewhere deep inside him another voice was reminding him that there were far more unpleasant matters than breakfast to investigate. A murder in the fog, and the disappearance of the murderess, for instance. Perhaps just a few more minutes of oblivion. . .

Duty was, however, victorious and within thirty minutes Auguste was taking his place in the breakfast room, narrowly beating the first of the guests to brave a downstairs appearance as opposed to taking a tray in their room. His eagle eye quickly moved over the delicacies in their chafing dishes, and noticed the waiter's defensive face. Auguste for the first time was aware of a gulf between the staff and himself, something lost, something gained.

Carruthers was the first, upright in tweed lounge suit. 'Morning,' he greeted Auguste gruffly before opening the breakfast campaign. 'See you've done the decent thing and put some kedgeree on,' he grunted. 'Not like the ones we had at Chitral. But it'll do.'

'Not for me.' Dalmaine had followed him in. 'I'm not

used to these rich dishes *out there,*' he announced offhandedly.

Carruthers glared. 'Eat acorns, do you?' he asked sarcastically. 'Like in the Peninsula?'

Dalmaine maintained a dignified silence, taking his seat at the opposite end of the long table, and ostentatiously arranging his napkin. He had no sooner done so than the Baroness and her companion entered and he was forced to rise again. He bowed in as soldierly a manner as was possible behind a plate of mundane porridge.

'I trust you slept well, gentlemen.' Thérèse ignored the tempting offerings on the side tables and contented herself with muffins.

'Like a baby, ma'am,' barked Carruthers, 'thank you.'

'The beds are too soft here,' commented Dalmaine immediately with a light laugh. 'Used to a hard pallet.' He was hoping Rosanna would enter in the wake of her twin sisters, but she evidently did not share their stamina.

Animosity crinkled the length of the table as if through an electric wire.

One by one the gentlemen of the party joined the table. Eva, Gladys and Bella had elected to refrain from exposing their morning complexions to public scrutiny, but Rosanna at last bestowed her sweet smile upon the assembled company with no adverse criticism of her pink and white beauty. Thérèse, whose wrinkles were deepset, giving character to her face, and the twins had no reason to fear early exposure, and Marie-Paul clearly had no option. A certain resentful obstinacy was clear in every muscle of her thin figure as she glared wistfully at the steaming hot dishes on the side tables. Thérèse handed her another muffin.

Auguste was well aware of his duties to keep conversation flowing. Not quite as important at breakfast as other meals, but nevertheless this was a Christmas party. 'I think it will keep fine today. That is good, is it not?' It was a brave if uninspired effort.

Only the Marquis de Castillon considered it worthy of reply. 'Indeed, monsieur, far better than your English fogs.'

Auguste stiffened. This was hardly a reply he welcomed.

'Out in Zululand,' said Carruthers loudly, 'it was so hot at Christmas even the ice was warm.' It was a joke that fell flat.

'Our parents are in Africa,' remarked Rosanna, fully conscious of Dalmaine's admiring gaze upon her.

'A strife-torn land,' he murmured. 'Where are your parents?'

'Cape Town, I think,' said Rosanna doubtfully.

'Johannesburg,' announced Evelyn.

'No, it's not,' said Ethel brightly. 'I think it's Lagos. Or is it Kumasi?'

'Somewhere near there, anyway,' Evelyn informed them, reaching for buttered toast and helping herself to a large portion of lemon cheese.

'Durban!' cut in Sir John crossly. 'Kumasi indeed.'

A small smile played on the lips of the Marquis. 'Such a troubled area, Sir John. Will the Ashantis ever accept British rule? We French seem to have better fortune with our colonies.'

'And look how—' Sir John broke off, remembering their diplomatic status. 'A muffin, Mr Bowman?'

'No, thank you, sir. I've done very well. Very well indeed. Beats me how you Frenchies keep going without a good solid breakfast inside you. Nearly starved to death when I was in Paris.'

Auguste deferred politely. 'There is much to be said

71

for a heavy breakfast for those with heavy work to do, monsieur.'

'When I was in Brussels I ate cheese,' put in Harbottle, nervously remembering they were all supposed to be one happy party. 'For breakfast,' he added unhappily, in case there was any doubt. 'I am in banking,' in a burst of confidence, looking round defiantly as if expecting it to be pointed out that this was no occupation for gentlemen. It had been pointed out often enough by his father. 'I travel on business.'

'Seen the "Manekin Pis" have you?' rumbled Bowman.

'There are ladies present,' said Harbottle nervously. Small children immortalised in stone while urinating were not a fit subject for mixed company.

'It's art,' pointed out Bowman, guffawing.

'What a man,' said Carruthers, following a line of thought of his own. 'Duchess of Richmond's Ball one day, Waterloo begins the next.'

'And thus the Duke was not at the front where he should have been,' pointed out Dalmaine, pouncing on the opportunity. 'Had he been so, he would not have had to wait until the afternoon to hear of Napoleon's attack on the Prussians. An error.'

'Sign of greatness,' snarled Carruthers. 'Hold your horses till you see the whites of their eyes.'

Thérèse with pleasant determination decided to break into this unseasonable discussion.

'For myself, I prefer always my native Paris to Brussels. And you too, Mr Didier.'

Auguste glanced at her curiously. 'I come from Provence. But Paris I know very well. You must miss it at the Kaiser's court.'

'You visit Paris often, monsieur?' Marie-Paul ventured quickly.

'*Non*,' said Auguste. How could he explain that

Tatiana lived in Paris, that to be there so near would not be possible. Impossible even to think of cuisine if Tatiana was in the same city. Feeling this sounded blunt, he continued, 'And you, mademoiselle, you are not from Paris, I think?'

A glance at the Baroness as if requesting permission to speak, then a colourless, '*Non*, monsieur, I am from Alsace, and my mother was Austrian.'

'The land of waltzing, and songs, and fair women,' Auguste said gallantly.

'Alsace, too, is German now,' remarked the Baroness complacently.

Marie-Paul's eyes flashed. 'I am *French*, madame.'

'*Oh, la, la* the worm turns, *mon chat égratigne*,' Thérèse said lightly, but slightly mockingly, to her companion, who had relapsed into her normal silence after this show of individuality.

'But Austria, Mr Didier,' Bella de Castillon, superbly and simply gowned by Worth, had swept into the room in a waft of perfume and fur, 'is not the only land, I trust, to contain such marvels.'

'Ah, *non*, madame,' murmured Auguste, distracted by her entrance and avoiding her eye.

It must surely have been his imagination that during the night the handle on his door turned, and in had floated an entrancing vision clad in pale blue satin and lace. Cowardly – but pardonably since the lady's husband might, after all, notice her absence from the adjoining room – he had pretended to be asleep, and the vision after murmuring a few words that still made him blush wafted away. Tonight he would lock his door. His regard for the sanctity of marriage could only be taken so far, and after all, if the Marquis did not prevent his wife wandering at night, he had only himself to blame. Nevertheless, Auguste felt distinctly uncomfortable this morning, faced with the reality of his dream. Fantasy? Bella shot a sweet smile at him. 'Did you sleep well, Mr Didier?'

'Extremely soundly,' he replied fervently. 'How kind of you to enquire.'

'Are you in banking, Bowman?' Sir John asked abruptly. He had been ruminating.

'No, sir.' Loud laugh. 'I'm in iron. Gates and railings, Sir John, that's me. Cast and wrought.'

'Indeed.' Sir John shot a faint look of disgust at this palpable evidence of trade.

Fourteen people, thought Auguste, glancing round the specimens here gathered. All here to weld together as best they may for the duration of twelve days. Then they would part again, probably never to meet unless by chance. This was a pause in their ordinary concerns, before taking up the burdens of everyday life again, just like the porters from the fardel rest in Piccadilly. Here, however, Auguste was entirely wrong, for several of his guests were not in fact escaping from the affairs of everyday life, but actively pursuing them.

'It is about that murder in the fog, *mon ami*,' Auguste said nervously. The note in Egbert's voice as they exchanged cautious Christmas pleasantries on the telephone did not bode well for relaying even news of such value as he had. There was a silence.

'I have found the murderess. I recognised the voice.'

'Where?' The tone was noncommittal.

'Here – at Cranton's. Ah *non*, not here. She has run away,' said Auguste unhappily.

Another silence. Then the words he had feared to hear: 'Two disappearing bodies, eh Auguste? You don't have much luck, do you?'

Rose had had a bad morning. Everyone from the Commissioner and the Chief Constable down to the bootblack, he thought grumpily, wanted to know what he was doing about the threat to His Royal Highness. The answer was quite a lot, but unfortunately the results were nil. All ports were watched – but for whom? All known agitators, Fenian anarchists, objectors to everything from the South African War to Aunt Jemima's hat had been interrogated fruitlessly. Nothing. And now Auguste was offering him yet another vain pursuit.

'Tell you what, Auguste,' Rose told him sourly, 'when you find even one of your ladies, just let me know.'

Smarting from injustice, Auguste stomped out of his hotel office to be greeted by the jolly strains of the Drinking Song from *Traviata*. He sniffed. Could he not smell curry? What was worse, he could almost swear it was curry *powder*. There was something about its lack of subtlety that—Full of rage, he set off down the stairs to the kitchens. True, he had promised Fancelli to remain away from the kitchens this morning, but this was something he could not be expected to ignore.

Fancelli looked up from his inspection of *la soupe* as Auguste entered, correctly divined his mood, and continued to sing Mr Verdi's rousing song. But an obstinate expression settled on his Latin face; eyes prepared to flash at the slightest provocation. In other circumstances, for lesser crimes, Auguste might have backed down.

'Might I have a word with you, Signor Fancelli? Alone.'

It transpired that the only place where solitude was guaranteed at least temporarily was a larder and here surrounded by pies and pickles and by undoubted evidence that it was not only curry powder that had been used, but his rival's curry powder. Mrs Marshall's! Auguste came quickly to the point.

'Yes, Monsieur Didier, I use curry powder for the

réchauffé turkey. It is good curry powder.' Fancelli folded his arms. 'Is prevalent in the Madras presidency.'

'I am acquainted with the wording of Mrs Marshall's advertisements *and* with her curry powder,' Auguste stated firmly. 'All I would say, signor, is would you add Mrs Marshall's gelatine to a zabaglione? Would you colour a *ragu* with Mrs Marshall's redfood colouring? Would you add Mrs Marshall's coralline pepper to a *risotto alla Fagiano*?'

'Eef,' Fancelli retorted heavily, 'my honour as a chef tells me thees ees good, I do it.'

'*Thees* is not good,' Auguste said firmly, waving a hand towards the kitchen. 'We are not a backstreet dining rooms, we are –' he drew himself up – 'Cranton's. We make our spices, our powders *ourselves*.'

'You will fetch me fresh ginger, Mr Didier, coriander seed, the fruit of the cardamon—' Fancelli was getting excited.

Auguste waved him aside. 'Without proper ingredients, no *maître chef* would condescend to prepare a dish at all.'

'Eh. You say I am no good chef?' Fancelli was torn between tears and anger.

Auguste perceived he had gone too far. True, he was justified, but in the interests of smooth co-operation, not to mention luncheon, more tact might be required.

'Your galantine, on the other hand, Signor Fancelli, looks superb. And I am somewhat of a specialist in galantine. The balance of colour is of the greatest importance. The black of the truffles should not overbalance the occasional touch of red and green.' He paused. 'The old English plant the galingale. Have you ever followed the fourteenth-century recipe from the *Forms of Curry*, Signor Fancelli?'

The look Fancelli gave him indicated he had not, but

that as a gesture had been made he was prepared to be conciliatory. He led the way from the larder in flamboyant style, as Auguste surreptitiously donned a spare apron and hat. He might be forced to intervene.

'*Il mio pudding!* And a *granite*. Sorbets. Ice creams.'

'But where is *the* pudding?' asked Auguste with awful premonition.

'*Si*, pudding.'

'No, English pudding.'

Fancelli eyed him warily. 'Yesterday I do English pudding. Today, I do *my* pudding. *Torciglione*.'

Auguste looked at the unappetising long thin objects coiled on a pastry board ready for baking. He gulped. 'Delicious, I am sure,' he said, 'but not *English*. Pond pudding, chocolate pudding, lemon pudding, *le* spotted dick, but there *must be a pudding*!'

One Latin eye met another. Fancelli's fell first. 'Fruit jellies,' he offered feebly. 'Charlotte—'

'English,' said Auguste succinctly.

Fancelli's temper snapped. 'Very well, I do the spotted dick. I do a very large spotted dick, so they all be fat. But it not be my dish. It be called Didier's spotted dick. And after that I do everything *à la Fancelli* or that is all.'

Quivering with fury, Auguste stormed from the kitchen, thankful that the majority of his guests had joined Maisie in a brisk walk in Hyde Park. Oblivious of the fact he was still clad in the apparel of his superseded profession, he hurried to the haven of his office. He was clearly not designed by nature to be a manager of men. He was a *maître chef*, not a hotelier. Yet had he not the right to say what should—

A scream rent the air. A female scream. He catapulted out of his chair, through the door into the corridor. Flying towards him was a twin. Which one, he neither knew nor cared. His face darkened. He had not forgiven them for their practical joke of the evening before.

'*Non*,' he said firmly. 'I am busy. I am not in the mood for jests.'

'But Mr Didier,' came the anguished cry.

'*Non*.' He went back into his office, but the hallowed sanctum was immediately invaded, as the door was flung open again with a crash.

'You must, you must,' she shrieked.

Auguste Didier had had enough. '*Non*, there is no must.'

'It's the old oak chest. There's something . . . Oh, you *must*.'

'The chest? Your sister again?' He went pale with anger, just as Ethel burst into tears.

'No, and I'm telling you the truth.'

Tears? Could they manage false tears too? Whether they could or not, Auguste was not proof against a young girl in tears. Very well, he sighed, he supposed he would play along with this stupid game.

'*Ma fille*,' he patted her shoulder in avuncular manner, 'do not worry. Auguste Didier is here. Let us investigate ze 'orrible crime,' he said melodramatically. 'I, Sherlock, will solve it.'

Taking her firmly by the hand, he led her still sobbing to the drawing room, where unaccountably she drew back. 'You go,' she quavered. 'I couldn't look again.'

Auguste gave a heavy melodramatic sigh. 'I understand, *ma fille*. This is man's work,' walking up to the chest, squaring his shoulders. He posed dramatically before it. 'I, Auguste Didier, the famous detective, will now investigate the terrible death of Ginevra, beautiful bride of Lord Lovell.'

He flung open the lid – and froze. No ghost, but quite clearly dead. She had been stabbed. There was no doubt about that, for the stiletto dagger was still stuck into the corpse's breast, congealed blood evident on the thick cotton of her apron. It was the missing housemaid.

Egbert Rose's telephone was ringing. Sometimes, he thought sourly, Bell had done the world a distinct disservice. Semaphore was just as good. It took only two minutes to get orders from London to the coast at the time of the threatened invasion, and that was nearly a hundred years ago. His mind played with the idea of standing out on his balcony with a few flags, and crossly returned to reality as he barked into the telephone.

'I have found you your body, Egbert,' came Auguste's quiet voice.

Rose's mind went blank. Body? What body? A rare anger overcame him. 'If you're making another monkey out of me—' Rose took hold of himself. 'Is this one going to disappear by the time I get there?' he asked sarcastically, then was immediately ashamed of himself as he took in the tone of Auguste's voice.

'No, Egbert, it will not disappear.'

A body? He'd have to send Twitch, was his instant reaction. He couldn't go himself, take time away from this all-important job. Then he reconsidered. Why not? Nothing was happening. He could at least see this corpse. He owed Auguste that.

Auguste reminded himself that he was looking on the face of a murderess, not the bride of young Lovell. But in death she might well have been. For all the impersonality of death, her face was fair. The face of a girl too young to die. Like the girl in the fog, her victim. He shut the lid again hurriedly, hearing again the voice of this girl crying: 'At Cranton's? Christmas?' And then had come the muffled choking. Now the murderess

79

herself lay dead, murdered in the same way. Odd. Or was it vengeance? But if vengeance, how had the avenger known how the girl in the fog had died?

He puzzled over this for a few minutes; partly to take his mind off the awful object so near to him. Egbert would soon be here. He would need to be told again everything that happened on that November night. A small twinge of satisfaction caught Auguste even in the midst of such tragic surroundings that Twitch might have the grace to apologise for his crude gloating.

He ran over in his mind all that had happened on that foggy afternoon. Finding Portman Mews, realising where he was, crawling along the railings that guarded the semi-basement kitchen area, then the words ahead of him coming out of bleak dampness. Those words: Cranton's and Christmas. A pause. Then the chilling sound of choking. Then nothing, only himself left alone with a body. The murderess had escaped – until he had recognised her voice again.

Then he realised that like Fancelli's forcemeat, something was not quite right here. Left alone with a body . . . *How did he know that*? He, Auguste Didier, had been guilty of jumping to conclusions. Because he had heard only two female voices, because he had heard this girl's voice, he had assumed she was the murderess. But suppose there had been a third person present at the scene, a man or woman who had crept up and murdered the one girl as the other departed. Then, he reasoned, knowing that the fatal words Cranton's and Christmas had been passed on, he or she had bided his time, assuming his prey would be present. The girl murdered in the fog could have passed on more information to this unfortunate girl in the chest, information that made her removal imperative. Yet the girl in the fog had been a housemaid – that was strange. What could a young housemaid know that would threaten someone enough to commit murder? And how, he wondered suddenly, did she know about Cranton's when staff were not hired until early December, after the murder? Perhaps she was not really a housemaid. Yet what evidence did he have for absolving this girl from murder? This girl so young, in her early twenties, deprived of life, so that now he fiercely wanted to prove her victim, not murderess. Evidence? Yes. There had been silence after the cry. No running footsteps. Did that not imply the murderer was there, all the time, as he, Auguste, had found the body? He shivered.

'Morning, Auguste.'

Deep in his thoughts, he had been unaware of Egbert Rose entering the room behind him. 'Not pretty,' Rose said at last as Auguste opened the heavy rounded lid to show him the contents.

'*Non*.'

'Who found it?'

'One of my guests,' he replied mechanically.

'*Your* guests?' Rose looked at him curiously.

Auguste shrugged. It seemed so unimportant now, this clutch at a lifetime's dream. 'I am the manager,' he told him.

'Nice place.' Rose looked round approvingly at some of Adam's best work. 'Who is she?' he went on. 'The girl in the fog?'

Auguste looked at him gratefully. 'No. The girl I told you had disappeared. One of the staff.'

'And you reckon she's your murderess?' Rose stared down at the corpse.

'I had thought so.' Auguste hesitated. 'I have been guilty, Inspector Rose,' (this was a formal occasion) 'of a perhaps incorrect conclusion. When I was present at the murder in the fog,' he said with some emphasis, 'I heard this woman's voice; of that I am sure. I had assumed, perhaps wrongly, that she was the murderess, for I was only aware of the two persons. But there was a gap between her voice and the choking cry. Suppose someone else was there?'

'Still got to find your first body,' Rose pointed out, after digesting this.

'I have *one* body for you, Egbert,' Auguste burst out. 'As you requested. Is one not enough to make you believe what I say?'

Rose looked at him for a moment. 'Yes,' he said simply. 'I'll put some men on it. River search. Mortuary search. Some of the bodies that come out of that river don't get too much investigation.'

'And this unfortunate girl?' Auguste asked quietly. 'I –' he hesitated, then continued, 'I have a hotel to run. It is not usual to present a Christmas party with a real corpse in the drawing room. It *is* my first hotel,' he added rather pathetically.

Rose considered this. Normally he wouldn't, but this was Auguste pleading. 'Where are your guests now?'

'Most are in the park. Colonel Carruthers, I believe, is in the study. Miss Ethel who found the body has returned to her room with her maid.'

Rose mused for a moment, as the front doors opened and Twitch appeared self-importantly, leading a phalanx of police constables and, in their midst, the police doctor.

'No help for it,' Rose said reluctantly. 'We'll have to block this room off for a while, both entrances. And search the bedrooms.'

'Where are my guests to go?' moaned Auguste white-faced, feeling personally responsible and remembering his all too public wish on the turkey bone. They would blame him. Of course they would.

Seeing Auguste's pale face, Rose said to him kindly, 'Why don't we go to your office, Auguste? We've got a lot of talking to do.'

It was out of his hands, thought Auguste wretchedly. A murder had taken place at Cranton's; and what was worse, publicly. It could not be swept aside, removed to the servants' quarters. It affected them all. Even the kitchens. A terrible thought struck him.

'Luncheon?' he asked miserably.

Rose understood his problem immediately. 'Where's the dining room?'

'Opposite. The other side of the front door.'

'Put them in there straightaway,' suggested Rose with all the optimism of one who had never attempted to organise fourteen people into doing something they had no inclination to do.

Auguste sighed as he entered the dining room. He had spent an exhausting hour with Egbert, recounting yet again every detail of that November night. They had even gone out into the mews and retraced his footsteps.

'So you were here, you reckon, when you heard these sounds. Choking like?'

'Perhaps the murderer put a hand over her mouth to muffle the sound.'

'Because of the pub, maybe.' Rose stared at the Three Tuns. 'You say you didn't see it was here. Odd,' he remarked without emphasis. 'It's big enough.'

'No,' said Auguste sharply. 'I concentrated on going forward. The sound was *in front*. And this was a peasouper. It was late afternoon. There would be little sound from the pub.'

'True,' said Rose. 'We'll talk to them anyway. So what then? You heard the sound – where did you find the body?'

Auguste shut his eyes, clung to the railings, and tried to remember. He inched forward, feeling out for obstacles, to the great interest of a passing ten-year-old chimney sweep for whom Christmas festivity was a matter for others. 'Been on the gin, "as 'e, mister?' he asked Rose, one man to another.

'That he has, laddy. The Yard keeps an eye on 'im, don't you worry.'

'Cor!' said the lad, impressed.

'I think *here* was the body,' announced Auguste with dignity, having advanced ten yards or so.

Rose joined him. He looked around. 'Difficult to get rid of in a peasouper. And it was only two hours or so later that I got here. Not a lot of time to get rid of it, in that weather, even if you were in the pub by that time.'

'Unless,' said Auguste, struck by a sudden thought, 'it was kept down there in Cranton's basement area till night-time.'

'Searched there,' grunted Rose. 'Looked there myself.'

'Even in the rubbish cupboard?' asked Auguste quickly, pointing to a door out of sight on the pavement side.

Rose almost blushed. 'Couldn't swear to it.' They exchanged a doubtful look.

'No,' said Auguste, 'surely it couldn't still be there. It has been used since.'

They both relaxed. One body was quite enough for a Boxing Day.

'He could have broken into the hotel to hide it in the cellars,' pointed out Auguste, anxious to absolve Rose from any hint of blame.

'Could be. One broken door here or there wouldn't be noticed when our Maisie's builders moved in.' Rose brightened up. 'Funny feet the Queen must have,' he said thoughtfully as they walked back.

'*Pardon?*' Auguste enquired, startled.

'That sign up there.' He jerked a finger at the building opposite. 'Rodways Patent Concave Shoes. It's got the royal arms above it. Perhaps the Prince of

Wales patronises them – he has a lot of standing about to do.' He spoke lightly, but the disagreeable thought struck him that unless he got a move on, His Royal Highness's standing about could be cut short very suddenly indeed.

Now, however, Auguste was on his own once more, to face his disgruntled guests in the dining room, disgruntled through no fault of his.

'I don't want a drink from the damned wassail bowl. I want to go to my room.' Colonel Carruthers's pithy statements seemed to sum up the general mood.

'I regret it is not possible to visit your rooms for the moment.' Auguste looked anxiously round his flock, whose expressions varied from impatience to curiosity. Even Maisie looked somewhat annoyed.

'Come on, Auguste. Stop playing games!' she ordered him informally. 'Why's there a policeman on the front door, and why have we been herded in here like a load of pigs to a trough?'

'Murder,' announced Auguste succinctly.

An astounded silence.

'*Murder*?' repeated Thérèse. She laughed. 'But we are all here.'

'One of the maids.'

'One of *them*?' Harbottle pointed a somewhat disdainful thumb towards the nether regions. 'But why should we be put to inconvenience?'

Colonel Carruthers had been thinking. Now he exploded. 'Good God, you mean we're suspects, don't you? That's why we're here in the dining room. Sorry for the girl. But what about our luncheon? No sign of it yet.'

'The body has only just been discovered,' said Auguste quietly. 'The police must examine the scene, and we must avoid it for a short time. Arrangements are being made for luncheon.'

85

'Where was the body found?' asked Bowman, for once not laughing.

'In a large chest by the window,' replied Auguste reluctantly.

A moment for this to sink in, then: 'You mean where I was last night?' shrieked Evelyn.

'Yes, Miss Pembrey. I regret that your sister found the body. She is lying down, being tended by her maid.'

'Oh, it was my fault. She said she would look for the brooch that I lost last night,' cried Evelyn, woebegone. 'She said she wanted to stay here, so she might as well hunt for it. She must have thought of the chest. Oh!' Rosanna put her arm round her to comfort her.

'It's just like your story of the Bride in the Chest, isn't it?' chattered Gladys, eyes glowing. 'Murder under the Kissing Bough. The Skeleton at the Feast. So she was murdered while we were out,' she added inconsequentially.

'Or during the night,' said Auguste. 'She was missing yesterday however. I was making enquiries.' No indiscretion in his saying so, for his enquiries had been public enough.

'Why were you looking for her?' asked Thérèse curiously.

'I – I thought I recognised her and wished to speak to her, but I could not find her. She might have been killed yesterday.'

'No,' wailed Evelyn, 'I was in the chest last night. It must have been today.'

'Then that would be a good place to hide the body,' observed Gladys. 'No one would think of searching there after Miss Pembrey had been in it.' Her eyes were agleam. She was a devotee of the adventures of Lady Molly of Scotland Yard, and was now demonstrating her methods.

'Since we have mostly come from overseas, I do no

see how we can be suspects,' said Harbottle nervously.

Sir John Harnet, Bowman and Carruthers looked at each other. 'Stuff and nonsense,' they said in unison, as the enormity of this statement sank in.

'Are the police looking for a jealous lover?' asked Gladys excitedly. 'It's usually them, you know.'

The Marquis stood up. 'I have diplomatic immunity, Mr Didier. My wife and I will leave immediately.'

'Oh no, Gaston,' cried Bella instantly. 'Think how bad that will look. And think what excitement we will miss.'

The Marquis fastened on to the important words: 'look bad'. 'French Colonial Office diplomat hurriedly leaves scene of crime,' he imagined the English newspapers shouting to the world. He slowly resumed his seat. 'Very well, we will remain – for a short period only.'

Egbert Rose came in. 'Mr Didier will have explained to you what has happened. We're sorry to have to keep you here a while longer, but we need to make a search of your rooms, I'm afraid. Do any of you have any objection?'

There was instant uproar. The words 'Diplomatic immunity', 'private papers, *very* private papers' could just be discerned in the outrage. When it had died down, Bella's voice could be heard remarking cheerfully, 'You are at liberty to search among my chemises and stays, if you wish, Inspector.'

'Thank you, ma'am,' Rose replied stolidly, as reluctant permission seemed forthcoming from the assembled guests. 'Meanwhile,' his eye caught Auguste's, 'luncheon is ready for you below. We need to search this room now. Mr Didier will show you the way.'

Reluctantly, Auguste rose. The moment he had feared. The moment when, as a reluctant Pied Piper, he must herd his band down the cellar steps, out along a candlelit, cold corridor, past the laundry, scullery and kitchens, and into the basement room normally devoted to the repasts of maids, valets and staff. Even luncheon could not compensate for this indignity to a manager's self-respect.

'Been dead some hours at least, the doc says. She was probably killed during the night – the risk would be too great otherwise. We won't know for sure until the PM.'

'Was she killed there?' asked Auguste, then realised his stupidity. Of course she could not have been killed in the chest or even in the drawing room, unless it was a crime on the spur of the moment and that was very unlikely. One did not choose a midnight encounter for casual conversation.

'No,' said Rose. 'And the men have come up with precious little from the search of the bedrooms. No helpful bloodstained clothes. And the top floor is kept locked, you say?'

'On the eastern side, and I myself have the only key. On the other are lumber rooms and staff bedrooms, although most of the staff are lodged nearby.'

Rose's face grew long. Any moment now he was going to break the news to Auguste that he wasn't going to be here to look after this case. Twitch was. He looked up as he heard footsteps. It wasn't Twitch. It was a proud-looking police constable who was unceremoniously escorting a burly young man in a cap.

'Found him down in one of those cellars, sir. He's been sleeping there, I reckon. Here's our man, sir.'

The young man tore himself free and planted his hands on the desk belligerently. 'Rot. I'm waiting for Nancy Watkins. Why are you all here? Is anything wrong?'

Rose looked at him sharply. 'Why should it be? And who's Nancy Watkins and what's she to you? And what are you doing in the cellars?' He motioned to the constable to take notes.

'I had an arrangement to meet her downstairs at seven thirty this morning. She didn't come. She's one of the maids here.'

'Seems an odd sort of time for a maid to arrange to meet her young man?'

'She isn't really a maid. And I'm not her young man.' Anxiety gave an edge to his tone. 'She writes a column for *London Watchman*, and I'm on their staff too. Danny Nash. She was here about an important news story she was after for the magazine.'

'What story?' Rose was suddenly very interested. It was a long shot, but—

Danny shook his head. 'She wouldn't tell me. She kept things very close, you see. And it was her first big story. Normally she does Household Hints. But she did say she had to be careful because it might be dangerous. That's why I said I'd camp here in the cellars and she was to slip out to see me each day.' There was another reason for his presence too, but he'd keep that to himself. 'Yesterday she came, but not today.' He looked from Rose to Auguste, picking up their silence. 'Something's wrong, isn't it? Something's happened to her.'

Rose got up from his chair. 'Bad,' he said gruffly. 'She's dead.'

'Dead.' The young man stared at them aghast. 'Murdered?'

'You think that was likely?' Rose shot at him.

'I believe *she* did,' he said soberly. 'I see that now, otherwise she wouldn't even have agreed to my camping here. She would do it all herself. Women need a man in a job like ours.' He banged a fist on the table. 'I'll help you,' he said vehemently. 'I'll find out who killed her.' He paused. 'She did say she'd give me one clue, but I couldn't make anything of it without some more to go on. It was Marlborough.'

'What about Marlborough?' said Rose sharply.

'Nothing more – just that. She liked being mysterious,' said Danny, in despair at the ways of women.

The editor of the *London Watchman* led his unwelcome visitors into his study, irritated at being caught in carpet slippers and playing at toy theatres on the floor. Boxing Day was no time to have to think of work. There he was given the unwelcome news of the death of one of his staff and the fact that another was by no means clear of suspicion.

'Nancy? Murdered? But we're the *Watchman*,' he babbled. 'Surely it can't have anything to do with us? That sort of thing doesn't happen nowadays, does it? It must be a gentleman friend of hers,' he diagnosed with relief. 'Or a lunatic! I liked Nancy,' he added sadly. 'Nice young lady. Orphan, you know. Made her own way in life. Didn't land up on the streets like so many others. She did well. Must have been a *crime passionnel*.'

'Perhaps, sir, but if so it was committed by someone in the hotel; no one came in or out during the night, so the porter said.' Not the front entrance, anyway, Rose was thinking to himself. 'What was the story she was working on?'

The editor gave an exclamation of combined relief and annoyance. 'She wouldn't tell me! She wrote a column of household hints, and I told her she didn't have time to go gallivanting after stories. But she would have it. She'd do it over Christmas, she said.'

'She told you nothing else?' Rose stared gloomily round the untidy cubbyhole, wondering how editorial words of such weight and wisdom could emanate from here each month and disgorge themselves into the highly regarded *Watchman*. Then he remembered that his own office at the Factory bore a great resemblance to this cubbyhole – to the outside eye – and warmed to Mr Jonus Martin.

'Told me, no. I did get, um, a little extra curious one day, and wanted to know just when I would be getting an article. She said it was more important than just an article: it was a matter of preventing something very important from happening in the public interest. But there would definitely be an article too? I asked. After all, I *am* an editor.' He looked defensive. '"Oh yes," she said, "the definite article is all-important." And then laughed as if it were funny. Women are odd creatures.' He pondered this for a moment as though it might form the basis of an article for his next issue. Very odd, he concluded. Then he recalled that Nancy Watkins was odd no longer. 'I'm sorry to hear about Nancy,' he said sincerely. 'The *Watchman* will do anything it can to catch the fellow.'

'I've bad news for you, Auguste. I'm going to have to leave you with Twitch on this one,' Rose told him after they arrived back at Cranton's, as he finished his last tour of the drawing room to ensure that nobody had broken in from the outside. Even the chest was in place, having been checked and yielded no further information. Wait till they got this fingerprinting idea in operation. It was taking them long enough, that was for sure.

Auguste stared at him unbelievingly. '*Why*?' he burst out indignantly.

'I've something more important on hand. I came today to start things off, but I've got to get back to the Yard.'

'More important matters than murder?' Auguste demanded.

'Yes. Preventing one,' said Rose grimly. He hesitated. 'Between you and me, the murder of the Prince of Wales. A threat of an assassination attempt. We got wind of it in November and are no closer yet, except that it's most likely to take place on the third of January.' And he explained the background.

'Does the Prince know?' asked Auguste quietly. Now he saw Rose's dilemma, saw the reason for his lack of sympathy over his own plight, and forgave him. Almost.

'He knows all right. Mind you, threats are two a penny. Most of them are cranks, nothing serious. But this one,' Rose paused, 'it's different. There's already been one body found murdered in connection with it. An agent of the French Sûreté. Diplomacy is topsy-turvy on the Continent. Because of the Boxer trouble in China, Kaiser Wilhelm feels indebted to us for a change, so he slights his chum Kruger, ex-President of the Transvaal. You can imagine how the Boers liked that. And with rumours flying around about the Queen's health, what better time to make an attempt? Especially with all the victory celebrations for Roberts's return. The Prince of Wales is to meet him at Paddington on the third, in just over a week's time.'

'He will go through with this reception?' Auguste was horror-stricken.

'You know what he said to me? "Anarchists are bad shots." I reminded him that the chap who shot the King of Italy in July didn't do too badly and the Shah only escaped because the Grand Vizier acted quickly. But no. Refuses to alter his plans. I'll have the place swarming with men, of course.'

Auguste digested this news. He had twice saved the Prince of Wales from becoming involved in the aftermath of murder. To prevent his own was a far different matter.

'I'll meet you tonight with the results of the PM on Nancy Watkins, but otherwise I'll have to leave you to Twitch's tender mercies.'

As if on cue, Sergeant Stitch marched in like Hannibal intent on taking Rome. Far from contrition, he seemed to ooze triumph as he addressed Auguste. 'There's no doubt,' he said, delighted, 'bodies do seem to follow you, Mr Didier. Someone will be putting two and two together one day, won't they?'

'And with your detective powers, Sergeant Stitch,' Auguste retorted, 'no doubt they will still make two of it.'

'Now, now, Auguste,' murmured Rose indulgently. 'You're colleagues, remember.'

Was there ever such tension and excitement as the moment before the rise of the curtain at a theatre, especially at a pantomime, the orchestra playing a crescendo, childish voices whispering, shushing, crying? Even Auguste was excited, as though a child again. Not that pantomime was a French pastime, particularly not in Cannes. But he loved it still, especially the magic of Drury Lane and the inestimable Dan Leno.

Some of the guests had not taken up their tickets for *Sleeping Beauty and the Beast*, preferring to remain at the hotel partaking of a supper with which Fancelli had excelled himself, though this was not saying a great deal in Auguste's opinion. Thus there had been spare seats which he had offered as a gesture of reconciliation to Egbert and his family. Rose had hesitated, refused on his own account, but accepted on his family's. Edith, Oswald, Ermyntrude and their brood thus joined Lady Gincrack's select party in the stalls.

Auguste watched the pantomime entranced, as the set moved to a street where two closed palanquins moved slowly across the stage, by courtesy of their occupants' feet protruding below. From within came the unmistakable voice of Dan Leno's comic genius. True, he could not understand quite the humour of his quick patter, but his very voice was funny, a true clown. And then there was the spectacle of the harlequinade, more decorative and beautiful at Drury Lane than anywhere else. Perhaps these floating ladies and wondrous translucent colours were the results of modern marvels backstage, but the illusion was enough. He was himself Harlequin. Would he ever see his Columbine again, let alone possess her? He firmly removed his mind from Tatiana, suddenly aware that Bella's thigh was pleasantly near his own, indeed much nearer than it had any right to be. He concentrated quickly on the Beast's Palace.

Marble columns, rather like the kitchens of the Reform Club when Soyer moved in there in the 1840s. The Reform Club had had many such master chefs – Francatelli, Rosa Lewis, Emma Pryde, all had passed through those eminent Pall Mall doors. Pall Mall was the southern boundary of clubland, containing not only the Reform and the Guards Clubs, but the Marlborough Club and – he stopped. Marlborough? Nonsense. That was a club. A man was safe in his club. He remembered affectionately his days at Plum's. No, not always safe, he reminded himself uneasily; Plum's was not always so. Not even a prince would be safe at a club, even one founded by himself, because no one would expect—

He stood up suddenly, jerking Edith's box of chocolates from her hand by mistake and stammering apologies as he made his way to the exit. He could not wait for Egbert to meet them at the end of the performance. He must tell him *now*.

★ ★ ★

Rose looked up from his desk impatiently, but his irritation soon changed to interest. 'Pall Mall?' he repeated, seeing again that scrap of paper, the blurred ink. 'Perhaps,' he said, 'Pall Mall, not Paddington. Not Padd, but Pall.'

He couldn't afford to ignore Paddington though. But nor could he afford to ignore the link with the word Marlborough. And if the Marlborough, then somehow it was all linked to Cranton's Hotel. He made his mind up quickly. He scowled at Auguste in his old familiar fashion and the last remnants of the rift vanished. 'I reckon you thought this up just because you don't want to be left to Twitch's tender mercies,' he grunted. 'Now you're here, look at this.'

He pushed the post-mortem report across the desk to Auguste, who scanned it quickly, then read it again more slowly. He looked up questioningly.

Rose nodded. 'That's right. The dagger was taken out. Then replaced in the wound later. And she'd been dead well over a few hours. Rigor mortis was wearing off. They reckon she was killed over twenty-four hours before you found her.'

Auguste wrestled with this problem. 'But—'

'The four Ws,' interrupted Rose. 'Where? Certainly not in the drawing room or chest. When? Might be possible to determine according to her duty list. Who? An open question at the moment. And why—'

'Why was she murdered? But this we can guess.'

'No. Why was the body put in the chest? And why was the dagger replaced? To make us think it happened on Boxing Day, I suppose.'

'And what better place to hide a weapon, *mon ami*?' asked Auguste simply.

Chapter Four

Slowly London bestirred herself, rumbled into life, uneasily aware that by rights Christmas was over and that in normal years Wordsworth's Stern Daughter of the Voice of God, Duty, would issue instructions to bury it quickly and efficiently in the interests of Queen, Empire and Industry. However, 1900 was not a normal year, for in a few days another great event would be celebrated. This new year celebration would carry an extra frisson, an occasion for reflection, for self-congratulation and for confident expectation. This new year would usher in the twentieth century, and only a minority doubted that it was a century that would see yet more laurel boughs of victory set on the forehead of mankind's conquest of the elements. And the old Widow of Windsor would march at its head to lead her people into the new dawn. Buoyed up with encouraging reports that the Queen's health remained excellent, and that rumours of her deteriorating strength were not merely greatly exaggerated but completely unfounded, London waited breathlessly to greet firstly the new century, then its returning hero, Field Marshal Lord Roberts, and in due course its Queen returning from Osborne House.

It was the second of these events that was giving Inspector Egbert Rose severe anxiety as he awoke this Thursday morning. Duty was not merely shouting in his ear; she seemed to be sitting on his stomach and pounding it up and down. For this he blamed Auguste.

It was all very well to insist he accompany the party to the new Carlton Hotel for a little late supper after the pantomime, but did he have to recommend Mr Escoffier's personally prepared *dindonneau aux perles noires* followed by *suprêmes de foie gras au Champagne*, not to mention his famous *pêches melba*? Furthermore, as he had staggered from the private room, his cup as well as his stomach was full when Auguste soberly pointed out the name of the private suite opposite to the one in which they had been dining: the Marlborough. They had looked at each other in unspoken agreement. This they would consider in the morning.

Now that morning had arrived – and far too early for Rose's head. After palely refusing all Edith's blandishments of a nice fried egg, he arrived at Cranton's at 7 a.m. to find a distraught Auguste, drawn between a desire to superintend the arrival of breakfast and the safeguarding of his office from the increasing number of policemen who seemed to have designs on it. He lost on both counts. Fancelli ignored his tactful comments on what was expected of English breakfast and Rose promptly commandeered his office.

Auguste had only had an office of his own for four days, and now he was to lose it because of a murder which was undoubtedly linked to another murder which he had reported only to be laughed at. He smarted with injustice. Really, life was most unfair. He was forced to content himself with the cubby hole adjoining the library, despite the fact that it was not as near the kitchens as he could have wished.

'Marlborough,' said Rose glumly, considering widening horizons unenthusiastically.

'Marlborough House, the Prince's own residence in Pall Mall.'

'Marlborough Club at No. 52 Pall Mall, and now

this. The Carlton – in Pall Mall. What's the odds that HRH is a frequent visitor to Monsieur Ritz's new establishment?'

'I do not offer odds,' said Auguste slowly. 'I remember only that His Royal Highness once stated that "Where Ritz goes, we shall follow". For where Ritz goes, Monsieur Escoffier also follows, with his *poularde Derby* and countless other dishes to appeal to the Prince's taste. I have no doubt he is a frequent visitor.'

'Right. I'll get Twitch down to the club to sniff around a bit. And to the Carlton. Meanwhile, we'll take the routine side again here.' Rose paused. 'You'll be helping me, Auguste.' There was a slight query in his voice.

'As,' replied Auguste with dignity, 'Sergeant Stitch will undoubtedly arrest me for murder unless I do—'

'Don't think I'm capable of it, eh?' commented Rose abstractedly.

'This is my *first* hotel,' said Auguste vehemently, 'although only for twelve days. My own honour demands that I help bring the perpetrators of this crime to justice.'

'With not much time to find them in,' Rose pointed out grimly. 'We'd better make a start. We know the girl was alive at seven thirty on Christmas morning because young Nash spoke to her. And we'll need another word with that young man too. It's likely she disappeared sometime between then and the time you were looking for her.'

'Yes, about ten o'clock.'

Somehow it made murder all the worse for its having happened when it did, Auguste reflected. The morning Christ had been born to make the world a more loving place.

99

'Right.' Rose took a deep breath. 'Bring on the chorus girls.'

Mrs Pomfret was shown in first, bridling under the stern eye of Twitch, and an unlikely candidate for the chorus line. 'I haven't done anything wrong,' she informed both police and manager, twitching her bombasine skirt nervously. Her trustworthiness thus established, she took the seat Rose waved her to, chatelaine's keys rattling at her waist.

'Nancy was a good worker,' she replied doubtfully to Rose's first question. 'I only met the girl on Sunday, didn't I, but I prides myself I'm a judge of character. I didn't expect her to end up in a chest,' she added, torn between horror and indignation that this could happen to someone under her command.

'Remember exactly when you saw Nancy on Christmas morning?'

'She was there for the teas, that I remember. Bessie was with her – you can speak to her.'

'And when did you see her after that?' He consulted a timetable drawn up for him by Auguste. 'Servants' breakfast?'

She wrinkled her brow. 'I can't rightly remember if she was at breakfast. We was all new to one another, you see. I wouldn't have noticed if one had been missing without some special reason to do so. There ain't a lot of time at servants' breakfasts.'

Auguste knew that only too well. He remembered at Stockbery Towers that for the housemaids it was a matter of a quick half-hour, if that, between the polishing, the blacking, the cleaning, the hot water carrying . . . Ah, Stockbery Towers. He wondered if his dear kitchen was being properly run now he had gone. Stockbery Towers had, after all, started him off on his life of crime. That matter, too, had begun with the murder of a servant, but see how far its tentacles had spread. Now Nancy Watkins' death boded much the same.

Bessie, when summoned, burst through the door ahead of Twitch in excitement at meeting real London policemen. She also seemed to be bursting through stays and print gown, plump with glowing health. Auguste was hardly surprised to find this was her first London post. Even the presence of her manager and the housekeeper did not quell her exuberance.

'Are we safe 'ere, sir? Mrs Pomfret didn't tell us about no murderers being in the house. And my mum, she said, look out for the butler; he's a caution most places.'

'Mr Didier's the nearest thing you got to a butler here, Bessie. You're quite safe,' said Rose kindly.

Auguste glared at him. 'The Inspector and his invaluable assistant Sergeant Stitch will catch this murderer in no time. Do not fear, Bessie. We understand you served the early morning teas with Nancy?'

'That's right,' answered Bessie cheerfully. Then the enormity struck her. 'So it might have been me,' she whispered.

'I doubt it,' grunted Rose reassuringly. 'The murderer was definitely after Nancy. All we need to know from you, miss, is which rooms you took tea to.'

'Nancy were supposed to do one side of the staircase and me the other, that was on the first floor, and she did the three rooms on the second floor, seeing as how I had further to walk on the first, my rooms being further from the lift,' she told them all in one breath. 'I offered to help, but she said she could manage,' she announced, sounding a trifle regretful that her beneficence had been so unappreciated.

'Where's that plan of the rooms, Mr Didier?'

Auguste produced it, and Bessie pored over it, one pudgy finger pointing to the west side of the hotel where Sir John Harnet, Miss Rosanna Pembrey, the de Castillons and Colonel Carruthers slept.

'So Nancy was responsible for Mr and Mrs Harbottle, Misses Ethel and Evelyn Pembrey, Major Dalmaine, and Miss Guessings, and on the next floor the Baroness, her companion, and Mr Bowman. And so far as you know, miss, they all got their tea.'

Bessie nodded vigorously. 'Course they did. There'd have been a tray left in the lift otherwise, eh?' She beamed at her percipience.

'And there wasn't?'

'Can't have bin. 'Cos I collected all the empties after, 'cos Nancy would have bin at breakfast by then, so she could start her dusting at nine. An' I collected *all* the trays.'

'Everyone had tea then, if you know you collected them all?'

Her face fell as slowly she took this in.

'I don't know, do I?' she said a little pettishly. 'You want dahn below.'

The term 'dahn below' in fact encompassed several rooms, the main kitchen itself, the subsidiary kitchen used as the staff dining room, scullery, larders, still room, cold room and wine cellars, together with a laundry and delivery room. It was the main kitchen, however, that immediately riveted Auguste's attention.

Fancelli, as soon as he saw Auguste, leaned nonchalantly back against the range. He had something to hide. What was it? was Auguste's fearful reaction. He had approved the menu both for luncheon and for dinner. Ergo, his detective instinct told him, Fancelli had altered something. All around, fresh wares from Covent Garden, Billingsgate and Smithfield lay awaiting attention, breakfast now being over. And there Auguste saw a distressing sight. He marched up to it, inspected and turned on the culprit.

'A fish with a dull eye is as bad as a detective with one,' he informed Fancelli none too gently. 'A cod's eye should be as bright as Inspector Rose's.'

'Very well, I will make him into soup,' Fancelli hissed clearly, wishing he could do the same with Auguste.

Rose suppressed a grin as he parted the warring cooks. 'What I want to know is who was responsible for loading the service lift with early morning tea trays?'

'Me.' An unhappy spotty youth was propelled forward by eager comrades none too anxious to be at closer quarters with the police.

'Any trays left unclaimed in the lift, son?' Rose asked him.

'No, sir. Thirteen trays went up as ordered.'

'And,' put in Bessie, 'I sends thirteen dahn again. And please, sir, I've been thinking. You was asking me about the teas. Well, if she was, like, killed *then*, where was the body put?'

'What do you mean, Bessie?' Auguste enquired. 'Either she was killed in the last room she visited with tea, or after that. Probably not in a public room, but in a bedroom. You may leave that to Inspector Rose to consider,' he told her gravely.

Bessie had no intention of leaving the limelight. 'Can't have been like that,' she said, pleased as Christmas punch. 'It can't have been put in the chest till late that evening, what with that young lady's joke. *Where* was the body hid in the meantime? You see, we girls would have noticed a body when we did the rooms proper, even if they 'id it when I collected the tea trays.'

Rose silently cursed last night's *foie gras* which had dulled mind as well as stomach.

'Hidden,' said Rose, less than adequately.

'But where?' asked Bessie, emboldened.

103

'Under the bed?'

A look of scorn from Bessie. 'Nah. Not with Mrs Pomfret around. Much as our life's worth not to do under the beds.'

'Wardrobe?'

'Nah. We opens them to put the day covers and cushions out for the beds.' Bessie was openly gloating now, looking round triumphantly to make sure her listening colleagues absorbed this triumph over the police, not to mention the all-powerful manager.

'A guest's trunk or another chest?'

'All the trunks are in the baggage room, Inspector,' Auguste told him, interested now. 'And as for chests, there are none in the bedrooms.'

'There must be many places in a hotel this size where a body could be hidden. Down in the cellars, for example.'

Fancelli, passing casually by, ostensibly with a half-eaten cold turkey but in fact to ensure Auguste was not putting the blame on him for murder, quickly intervened. 'No in my cellar. No in my kitchens.'

'Down the servants' stairs? Outside?'

'Then why bring it back?' asked Auguste reasonably. 'The guests,' he told Rose when they were alone in his office once more, having established that after about eight thirty none of the staff recalled seeing Nancy, and that apart from the other housemaids, all the staff were busy with Christmas luncheon and not bent on murder. 'It seems most likely to have been one of them.'

'What about maids and valets?' asked Rose sharply, remembering Stockbery Towers.

'The de Castillons have a maid and valet with them, as do Sir John Harnet and the Pembrey girls. They are lodged in nearby houses with some of the staff.'

'How do they get in?'

'Through the tradesmen's entrance.'

'So anyone could have got in.'

'My friend,' said Auguste gently, 'it is possible. But hardly likely. Remember – "At Cranton's? Christmas?" '

'Might we take a stroll round Portman Square, Mr Bowman? I would be so grateful for your company.' Gladys's kid-gloved hand stole inexorably round the crook of his arm.

'Never fear, dear lady, they'll arrest you over my dead body.' Alfred Bowman perceived his joke was not well received, and a guffaw was hastily turned into a cough. The gardens, though well-kept, were barren at this time of year, life represented only by one or two intrepid guests from the hotel like themselves, whom Gladys appeared to eye with alarm.

'Now,' began Bowman genially, 'how can I help you, dear lady? I can see you are troubled.'

'I knew her, you see,' Gladys burst out.

'Who?' asked Bowman cautiously.

'The girl. Nancy. The one who was murdered. I didn't know who it was dead till last night, and since I found out I've worried and worried. Oh, Mr Bowman, do you think I ought to tell the police? Will they think I did it?'

'Of course not,' replied Bowman offhandedly and far from reassuringly. 'How did you know her, my dear Gladys, if I might so address you?'

'They said a *maid* had been murdered, you see. And Nancy wasn't a maid. Well, not really. I recognised her on Christmas Eve – she was so startled to see me here, that's when she dropped that chestnut purée. Oh dear, I don't suppose the Baroness will be very grateful to me either. She comes from Much Wallop, you see.'

'Pardon?'

'The village where I live. She's the ward of an acquaintance of mine. Went to the *bad*, you know.'

'You mean, she became an unfortunate?' Bowman just held himself back from his usual word for the oldest profession.

A shocked silence. Then, 'No. But nearly as bad. She went to work for a *newspaper*.'

'Your just knowing her isn't going to worry the Inspector, dear lady. Shall I come with you to see him? Ten to one they've discovered already who the girl was.'

'But it's worse than that, Mr Bowman,' Gladys cried, determined to tell all. Or nearly. 'You see, when she brought my tea in on Christmas morning, she told me what she was doing here. And, oh, Mr Bowman, what do you think? She said she was working on a story for her magazine.'

'What story?' Sharply.

'She writes a household hints column, so I did just wonder. . .'

'Yes, dear lady?'

Gladys grew a trifle pink. 'She said something odd. I asked her if she couldn't make a little visit at New Year to Much Wallop, for her guardian would so like to see her. But she said no, it was urgent, for there was something she had to stop happening. It was still going on, she said. I wondered,' Gladys added diffidently, 'if she had something like the adulteration of honey in mind,' looking at Mr Bowman for his views. But he had no views to offer on honey.

'I suggest,' he said heartily, 'that you tell the Inspector at the earliest opportunity everything you've told me. Especially about the household hints. It might give them a lead.'

Thérèse von Bechlein, too, was walking in Portman Square, with Marie-Paul. There they came upon Thomas and Eva Harbottle, the latter being subjected to

106

the complete Baedeker guide pouring forth from the lips of her husband. 'That,' he pointed to the northern corner of the square, 'was the home of Monsieur Otto, the French ambassador who at the time of peace being concluded between England and France in 1802 hung lights to spell the word "Concord" outside it. The crowd outside construed it as "Conquered" and took great exception.'

'Was that not rather foolish of your countrymen, Thomas?' enquired his bride not entirely innocently.

He turned pink. 'Nonsense, my dear. It was but the misreading of the moment.'

'Unfortunately, Mr Harbottle,' interjected Thérèse, overhearing, 'Monsieur Otto's subsequent attempt "*Amitié*" was also misread as "Enmity". You see how hard we French endeavour to please you English in vain.'

'As you say, Baroness,' retorted Mr Harbottle. 'Unfortunately, every country has its mob. Even France.'

'*Oh la, la*, Marie-Paul, we have aroused the sleeping lion. My apologies, Mr Harbottle.'

He bowed, but as the Baroness walked away, she remarked to her companion, 'Not a lion, but a sleeping tiger, that one, Marie-Paul.'

'The Englishman?'

'Ah *non*. His wife, I meant.'

'Can't keep out of a good murder, can you, Auguste?'

Maisie's head appeared round the door of his cubby-hole, surmounted by a large pink feathered hat and muffled in white fur.

'Dear Maisie.' He leapt up and embraced her; chastely, with merely two kisses. 'It follows me, as you well know.'

'*Cherchez l'homme*, say I,' pulling off her gloves.

'Which *homme* had you in mind?' asked Auguste drily.

'Her young man,' said Maisie cheerfully. 'He's the obvious suspect. Ten to one they had a quarrel when they met that morning, he stabbed her and there you are.'

'And then she arose and served seven trays of tea?' he enquired.

'He lied about the time,' she said shortly.

'And how did the body walk inside the hotel again unnoticed?' enquired Auguste patiently.

'Elementary, Watson,' said Maisie, twinkling now. 'I reckon he hid it in the cellars where he was sleeping, then popped it up into the chest during the night. At *eight* thirty there wouldn't be too much risk when he stabbed her. The servants would be in the kitchens, not the cellars.'

'This body was not yet released from rigor mortis. You think he could "pop" it up a staircase into the drawing room just like that?'

'I can't solve everything for you, Auguste. I have to leave something to you,' she said impatiently, then soberly: 'Poor girl. Like the others. Remember?'

A glance between them, and six years fell away once more. They were back in the Galaxy Theatre, that place of enchantment, now being swept away under the beginnings of a new roadway, the Aldwych. Soon the theatre would open again elsewhere, yet the old building had gone with its years of happy memories. True, of the time he and Maisie had been there, not all the memories were happy.

'We both remember,' he said quietly.

She sighed. 'That's why I want to help find who murdered this girl.'

'Then, Maisie, tell me. How, when did the staff come to you? Where and when did your guests hear of this party? It is, Egbert and I know, of great significance.'

'We advertised in *The Times* for guests, of course.'

'When?'

'I think October.'

'So we can rule out all those who live so far away that the news could not have reached them in time.'

'Oh no,' Maisie said, highly pleased. 'You're losing your touch. Perhaps they have relatives in this country, who arranged it for them.'

'True,' he agreed regretfully. 'And the staff were all hired in early December?'

'Yes, at about the same time I approached you.'

'You came to me first?' he asked suspiciously.

'Naturally, I *thought* of you first,' said Maisie smoothly, 'but it never occurred to me that you would be free. Not until one of your former pupils applied for a job, and mentioned it.'

'Why, as a pupil of Auguste Didier, did he not get a position?' he demanded indignantly, diverted for the moment from the thread of his enquiries.

'Because I'd already appointed Fancelli,' retorted Maisie. 'And nothing but the best posts, naturally, would suit your pupils, Auguste.'

'Ah.' Auguste was mollified.

Egbert Rose had arranged to see the guests one by one and Maisie was deputed to search her offices for all correspondence likely to be of interest. Highly incensed at being banished, she went off, head in air.

Rose had elected to see the Marquise first, but to his surprise it was Gladys Guessings who swept in first, hat askew, nose pink, to explain her mission.

'Why didn't you tell us earlier you knew the young lady?' he asked resignedly. 'It would have saved a great deal of work tracing her relations.'

'Oh!' Her face was anxious. 'Has her poor guardian

been told? I didn't know, you see. I just thought of her as poor Nancy Watkins gone to the bad.'

'To the *London Watchman*, in fact,' observed Rose drily.

'Yes. She was working on honey, I believe,' Gladys announced in a hushed voice.

'Honey?' Rose asked blankly.

'It's very wicked, you know, what goes on in our food.' She leant across the table confidentially. 'They adulterate it. I've read about it. And other foods. All sorts of things in there that shouldn't be. *And* our water. Food was put on earth to be clean, Inspector Rose.' The bobble on her hat emphasised its agreement with her. 'What is mankind doing to it? That's what we need to know. I think Nancy was quite right, although she'd gone to the bad.'

'To the bad, madame?' asked Auguste, just entering. 'You mean she . . .' Visions of white slavers, the Haymarket, the brothels of Soho, flooded through his mind.

'Oh no. Why must you gentlemen always be thinking of *that*?' Gladys blushed half in annoyance, half in embarrassment.

'He's French, ma'am,' Rose retorted gravely, shooting a sidelong look at a highly annoyed Auguste. 'Did she talk to you after she had recognised you?'

'Oh yes, we had quite a chat when she brought the tea in in the morning, and she asked me not to tell anyone why she was there. I suppose it's all right now though,' she added sadly. 'She said she was after an important story, you see. That it was all happening again. About the food.'

'I think the story she was after might have been bigger than that, ma'am.'

'Oh no, it was definitely food. Particularly puddings.'

'Puddings?' repeated Rose blankly.

110

'Yes, I remember that clearly because she mentioned my favourite. My father brought the recipe home from his club one day for Mother, but I fear,' she giggled, 'I used to eat the greater part. It was called Emma Pryde's Pall Mall Pudding. That's Emma Pryde, the famous cook, you know,' she added.

'*Oui*, madame, I know,' Auguste said, well aware of Emma's specialities. Pall Mall Pudding was not a recipe he was acquainted with, but with its inventor – ah, that was a different matter.

'So when Nancy mentioned Pall Mall, I told her at once I understood,' Gladys added proudly.

'She mentioned Pall Mall – you're sure of that?' Rose asked sharply.

'She did so like to be mysterious, but she knew my little weakness and so naturally confided. It's about ginger, isn't it? And honey and so on. And the pudding. "Oh yes," she said, "you're right, Miss Guessings. My story is about the Pall Mall Pudding with a dangerous mix." I can hear her now. Saying those very words. I've read about it, you see, ginger being a little weakness of mine. They sweep up sand and dirt from the warehouse floors and put them in the ground ginger, you know. And sometimes they add Plaster of Paris and gypsum too. I do hope,' she rushed on, 'Scotland Yard are investigating.'

'We've got a Food and Drugs Act for that, ma'am,' said Rose patiently. 'Now—'

'And honey – that's mainly sugar – starch. And jams, they're all made of turnips.'

'Not my jams, Miss Guessings,' said Auguste firmly. 'Mine are made from the purest ingredients.'

She eyed him doubtfully. 'Even ground ginger? What can a gentleman know about puddings? Oh, I forgot, you're a cook, aren't you?'

'Madame, I am *the* cook, the *maître chef*. And you

may be assured no pudding or food for which I am responsible, as I am here, is adulterated with Plaster of Paris.'

Colonel Carruthers marched in as if a Wellington advancing to his Waterloo. He almost saluted, but instead sat down with a harrumph.

'Gather you want to see me. Nothing I can tell you. Never notice girls. Why can't you have men servants here?' he shot at Auguste. 'Girls should keep out of sight, that's my view.'

'Did you notice the murdered girl, sir, either at table on Christmas Eve or on Christmas morning?' Rose showed the Colonel a photograph, and he turned pale.

Then recovering, 'No. She could have been serving me dinner and tea for the last twenty years and I still wouldn't recognise her face. Why?' he shot out as if on parade at Oudenarde.

'The girl was a journalist, sir, involved in investigating a crime.'

'Crime?'

'We think perhaps a series of art thefts in London,' lied Rose blandly.

'Convenient,' snorted Carruthers. 'So that's why we're being marched off to Hertford House this afternoon.' He scowled at Auguste. 'You behind all this, are you?'

'*Non, monsieur*, I am not a robber. I am a cook by profession.'

'So you're the one responsible for that blasted mess you dare call kedgeree?'

'Not this one, sir. It is the chef's.'

'In overall command, aren't you?' barked Carruthers. 'In my day you'd have done the decent thing. You'd have been found dead with a Martini-Henry beside you.'

★ ★ ★

'I think, Inspector, as a visitor from Germany, it is hardly likely that I would choose to spend Christmas murdering a girl I'd never set eyes on before.'

'No, ma'am,' said Rose. 'On the other hand we have to speak to everyone.'

'Another servant seems the most likely culprit,' offered Thérèse helpfully.

'Possibly, but unlikely, given who she was.'

The beautifully arched eyebrows were raised.

'A news reporter working on a story about art thefts.'

'Indeed?' A flicker of interest passed over Thérèse's face. 'I must mention this to my husband. He is a connoisseur of art.'

'A diplomat at the Kaiser's court, isn't he?'

'He is,' agreed Thérèse. 'He is at the moment in Hungary, however, a place I have no liking for, hence my visit to your country.'

'Do you recall the young lady who brought your tea?'

'I recall receiving tea,' she answered. 'Does this make me a suspect, Inspector?'

'No more than everyone else, ma'am. You and your companion and Mr Bowman would have been at the end of her round, being on the second floor.'

Her eyes flickered sharply. 'You mean if any of those served earlier murdered this poor girl, there would have been complaints from other guests that their tea had not arrived. Therefore, if I am last, I had the best opportunity to murder her.' She smiled. 'Might I point out, Inspector, that if as you say this young lady was a reporter, she clearly had reason for being here. If she wished to speak to one of the guests about this reason, she would naturally leave them till last and serve us out of order. How, Inspector, can you tell that I was last?'

'She's right of course,' said Rose after she had

departed. 'It could have been any order. Bessie wouldn't notice, she'd be busy.'

'Or it could have been any of the people Bessie served after Bessie had left for breakfast,' Auguste pointed out.

'Or even you,' grunted Rose crossly, regretting it as he saw Auguste's hurt face.

'Marie-Paul Gonnet,' announced the companion, in a low voice, keeping her eyes down as though even here she must remember her position.

'Have you been to England before, Miss Gonnet?'

'It is my first visit.'

'You speak English well.'

'I learn it from my employer.'

'In Germany?'

'No, in Paris where we spend much time.' She folded her hands in her brown silk lap, a curious stillness about her body that reminded Auguste of something he could not identify. She sat obediently, he noticed, waiting to be asked questions, never volunteering. The perfect companion.

'Did you receive tea that morning?' Rose went on.

'I do not take tea. I go into Madame's room at about eight thirty.'

'To help her dress?'

For the first time a flash of individuality. 'I am not a maid, monsieur, I am a companion.'

'Madame has a maid with her?'

'*Non*. I –' she hesitated. 'I do assist Madame with her dresses if she requires, and the hotel has excellent services if required. Madame had only to ring the bell.'

Auguste preened himself. Naturally his hotel was well run.

Bella flashed a smile at Auguste. 'Isn't this fun? I feel

like one of those damsels in distress in the *Strand Magazine*.'

'Far more beautiful and intelligent than they, madame,' he murmured gallantly, then wished fervently that he had not, since the warmth of the ensuing smile and the twinkle in her eyes boded ill for the future.

'Yes, a girl did bring me tea – I hardly noticed her, save that she was plump,' she answered Rose's question. 'I was asleep. It was a little late when I awoke. I had had rather a disturbed night,' she added innocently.

'Why did you decide to come to England for Christmas, madame?' Auguste tried to ignore the dancing eyes of invitation.

'Paris is not entertaining at Christmas. England is. My husband finds my family in Hungary – shall we say, uncongenial. So we come here,' she explained.

She spoke easily, frankly, yet why did it seem to him just a little too easily, as though these were words she had rehearsed? Auguste shrugged the sudden feeling off; he must not let the lovely Bella prey on his mind – or his body.

Egbert Rose pondered on the Marquis. Difficult, these diplomatic types. He'd already thrown Auguste out of the room, as a condition of his condescending to speak to the police at all. 'I'm going to be frank with you, sir.'

A flicker of an eyebrow.

'It's rather more than the murder of a housemaid I'm concerned with. The girl was here on a story – she picked up the whiff of a plot to kill the Prince of Wales.'

'Ah.' The Marquis was at once most interested. 'Does this have connections with Paris also?'

'It does, sir. The Sûreté passed the information to me.'

'And I, Inspector, passed it to them.' He paused, his face impassive. 'I do not approve of the British handling of affairs in Africa. Nevertheless, I cannot approve of assassination either. Through our African sources we have contacts with the Transvaal government. It is indeed disturbed by the sudden friendship of the Kaiser with your country, monsieur, since, as you know, Germany is one of the main sources of their armaments. There are factions that see the war as by no means over, despite Lord Roberts's temporary achievements – if achievements they are. They wish to make the task of Lord Kitchener most difficult and there are arms dealers everywhere, sir, and manufacturers – in our country and even in yours too – that have every desire to support them. And that was well before Kruger was refused an audience by the Kaiser on his visit to Germany. At that point one of his party with business reasons of his own for continuing the war came immediately to Paris, and then to Brussels, we gather, there to plan a blow that would throw not only Britain into turmoil, but undoubtedly prolong the coming of true peace in South Africa.'

'Names?'

The Marquis shrugged. 'Inspector, you ask the impossible. The Boer is on his way back to South Africa, the Sûreté agent was murdered on his way back to Paris – and we do not know whom the Boer met in Brussels. The man is a shadow.'

'Or woman.'

'Or, as you say, woman.'

Sir John Harnet bristled. 'Stuff and nonsense. De Castillon's trying to make himself important again. He's a provincial, you see. Trying to show he's as good

116

as his Parisian colleagues. No one would dare try to assassinate the Prince of Wales.'

'How about Sipido in Brussels last April?' Rose asked quietly. 'He tried all right, got close to the carriage window and fired several bullets. Only the fact he was a bad shot saved the Prince and the Princess.'

'That was different. Sipido was a crazed youngster acting alone. If there was a conspiracy with the Boers involved, I'd know about it.'

'Nevertheless, we have to take the threat seriously.'

Sir John ruminated. 'Did he tell you about the Ashantis?'

'Ashantis?' repeated Rose blankly, envisaging painted warriors with spears launching an assegai attack on His Royal Highness in the midst of Paddington Station.

'Thought not,' Sir John rumbled with satisfaction. 'If that girl was after a story, ten to one it's about that, not some cock and bull tale about shooting Albert Edward. The Golden Stool of the Ashantis, their symbol of kingship.'

'Something like the Coronation Stone in Westminster Abbey?'

'Entirely different,' said Sir John testily. 'They're Africans.'

This was not the moment for an anthropological discussion of ancient kingship beliefs, Rose decided. Edith was a fervent reader of folklore. Sometimes he thought she believed King Arthur was waiting in Epping Forest to be summoned by Egbert Rose whenever he had a difficult case. It was a comforting thought, but impractical.

'The Ashantis hid it in ninety-six when King Prempeh agreed to co-operate with the Governor.'

Agreed to co-operate was not how Egbert Rose had read the news, but he remained tactfully silent.

★ ★ ★

Major Dalmaine limped in, sank down in the chair, stretched out his leg. He had been gratified that Rosanna had enquired after his wound at breakfast. 'Volunteer battalion, the Queen's Own the Royal West Kents. Home – ' he hesitated – 'on leave.' No need to specify just how uncertain his military career looked.

'Seems odd to choose to come home for a Christmas alone, sir,' Rose commented mildly.

He reddened. 'Yes. Unfortunately my sister was called away, and so planned for me to spend Christmas here.'

'When was that arranged, sir?'

'I've no idea. Early in December, I expect.'

'What do you do out there, Major? On the staff, are you?'

'Staff, Inspector?' He looked astounded. 'I fight, sir. I fight.'

'You weren't connected with the annexation celebrations at all, then? Had no contact with the top brass on the Boer side?'

Dalmaine stiffened. 'No,' he said coldly. 'I did not. I am a fighting man, as I told you.'

'Tea, sir.'

'Tea?' Dalmaine was thrown.

'You received it on Christmas morning?'

'Yes. I don't remember who brought it. A fat girl picked up the tray,' he announced unenthusiastically.

'But you don't recall the girl who brought it?'

'No,' he replied abruptly.

Thomas and Eva Harbottle insisted on being interviewed together, though this did little to sustain their morale since they seemed ill at ease.

'Did you both receive your tea on Christmas morning?'

118

'We are married, Inspector.' A mixture of pride and coolness in his tone at the implied suggestion that they might have been separated. 'Yes, we did, thank you. I'm afraid there is little we can tell you about the girl that brought it, except that she seemed preoccupied, in a hurry. I remember Eva,' he smiled fondly at his wife, 'made a joke and said she must be anxious to get to breakfast.'

Rose smiled politely. 'You're not English, are you, Mrs Harbottle?'

'We met in Amsterdam,' Thomas answered quickly for her.

'Is that where you were born, Mrs Harbottle?'

'No, I am German,' she announced quickly.

'A very interesting city, Amsterdam,' began Thomas loudly. 'We are on our way to settle in England. Eva has not yet met my parents. We are looking forward to visiting them, aren't we, Eva?'

'Oh yes,' his wife replied obediently.

Rosanna entered briskly, her cheeks glowing, her eyes bright. 'I must warn you, Inspector, my sisters have no intention of being separated. They are outside now planning something.' Her eyes danced, belying her apologetic tones.

'Your choice to come here, was it, Miss Pembrey?'

'No,' she sighed. 'But I am only twenty and Sir John looks after us in England until I am twenty-one. And if I am not married by then, I suppose, longer than that. I *intend* to be married by then,' she added firmly.

'To Major Dalmaine?'

She hooted with laughter in an unladylike way, for the first time resembling the twins.

'No, Inspector. I have my own plans.' She smiled brightly. 'It is of course a most unsuitable match. The *Strand Magazine* and *Peg's Companion* would both approve. He is the completely penniless son of a good family of impoverished means. And it just so happens he lives in London,' she added artlessly.

The twins followed her in, endeavouring to look extremely solemn. One wore a Sherlock Holmes-type deerstalker perched over her blonde curls; the other carried an attaché case and a magnifying glass.

'We're here to help all we can, Inspector,' Ethel announced importantly in a deep voice. 'Aren't we, my dear Watson?'

'Right you are, Holmes!' announced her sister.

Rose sighed. Auguste shrank back, feeling he could cope with twenty Fancellis more easily than this pair.

'What we plan to do,' Evelyn announced brightly, 'is to make it a sort of parlour game.'

'*Game?*' Rose frowned. 'Murder ain't a game, young lady.'

'We know that,' retorted Ethel severely. 'After all, I was the one who found the body.' When she judged Rose looked sufficiently penitent she went on: 'We thought if we made it a Sherlock and Watson investigation, and got all the guests talking amongst themselves, we could find out things for you. After all, there can only be one guilty party, can't there? So if the others became interested and started talking, all sorts of things might come out that you would never think of asking.'

'No,' shouted Auguste, seeing trouble lying ahead. Reproachfully they turned their full charm on Rose.

Charm he was impervious to, potential he was not. But in this case – 'Theoretically, young ladies, you're right. But I can't let you do it.' Their faces fell. 'You forget,' he told them soberly, 'there's a murderer amongst us. And murderers, young ladies, after they've tried it once, sometimes get a taste for it.'

The twins were impressed, or seemed so. Nevertheless, when they left, Auguste distinctly heard one say, 'We have our methods, Watson.'

'She came at seven thirty,' said Danny obstinately, glaring at Rose. 'Then she left. You know she did, she served teas.'

'How do we know it wasn't eight thirty?' enquired Rose grimly.

Danny blenched. 'Why would I have killed her?' he asked vehemently. 'Why?'

'Same reason any young man kills a girl,' Rose informed him.

'Your passions may get aroused in cellars at seven thirty in the morning, Inspector, but—'

'What the Inspector means, Danny,' Auguste hurriedly interrupted, seeing Rose's usually impassive face begin to show more than a few signs of dislike of Danny Nash, 'is that it seems strange that you should be so devoted to protecting a colleague that you give up Christmas to sleep in a cellar.'

Danny opened his mouth, then shut it again, his face slowly turning brick red.

'I've good news for you, Mr Nash,' said Rose grimly. 'You can move out of your cellar – and into the hotel. Where my men can keep an eye on you. A close eye.'

'Now we're permitted in here again,' said Bella, following Auguste into the drawing room where he had superintended the hasty dusting of the room, 'I can take advantage of you,' advancing on him meaningfully.

'Not here, madame!' he cried aghast. 'Just think, if we were to be discovered on the sofa *en déshabillé*, your husband—'

'Why, Auguste, I only meant a tiny kiss under the

mistletoe.' Laughter bubbled up as her hands stole round his neck. 'What did you think I meant?'

The kissing bough twirled and turned above them in the slight draught through the windows, as her lips met his, and for once luncheon was not top of the manager's list of priorities.

'If an art theft is supposed to be the reason for that girl getting murdered, are you sure,' enquired Sir John somewhat querulously, 'that we are safe here with merely one constable?' He gazed suspiciously around the Wallace Collection newly open to the public as though the Watteau before him might be snatched before his very eyes.

'Quite safe,' Auguste assured him, wondering in fact how he could keep an eye on his brood in such a vast place, even though they were the only visitors. Hertford House had been opened especially for them today. Already he thought he had counted fifteen, not fourteen heads, but Miss Pembrey had assured him the fifteenth was her maid.

'I wonder if you are aware, Eva,' announced her husband loudly, 'that Simon Bolivar stayed in a house near here in 1810?'

Eva for once reacted. 'He fought for his country,' she said fiercely. 'He was a hero.'

'Quite,' said Thomas uneasily, steering her to a peaceful contemplation of Caillot's Cupid and Psyche.

'Stolen by that man,' Carruthers was remarking at the moment some way away in the armoury, a portion of the museum ignored by all but himself and that damned Napoleon-lover, Dalmaine.

Dalmaine stared at the equestrian suit in black and gold ascribed to the Elector Joseph of Bavaria and removed from his arsenal by Napoleon.

'Good general, though. Didn't make as many mistakes as Wellington, I maintain,' said Dalmaine stoutly, moving on to powder flasks.

'Justify that, sir!' Carruthers glared.

'Failure to supply more ammunition at La Haye Sainte,' said Dalmaine promptly.

'Good God, man, the C-in-C can't be held responsible for everything? Can he, sir?' whirling on Auguste who arrived at this critical moment.

'Indeed not, sir,' replied Auguste smoothly and ignobly. 'No more than a manager for his cook's kedgeree. . .'

Some miles away to the east, Egbert Rose climbed from a hansom in less salubrious surroundings. Behind him the Thames flowed on, grey and uninviting, hugging its secrets to itself. Ahead were several small lanes leading down to the waterfront. A group of ill-clad children broke off their hopscotch to watch him as he turned up the collar of his overcoat and decided which way to go. They knew a crusher when they saw one. If they had been older, they would have known even more about this one, for he was no stranger to Stepney. From the lighted windows of two public houses, seamen paused in the drinking of porter to watch, some in idle curiosity, others less idle, and at least two who abandoned their drink and slunk off into the network of alleys, rats back to their holes to spread the news.

Aware of their scrutiny, Rose struck off up one alley through another, and another. He turned into the dark, damp covered passageway between two rows of small terraced houses, and glancing back when he was at the end, turned quickly left, and then in at a back doorway, through the yard into a house. The man vigorously mending boots hardly paused to look up, as Rose re-emerged into the street, no bowler hat now, but cap and shabby jacket, clutching a bundle. He let himself out, walked quickly for two hundred yards or so and into another house.

He thrust open the door, and clouds of steam enveloped him, making him cough with the smell of Sunlight soap, of mangles, of damp washing. It was better than the smells that usually reached him in this part of the world.

In the steam he could dimly make out a shape.

'What d'yer want?'

An enormous figure, sixteen-stone, copper dolly-wielding, a laundress who in this area of dirt and filth produced the cleanest clothes Rose ever saw in the whole of his travels.

'Afternoon, Ma.'

The figure loomed more closely, emerging from the fog, wiping her hands, peering at the visitor.

'Oh. It's you.'

Ma Bisley was at home.

Chapter Five

Say what you like, but Norfolk was a long way away, and much too flat. Rose gazed out of the window of the Royal Train at dull green fields and barren fields. Trouble was with the country it was all the same. Nothing to oil the brain. Give him houses, shops, people, public houses, theatres even, anywhere that things happened. It might suit some folks to live in the country, but he couldn't see it for him – or for Edith. Highbury Fields were country enough for them. Mr Pinpole the butcher and the Maypole and Liptons were just down the road, and Mr Waskett the greengrocer was just a few steps further, and always very civil to Edith. Life was uncomplicated in Highbury, and that was something, after a day at the Factory, he could do with.

It had been a pity not to be able to tell Edith this morning he was going to see Albert Edward, Prince of Wales, to report progress – or lack of it. The fact that he had put on his best waistcoat had not escaped her, he was sure of that. After it was all over, he could look forward to telling her. 'Oh Egbert,' he could hear her saying, 'What was Her Royal Highness wearing?' So far the journey had proved a disappointment. He had felt somehow cheated to discover that travelling on the Royal Train merely meant a halt on Sandringham estate, not that he would be cushioned in regal splendour.

His spirits rose to see the line of royal carriages and

baggage wagons at Wolferton railway station. It wasn't every day he rode in a carriage with the Prince of Wales's crest on it. Rather to his surprise, he seemed to be taking precedence over the undoubtedly far more aristocratic Saturday-to-Monday guests arriving by the same train, until he reflected that His Royal Highness was no doubt eager to pack business out of the way at the earliest opportunity.

It was a nice enough drive, if you liked this kind of thing, long road bordered with grass and trees, birds singing, squirrels scurrying about – bit of contrast to Ma Bisley's place. He grinned. He liked Ma. They understood each other. Ma was the Piccadilly Circus of all roads of information; if it didn't come to Ma Bisley's ears, it weren't a villainy worth knowing about.

The carriage turned a curve in the road and there were the massive gates of Sandringham, with crowns, feathers and shields all over them, only one policeman on duty. He showed his pass; the policeman was unimpressed. After all, he had the security of the throne to ensure, that of the nation rated second in his book of precedence. Rose grinned as the carriage proceeded up the avenue, then under a covered way to a door somewhat less imposing than the principal front entrance to which he observed subsequent carriages were heading.

Albert Edward, Prince of Wales, advanced towards the waiting room as he might towards his dentist – a disagreeable but necessary visit before he might enjoy luncheon. And receive his Saturday-to-Monday guests of course. Shooting this afternoon, perhaps, while the ladies disported themselves in the bowling alley. And this evening – he encouraged his mind to wander over the delights of the evening to come – not so delightful as they might have been in London without the Princess's presence, but nevertheless jolly. At his time of life there was quite a lot to be said for a game of billiards and a good smoke. Then his arrival at the waiting room reminded him disagreeably that life might not be there much longer unless he took this matter seriously.

He regarded Inspector Egbert Rose thoughtfully. 'Progress?' he asked in his guttural voice.

'Sorry, sir,' said Rose guardedly.

The heir to the throne of the British Empire walked to the window and stared out over acres of peaceful England. 'Madmen I can understand,' he said at last. 'A plot, conspiracy – no.'

'England has enemies, sir.'

'Germany?' rumbled the royal voice. 'The Kaiser would never dare.'

'It doesn't have to stem from His Majesty himself, sir,' Rose pointed out. 'South Africa though, that's what we fear.'

His Royal Highness considered this. 'Then it's Field Marshal Roberts they're after.'

'Why at Paddington then, and not at Cowes where the Field Marshal is landing to meet the Queen?'

'Wouldn't dare. Might harm Her Majesty. Wouldn't do them any good,' said her son simply. 'It would have a better result if they killed me.'

'Sir, it is just possible that the attack will be made not at Paddington, but in the Marlborough Club or at the Carlton. Do you have plans to go there, sir?'

Royalty seemed extremely unwilling to answer, but finally intimated that if he could not drop into his club without being surrounded by half the British army and police force guarding him, a club that he had founded for this very purpose, then life was not worth living anyway. Somewhat grudgingly, however, he admitted to having plans to go to the Carlton with a private party in the middle of January, and yes, he did usually dine in the Marlborough Room.

Something in Rose's stomach, which could not be blamed on last night's cold mutton chop, stirred uncomfortably.

'And Cranton's, sir – do you have any connection in Cranton's?'

'*Cranton's*?' The Prince was startled. 'Why?' he asked cautiously.

'We think the plot has something to do with Cranton's.'

'I remember it,' His Highness answered slowly and noncommittally. 'I heard it was being opened again by—' He said no more. One of the irksome duties of his position was to vet for his mother, the comings and goings of all his relations, whom they intended to marry, where they intended to live, what they had for dinner. He brought himself back to the matter in hand. 'If you're right, the conspirators would stay at the Carlton, not Cranton's.'

'Wouldn't that draw too much attention to the villains' presence?'

'They can't just pop up in the middle of a cake and shoot me,' the Prince pointed out. 'They would have to plan some method of being there.'

'Yes, sir, but the reason Cranton's is involved is that a young lady who was, we think, investigating a rumour about this affair, has been murdered there.'

'Murder?' This was definitely unwelcome news. A shiver ran through the Prince at the thought of murder. He did his best to avoid it and it seemed to hurl itself directly into his path. That settled it. He'd keep well away from Cranton's. Then an amusing thought struck him.

'That French cook fellow hasn't got himself mixed up in this, has he?'

'As a matter of fact, he has, sir.'

'I'm sorry, Auguste.' Maisie's normally cheerful face was rueful. 'I'm afraid George has put his foot down.'

'How did his foot hear of it in St Moritz?' asked Auguste crossly.

'Now, now, Auguste. There's newspapers, you know. George doesn't want me involved.'

Auguste knew all too well that there were newspapers. The news had not taken long to reach them that one of their own had been murdered. True, it was a lady reporter, but the issue was all the more emotional for that. It had been with more than usual difficulty that they had been persuaded by Twitch to refrain from broadcasting the fact to the far corners of the earth. Sulkily, Fleet Street recorded that a housemaid had been found dead in the old Cranton's Hotel. The death was entirely unconnected with a series of major art thefts being planned, it was believed, with foreign connections. The police were watching for suspected criminals entering or leaving the country.

Fleet Street took its revenge by haunting Cranton's entrance. The doormen shooed them away like pigeons periodically when their numbers grew, and like pigeons they returned. One or two took to trailing guests, and Auguste was on tenterhooks lest his guests object to the attention they were receiving. Furthermore it had not escaped his notice that Danny Nash was keeping remarkably quiet, coming in late at night, and disappearing at breakfast time.

'But if you are not here, Maisie, how am I to do everything?' Auguste despaired. 'How can I escort the guests on their visits, be host *and* hostess, oversee Fancelli, how can I *Manage*?'

'Good practice,' replied Maisie reassuringly, 'for when you're a hotelier.'

'I am not sure,' Auguste remarked gloomily, 'that I wish now to be one. It seems to me that being a chef has rewards enough.'

'Don't worry. You won't get a murder with every hotel.'

'And that is another matter. Inspector Rose asks me to help solve the murder—'

'There now, me old duck, you'll be admirably placed for sniffing out clues,' said Maisie, relieved. 'And as for hostessing, I've asked Bella to help you. She'd be delighted, she told me.'

Auguste digested this news with mixed feelings. Delightful though Bella was, the opportunities for têtes-à-têtes would undoubtedly increase with such proximity. He looked round his domain when Maisie had gone. He was a regent in temporary possession of a kingdom. Around him were the signs of Christmas, the decorations, the festive twinkling coloured paper lanterns. And there through the open doorway of the drawing room he could see the kissing bough, a symbol going back into the dark ages that told of sinister rituals of the druids that had little to do with a festival of goodwill to all men. And death had come again beneath its innocent-looking berries and greenery. An unsolved death as yet. Suddenly he was angry with fate for throwing him this opportunity and then mocking it with murder. He would solve the crime, and quickly. He had not been thinking as had been his wont in former times. Perhaps he needed the stimulation of cooking to make him detect correctly. But on this occasion, he remembered with frustration, Signor Fancelli was in the kitchens, not himself.

As if on cue, the hated voice rose in unnatural bass from its underworld kingdom. 'What has swept you from the sunshine of your native land?' Filled with a rage he could not identify, Auguste ran downstairs. Not in his hotel. And not an aria about *Provence*. That was *his* home, not that of this fat parvenu Italian. Fancelli beamed on his arrival, albeit a smile of contented possessiveness, a usurper unafraid of his Hamlet. Auguste did not return the beam.

'No singing, signor, I beg.' He said sternly.

'Ah. You no like. I forget.' Fancelli beamed again.

'And I no like this either.' Auguste marched grimly to the ovens where a haunch of venison awaited its entrance.

'What wrong?' Fancelli asked warily. 'Turtle soup and venison, the Gog and Magog of English cooking, so Soyer say,' he brought out with pride.

'Perhaps.' Auguste's tones were clipped. He did not need to be reminded of the glories of the great Alexis Soyer today or any day. 'But this, if I am not mistaken, is *roebuck* venison.'

'So?'

'The English eat only fallow deer from English parks. And where, Signor Fancelli, is the fat? It is not worth roasting without,' Auguste hissed reprovingly, keeping his voice quiet so that underlings would not hear this dispute.

'Signor Didier, if you think you cook venison better than Fancelli, then you—' Fancelli stopped short, as if reconsidering this gauntlet before he flung it. Auguste, by the look of his face, would be all too ready to pick it up.

'If you believe this is edible, then you may serve it to your staff. My guests will not eat it. Preferable they eat an omelette Didier to this,' he flicked it disdainfully, 'boot leather.'

'I do this, Signor Didier, but beware. Fancelli is not to be insulted.' The smile reappeared on his face, and he hummed happily – to himself – Signor Verdi's

Grand Victory March from *Aida*.

Auguste returned to his office and tried to study the menus for the next day. *Chartreuse de perdreaux*, almond pudding, duck simmered in claret, oyster quenelles, stewed lampreys – the names swam before him, for once not conjuring up to his mind delightful aromas and memories, but remaining there stolidly before him, uninspired and uninspiring. He remembered how in the past he solved murder by considering it as the ingredients of a *plat*. In the kitchens below now, however, there was no order. It was chaos. Like in this murder itself. So many people could have done it that patient logic was necessary, but how could this be achieved if all were not well below?

He forced himself to try to think calmly, to assemble the ingredients for this recipe that had ended in the murder of a girl. To take a simple receipt such as the making of an Indian curry: first the assembling of the implements – here we had an oak chest, a stiletto dagger. Let us consider the instrument – Italian, and there was only one Italian on the premises.

Try as he could, Auguste could not see Fancelli murdering the girl. He had not the intelligence to plan this crime. Besides, Fancelli, so Egbert had informed him rather more pragmatically, had been in sight of all the other kitchen staff at the time. Regretfully Fancelli was tentatively ruled out. Who else? Anyone who came prepared for murder, logic told him. *Prepared?* Yet how could this be unless Nancy's murderer knew she would be there. Was this possible? Yes. If he, Auguste, had heard those words in the fog, the murderer might have done also and arranged to come here. And that presumed that he, being present, was indeed the murderer of the girl in the fog, and not Nancy herself. The murderer had two choices after realising the presence of an unseen stranger (himself, Auguste): to chase after

Nancy, or to stay to remove the body. He chose the latter.

Yes, that fitted. But so also did the thesis that the murderer was prepared because he intended to kill the Prince of Wales. Yet with a stiletto? How could he – or she – hope to get close enough?

Now for the ingredients, so important in a recipe. The least mistake, and the whole recipe was thrown out. Suppose no chillis were included, or no cayenne, would that not alter the whole? And here there were a lady reporter, a story, a planned assassination, a group of people – some of whom had something to hide, of that he was sure. The Baroness, Dalmaine, Rosanna . . . However innocent, there were secrets here that needed revealing.

He had argued that this was the plan of an intelligent person, whether conceived before he came to Cranton's or when he saw Nancy serving supper. No, it must be the former, for how otherwise would he recognise her? And that meant he had been close to her in the fog; yet if he had seen her, she had seen him. Did she not know the girl had been murdered? Yes, she must have known. Why, then, not be on her guard when serving tea? This would suggest either that she was murdered by one of those to whom she did not take tea – Bessie's rooms – or Mademoiselle Gonnet. Or, he had a happy thought, there were two people involved. Ah yes! Much more likely. Two people to support the body, to lift it into the chest.

He took another piece of meat for this splendid curry he was concocting. If this was an intelligent murderer, why the clumsy attempt to make them believe the murder took place on Boxing morning by replacing the dagger? Only a fool would think this undetectable? True, as he had pointed out, it was an ideal place to hide a weapon, but suppose this meat should be cut across the grain, not along it? Why, after all, had the dagger to be taken out in the first place? There was but one answer. Unlike the chest with its convex lid, wherever the body remained during the Christmas Day festivities, it would not allow room for a knife.

Ah yes. And now this meat must be chopped even finer: *where* was the body while the rooms were cleaned? And when and why was it moved? It would be heavy, there would be the risk of observation. The hiding place could not be far from the room.

Now the vegetables, whose appearance, like the meat, would all be subtly changed by the spices, the hidden threads at work behind the scenes. The Baroness lived in Berlin, though she spent much time in Paris. Was her reason for being here the true one? Bella was Hungarian, with a French diplomatist for husband. Why should they be here? And Thomas Harbottle and his German wife – why not stay with his family? Colonel Carruthers and Dalmaine were unmistakably English; Dalmaine had come back from the South African War, Carruthers had been widowed, Maisie told him. The Pembrey girls were English with parents in Africa. Mr Bowman and Miss Guessings were English. All had reasons to be here at Christmas – and Miss Guessings had confessed to knowing Nancy before. And there was one other vegetable in his curry: Danny Nash, who still obstinately clung to his story that he was here merely to protect a colleague. And the staff? Egbert had ruled them out. Mrs Pomfret and the other maids could enjoy no such immunity, but Twitch had been busy checking their backgrounds. None seemed a likely candidate for stabbing either Nancy Watkins or the Prince of Wales.

And mixing the curry, if two worked together? The Baroness, perhaps on behalf of her husband and acting with her companion. Possible. Bowman and Gladys

Guessings? Motive? None yet. The Harbottles? The same applied to them. Dalmaine could possibly have been suborned while in South Africa, but it seemed unlikely. None of the three girls could be imagined villains of the deepest dye – not in the sense of murder anyway, he thought bitterly. Sir John Harnet and the Marquis were respected diplomats. Of them all, Miss Guessings was the only one with a known link to Nancy.

Pall Mall Pudding indeed. He wondered idly what might be the recipe. He would visit Gwynne's and ask Emma. Yet, he reminded himself, for him not the pudding, but the Pall Mall was all-important.

His master chef's instinct told him this curry he had invented had an indefinable quality that was entirely Didier. But what was it? If his hand had put the final touch, had created a whole from the mass of separate facts and suspicions, he could not yet discern what it might be. The art of a master chef, perhaps, but less than useful for a detective.

One of the problems of history, thought Auguste gloomily to himself after luncheon, regarding the itinerary Maisie had given him with trepidation, was that there was a lot of it. The morning had begun well, so the Baroness informed him on their return from a visit to Westminster Abbey, though it was true the most enthusiastic response seemed to be for the waxwork show of some of the Kings and Queens of England, taken from casts of their faces and in some cases clad in their actual clothes, which had been carried in their funeral processions and for many years had stood by the graves. Animated discussion had followed as to why Charles II's head remained on his shoulders, so animated that Harbottle was unable to make himself heard to correct their historical knowledge. Consequently he was out of sorts at luncheon, only reviving sufficiently when they reached the Post Office Station in the afternoon. A journey by the new Central London Underground Railway was voted a most pleasurable and unusual experience, and St Paul's evoked equal new enthusiasm, especially with Harbottle. He cleared his throat.

'I wonder if you are aware, Mr Didier, that the bells of St Paul's if rung continually for twenty years would only then exhaust the number of changes.'

'Indeed, monsieur.' Auguste managed a look of great interest. Why could not the bells play tunes, he asked himself, and then the number would be limitless.

'Thomas, let us go to the Whispering Gallery,' demanded Eva, a suggestion taken up with enthusiasm by the rest of the party, now weary of stone tombs. Conscious of his role as leader of the party, Auguste followed his charges.

'I'll race you up, Evelyn.' Ethel raised her skirts to show a shocking glimpse of shapely ankle, and sped to the stairs to the Gallery.

Behind them Marie-Paul turned to the Baroness. 'May we?' she asked, her usual low voice almost animated.

Thérèse shrugged. 'We are in England. Of course we must go to the Gallery.'

'Pray take care, Miss Pembrey. If I might offer you an arm?'

Rosanna looked up at Dalmaine and smiled. 'How kind, Major Dalmaine.' She had little else to do really. She had captured her beloved in Westminster Abbey this morning. There was no sense in wasting the rest of the day. Besides, this major had a certain stiff-necked charm. She accepted the arm.

In front, Alfred Bowman had Gladys's arm firmly in his already. 'Can't have you falling, can we?'

Bella glanced at Auguste, dimpled and took the Colonel's arm. 'I wonder if I might cling to you, sir. I would feel so much safer.'

Colonel Carruthers stiffened. He could hardly say no; besides, the lady was deuced attractive. He straightened his shoulders.

'Madam, I'd be honoured.' He felt twenty years younger.

Behind them, jostling with a crowd of other tourists, Auguste stomped up the stairs alone. A cacophony of words were echoing round the Whispering Gallery as he came up. He was just in time to hear, as did everybody else, a hoarse, unrecognisable voice inform the echo: 'I know how it was done. I know who did it.'

It had nothing to do with the murder. How could it? he argued. Yet it was undeniable that a marked silence fell on the party, especially on Rosanna, who seemed to find nothing at all to say to the gallant major.

Gray's Inn was by no means a success. The party listened politely as Auguste explained the history from Maisie's notes, but he could not help but feel that the information that 'Gray's Inn Road was, at its junction with Holborn, the toll-paying entrance to the City of London, and thus in earlier times called Portpool Lane (it being near a pond)' was not received with much enthusiasm. Sir John caused a surprising stir by uncharacteristically informing the company that in earlier times the legal profession had to sleep two to a bed in the Inns of Court. Harbottle's defiant 'I wonder if you are aware that this catalpa tree was brought back by Raleigh, and Bacon planted it' aroused less interest.

'Bacon burnt a bit?' grunted Carruthers, slightly deaf when he wanted to be. 'I agree with you, sir. Charred to cinders. That cook of yours should be shot,' a glare at Auguste.

Harbottle raised his voice. 'I wonder if you are aware

that in 1622 on Twelfth Night, some young barristers here stole the cannon from Tower Hill and set it off. King James thought it another Gunpowder Plot.'

'The Boers have a nasty trick with gunpowder,' remarked Dalmaine in a loud voice, impressively to Rosanna. 'They set a cocked pistol on the line – railway engine passes over it, sets it off. Spark ignites a connected load of dynamite. End of train, and occupants, too.'

'That's murder,' cried Gladys, shocked.

'Assassination,' corrected Thérèse.

'War,' said Eva Harbottle in her thick accent. So rarely did she speak, her voice startled everyone.

Assassination? Murder? Was this just a general discussion, or was there more involved, more passion in these few words than was apparent? He must be careful, Auguste thought, not to read too much into casual conversation. But he should not ignore it. It must be stored in the larder of his mind, ready for use with other ingredients.

There seemed surprisingly little enthusiasm for Lincoln's Inn, despite his cunning promise of tea thereafter. Lincoln's Inn was never reached, however. Crossing the wide thoroughfare of Holborn, expounding obediently from Maisie's notes on the Dickensian associations of the area, Auguste was suddenly aware that his party had considerably reduced in size. Only Thérèse and her companion remained loyal. She smiled at his perplexity, and pointed. The vast emporium of Gamages was a mecca few could resist.

'I cannot see, *ma chère*, why this store is of such attraction.' Gaston de Castillon wrinkled his nose at the peculiar smell that was Gamages. An English smell, of wood, ironmongery and, he sniffed delicately, of the Paris Zoological Gardens. 'On Monday we can visit

Woollands, or the Army and Navy Stores if you wish to shop.'

'They're not the same,' announced Bella cheerfully, sweeping her fur-trimmed mantle past displays of strange-looking cheap machines and into another little room filled with confectionery of gaudy packing; then she turned a corner straight into the smell, it seemed to him, and a raucous voice that informed him he was 'a jammy old jelly-belly'. It was, so the salesmen instructed them, a Chattering Lory.

'Think how well he'd go down at one of your stiff dinner parties, Gaston.'

A rare smile reluctantly forced itself to his lips as he contemplated *le ministre* dining with competition of this sort. Then he remembered he was annoyed with Bella.

'*Ma chère,*' he said, 'how much longer do we have to endure this torment?'

'Now, now, Gaston. You know what we're here for and why we must stay.'

'I do not approve,' eyeing his wife's purchase of Ogden's Otto de Rose cigarettes. Whether he spoke of her acquisition or her Christmas mission was not clear.

'Nonsense, Gaston,' she said lightly. And he didn't know the half of it.

Colonel Carruthers, after ensuring he was on his own, marched through Cycles and Cycle Accessories to Toys and Musical Instruments and, with a short stop at model trains, arrived triumphantly at toy soldiers. From the opposite direction, having come through Magic Lanterns, and Cigars and Tobaccos, marched Dalmaine. (Rosanna had disappeared into Umbrellas.) They stopped short at twenty paces on sighting each other, then the attraction of toy soldiers outweighing dislike, they advanced till they stood side by side, hands behind backs.

'The Dirty Half Hundreds.' Carruthers broke silence with an insult.

'The Fiftieth, sir, was beyond reproach.' After all, the 50th had become the West Kents.

'No reproach intended, sir,' said Carruthers hastily. 'Affectionate nickname, that's all.' It was an olive branch and seized.

'Fine regiment, the Buffs,' Dalmaine commented.

'The best,' responded Carruthers quietly, contemplating his imminent purchase of a 10d box of seven Buff infantry.

Dalmaine too selected a purchase, with a quick glance to see if Carruthers was watching. He was.

'For my nephew,' Dalmaine said lightly.

'West Yorkshires?' grunted Carruthers. 'Made a mistake, have you?'

'No. My brother-in-law is in the regiment,' Dalmaine said stiffly.

Carruthers' brow puckered. 'Weren't they in the Ashanti affair of ninety-six?'

Dalmaine did not reply. He appeared to be contemplating the further purchase of some Egyptian Camel Corps with detachable men.

'They know. I'm sure they do,' Eva Harbottle was whispering desperately to her husband in Guns and Fishing Tackle.

'Of course not. How could they?' he soothed her.

'But suppose they do? Suppose your family—'

'When they know you,' Thomas said firmly, 'they will love you. Nothing else will be important any more.'

'If only it all goes right,' Eva sighed to a display of double-barrelled hammer guns complete with all accessories.

Auguste, left to himself, wandered through the theatrical department. How he remembered the Galaxy – and Plum's. Those days of Maskelyne and Cooke at the Egyptian House. Illusion – all illusion. He debated whether the purchase of a Crystal Gazing Ball might add to the failing festive atmosphere at Cranton's and decided it would not, though it might have some other uses. He tried on some false Dundreary whiskers together with an old gent's bald head mask and was engrossed in contemplating the result only to be interrupted by the Baroness and Marie-Paul, returning from their shopping purchases.

'How very handsome, Mr Didier. Do pray keep them. A most suitable disguise for a detective.' Thérèse tried not to laugh, but failed. She and Marie-Paul Gonnet had already been through the department once in their search for Gamage's Powder.

'I have read of it, madame,' explained Marie-Paul, perhaps to excuse this extraordinary desire to exert her personality and adorn her person. 'Also Regent Cream.'

'Very well.' Thérèse seemed amused and stood patiently while her companion made her purchases, contemplating lipstick and eye pencil thoughtfully. 'You had better be careful, Marie-Paul. You don't want to catch the murderer's eye as did Miss Watkins.'

The companion looked at her. 'I think there is no fear of that, madame. I am not unduly curious, unlike Miss Watkins.'

'A foolish girl,' agreed Thérèse shortly. 'But you are not foolish, are you, my dear?'

For some reason, Marie-Paul laughed. '*Ah non, madame. Non.*'

Gladys Guessings was in seventh heaven as she wandered idly through the jewellery department with Mr Bowman. True, Gamages was not the ideal place to

141

purchase an engagement ring, which would hardly be something to boast about, but nevertheless it might put the correct idea in Alfred's head. And after all, the store was not that cheap. She could see a ring there priced at £15. She felt very bold. After all, last evening Alfred had kissed her very energetically under the kissing bough in the drawing room. True, it had not been an entirely satisfactory experience, but no doubt she could grow to like it in time. That revived memories of the contents of the oak chest so close by. She shivered. If only she could expunge it from her conscience. Or find the courage to tell the Inspector everything.

Alfred Bowman held on to her arm determinedly. He was well aware of Gladys's intention. He didn't mind going along with it at all. For his own reasons of course.

'Some jolly things here, Gladys. Like a belated Christmas present, would you?'

'Oh, *Alfred*!'

'Fancy this hatpin, do you? Or how about a nice Toby jug?'

The warm cocoon of Daly's Theatre in Cranbourne Street had been exchanged for two further cocoons, the short cab ride to the Carlton for a light supper, and the Carlton itself. The party had entered the yellow stone building of Daly's with the highest expectations. After all, was not *San Toy* the notorious show where Marie Tempest had quit after only a few weeks, on a point of principle: being forced to wear short pants? Gentlemen and ladies alike in the party were looking forward to seeing the present San Toy for this reason alone; the gentlemen since the prospect of viewing Miss Ada Reeve's legs was pleasantly titillating, the ladies because they wished to be shocked or envious according to their age and dispositions. In the event, such was the fascination and delight of the show that the legs were almost forgotten. The dance of the Pas Seul captivated the ladies, and San Toy's song 'All I want is a little bit fun' left every gentleman only too willing to provide her with it. Damn good theme, Oriental girls and Western officers, who suitably late in the action see the error of their philandering ways.

'I think it's all wrong,' said Gladys volubly over a glass of champagne, 'women dressing up as men. Like that Vesta Tilley. Everyone knows she's a woman, so what's the point?'

Alfred Bowman could have told her, but didn't.

'The Chevalier d'Eon passed half his life both in England and France as a woman,' observed Auguste, 'with high odds being laid as to which he was. No one was certain until his death.'

Colonel Carruthers thought this over. 'Damned nancy,' he muttered to Dalmaine.

'Not at all,' remarked Thérèse, overhearing. 'He was a master fencer. And after all, what are clothes? Merely the custom of a country. In China women do wear trousers.'

'The East is a mysterious place,' said the Marquis. 'As you British know with your opium dealings,' he added.

'That's over,' barked Carruthers.

'No, it's not,' said Evelyn brightly. 'What about opium dens?'

'A young lady shouldn't know about opium dens.' Sir John bore down on her.

'It was in that old copy of the *Strand Magazine* that you gave me,' replied Evelyn innocently.

Sir John glared.

'Opium goes with white slavers,' shivered Ethel.

'Don't be foolish, you two,' announced their elder

143

sister. 'No need for you to worry. The white slavers would send you right back.'

Opium – Auguste thought back to the day in the fog, which Egbert still half thought was the result of an opium-based medicine. He stared at *le maître*'s *Cailles Souvarow* before him. How could he do justice to it while murder hung over him? Yet to ignore it was the greater crime. At the first taste, his spirits began to rise. Truly, he was in the presence of greatness. He longed himself to be back in his beloved kitchen – ah, that was where a man belonged, not as a hotelier, but like Monsieur Escoffier himself, a king in his own undisputed kingdom.

He was brought sharply back to murder by an avid discussion at the table which seemed to have replaced admiration for *le maître*'s best work before them. First it concerned peach melba and whether Monsieur Escoffier's famous dish would appear again that evening on the dessert menu. Second, it concerned the murder of Nancy Watkins.

'I don't believe all this talk about art thefts,' announced Bella. 'It seems very strange to me. Why should an art thief bother to come to Cranton's?'

'I agree,' said the Baroness. 'I do not think we should have the presence of quite so many policemen if art thefts were the matter at stake. What do you think, Mr Didier? You must know, being in Inspector Rose's confidence.' She gazed at him challengingly, almost daring him to try to escape answering.

He was saved by Gladys.

'Puddings,' she said confidentially.

Evelyn giggled.

'It's all very well for you young folks to laugh,' Gladys continued indignantly, 'but we – slightly older – people know what goes on. There's money at stake.'

'How?' asked Harbottle, bewildered.

'Adulterated food,' said Gladys, and sat back smugly.

'Is this so, Mr Didier?' asked Thérèse solemnly. 'Are we all at risk from poisoning?'

'I think,' said Auguste diplomatically, 'that we need fear nothing from Mr Escoffier – or from Cranton's.' Despite Fancelli, he thought savagely to himself.

'And it was not the reason Miss Watkins was murdered?' Thérèse pressed sweetly.

'I do not think—' Auguste was again saved, by an exclamation from Dalmaine.

'I say, look at that.'

Their eyes followed him, gazing out into the dark December street, where a hopeful late-night newsboy still plied for custom. Through the glass they could not hear what he was crying, but the newspaper placards were clear enough: 'Missing Bride Found in Chest. Murder of Lady Journalist.'

'Oh Evelyn,' said Ethel delightedly. 'Look what that nasty newspaper has printed. And that nice young man said he just wanted to write about poor Miss Watkins' job at Cranton's.'

Back at Scotland Yard, Egbert Rose too was putting in a long day. He had had a bad journey home from Norfolk. The LNER smoke still seemed to be in his eyes, his clothes were sooty, and the meal on the railway train was a distinct disappointment to one who had visited Sandringham. There he had received sandwiches and ale from the housekeeper, and in compensation had dinner on the railway train. To one who undulated between Edith's cooking and Auguste's, the railway train came somewhere towards the lower end, but then he did not have the same affectionate loyalty to the railway cook as he did to Edith. It had been a rum place, Sandringham, all those various shooting gentlemen wandering in and out. Just like Stockbery Towers. Far more danger of the Prince getting shot there in his own home than on Paddington railway station.

Awaiting his arrival back was a memorandum from Twitch, who had no doubt repaired home long since, Rose thought savagely. In answer to his enquiries of five weeks ago, the Thames Police had a body they'd like him to look at.

Chapter Six

The blue lamp shone encouragingly in the early morning gloom as Rose and Auguste climbed the wooden steps from the muddy banks of the Thames up to the Wapping Wharf headquarters of the Thames Police. The police boats rocked gently behind them by their mooring posts, each with its boatman standing sentinel over it. The skipper of theirs, whose old man o' war's hat proclaimed a Navy veteran even had his eyes, with their air of searching faraway horizons, and his weather-beaten face not done so, had regaled their journey with tales of the loss of the *Princess Alice* in '78. Auguste was appalled by the story, but it wasn't new to Rose. He'd been on the Ratcliffe Highway beat then and been witness to the misery and heartbreak at the loss of life when the pleasure steamer went down.

A thin swarthy man pushed past them as they entered the police station, eyes set on freedom, intent on disappearing into the warrens of Wapping as soon as he might, relieved and surprised at his release from the dock. Inspector Robbins, a short, worried man, was waiting for them impatiently. He'd been on duty all night, and the sooner he could get home to his kipper, the happier he'd be.

Ten minutes later they were staring down at the very dead body of what had once been a young girl.

'It's not my men's fault we didn't find it sooner, Inspector,' defending the honour of the Thames Police. 'Weighted, you see, otherwise they'd have had her out in days.' It was hardly necessary to point this out. The rope binding the body, with its cut ends, was evidence enough. 'Only because he had a report of a suicide that he found it at all.'

'Well, Auguste?' Rose asked evenly. 'Recognise her?' Slight emphasis on the 'her'. To Robbins it was a corpse, an 'it'. To them it was a girl, with a life that had to be reconstructed, an identity revealed – and a motive for murder discovered.

'Yes, Inspector.' Auguste gulped. 'Not the face.' He made an effort to overcome nausea, swallowing hard. There was little left. 'But that dress, oh yes, I recognise that.' The dark brown print under the inadequate shawl, the red of the blood against it – he would not forget that.

'As I told you, she's been stabbed, sir,' Inspector Robbins said.

Rose nodded and Auguste relaxed, realising Egbert had not passed on this information at first in case it inclined him to make a false identification. He understood. Egbert after all was the professional through and through.

'The body must have been hidden down in the cellars by the time we arrived on the scene,' said Rose, considering. What yet remained unspoken between himself and Auguste could come later. 'And then moved at night, probably the same night.'

'Why as far as here?' asked Auguste quietly.

'I can tell you that, sir. My men are very vigilant round the Waterloo area, and Charing Cross. The Bridge of Sighs we call Waterloo because so many throw themselves off it. Always a policeman on watch there. Down here it's different. There are plenty of men round here wouldn't mind earning themselves a bit and no questions asked, helping to move a body. There's more in this old river than you can see from your window at the Yard, sir. I could tell you tales. . .'

Rose didn't want to hear them. The sight before them was tale enough for the moment. By common assent he and Auguste took a hansom back.

'You were right, and I was wrong, Auguste,' Rose broke the long silence as they came into the purlieus of the City.

'You could not know it was not the medicine,' said Auguste, trying to be fair.

'I could. I know you, after all. I remember enough of the effects of opium on the Ratcliffe Highway for all it was twenty-odd years ago. More opium dens than bakers, and still are. But it wasn't opium in your case, and now we've got the body to prove it. We'll look at that missing persons file again to see if anything new's come in.'

It hadn't, not at least in respect of young girls missing for over a month. Rose closed the file and looked up at his ever-present, ever-eager sergeant, who had followed them up to his office as keenly as an insurance gentleman a fire engine.

Rose sighed. 'What does this suggest to you, Stitch?'

'That the murderer was one of her own family,' stated Sergeant Stitch brightly. There was no query in his voice.

'Sometimes,' Rose remarked, 'you show positive signs of brilliance, Sergeant. I hadn't thought of that. But I don't reckon it's so here. There's usually neighbours keeping a helpful eye out in a case like that.'

'From a Norphanage,' offered Twitch, ignoring Auguste. No room for laymen. This was a case for professionals. 'Or a Nome.'

'Even more likely to report her missing.'

'On the streets then.' Twitch folded his arms complacently.

'She was not wearing the dress of a streetwalker,'

149

said Auguste firmly. 'It was a maid's dress.'

'A Nousemaid, did you say, Didier? Even more likely to be reported missing,' Twitch sniggered. 'Harder to get, nowadays, 'ousemaids are. No, the streets,' Twitch informed them. 'We'll have to follow that up. It's the obvious answer.'

'There is one puzzling matter, Inspector,' said Auguste thoughtfully, 'about this crime. At one end we have this girl, clearly poor, and without access to matters of State importance. At the other end is the Prince of Wales himself. Somewhere there is a chain that connects the two – a binding of egg to make this cold fare into Soyer's *fritadella*, but as yet the egg is missing.'

'Unless we get a move on,' remarked Rose sourly, 'it'll be on my face.'

The calendar on the wall with Phiz's Dickens scenes on it showed only two days left of the old century. And three days after that the Prince of Wales would be at Paddington railway station.

The house looked much like its neighbours. Only a demure sign Home for the Protection of Young Females made its purpose clear – and its need of money obvious. The manageress, a dour-looking woman in her forties, led the way to her sanctum without surprise. Visits from the constabulary were frequent on one mission or another. Sometimes they brought new girls in, sometimes removed occupants for whom the home had unwittingly provided protection from arrest.

'A missing girl?' Her eyebrows arched. 'Not one of ours, I can assure you.'

'Girls never go missing? Run away? Go back to the streets?'

She inclined her head. 'Rarely, Inspector. What we have to offer is little, but it is better than what lies outside. We try to keep a central register for our homes, where up-to-date information is kept on the whereabouts of any of our girls who revert to their old ways, or who succumb after having left us to take remunerative and respectable employment. I fear that a housemaid's wages are scarcely an attraction besides the lights of Piccadilly.'

'Is that what happens to them? Housemaids? Nothing else?'

'Of course, according to their abilities. Some can be trained as governesses, often to be sent abroad. Miss Rye runs an admirable home in Peckham for sending girls to Canada, and even Mrs Crosby's training establishment in Battersea for the Continent.'

'Governesses? Wasn't that once a cover for white-slaving? Girls escorted across the Channel in groups by the owner of a so-called high-class agency for tutors and domestics?'

She looked disapproving. 'Once, Inspector, is the operative word. Now that the Criminal Law Amendment Act is working well, the National Vigilance Associations well-established and the harbours carefully watched, it could not happen again.'

'The girl we're trying to trace was wearing a brown print gown,' said Auguste. 'It seems hardly likely a girl on the streets would wear something of the sort.'

She gave him a look of scorn. 'I see you know little of the night life of London, sir, being a foreigner. Girls wear what they have. If this girl you are seeking had just left her home, or a housemaid's position, she would wear the dress she possessed. Not every unfortunate wears silks and satins, you know. Here,' she announced, 'my girls are each given a serviceable brown linsey-woolsey frock. *And*,' she informed them with pride, 'a holland apron. I believe most homes have some such plain uniform.'

'So all we know is that she is unlikely to have come from a shelter for unfortunate women, but was probably a housemaid at the murderer's home. Yet, Egbert, there is something strange about that. Why was she not wearing black?'

'Pardon, Auguste? I don't follow.'

'If you recall, at Stockbery Towers the housemaids wore their print dresses in the morning, but in the afternoon they changed into black. And this poor girl was killed in the afternoon.'

'Out at Highbury we're not so particular about that kind of thing,' observed Rose drily.

'So that suggests,' Auguste continued, 'that the girl was working in a not very aristocratic home. A maid of all work, perhaps. And who does that fit? The Harbottles? No, they came from abroad – or so they say. She could work for his parents, though. And Miss Guessings would have a maid of all work.'

'It would take more than one maid to look after her,' Rose commented.

'You are right. But it *is* possible. Mr Bowman would employ a maid. The Baroness comes from abroad, and so does her companion.'

'This girl could be French,' Rose pointed out.

Auguste shook his head decisively. 'No, her whole look is English, and she had clearly been speaking in English when I arrived.'

'Colonel Carruthers? His housemaid would hardly travel up from Dorset. Dalmaine – could be his, except that he's come more or less straight from the boat. The Pembreys? Too aristocratic a household for this girl, and the de Castillons live in Paris.'

'Perhaps we should check whether anybody is missing from the English households.' He glanced at Rose, and they spoke together.

'Twitch can do it.'

Clouds of steam swirled, cleared and gathered again. Through it, like a Cheshire cat, Ma Bisley's round grinning face appeared at intervals, sleeves rolled up to the elbows.

'Waiter minute!' bawled her stentorian voice. Then reappearing, waving a bar of Sunlight soap in one hand and a washing dolly in the other. 'Oh it's you. Can't be too careful.' She had her reputation to consider.

Egbert Rose sat down amid carefully sorted and ticketed bundles of dirty washing, some in newspaper, some respectable bags, some open to full public scrutiny.

'Takes all sorts,' remarked Ma disparagingly, seeing him looking at the heaps and plumping her large body in the chair next to him.

'Any news?'

'Maybe,' she said guardedly. 'Maybe not yet.'

He knew better than to rush her.

'See that? I always tells a man by his washing.' She looked at one opened parcel dispassionately. 'Look at this lot: good quality shirt, bought from Jermyn Street, cheap flannels – Gamages. No socks – maid washes 'em. Fine quality handkerchiefs, and this one,' she picked up a pair of combinations disdainfully, 'this here. What does that tell you?' She paused impressively, and Rose knew not to answer her rhetorical question. 'Worn out, that's what they are. You look now. I'll tell you what all this tells you. It tells you he 'as a job where his shirt's going to be seen *and* his pocket handkerchief, and not just any job – where he's got to keep his end up. Lives aht this way – wife does her shopping in the Lane – but 'e shops for his long johns. Too mean to buy 'em up West, but not going to buy 'em in the Lane like other folks round 'ere. So 'e

153

don't buy very many. Ho, yes, a man who 'as ideas above his station is Ticket No. 22.'

'You'll have my job next, Ma.'

Gratified, she continued, 'And that's not all. Where does 'e buy 'is shirts? Not at Selfridges. Not at John Lewis. No, 'e buys 'em in Jermyn Street. Orl right, 'e's hambitious, but any number of places would do for 'is shirts. Yet 'e goes to Jermyn Street. Must be 'andy for 'im. 'Andy. A shop assistant, you'll say. Maybe in a shirt shop. Hoh no. Look at these dirty combis.'

Rose eyed the offending articles with some disaste. 'What about 'em, Ma?'

'Baggy!' she said triumphantly. 'Baggy, sir.'

'They do go baggy, Ma.'

'But it's where. Baggy bum, sir – begging your pardon. And baggy knees. All the same – look.' She delved into the unfortunate No. 22's pile. 'This little man's a sitter, sir. He sits. Now where does you sit?'

'An office?'

'Orfice? Come, sir, you aren't trying. He's on view, not just neat and tidy, but on view. I think what we have 'ere is a bank clerk with aspirations. I think if you was to drop into the banks of Piccadilly you'd find a Mr Edgar Prentice there all right.'

'I see you're an admirer of Sherlock Holmes, Ma.'

''Oo?'

'Sherlock Holmes, the great detective whose adventures appear in the *Strand Magazine*.'

'Oh.' Mrs Bisley lost interest. 'Can't read, sir. Know me numbers, that's all, for the tickets.'

'In that case, Ma, I reckon Sherlock knows you.' He paused. 'I brought you some clothes. Can you do the same for these?' He carefully unwrapped the ragged remains of the clothes of the murdered girl.

She gave him a sharp look and turned the dress over for a few minutes.

'Poor lass. In the river, eh?'

'How can you tell?'

'Easy to see from the way the cotton's gone. Besides, I seen one or two who've gone in over the years. This one, though.' Her sharp eyes examined it closely. 'You wouldn't be interested in no suicide. This is murder, ain't it? And one of our own, from round 'ere. Or was once.'

'How can you tell?' he asked sharply.

'This dress – it's old, nearly all the dye washed out, but it's been carefully looked after. Neat hem and seams. But it's been taken up – see the old hemline inside? *And* taken in, I wouldn't wonder. No stains, – but someone's been careless with the acid. See that patch?' She pointed to a filled in hole at the back of the dress. 'These old fastenings – they don't use 'em now – used to leave rust marks, and only acid would get rid of them. That shows its age. Nah, the red flannel petticoat, that's not so old. Only a few years is my guess. But look at it! I ask you, that's been *rubbed* and it's shrunk. Might be the water, but more like it's been left too near a fire. What does all this tell you?' She looked sharply at her pupil.

'Second-hand, Ma?'

'Right.' Ma was pleased. 'Or an anmedahn.'

'A what?'

''And-me-down,' she repeated impatiently. 'Now, these drawers – and stays, what there is of them. Same thing. Old. No shape in these corsets. Wouldn't hold a sparrow's arse up. Poor little mite. Not much of a life, 'ad she?'

'We'll find 'im, Ma.'

'That dress – 'ousemaid's uniform, is it?'

'Looks like it. Any ideas?'

'I'll put the word out. See if my lads can come back with anything. And on that other matter, sir. The matter of royalty. The lads say they ain't heard nothing. Now that is peculiar. Very, very peculiar.'

'Why?' From his immediate sense of let-down, Rose realised how much he'd been banking on Ma Bisley's runners coming back with something positive.

'If there was anything to hear round 'ere, they'd have heard it. Unless,' Ma heaved her bulk off her chair, 'unless it were foreigners. Now I must get back to blue me nose-wipers. I've got a business to run.'

Auguste pushed his way through Cranton's door, an eager group of gentlemen of the press crowding after him. They were firmly discouraged by Wilkins the doorman. Auguste silently and fervently blessed Maisie for choosing a retired sergeant major from the Indian frontier for this role. How delightful it would be to be returning to Cranton's if this were indeed his own hotel and if it had not been sullied by murder. He spoke a silent word of encouragement to the shade of Robert Adam, assuring him that the stain of murder would certainly be lifted soon from his handiwork.

In the entrance hall, a reassuring smell came over him – a haven in normal times. Luncheon, and all the thoughts that it evoked. Every instinct in him urged him towards the source of those smells, to taste, to check, to glory in. But he must restrain himself. For these were not normal times.

As if to remind him of the alien presence, the sounds of *La Donna è Mobile* floated up from his Orpheus in the Underworld. Auguste clenched his fists to distract himself from temptation. How easy to run below to glance at luncheon, but he would not. Fancelli had proved himself just about adequate, though not, he reminded himself, in the matter of curries. He was not a *maître* and never would be one. Nevertheless he, Auguste, would not get involved – except in cases of

156

dire emergency, he promised himself. Emergencies could include the use of coralline pepper or the intrusion of Soyer-like principles into his kitchen. *La Donna è Mobile* . . . Ah, faithless woman!

As if on cue, Bella wafted serenely towards him from the drawing room. 'Ah, Monsieur Didier, how delightful. If you have a moment . . .' There was, from the tone of her voice, to be no escape by claiming that his moments were all required elsewhere. Alone and unprotected, he yielded as gracefully as possible, following her back into the drawing room, which with sinking heart, but unsurprised, he noted was empty.

'Monsieur Didier,' really she did look so delightful with her pretty toque hat and fur-trimmed collar, it occurred to Auguste, 'I wish to confess—'

'Confess?' His heart lurched. *Bella?* A moment's horror at the thought of this lovely face contorted by hatred, engaged in murder.

'I confess that I have been quite overcome once more by the proximity of this kissing bough, Monsieur Didier, and as I should like to kiss you again very much, I propose to take advantage of it.' The delicious smell of Floris perfume assailed his nose, his senses and his common sense as her silk-clad arms stole round his neck and her warm body burrowed against his. Even at eleven thirty in the morning, this could not be resisted, even if it were polite to do so. So. . .

'There, Monsieur Didier, was not that delightful? However,' she added regretfully, 'Gaston will be here any moment, so I fear we had better not pursue this experience to a further stage. He might be here already in fact.' Bella looked vaguely round at cupboards and concealing high-backed chairs.

Auguste jumped back in alarm, unflatteringly quickly.

Bella did not seem perturbed. 'Now I *know* you

157

care.' She smiled at him delightfully, whisking out of the room leaving Auguste to stare at the Christmas tree as though it might provide some answer to the ways of women. And Bella in particular. Beautiful though she was, and undoubtedly most attractive, it was hardly the way a manager should behave towards a guest – even with a complaisant husband such as the Marquis appeared to be. He wondered idly once more what brought the pair to Cranton's. If she were on her way to visit her father, and de Castillon was as little interested in his wife as she intimated, why did he accompany her? He pondered this for some time, but could not provide an answer.

Auguste emerged from the drawing room cautiously. True, Bella would surely have departed now, but one never knew when the Terrible Twins, as he had named them, might be lying in wait for the unwary. Only yesterday they had pleaded to take his photograph, and when he had agreed to this innocent request, and had posed elegantly against Cranton's door, a long toy snake had shot out of the camera. It had amused the Misses Pembrey greatly.

On this occasion there was no sign of them, and, determinedly steering his thoughts and feet away from the lure of the kitchens below, he walked up the staircase towards the hotel bedrooms. Somewhere there must be an answer.

The eighteenth-century oil paintings of the public rooms gave way on the corridors to less valuable artistic endeavours including a set of Cecil Aldin prints of the Fallowfield Hunt, one or two younger artists who for some reason had caught Maisie's eye – for eccentricity perhaps, especially this oddly named Picasso. He wondered fleetingly, and without rancour, if it were not the art so much as the artist in which she was interested.

Dear Maisie. Now he acknowledged that it was

indeed in the past. No love so tender as that for one that was gone, that warmed the heart with memory and paved the path to the future with hope. Hope? For him there could be no love without Tatiana. Life would merely be a series of Bellas. He considered this prospect for a moment. It might have compensations, true, but lacked reward. He drew his mind back to murder. For if he could not think of love, and should not of cuisine, there still remained open for his thoughts the world of detection.

Somewhere a girl had disappeared on Christmas morning, probably at about eight o'clock and for over twenty-four hours had remained hidden in a confined space that allowed no room for a protruding stiletto. He and Egbert had searched the bedrooms now themselves, and found no such hiding place. Trunks were in the baggage room in the basement; beds and wardrobes offered no safe refuge. It seemed certain the murderer could not have risked discovery by keeping the body in the bedroom.

Auguste walked slowly along the corridor of the first floor, first to the west, the side that had been served by Bessie. Here, facing the guests' bedrooms and overlooking the mews at the back of the hotel, were the housekeeper's room, the linen rooms, and one or two spare rooms, which were kept locked. Impossible that the murderer could have taken the risk of bringing the body up this end of the corridor. No, it must be as they thought, the murder was done on the eastern side of the building where Nancy herself had served tea on the first and second floors. Opposite the bedrooms were bathrooms. A hiding place? Excitement sprang to life, flickered and died as he flung a door open and contemplated the Turko-Russian (self-purifying) Folding Bath Cabinet. Alas, these too would need to be cleaned and would not be a safe refuge. Perhaps the body could be taken there with the murderer remaining locked inside the bathroom with it, while the bedroom was cleaned? No, impossible. How to know the right moment to leave – and how to leave with housemaids constantly hovering. Moreover, if a bathroom had remained occupied for a great length of time it would be noticed, and remembered. This he knew now, from his brief experience as hotelier, dealing with complaints.

Disconsolate, he walked up the staircase to the next floor. Only two – three, he had forgotten Marie-Paul Gonnet – bedrooms had been occupied here and none on the west side. This alone would centre attention here, for these were the last rooms that Nancy would have visited – if she kept to her strict order. One had to start somewhere and to roll out the pastry by considering the second floor first was by no means a bad idea, since the risk of observation by Bessie was greater on the first floor.

But where could the body have been hidden? This case, he thought glumly, seemed to centre on disappearing bodies. True, this one had only disappeared for a day, but the murderer could hardly have expected it to be found as early as it was. That night it too might have disappeared into anonymity into the Thames like its predecessor.

'What are you doing, Mr Didier? Those carpets are *clean!*' Mrs Pomfret's indignant voice roused him to the fact that he was striding along the corridor, hands behind back, eyes fixed on the pink patterned Wilton as if some clue lay woven into it.

'My apologies, Mrs Pomfret. I grow too like Sherlock Holmes, I fear.'

She sniffed, unmollified.

'Mrs Pomfret, those rooms that are unused—'

'Are locked, Mr Didier. No one gets into them without my keys. Or yours, of course,' she added without interest. 'And I lent my keys to no one. Besides, nothing in them but peeling plaster and wallpaper.'

'This is Cranton's, Mrs Pomfret. This is history,' Auguste informed her.

The expression on Mrs Pomfret's face indicated that history was all very well in its way, provided it didn't get in hers.

'So you have the keys to all rooms on these two floors, and only the bathroom, linen cupboard and your room would be unlocked.'

'That's right, Mr Didier. And if you're thinking of the next floor up, one side is staff and the other side is empty and locked. I don't have a key. Only you do,' she said somewhat accusingly.

'Yes, yes, Mrs Pomfret,' he soothed her absently. There must be something he had missed. He ran his eye up and down the corridor.

'There are no cupboards for brooms?'

'Brooms are in the room next to mine.' Her tone dared any murderer to get past her.

'And that?' He pointed to a door by the side of the central stairs.

'That's not a cupboard,' she declared, glad to have caught him out. 'That's only the service lift.'

Inspector Rose looked up eagerly from behind Auguste's appropriated desk as its rightful owner shot into the room. 'The Prince?' he asked sharply.

'No, *mon ami*. But I have discovered where the body was while the rooms were being cleaned. Come!'

Two minutes later Rose was peering into the large square hole of the service lift.

'It has access to both the first and second floors,' Auguste said excitedly. 'It is just for food, and after the tea trays had been sent down at eight thirty it would not be in use again normally until the evenings, and on Christmas Day not at all when everyone dined down-stairs.'

'It couldn't have been in there long without the body getting distorted as it stiffened,' Rose pointed out cautiously. 'And how would your villain get the body in without being noticed? As much of a risk as keeping it in the room, eh? Suppose the maids caught sight of what was going on?'

'It was moved during servants' breakfast,' said Auguste simply.

'Possible.' Rose stood deep in thought, then shot at him: 'How would the murderer know when servants' breakfast was? Suppose the lift had been used? Sup-pose—'

'One moment, Egbert,' Auguste said quietly. 'I have some supposes of my own. Even suppose it had been used and the body arrived in the kitchens, there would be no more clues as to who had put it in there than there are now. But more likely, suppose our villains simply jammed the lift to stop it moving? Risks had to be taken by these people.'

'These people?' Rose's tone was sharp. 'Why do you say "*these*", Auguste?'

'Because I think two must have been involved, my friend. I have thought it out logically as I would a receipt for a sauce to complement a *plat*. The basis, then the added ingredients, and the flavourings, or herbs or spices. All must be in harmony. There must be more than one person involved in a plot to kill the Prince. True, Sipido acted alone in Brussels last April – but he was crazed. For a plot, there must be brains to plan and perhaps technical knowledge to carry it out.'

'There's both here all right,' observed Rose. 'Strength to put a girl's body into a lift, strength to get rid of it at night into the chest. And why the chest,

162

Auguste? Why not leave it in the lift, lower it right down to the service area and get rid of it the same way as the last one – out through the cellars? Why the chest?'

'They would have taken it from the lift back into the room of course,' said Auguste irritably, hurt at these flaws being picked in his perfect theory, 'once the room had been cleaned, and . . . and. . .'

'Why not put it back in the lift at night?' Rose pressed on inexorably.

Auguste glared. There had to be an answer. There was no other solution, and so he must be right. Then the answer helpfully supplied itself. 'Because by that time, *mon brave*, the lift was back in the kitchens, perhaps set with teacups for the morning. Moreover, these lifts are not silent, Egbert. They could not raise it without arousing the curiosity of the night porter.'

Rose considered this. 'Right,' he said, 'but whichever way you look at it, the body is in the chest, and no reason for being there that I can see. But I agree. It must have taken some handling. Brains and brawn again – in the form of one person or two.'

'Two, I am sure,' said Auguste simply. 'Like bubble and squeak.'

'Or fish and chips,' grunted Rose as they walked down towards the kitchens. 'Unusual to hear you talk so plain, Auguste.'

'*Non*,' said Auguste indignantly. 'It is a delightful dish. It all depends on the cook. Of course I would add *un peu d'ail*—'

From below came a mournful wail. The composer was not recognisable, but today it resembled the doleful chorus of the Hebrew Slaves more than *La Donna è Mobile*.

Auguste paused on the stairs, like a Dante wondering whether he really wished to enter Hell. Not only were the six assistant cooks running around like Mr Carroll's caucus race, without beginning or end, but Fancelli himself seemed to have joined them.

Every table was full. Occasionally scullerymaids made darting attacks to remove dirty dishes, but as fast as a space was made, a cook with a cry of triumph would plomp down chopping board, knife and ingredients, and begin another task of beating food into submission. Auguste agonised with the truffles. Like beautiful women, they required delicate handling, each according to its shape, nationality and individuality. Before his very eyes they were being hacked like logs, deflowered of their innocence and fragrance by monsters.

'Signor Fancelli!'

A white-coated figure looked up at Retribution on the stairs, scorned it, and continued feverishly to pound what might be quenelles. Or suet dumplings. Impossible to tell under those flailing fists.

'Signor Fancelli.' This time a note of steel in Auguste's voice persuaded Fancelli that attention was in order.

'Signor Fancelli,' Auguste enquired dangerously, 'what is amiss here? These seem rather late preparations for luncheon.'

'Is for tonight,' Fancelli explained.

Auguste ran his eye over the table. Preparations for *ballotines* of turkey, *cannelons* of beef, *foie gras*, galantines, cutlets in aspic, *coquilles* of mutton, mousse of pheasant. He could not comprehend, absorb the terrible truth. He looked again. No, he had not been deceived by his eyes. It was all *cold*. He turned to Signor Fancelli and spoke with strangled voice:

'You do not cook tonight?'

'Is my evening off.'

'Evening off?' Auguste struggled for composure.

164

'There *is* no evening off in a twelve-day assignment.'

'Lady Gincrack say yis. Is Sunday. I go to church.'

'In the morning,' Auguste said in a voice that did not seem to be his own.

'Evening,' announced Fancelli.

'Cranton's does not serve cold meats for Sunday dinner. This is not a seaside temperance hotel,' Auguste almost snarled. 'You will be here—'

'Lady Gincrack say yis, and I work for Lady Gincrack.'

So, this was being a manager. What was the world coming to when cooks defied you? No true cook could leave his clients with cold food. If this was to be the way of the twentieth century, Auguste did not approve.

'You will provide *soup*. And a *réchauffé* dish. As we agreed.'

'Soup. No *réchauffé*.'

'Devilled turkey. Or *I* come to cook.'

Latin eye met Latin eye. 'Fowl devil,' Fancelli said sulkily and ambiguously. 'Then I *go*.'

'Staff,' said Auguste despairingly to Egbert Rose, an amused spectator.

'I have the same trouble with Twitch,' he replied. 'They don't make 'em like they used to.'

'I wonder, Egbert,' Auguste began, then as Rose looked at him enquiringly, continued haltingly, 'whether I am entirely suited to be a manager.'

'You'll learn,' Rose replied encouragingly. 'It's all a matter of making clear who's the brains and who's the brawn.'

'The brace of pheasant,' said Auguste thoughtfully. 'You like this idea, don't you, Egbert?'

'Very good of you, Auguste. Plucked of course, if you please. Edith usually gets Mr Pinpole to do it.'

'I did not mean a real brace, Egbert, though I am of course delighted to give you as many as you wish for dear Edith. But for once I did not think of food. *Pardon*. I think instead of our murderers. One the liaison with the foreign government, and one the man who does the deed.'

'Miss Guessings and Mr Bowman? The Baroness von Bechlein and – but who? Miss Gonnet is too thin to lift a cabbage, let alone a body.'

'She has strong hands, Egbert,' said Auguste, vivid memories of the companion peeling back the skin of an orange. Delicate fingers, but powerful.

'You need more than hands, and stabbing ain't exactly a woman's crime, or assassination.'

'No, if the Baroness is our quarry she must have had the help of one of the staff, the footman or—' He broke off.

'Or the kitchen staff,' Rose supplied.

'No cook would . . .' began Auguste heatedly, until he remembered several gentlemen of his past acquaintance engaged in culinary activities who would have slaughtered their fellow beings as cheerfully as wringing the neck of a chicken. 'I was going to suggest young Mr Nash. He is strong enough even to have carried the task out alone.'

'I've glad you've remembered him, Auguste.,' Rose said grimly.

'There are also the Harbottles – or our army gentlemen. We have plenty of pheasants in our larder,' said Auguste wryly.

'And only four days left to pluck 'em in.'

Somehow, somewhere, there had been collusion between kitchens and guests. Such a thing should not happen in a well-ordered establishment. It was a sign that things were not correct at Cranton's. News of the dinner to come that evening percolated to its intending partakers, and was not received well by some. Thus it was that Auguste arrived at the dinner table to find empty spaces. It was a direct slight to his competence, a load he was forced to bear.

The Colonel had decided to pay a long overdue visit to his club, and had invited Dalmaine to join him to discuss the influence of Blücher's forces, and whether or not they had been misdirected by the Great Man as to where precisely his forces were. The invitation had been rejected. The de Castillons and the Harbottles too were absent. The Pembrey girls, with Dalmaine in attentive attendance, were, however, gracing the table, as were the Baroness, Miss Gonnet, Mr Bowman and Miss Guessings. But the shame of the empty spaces obsessed Auguste. How could this happen at a dinner for which he was responsible? Never, never would he desert his post as had Fancelli, who could not even claim the title of chef let alone *maître chef* after such enormity.

Tomorrow he would have further words with this gentleman, for tomorrow was the all-important New Year's Eve. The last banquet of the nineteenth century should be a banquet to remember. If only he, Auguste Didier, were in command instead of Fancelli . . . Meanwhile, his conscience as a manager reminded him that this evening must first be rescued from catastrophe.

When they gathered in the drawing room for their Sunday musical evening, he would offer them a Locomotive Cup to cheer the proceedings. He was proud of his version of Francatelli's somewhat rich drink and on this cold evening it would indeed add warmth. A snap of his fingers (there were some pleasures in being a manager), a few whispered words and several pints of Burgundy were coaxed into warm fusion with honey, Curaçao and cloves.

The absent diners returned to find a harmonious

scene in the drawing room. Steaming bowls of red liquid stood in chafing dishes on a side table. Glasses in hands showed various levels of consumption. The kissing bough swayed above their heads, as logs flickered and sputtered on the hearth. A deep dish displayed evidence of a game of Snapdragon having been completed; the noise level was high. At the piano Rosanna was playing, while Thomas Harbottle rendered 'The Miner's Dream of Home'.

'Oh Thomas,' breathed Eva, tears rolling down pink cheeks. 'That was *beautiful*.'

'How well you sing,' agreed his pianist.

Frederick Dalmaine almost pushed, or so it seemed to Auguste's dazed eyes, Harbottle from his path in order to render 'Come into the Garden, Maud'.

Auguste felt an unaccountable lifting of the spirits, a sudden desire to join with the singer, a desire apparently shared by the rest of the room enthusiastically shouting the chorus. He noticed his glass was empty, and went to refill it, performing the same function for all the other empty glasses – of which there were many – in the room. He noticed the twins standing by the piano, innocence shining from their faces, and felt a new and glowing warmth towards them. Indeed, a warmth towards everyone – especially Bella who had never looked lovelier.

'Ah Auguste,' she said, her face near his, 'what a splendid time is Christmas.'

'You who would feast us paupers, what of my *murdered wife*?' bawled Colonel Carruthers, who for some unaccountable reason had felt the need to recite all twenty-one verses of 'Christmas Day in the Workhouse'.

Auguste rose with dignity. 'Do not fear, Colonel, I will discover this murderer,' announced his very slightly slurred voice.

There was something strange about this statement, he thought, as, his legs feeling somewhat unsteady, he resumed his seat. No one else seemed to think so, for he received a round of applause. No, it was the drink there was something strange about. He glanced up sharply, saw the innocent gaze of the twins upon him – and realised the worst. He made his way as steadily as he could manage to the steaming bowls. The twins hastily took Rosanna's place at the piano, as Auguste's glazed eyes noticed three gin bottles behind the Christmas tree. Empty.

In his condition this seemed to have been an excellent idea and he nodded approvingly. Eva Harbottle was giggling with Gladys, who was clasping Alfred Bowman's hand possessively, and waving away Auguste's offerings. She had her very own liquor-free punch. Indeed she had, adulterated with half a bottle of gin. Auguste filled Bowman's glass just as Bowman decided it would be a good idea to impress Gladys. He clambered to his feet, and shakily began regaling the company with 'Daisy, Daisy, give me your answer do'.

'Oh Alfred, I will, I will!' cried Gladys, standing up to rush to her apparently betrothed, and immediately collapsing. Auguste rushed to her, but Marie-Paul had already hauled her upright, removed her to the Chesterfield and deposited her again to stare foolishly at Bowman while he bawled out: 'That daring young man on the flying trapeze, he flies through the air with the greatest of ease,' imitating a bird and standing on one leg.

'That's how they'll do it, I expect,' observed Ethel brightly, standing by her twin who had picked up the melody on the piano. 'Don't you think so, Evelyn?'

A crash on the piano.

'What do you mean, Holmes?' Evelyn retorted gruffly, coming to a triumphant finale.

'When they try to assassinate the Prince of Wales on Thursday, he'll be heavily guarded, so I think a daring young man will do it by flying trapeze.'

A quiet stillness. A sudden chill in that close warm atmosphere. Then the Baroness's throaty laugh broke the sudden silence. 'What imagination you have, my dear. Assassination indeed.'

'Stuff and nonsense,' declared Bowman. 'Balloon, that's how he'll get there.'

Auguste fought his muddled head. What was happening? How alcohol distracted and confused. Surely no one save he and Egbert had known of the assassination threat? And yet no one had queried it. No one had shown surprise. Was it merely alcohol, or guilt? His mind fought, and lost. Around him the party swirled on as dancers to the piano played faster and faster. Bella was in his arms, dancing under the kissing bough. Then he seemed to be swearing undying love to the Baroness. To the *Baroness*? Surely Rosanna. Or was it Mademoiselle Gonnet, whose eyes were alight with sudden mischief, as her hands crept round his neck, and she held him close. His senses were on fire. Oh happy Christmas. He murmured in her ear endearments of their native France, for Alsace was French in its heart, despite its German rulers. Streams of love poured from his lips, words he would have spoken to another had he been able. But now to Mademoiselle Gonnet, for once full of grace and femininity. Only her shocked 'Monsieur Didier' made him aware that he had been guilty of suggesting a nocturnal assignation.

'A thousand pardons,' he murmured happily, drawing her closer.

'Only because the Baroness is so close, Auguste,' came a throaty murmur in his ear. 'Otherwise, who knows?'

And the twins played on.

★ ★ ★

Egbert Rose was on duty, though at first sight he did not appear so. The evening suit he kept was far more often used on duty than on social activities enjoyed by himself and Edith. But if he walked into Jimmy's at midnight in bowler hat and overcoat, he'd get less help than a Smithfield man at Billingsgate.

He glanced towards Vine Street police station as he walked through to Piccadilly. He reckoned they saw pretty nearly as many villains on this beat as ever walked the Ratcliffe Highway. The best and the worst you saw on Piccadilly. And it was the latter he was in search of now. If that girl had been on the streets, he knew who'd be able to help him.

''Allo, darling.'

He turned to his accoster and grinned. 'Me? Sure?' The hand fell away, the form slunk back to join her sisters jostling for trade on the pavement. He walked into Jimmy's. Same trade, different levels. As different as Auguste from the cook at Charley's Café was the world of the demi-monde from the pavement trade. The front of the restaurant was full of men staring into the dining rooms. Rose walked past in search of his quarry.

'Emmy,' he said quietly.

She hadn't noticed him at first, laughing and talking to her three companions. She turned her head, the red taffeta of her gaudy, low-cut gown rustling as she realised who was with her.

'Looks like I've trade,' she told the three other women offhandedly. Obediently they moved to another table.

'Anywhere private we can talk, Emmy?'

She shrugged, lighting a cigarette. ''Ere's good enough. No one'll hear. All too busy on the jaw. Ain't seen you in long time, Egbert.' She eyed him provoca-

171

tively. 'Come for a bit, 'ave yer?'

'Information,' he replied.

'Yer oughter get off the straight and narrow.'

'Land in the river that way, Emmy, you know that.'

'Begin at Jimmy's, end up over the Bridge of Sighs, eh? Or out there selling matches. A bright life and a short one, eh?' Her hands trembled slightly as she held the cigarette. 'D'yer come 'ere to cart me off to an 'ome, Inspector? Turn me into a nice little 'ousemaid and pack me off to Paris?'

'Lassie in the river. Thought you might recognise her.' Rose had no compunction about showing her the photograph. If she felt emotion, she did not display it. 'Murdered north of Oxford Street. We think she was a housemaid, but might have been on the streets. No one's reported her missing.'

She studied it and shook her head. 'Difficult to tell. Don't recognise her. Try the 'omes.'

'Homes?'

'Those training places. Some girls they pick up from the streets, or buy 'em from crowded 'omes. Like they used to do when they wanted young girls for the foreign whorehouses.'

'That's all stopped.'

'There's an overseas trade in 'ousemaids, Egbert,' she addressed him familiarly, 'mostly to Belgium. And Canada. I'll put the word out round here, but the girl looks, well, not quite our class, if you know what I mean. Print dresses don't find much in the way of pickings in Piccadilly.'

Auguste staggered into his bedroom, tucked well to the rear of the ground floor behind his office. He had barely been able to restrain himself from resorting to hands and knees to get here. Water, he must drink water before he slept or assuredly he would be in no fit state to greet the last day of the old century. Greedily he consumed the whole contents of his water flask and sank gratefully into bed. Half an hour later he awoke with a start, aware of an urgent need. Water might be beneficial for his head, but it reached parts where its immediate result was far from convenient. With a groan, he flung aside the bedclothes and swung his legs to the ground, his head throbbing. Just as he did so the door opened, and he smothered a shout of fear that the ghost of the bride of young Lovell was paying him a visit.

It was not a ghost. It was Bella, very much desirable flesh and blood, clad in white satin and lace. At least, under other circumstances, she would have been desirable. At this precise moment he had only one desire, and it was not Bella.

'Auguste!' She wafted towards him with open arms, and as he stood up in agitation, threw her arms round him with gusto, toppling him backwards on the bed. She had a fashionable figure, and fashion was not approving of girlish slenderness, thus Auguste was buried under her smothering warmth and kisses. Her arms slid up and down his body, arousing sensations delightful at other times but *not* now!

'Madame,' he cried into a mouthful of satin. 'Bella, don't,' as a particularly well-aimed hand found its target. 'I have sworn to remain faithful to my love,' he tried without much hope.

But the arms slightly relaxed their hold. 'She wouldn't know,' Bella's voice informed him from above.

'I would,' he cried eagerly. 'In my heart.'

'Ah well, I could leave your heart intact,' Bella murmured beguilingly.

'The two are linked,' Auguste shouted in desperation. 'I plead with you, madame. Would you have me betray another?'

'Why not?' Bella enquired, then laughed, rolled off her prey, sat up and patted her hair back into order. 'I hope your lady appreciates your sacrifice.'

'No,' said Auguste simply, 'for Tatiana is not my lady. Nor ever can be,' adding hastily lest Bella take this as encouragement to renew the offensive, 'but yet I cannot love another,' he perorated, cursing the predicaments in which body and social convention could combine to place one.

'What a waste,' sighed Bella. 'And I thought you liked me. I suppose I could always go to visit Gaston,' she announced without excitement as she floated out.

A few moments later, urgent needs fulfilled and the chamber pot replaced, Auguste climbed once more thankfully into bed, where he slept out the night, peacefully if regrettably chastely.

Chapter Seven

Auguste slowly emerged from his bedroom at seven thirty, not yet able to face the possibility of passing guests, to greet the last day of the old century. True, only a slight headache reminded him of his involuntary excesses of the evening before, but consciousness that he had been made to look foolish at least in his own eyes contributed to the distinct grumpiness that enveloped him this Monday morning. He felt a great desire just to go to his cubbyhole office and let the world pass him by. Conscience directed his footsteps elsewhere. To the dining room where guests would shortly be descending for breakfast.

A terrible sight met his eyes. Mary was on duty with two footmen, immaculately clad in livery. The garnish, yes, but where was the meat? Where was the usual array of steaming hot dishes, where were the succulent smells that should gently woo the breakfaster into a delightful awareness of the promise of the day to come? What met Auguste's nose was burnt devilled kidneys and the smell of old tired herrings that had lain uncalled for in their marinade for too long. Worse, where was the heart of breakfast, the breads? In the place usually occupied by freshly baked muffins, crumpets, Sally Lunns, Didier's breakfast cakes, anchovy toasts, sausage toasts and Scotch woodcock were what looked suspiciously like the bottom rounds of yesterday's cottage loaves, with their round roofs sitting on their own, doubling as rolls.

'What is this?' asked Auguste simply.

Mary quailed. She had the stamp of a true connoisseur, he noted dispassionately. She had an instinctive awareness of the correctness of things.

'Cook's a little busy this morning, sir,' she offered in misguided loyalty.

Auguste stared at her aghast. 'A little busy,' he repeated, dumbfounded. 'Too busy to—' He broke off. One should never criticise superiors before their underlings, no matter how great the provocation. And Fancelli was undoubtedly the chef in residence. His chest swelled. His muscles grew tense. The time had come for Showdown in the Kitchen Corral.

Quivering with rage, he ran down the staircase towards that underworld that should have been so entrancing but now was occupied by an alien presence. He spied his quarry, and marched straight to him.

'Signor Fancelli,' he began silkily, 'I understand you are a little busy this morning.'

Fancelli looked up briefly, and went back to his apparently engrossing task of desultorily stuffing a turkey. 'Yis,' he informed his superior.

Auguste examined the object of Fancelli's attention more closely and was transfixed. His whole consignment of delicately perfumed truffles – *fresh* truffles, 8 lb of *Kentish* truffles, supplied by His Grace the Duke as a favour to him – were being carelessly stuffed into one turkey. True, the art of cuisine had been known to demand such sacrifices in the past, but not unless for a centrepiece, a dish for the highest gourmets to appreciate.

'What is it you do?' he asked, voice rising uncontrollably. 'These truffles, at the peak of their condition, so delicately perfumed, snouted out by the Duke's own dogs, they cannot be wasted so when mushrooms would do as well.'

Fancelli's reply was muffled and far from cordial as he continued stuffing truffles into the cavity, followed by a noise that suggested he was about to break into song.

'We *have* no more truffles,' screamed Auguste. 'These must be saved for the garnish,' pulling the dish away.

Fancelli at last took notice, grabbing the dish back, and flourishing a precious truffle under Auguste's nose.

'*Attention!*' cried Auguste anxiously, the delicate perfume under his nose seeming to be pleading for its release.

'I take care,' snorted Fancelli. 'I take care with truffles. They all go in. See!' plunging one in as though it were a fistful of pug into a wall cavity.

'No, no,' Auguste plunging in his own hand as soon as Fancelli's was released, and removing the precious objects.

A silence fell in the kitchen as the staff began to watch, fascinated.

Fancelli's face bulged at this affront to his position; he picked up the truffles and replaced them before, too late, Auguste grabbed the dish to guard them against further assault.

'Signor Didier, you stuff your truffles where you like.' Fancelli's preferred choice was menacingly obvious.

'I, Signor Fancelli, am the manager here.'

'And I am the chef.'

'They are *my* truffles. Remove them from this turkey.'

Fancelli looked at him. Then he turned to the turkey. With great care he removed the truffles one by one; then he picked up one, weighed it in his hand, and hurled it at the menu blackboard.

A terrible silence, and at last: 'You, monsieur, are

not worthy of the name of chef. You will leave these kitchens *now*,' pronounced Auguste in deadly voice.

'I go,' snorted Fancelli in a mixture of grandeur and glee. 'I go and you have no chef for tonight, your New Century's Eve banquet.'

Auguste and his staff watched the portly figure don jacket and hat, exit through the tradesmen's entrance and puff up the steps to the outside world. The strains of *La Donna è Mobile* could just be heard till they faded into the distance.

August drew a deep breath in the stillness of his own domain. He looked at the open-mouthed faces watching him for his reactions, for guidance; he looked at the familiar objects of the kitchen, salt jars, chafing dishes, mousetraps, dough bins, salamanders, from which he had been temporarily banished. He looked at the tables, untidy but scrubbed ready for action. He looked at the menu blackboard, at the cook's knives inviting his use, he looked at the baskets delivered from the market, beautiful cauliflowers glowing white, green firm sprouts, red glossy apples. Oh, the textures, the colours. He smelled the fresh fish awaiting preparation, he saw the exotic fruits awaiting his master touch.

Scheherazade with all her jewels could not command as much as he before this riot of possibility, this wealth. Auguste drew a deep sigh of happiness. He beamed. He looked at his staff.

'*Alors, mes enfants*,' he said, spreading his arms wide in welcome. 'Come, we have work to do.'

Auguste Didier was himself again. He was home.

Fifteen minutes later, Cranton's kitchen resembled a maypole of flying figures dancing round it, woven into an intricate dance choreographed by a master chef. Maids flew upstairs with eggs and marrow toast, the smell of baking filled the kitchens. A kedgeree was somehow spirited into swift existence with just a hint of Colonel Kenny's curry paste. Auguste eyed Mrs Marshall's balefully. Not in his kitchen.

Auguste flew round the kitchens, a white-gowned banshee of activity, wailing at all and everyone. Breakfast time would no longer present disaster, but what of luncheon? Not to mention this evening's banquet. He cast an agonised glance at the blackboards. True, they were his menus, but somehow now they looked uninspired, they lacked the true flavour of a Didier banquet. And the ingredients – how could he be sure that *man*, for assuredly he was no chef, had obtained them correctly? He drew a deep breath. He was the general: he must study the plan of campaign, then inspect the battlefield, and lastly review his troops and send them into battle.

His eye fell on a few dishes at random, purée of partridge soup, supreme of turkey fillets *à l'écarlate*, *bavarois de marasquin*, apples *à la crémone*, Indian trifle, London syllabub, the sorbets, the ices—Panic seized him. The ices – he had not noticed any. He flew to the ice boxes with sinking heart. As he thought, no sign of ice, no sign of sorbet. Panic momentarily overwhelmed him. He had a matter of hours only. Then he reminded himself firmly that it was for emergencies such as this that Maître Escoffier had trained him.

'*Alors*,' he informed his henchmen briskly, 'we will make junkets, trifles, orange custards – even, yes, Pall Mall Pudding,' he said triumphantly. Obtaining the recipe from a reluctant Emma Pryde on behalf of Miss Guessings had taken all his considerable arts of blandishment.

Ovens were lit, scullerymaids rushed cooking pots to the fore, kitchenmaids eagerly sorted ingredients as their new master dictated. Footmen were despatched speedily to Senns High Class Delicacies for missing ingredients. By ten o'clock the kitchen was beginning to show some evidence of order, and work in progress. The banquet, Auguste told himself thankfully, was under way. It could be achieved, and better, oh how much better than it would have been under the direction of Signor Fancelli. He gazed round happily.

'What's for luncheon, Mr Didier?' piped up John, his underchef, brightly.

'*Quoi?*' asked Auguste impolitely, so taken aback was he.

John repeated his question, but there was no need. The awful truth had already dawned on the *maître chef*. *He had forgotten luncheon!* Should he fall on his sword like Vatel? Or rather his kitchen knife? He had forgotten a meal. Such a thing had never happened before! Truly, he grew old, past his prime, an overhung *faisan*. He should be put out to grass, donkey that he was. He gazed at John helplessly, wits deserting him.

'I hear your cook has left, Monsieur Didier.'

Glassy-eyed, Auguste looked up at this interruption and was appalled. Madame la Baronne was descending the steps of the kitchen in an elegant morning dress of blue wool, a high pearl dog collar at her neck. Such demeaning intrusion of guests to the nether regions must not be allowed. But he was past pretence.

'The *cook* has indeed departed, madame, but as you see, *le chef* remains.' He bowed, hoping to impress the Baroness that nothing was amiss.

He did not succeed.

She apparently took in the situation at a glance, and strode towards him. 'Monsieur Didier, I shall require an apron.'

'But madame – you cannot!' He was appalled. What were the aristocracy coming to?

'*Mais pourquoi?*' The elegant eyebrows were raised.

'I have nothing to do this morning other than to write letters and that does not amuse me. Mademoiselle Gonnet has gone to visit friends, and I am too old to wish continually to add to my store of knowledge by visiting museums.'

'But a baroness to help in the kitchens—'

'I was not always a baroness,' she said lightly. 'I was born Thérèse from Orléans. You need have no fear, monsieur. I have read my Brillat-Savarin, my Dumas, and furthermore I have my specialities. The apron, *s'il vous plaît*, monsieur.'

Somehow the Baroness inspired confidence. He did not understand her, doubtless there was some mystery attached to her, but he felt instinctively that he could rely on her. If she stated she could achieve miracles, then he was prepared to believe it. In fact, he had little choice with a minimum of forty dishes to prepare for this evening.

'In that case, madame,' he handed her the apron.

'And the task, monsieur?'

'Luncheon for fifteen.' By her reaction he would test her.

'And what do your larders possess that can provide the basis for this repast, monsieur?'

His respect grew. 'Cold goose, madame, it appears, for a *plat rechauffé*, and cold beef for another, brawn, salads, and the stockpot at your service.'

'And the desserts?' Her voice was as brisk as his, as set on the task before her as was he.

'Fruit, madame, would be simplest.'

She dismissed this. 'Soufflés.'

His respect shot up so high he had to reassure himself. 'You are bold, madame.'

'I achieve what I want, monsieur. And now, pray, let us return to our muttons. Or, in this case, our cooked goose.' She paused, looked round at the staff and her eyes fell on Mary. 'I will have you,' she pronounced, 'to assist me.'

'Yes, ma'am.' Mary cast a terrified look at Auguste who nodded approvingly. The Baroness, for the moment, could do no wrong.

This indeed appeared to be the case, for she worked efficiently and tidily so that he ceased to keep a wary eye on her and devoted himself to the banquet. A new spirit of goodwill seemed to be flourishing in the kitchens as the morning wore on, a liveliness of eye and step that had not been apparent before. Ah, this was truly where he belonged.

By some miracle, at twelve o'clock the Baroness pronounced herself ready for inspection. By now she would have had to have taken a sledgehammer to a delicate sole to earn his disapproval, and before him lay no evidence of that. He stiffened slightly as he saw the goose in a cream sauce, but the subtle taste of simmered garlic and vegetables within it reassured him. He beamed and nodded approval at a *chicon gratiné*; his eyes rose slightly when he saw spice cloves in the salad dressing, but before he could comment, his eye was drawn to a horror that he could not believe the Baroness capable of. Coralline pepper – furthermore, Mrs Marshall's coralline pepper – adorning the *rechauffé* dish of beef in sour cream. True, he was forced to admit, the taste could hardly be faulted, but the end did not always justify the means. An eye must be kept on the Baroness after all.

'I think you deliberately goaded Fancelli into walking out, Auguste,' announced Maisie crossly, far from pleased at the *fait accompli* that had resulted in an urgent appeal from him to reconsider her absence from Cranton's.

'Maisie, Fancelli is no true chef,' Auguste pleaded.

'No true chef would leave his guests unprovided for. He left them, Maisie, without making provision for luncheon.' He overlooked the fact that in the excitement of the moment he also had overlooked it.

'And what am I to do for a chef now?' she demanded belligerently.

'I will be your chef,' Auguste announced grandly.

'Splendid. And who will be manager then, while you're souffléing around the kitchen?'

'I will do that too. And the Baroness has kindly offered to assist. She has experience of hotels, it seems, from before her marriage.'

Maisie snorted. 'Fine thing, me organising holidays for gentlefolk who land up having to run them themselves. What a reputation that will give me!'

'It will indeed if I am to be the chef,' Auguste pointed out mildly.

'Chef? I thought you were the great detective. You're going to be busy one way and another this afternoon.'

He looked wildly round. It was a gross dereliction of duty, for he had found a letter from Egbert in his office instructing him to make full use of the afternoon – and why. But how could he leave the kitchens? That, too, was duty.

'Could you not. .?'

'Yes?' she asked dangerously.

'Escort our guests to the Tower of London and observe, listen?'

'What for? Want a potted history of the Tower straight from the Beefeater's mouth?'

'Non. This is *très sérieux*, Maisie. Listen to what the guests talk of amongst themselves. And in particular, any mention of Brussels.'

'Sprouts?'

'Now you try to provoke me,' he said crossly. 'I tell

you, Maisie, much depends on this. A murderer must be found, and an assassin, and the Inspector is beginning to think this plot may be connected with Sipido's failed attempt in April.'

A short pause. 'Anything to oblige, Auguste. What would you like me to do if I find him?' she enquired. 'Chop his head off on Tower Hill?'

'I wonder if you are aware,' announced Thomas Harbottle impartially to the party, emboldened by the flamboyance of today's choice of waistcoat, 'that if there are no ravens at the Tower, the fortress is doomed?'

Whether the rest of the party did or not, the Yeoman Warder assigned to it most certainly did and was not going to have his authority undermined by a pipsqueak like this. He puffed out his magnificent chest. They weren't called Beefeaters for nothing; the roast beef of old England had given him not only a heart of oak but a chest to match.

'This 'ere dungeon,' he boomed in a voice that had once terrified recruits on army parade – grounds in farflung parts of Her Majesty's Empire, 'is known as "Little Ease", where the arch-villain Guy Fawkes was imprisoned.'

Curiosity having been satisfied by one journey on the Underground Railway, it had been deemed desirable to hire carriages for the journey to the Tower. Maisie had led her flock across the drawbridge (less the Miss Pembreys who waived eight hundred years of history in favour of an examination of the delightful novelty of the new Tower Bridge) into the Tower precincts, waving her Governor's Pass to be admitted to regions where visitors were not normally allowed. This gave them the honour of seeing empty rooms in the White Tower in which Sir Walter Raleigh had been imprisoned and the even more dubious honour, in Maisie's view, of descending to the dungeons. The ladies, except for the Baroness, were not impressed.

'Guy Fawkes – did he not try to blow up Parliament?' whispered Eva Harbottle to her husband at Maisie's side as the party left in twos and threes.

'Yes,' answered Thomas shortly.

Hello, thought Maisie, why no historical diatribe on the subject?

'What happened to him?' Eva pressed on, uncharacteristically.

'He was tortured and killed.'

''E'd be given a medal today,' guffawed Bowman, turning round. 'One way to get rid of old Salisbury, eh?'

'But blowing up Parliament meant blowing up the King too, Alfred,' said Gladys, quite shocked.

'Those days are over, thank goodness,' put in Maisie brightly, provocatively. 'No one would want to blow up Her Majesty – or kill poor old Bertie.'

A sudden stillness – because of her disrespectful reference to the heir to the throne, or for some other reason?

'The Boers would,' pointed out the Marquis coolly.

'I'd like to see any get near enough to try. A Boer wouldn't get past Dover,' said Carruthers.

'Wouldn't they?' chortled Bowman. 'There's one right here. Your lady wife's a Boer, isn't she, Harbottle?'

'I don't know what you mean,' cried Eva, white in the face, simultaneously with her husband's 'Eva's German.'

'She wasn't when I saw her in Brussels at the Hôtel Midi. I just realised why I knew you. Eva Kruger was her name then. Related to the great man, are you?'

'It must have been someone else,' said Harbottle

185

stonily. 'You have never been to Brussels, have you, Eva?'

'Never,' said Eva listlessly. 'Never.'

'I wonder if you are aware that the uncut ruby,' announced Harbottle loudly, almost defiantly, as the party gathered round the iron cage protecting the crown jewels in the Wakefield Tower and gazed at the Queen's State crown, 'is said to have been worn by Henry V on his helmet at the Battle of Agincourt. The large sapphire below is said to have belonged to Edward the Confessor.'

'Why did a priest own it?' asked Marie-Paul.

'He was a king, madam,' the Beefeater informed her loudly. 'One of our great English kings.'

'Then where is his crown?'

'It ain't here, madam,' the Beefeater was forced to admit. 'All the royal jewels and crowns were sold orf after we cut off Charles I's head.'

'Is this not assassination?' demanded Eva sulkily.

The Beefeater looked nonplussed.

'Not when it's legal, madam,' Sir John stepped in.

'But it was not legal while the King lived,' argued Eva, 'so you say if an assassination is successful it is legal, and if it fails like poor Mr Fawkes's, it is not legal and you kill them.'

Sir John turned purple. Harbottle took his wife firmly by the arm. 'Come, dearest, let us view the Sword of Mercy.'

Colonel Carruthers was staring long and hard at the St Edward's Crown. 'One of my ancestors stole that, you know,' he announced to the assembly suddenly. 'Blood, his name was. Blood.'

The Beefeater edged closer, as did Maisie. This was a sidelight and a half on the Colonel. He coughed, aware of the interest he was causing. He looked round testily for Dalmaine. He had new arguments to present on the Iron Duke's choice of Waterloo as a battlefield and the damn fellow was nowhere to be found.

Dalmaine had in fact tired of jewels and was wondering where Rosanna might be. He had left the Wakefield Tower in search of her and found not the object of his desire, but de Castillon, who felt uncomfortable in this English fortress. Why did they still keep it fortified? Surely they no longer expected his government to invade? Or did they? In his view, France had more to worry about than its old enemy England. Even so, a little less stability in England would be no bad thing. The old Queen could not last much longer, and for the French to stir up anti-British sentiment was hardly necessary at the moment. The Boers were doing it for them. He greeted Dalmaine with some pleasure. He did not wish to return empty-handed from this holiday.

'How do you find this climate after Africa, Major Dalmaine?'

'Not to my liking, sir. Miss the sunshine.'

'But there is much rain also, is there not?'

'Not in the Transvaal, sir,' Dalmaine stared.

'But on the Gold Coast,' said de Castillon silkily.

'I don't know about West Africa,' replied Dalmaine quickly.

'My apologies, Major Dalmaine. Of course it was your brother involved in the Ashanti War of ninety-six, was it not? And did I not hear he went out again this year as a volunteer? No doubt now the Ashantis are subdued once more, he will be returned home. I wonder what may be in his trunk? How my government would like to know where the Stool might be found. Assuredly peace can never come to the Gold Coast while it is absent, and the French see their role as peacemakers. Ah,' he broke off, 'Lady Gincrack, how delightful to see you. Dalmaine and I were just discussing the unity of Africa under the wise guardianship of England and France. And Brussels too, of course, Dalmaine,' he added offhandedly. 'Don't forget the Congo. And now tell me, what is this we are looking at, pray?'

'Traitor's Gate,' answered Dalmaine unemotionally.

'My dear,' said Gladys, 'what a splendid party this is.' She gazed happily at the Queen's consort ring and imagined it adorning her own finger. 'Apart from poor dear Nancy, of course,' she added hastily.

'Where can Mr Bowman have got to?' asked Bella innocently.

'He went to talk to that young couple, the Harbottles,' said Gladys, trying to hide her disappointment that he had torn himself from her side even for a moment.

'He seems most attached to you,' said Bella politely.

Gladys flushed with pleasure. 'I believe he is,' she confided. 'I really think he is.' She pondered on life in Much Wallop and the greater glories that might lie ahead if she left it. There were still a few days left. It was not beyond the bounds of possibility that tonight, New Year's Eve, Alfred would propose. Her happiness would be complete. If only Nancy hadn't come along to complicate matters. How could she have expected to meet someone from Much Wallop in Cranton's? Poor Nancy. Gladys was genuinely sorry for her death, but there was no doubt it had removed a difficulty. Now no one knew about Much Wallop, least of all Mr Bowman.

'I read that it was here the murder took place,' Bella was saying conversationally, as Maisie returned to collect her flock.

Gladys jumped. 'Murder?' she repeated fearfully.

'Yes,' said Maisie. 'Henry VI.'

Outside, a plump man in a bowler hat and dark

overcoat walked swiftly out of the Tower and disappeared into the anonymity of London. Even had the party from Cranton's been accustomed to taking notice of cooks, they would hardly have recognised Fancelli without his cook's hat and apron.

'Drums captured at Blenheim,' Maisie read out.

'Fascinating,' said Thérèse stoutly.

'A great British victory.'

'Perhaps the enemy's books read differently,' said Thérèse drily.

'History's an odd thing,' agreed Maisie. 'It all depends which side you're on. Look at Joan of Arc. Heroine where you were born. And we burn her at the stake. And look at Sipido,' she added innocently, 'who tried to kill the Prince of Wales at the Gare de Midi in Brussels.'

'De Nord,' corrected Thérèse absently.

'Oh, you know Brussels do you?'

The Baroness raised her eyebrows. '*Naturellement*,' she said coldly. 'My husband is a diplomat, after all. The poor boy's deed is obviously known to us.'

'Oh, look at that,' said Maisie, anxiously pointing at the block on which Lord Lovat lost his head for treason. 'They'd have put Sipido on that if this were 1747.'

'Barbarians,' muttered Thérèse.

'Dear lady,' boomed Alfred Bowman, appearing suddenly behind Gladys as she gazed disconsolately at an English longbow recovered from the wreck of the *Mary Rose*, 'where *have* you been hiding?'

'Nowhere,' replied Gladys rather crossly. On the contrary, she had been hunting and had given up the search. One might almost think Alfred had lost interest in her. Surely it could not be so.

As if in affirmation of her confidence, he slipped a

possessive arm through hers. 'Take a look at these breechloaders, Gladys. Don't see many of those today. Or your Brown Besses. No, we've moved on a bit. The lads in South Africa are better equipped. Fine guns Krupp produces.'

'Aren't they what the Boers have?' said Gladys, frowning.

Alfred did not seem to hear her. Her arm had been returned to her and he was busy admiring a damascened suit of armour of the seventeenth century.

'Marlborough,' declared Gladys loudly as they reached the foot of the staircase leaving the White Tower where Maisie was waiting.

Bowman jumped. 'What?' he said quite rudely.

'Marlborough,' repeated Gladys crossly. Really, Alfred didn't seem to be listening at all. If this was what marriage was like . . . 'I said, there are some pieces of the old State barge, with the arms of the Duke of Marlborough.'

'Oudenarde, Ramillies, Waterloo,' muttered Bowman. 'Good for Belgium, eh? It's getting its own back now.'

'Ah, there you are,' said Carruthers gruffly, striding up to Dalmaine, trying not to appear too eager.

Dalmaine was surveying a showcase of early nineteenth-century helmets and swords. Colonel Carruthers surveyed it with him. 'Great days!' he said at last. 'Great days!'

'I'm prepared to admit,' Dalmaine offered magnanimously in a spirit to accord with their new-found comradeship, 'that Napoleon was remiss in not following up the Prussian retreat.'

Carruthers glowed. 'And that the Duke's strategy was flawless?' he pressed eagerly.

This was going too far. 'By no means,' said Dalmaine, genuinely amazed. 'His troops were far too widely disposed in view of the fact that Napoleon's intentions were not foreseeable.'

'If you'd walked the battlefields as I have, young man,' Carruthers began.

'I have,' retorted Dalmaine. 'I visited them with my brother last year.'

'Stayed in *Brussels*, I'll be bound.'

'Yes,' retorted Dalmaine. 'What's wrong with that?'

'Aha,' said Carruthers triumphantly. 'I'd had enough of that place after a day. No, out in the fields, camping, like me – then you'd understand.'

'In a tent?'

A laugh. 'Might as well have been. Stayed in one of the Belgian so-called hotels. No decent port.'

Dalmaine had the tactlessness to laugh. 'Brussels was good enough for the Duke and good enough for me.'

'Dammit, sir—' The Colonel broke off as Maisie approached. 'Come to my club, young man, and we'll settle this matter of the Duke's dispositions over a whisky.'

'I'd be glad to, sir,' Dalmaine retorted, with no sign of gladness at all. 'Er, which one?'

Colonel Carruthers glared. 'The Rag, my dear sir. What other club is there?'

'The Duke was Constable of the Tower for many years, wasn't he?' contributed Maisie brightly, wondering why the whole world seemed intent on discussing Brussels this afternoon.

'He was, madam. He was,' agreed Carruthers. 'He had the right idea. Get rid of its zoo, get rid of the sightseers, and arm the place to the teeth. He knew an enemy when he saw one. Never trusted the French, you know. Quite right. What do you think is going to happen when the old Queen goes? God bless 'er. This young Prince of Wales is going to be hobnobbing with the enemy all the time. Folies Bergères.' He snarled in disgust. 'He'll have us part of France again before you can say Wellington. England could breathe easy if that son of his were on the throne. He's no army man, mind you, but at least in the Navy he'll have got some idea of what the Channel's there for. Eh?' He glared at his silent audience. 'What are you staring for?' He was quite surprised. What the devil had he been saying to make them look like stunned trout?

'Darling!' Rosanna threw herself into her beloved's arms. 'Where have you been? I thought you'd never come,' she complained. 'I've been counting ravens—'

'The raven himself is hoarse,' quoted Danny Nash absently, returning her embrace without much enthusiasm.

'Which one?' asked Rosanna. 'I can't tell one from the other.'

'It's a quotation from *Macbeth*,' her beloved informed her.

'Isn't that the play it's unlucky to quote from?' asked Rosanna in a rare sign of erudition.

'What could possibly be unlucky about our meeting?'

'We are in the Bloody Tower,' Rosanna said soberly.

'That's all in the past. It's the present I need to know about,' said Danny impatiently. 'Now, did you find out anything about Brussels?'

Rosanna pouted. 'You're more interested in your old story than me.'

'Nonsense. But you know how important it is.'

'Do I?' she said carelessly, breaking away, just as Maisie entered with such of her flock as could be rounded up to admire the Bloody Tower, restored to its former self now that its stucco covering had been stripped. 'Bother Brussels,' she said pouting, to Maisie's great interest.

Danny was forced to wait impatiently as the Beef-eater worked his way through the history of the Bloody Tower and after the oohs and aahs had died down taken the party out again.

'Now,' he said, 'tell me.'

'Well—' Rosanna broke off with a scream as a wailing sound came from above, approaching. Whatever it was was coming nearer. She clutched at Danny as a particularly loud wail sounded outside the door, a black stockinged leg appeared round it, and a voice quavered: 'We are the ghosts of the poor little Princes.'

'And you know what happened to *them*, don't you?' shouted Rosanna in exasperation at her two younger sisters.

'They were murdered!' answered Evelyn and Ethel dolefully.

Egbert Rose stood for a few moments watching Auguste at work, the friend in him amused, the detective in him irritated. Precious moments were ticking by whilst Auguste was completely engrossed in garnishing a raised game pie.

'I see you're back home, Auguste,' he commented wrily.

Auguste's head shot up, forced out of his all-engrossing world like icing out of an icing bag. Even so, at the back of his mind he was running for the ump-teenth time through the last-minute tasks for the all-important evening ahead, the last meal of the old century, together with a few delicacies for a late supper, which would no doubt be the first of the new: Mrs de Salis's stuffed anchovies, some lobster in aspic, oyster soufflé, *tartines au pâté de fois gras* – was that sufficient? – with the usual cold meats, salads and so forth. And naturally dessert. He decided it might be sufficient considering the magnificence of the banquet *à la Didier* that would have preceded it. He dwelt lovingly on the banquet for a moment. There was one problem—

'And if we don't get to the bottom of *my* problem soon, the next King is going to be the Duke of York,' said Rose with asperity as Auguste voiced his concern aloud.

'You are right, Egbert. Some things are certainly more important than food. I have been wrong,' he acknowledged. 'It has not been a good day.'

'I thought you said you were going to the Tower,' said Rose grimly, leading the way out of the kitchens.

'Maisie has gone in my place,' Auguste told him shamefacedly. 'She is adept at gathering information.'

Rose eyed him. 'You are taking this little matter of murder and assassination seriously, Auguste? Sure you haven't more important things to do?'

Auguste raised doleful eyes to him. 'I found a corpse in November, *cher* Egbert,' he said hesitantly.

Rose sighed. He took the point. They'd maybe wasted weeks because of that, and he was cavilling over one afternoon. He rubbed his eyes. 'Only two days, Auguste. It's getting on top of me.'

'Will you stay and eat tonight, Egbert?' Auguste asked gently.

Rose thought of Highbury, of Edith waiting for him to return and of the probability that he would not get home in time, even if he left here now. He thought of the feast that awaited him here. Could he call this duty? He could. 'Duty calls, Auguste, duty calls,' he said cordially, rubbing his hands as he read the menu.

'My lips are sealed,' declared Danny defiantly, legs cockily apart, arms akimbo. He had declined the rickety chair.

'They're not when it comes to spreading the word on

194

matters the Yard want kept to themselves,' Rose said shortly. 'You've been playing fun and games, young man. You sleep here at night all right, but we don't see hair nor hide of you in the day.'

'I'm following up the story,' said Danny defiantly. 'It's my job. To avenge Nancy.'

'So you say. How do we know you didn't come here specially to murder her? Playing you up, was she?'

Danny gaped. 'Nancy? No, I've told you, it's the story.'

'Very gallant of you to sleep in a cellar all over Christmas, ain't it?'

Danny flushed. 'I had another reason to be here,' he muttered.

'I thought so,' Rose announced with satisfaction. 'Suspected her of having another bloke?'

'Darling! I'm here to save you.' Rosanna thrust herself into the room and threw her arms round him. 'He was here to see *me*, Inspector. We are in love.'

'This true, Mr Nash?'

'Yes – I—'

'Poor Danny couldn't have killed Nancy. I was with him.'

Danny turned red.

'When and where was that, miss?'

She hesitated. 'As soon as I had my tea I went down to see him,' she announced, 'to give him my present. And I stayed there until breakfast time. At least nine fifteen,' she concluded triumphantly.

'Chesnais' belief is that this plot was hatched in Brussels, probably by the anti-British group that gave Sipido the idea of shooting the Prince when Dr Leyds, who's Kruger's agent on the Continent, addressed them. Apparently Sipido got it into his head he had to kill the Prince because he was, Leyds said, "an accomplice of Chamberlain in killing the Boers". And he was very nearly successful. One shot right in the cushions beside the Prince and Princess, by all accounts. That's why I asked you to keep an ear open for any Belgian connections, Auguste.'

'It seems to me,' said Maisie, rocking to and fro on the rickety chair in Auguste's erstwhile office, 'that the whole world knows Brussels and they're all blooming well at Cranton's.' She massaged her feet lovingly if inelegantly.

Auguste looked hastily away. How well he remembered performing that function for her under more intimate circumstances. *Où sont les neiges d'antan*? His eyes misted over, as Maisie recited the results of the afternoon's work. They quickly cleared, however, when Rose said: 'There's Mr Fancelli too.'

Auguste looked at him sharply.

'Twitch found out this stuff about his parents working at the Café Royal is a load of *tripes de Caen*, if you get my meaning, so I got Chesnais to do some checking. Fancelli worked in Brussels at a hotel called the Midi before he came here six months ago. Since when he don't seem to have surfaced in the working market. Italian name, Brussels background. Who does that remind you of?'

'Sipido,' said Auguste immediately. 'But he was acting alone, not with a group.'

'So they thought. But as he got the idea at a pro-Boer gathering, I'm pretty sure Sipido wasn't acting alone. Suppose someone decided to do the job properly now?'

'But Fancelli would not have the brains,' Auguste said scathingly, 'to think such a plan out on his own.' He might have known. No true chef would have left guests to starve for the *Réveillon*. No true *maître chef* made use of curry powder, and coralline pepper – though, true, the Baroness had used it. An odd recollection flitted through his mind and vanished again, in his fury about Fancelli. He pulled himself back to the path of logic. 'It will be no ordinary train that pulls into Paddington on the third. The assassin must realise that police will be guarding it. This is not Brussels,' he added gratuitously.

'Fancelli could be at Cranton's,' said Rose, 'to meet the brains and have a base for operations. So why don't we persuade our friend Fancelli nice and gentle to have a chat with us and tell us who it is? Why don't we call him in now?' asked Rose lovingly.

Auguste's face sank. 'We cannot, Egbert.'

'Banquets are all very well, Auguste,' said Rose, his face losing some of its good humour, 'but this is priority. See?'

'But Egbert, I cannot call him,' cried Auguste in misery. 'I dismissed him this morning.'

It was almost twelve o'clock. Auguste snapped his fingers at the footmen to ensure all glasses were filled; the bowl had on this occasion been guarded by a particularly stalwart elderly footman, proof against any incursions from the twins.

The *réveillon* had been a success. One of the superb banquets of his career. He had turned each of the humdrum dishes planned by *that man*, for he would not call him cook, into a masterpiece, he told himself modestly, by adding '*un peu de Didier*' and naming each of the twenty dishes in honour of one of the guests. It was a master stroke. It would go down in culinary history. *Velouté Rosanna*, *concombres au curry Carruthers*, *suprême de dinde Dalmaine*, *poularde Marie-Paul*, *pêches Bella*, *homard au gratin de Castillon*, *mousse glacée Gladys*, *boeuf Bowman*, *soufflé surprise aux Dames Pembrey*, *haricots Harnet* and *terrine de poisson Thérèse accompagnée de crevettes roses enrobées d'un fin velouté au poivre de baies rose*, a compliment the latter acknowledged gracefully.

'So much more gentle than your paprika, Baroness,' he murmured.

A moment's stillness as though this were an impertinence, then she smiled. 'You are the true *maître*, Monsieur Didier. I must accept your judgment with the same pleasure as your *terrine Thérèse*.'

He bowed, relaxing at last in a glass of the wine, thinking muddledly that had he not also provided an *englefin Egbert*, the *sauce au paprika rose* might equally well compliment him. Rose and the Baroness. He smiled. What worlds apart – and yet a similarity. He could not place it, and indeed for the moment had no desire to think.

The dancing and the energetic games organised by the twins banished sleepiness, as once again he found himself in Bella's all too loving arms.

'Now I know you are not entirely devoted to your distant love, Auguste, I feel there is hope yet. Do you not?'

Auguste did not. Reflection in the cold light of morning had convinced him that however many Bella's charms, the drawbacks would always outweigh them. With dear Maisie, the current was clear; with Bella the waters were uncharted, and instinct told him that perilous reefs might well lie hidden for unwary vessels.

'We need a dark stranger,' shrieked Evelyn. 'You'll do, Inspector.'

The luckless Rose was pushed outside to shiver on Cranton's steps as the new century approached. At least this would have been Oswald's task had he been at home, he grumbled to himself, drawing his coat collar closer.

The door of Cranton's was flung open as on the wings of the wind came the sound of Big Ben chiming in the twentieth century. Maisie kissed Auguste on the cheek. 'Happy next hundred years, Auguste.'

'And you, Maisie, and you.' His eyes blurred. What would they hold, for him, for Tatiana, for mankind?

After the chimes ceased, the sound of cheering, and of thousands of voices singing God Save Our Gracious Queen filled the air, as Rose came through the door of Cranton's Hotel.

Before him, resplendent to greet the new century, were Thérèse von Bechlein in maroon lace over silk, a bertha at her neck, Marie-Paul Gonnet, a gawkish bird of paradise for once in bright green taffeta that did nothing for her sallow complexion, the Pembrey girls in blue and white, Gladys Guessings in a pink taffeta dress with feathers, Colonel Carruthers, Major Dalmaine, Gaston de Castillon, Sir John Harnet and Thomas Harbottle immaculately penguined in tails; Eva Harbottle stood close to her husband in bright yellow as though determined now to be noticed. Bella, her red hair piled high in curls upon her head, and wearing a simple primrose-coloured gown by Worth, overshadowed them all.

Rose's eye ran briefly over the faces that greeted the first dark stranger of the twentieth century. One was a murderer, and would-be assassin.

God save the Queen. And God save her son, thought Auguste soberly. Pray God he would have more than two and a half days to live.

Chapter Eight

'This Fancelli,' Rose wasted no time in recriminations, 'did he seem eager or reluctant to go? You see my drift?'

Auguste did. If Fancelli were indeed the murderer and assassin, and was acting on his own, he would no doubt be eager at this stage to seize any opportunity of removing himself from police scrutiny. On the other hand, if he were a lone operator, why should he come to Cranton's in the first place? Why not stay well away from any scrutiny? Yet if he had an accomplice in the hotel, one of the guests, surely he would not wish to depart before the crime and be out of touch with his mentor. Or would he? Auguste thought back carefully. A sudden and unpleasant thought.

Could it have been that Fancelli had been deliberately provoking him throughout, intentionally using tactics – not to mention ingredients – that would induce an outburst so that he could leave without arousing suspicion? That his use of Mrs Marshall's coralline pepper was merely, like the Duchess in Mr Carroll's story of Alice, to annoy? Worse, to *mock*? Auguste's self-esteem received a severe buffet. He, Auguste Didier, *maître chef*, had been *mocked*? Had it come to this? He braced himself to face facts. Even the greatest of cooks must one day lay down their ladle. The secret was to know when. He tried to reply to Rose's question with dignity.

'I think it possible it suited Fancelli to leave. The

business was arranged. The hare can go to ground.'

'Then this hare's got to be jugged again, and quickly. And I'm told young Nash has slipped the coop again. The kitchen can look after itself today.'

Auguste gave an anguished yelp. Look after itself? No kitchen looked after itself. Even Mrs Rose would know that. It needed loving protection and guidance. But of course Egbert was right. Even dinner must come second at the moment. The Baroness had already proved her cooking ability and she might superintend, if she had no objection, every now and again, and, with a few (very brief) moments' overall inspection given to it from time to time by himself, surely John, the underchef, might cope? He was no *maître chef*, but then these were no ordinary times. If John chose simple straightforward recipes, and resisted the temptation to add exotic sauces and to experiment, the guests might survive without starvation.

'Very well, Egbert,' Auguste told him bravely. 'I will inform John. If I go now he will still have time to give proper attention to the menus for the day.'

'Don't get tempted to taste the soups while you're down there,' Rose said warningly.

Useless to try to pretend that he had had no intention of doing other than having the briefest of words with John. 'Very well, Egbert,' he repeated.

He hurried from the office undecided whether to seek out the Baroness or to descend to the kitchen first. The matter was, however, settled for him. As he came into the entrance hall he stopped short in amazement. An altercation was in progress between a lady most unlike any guests that Cranton's had ever entertained and the doorkeeper, expressed in both verbal and physical terms, as she shouldered her mountainous way past her opponent through the swing doors with all the determination of Wyatt Earp to shoot from the hip.

Her height did little to detract from the huge, bulky figure wrapped in two coats, one worn frontwards, the other backwards, since neither fitted, big lace-up boots, and a tweed cap on her head.

'Can I help you, madam?' Auguste asked feebly, as Perkins, who had been temporarily set back by a swing door rebounding forcefully on him, rushed after her.

'I'm here to see Egbert. Tell him Ma's here.'

Ma Bisley's large feet trod the thinnest of lines between the lesser criminal fraternity and the police, both trusting in her ability to remain on it. Her own confidence never wavered, so nor did theirs. It was tacitly agreed by her supporters on both sides that serious crime was equally bad for both, and that both therefore had a common interest in combating it. Thus it was also tacitly understood that the Yard would not burrow into the lesser crimes of the East End more than was strictly necessary in the course of their inquiries, this being left to the province of the Metropolitan Police, which was counted as fair enough by the lesser villains of the east and west of London.

Rose had become a veritable Nelson, his blind eye working as hard as ever did Nelson's at the Nile, and for their part, those picking up an honest living by petty crime were anxious not to be seen harbouring villains that Rose might be after. Occasionally conflicts of interest were adjudicated on by Ma with stern and impartial standards. The West End seldom had the honour of welcoming Ma in person, her bulk making her prefer to stay at home, a Mycroft, not a Sherlock. When she stirred, the criminal world stirred with her.

'Hoped I'd find yer 'ere.' Ma Bisley panted in to Rose's sanctum, brushing aside such mere impediments as police constables. 'Got some news for you. One of my runners,' she told Rose. ''E's found out who got that body you wanted to know about away from 'ere and over the bridge.'

'Who?' Rose rapped out.

'This geezer got a new shirt, see, and socks. Joe got suspicious.' She glowed with pride on behalf of her underling.

'Who, Ma?' repeated Rose.

'Can't tell you, you know that, Egbert. Got to protect me sources. We'll make sure you get 'im when it's necessary. It was a chap he helped. Not English, though he didn't say much.'

'Right, Ma.' Rose clapped on his bowler hat. 'Sounds as if it's Fancelli all right, doesn't it, Auguste? Got runners in Soho, have you, Ma?'

A broad grin crossed her face. 'You know me, Egbert. More runners than a bean-tinning factory.'

'Then a-hunting we will go, Ma. Urgent-like.'

The horse looked round indignantly as Ma Bisley's bulk sank into the growler, after being heaved up by Rose, Auguste and the driver pushing together, and was with some difficulty persuaded by its driver to begin the journey to Soho. Cities, Auguste decided, were much the same anywhere, as the growler left the luxuries of Shaftesbury Avenue and turned into the overcrowded inner streets of the parish of Soho.

Left, then right, and left again, narrow streets, many of the ground floors turned into shops now, only dark doorways indicating the one-room tenements that lay behind the façade, with even now families living – and often dying – as many as eight to a rat-infested room.

'Not that you ever see eight,' Rose told Auguste. 'They usually have a system going that at a knock on the door half of them scoot to another room, 'case the rent goes up.'

'You hope to find Fancelli in Soho?' asked Auguste.

'We've checked the restaurant you said he worked at – they've never heard of him.'

Auguste blushed. That he could have been so foolish! When so much depended on Cranton's Christmas chef, he of all people had trusted that Fancelli had indeed been in the kitchens when he had eaten at the restaurant before Christmas.

Ma Bisley cast a kindly eye on the Inspector's recruit.

'I'm arter hinformation,' she told him. 'What with all the restaurants here, and the casual work, a feller like Fancelli can disappear for months, and no one the wiser. 'Cept me,' she told him matter-of-factly, resting her arms on her gamp umbrella. 'Only two places he can be hiding out, 'ere or Leather Lane, and this being closer to –' she paused and winked – 'the place hin which you are interested, Hinspector, I reckon we'll be trying here first. I've got me runners here.'

'What are these runners?' Auguste asked, puzzled, his mind reverting to beans.

'Ma's a laundress, Auguste. Takes in for hotels all over London, farms it out to her ladies.'

'I keeps me hand in too,' Ma Bisley announced with pride. 'Take you, for instance, those trousers. They're English, but not English.' She ran a sharp eye over Auguste. 'I'd say Redfern of Paris. Now that shirt, that *is* English. And very new. Yet you ain't new over here, that's for sure. All new save the unmentionables and they're the best. Trying to impress, eh? And that weskit. Fancy but not too fancy. Got a new job, 'ave you? Egbert taken you on? Nah, not with that weskit. You was at the hotel. Guest? Nah. Manager, and new to it. So, what were you doing before?' She shook her head regretfully. 'I'd have to look at your underwear to tell your trade.'

'Madame, I—' he began heatedly, only to hear her

bellow of laughter and even Egbert allowing himself a smile.

Ma leaned over and rapped the driver on the shoulder with her umbrella. 'This'll do, young man. We don't need to tell the Lord Mayor where we're going.'

The Lord Mayor would be unlikely to be greatly interested in this old decaying house, thought Auguste.

Ma clambered down. 'You two stay 'ere,' she commanded. ''E won't want to be compromised by a couple of toffs like you, one of 'em shouting nark from 'ere to 'Yde Park.'

Her bulk disappeared into the distance, turned a corner and vanished from view.

'Tailoring, tenements and tarts is all you find here,' said Rose. 'Not much of a life.'

Auguste agreed, although the restaurants, poor though they looked, held a certain interest. There was a smell, an indefinable smell, that held promise.

Ma returned five minutes later. 'Leather Lane, young man,' she told the driver grandly, after the decanting process had been reversed and she was once more seated. ''E's not 'ere,' she told Rose. ''E was, but 'e ain't. Ain't been seen since the summer.'

The driver took one look at the hordes swarming in Leather Lane and refused to go further. Selecting the least villainous of the bambinos playing their own version of hopscotch, he ensured the safety of his vehicle and horse in the time-honoured way, and disappeared into a public house.

Ma Bisley, with Rose on one side, Auguste on the other, waddled into the maelstrom of the Italian quarter at the far end of the Lane. Noise and smells assailed their senses. Smells from the ice-cream makers and roast chestnut vendors, intent on selling their wares, the latter doing a better trade than the former on this raw January day, and noise from the chatting women surrounding the old clothes stalls, dressed as brightly as for the Neapolitan sun. Children dived in among the crowds, shouting, squealing, intent on their own business. The sound of 'The Lost Chord' ground out on a piano organ emanated from the hiring company, where late traders bartered for cheap daily rates now that part of the day was spent, with monkeys on their shoulders, or children caught by the hand. Everyone here had his purpose in life, it seemed, even the women battling with such determination in the Piggy Wiggy porkshop. Here was none of the restless unemployment of Soho. If they could not work, why then they would dance or sing.

In the midst of this exoticism, Ma Bisley stood out, unmistakably English, unmistakably powerful. As she rapped on a door, one or two even fell silent to watch. Foreign communities like this were tolerated provided they kept the rules. And Ma Bisley's summonses fell into this category. No serious crime here, so Ma was safe. Only further east were her doings shrouded in secrecy from the casually curious.

Nevertheless, when the door was opened, a muttered exclamation was heard, and a hand shot out to suggest she and her escorts should enter. The short, bearded, dark-eyed Italian peered at them nervously in the narrow corridor, smells of Neapolitan sauce wafting interestingly down the stairs. Oregano, was it not? Not like the herbs of Provence – a subtle difference. Auguste pondered on this entrancing problem, sniffing again. One Giulio who spoke *Inglese*, they were told with some pride, appeared, a younger version of his father, minus the beard.

'Fancelli, Antonio Fancelli,' said Rose. 'Know him, do you?'

A hesitation, a discussion in rapid Italian, which Auguste only partly followed, a wary eye on Ma Bisley.

'Yis,' declared Giulio. 'We know him.'

'Where is he? Seen him in the last day or two, have you?'

'No.' The answer came quickly, but not too quickly, Rose judged.

'Before Christmas.' The signor was anxious to help. Fancelli lodged with a family in Little Bath Street and helped in the butcher's shop, Giulio amplified.

The family, when visited, confirmed the story. Equally anxious to help, or at least to avoid the wrath of Ma Bisley, the wife showed them the room where he had slept. 'With Rudolfo,' she told them. 'And Andrea. And Giulietta of course.' He had a bed of his own, she told them with pride. This was no mean lodging. A rough pallet lay still untenanted in the corner.

'Belongings?'

'He took them all at Christmas.'

'But the job was only for twelve days,' said Rose to Auguste.

''E say not coming back.'

'It fits,' said Rose gloomily. 'He wouldn't be retracing his steps after he'd made his attempt on the Prince's life. But it doesn't help.'

'Where would he go if he were trying to hide away?' asked Auguste in halting Italian. 'If he had committed a big crime?'

There was an outburst of indignation at the idea that any Italian might commit a major crime, which required a few moments to sort out and concluded only with Antonio's apologetic: 'Fancelli is a butcher by trade.'

Auguste pursed his lips. To think that he had tolerated Fancelli's presence in Cranton's kitchen for one day, let alone allowed him to stay for a week.

'Perhaps he go to Smithfield.'

It was a suggestion worth following up, but, after sending Ma back last in the growler, Rose returned to the hotel from Smithfield disgruntled and more overtly worried than Auguste had ever seen him. 'Like looking for a needle in a haystack. Might have been around, might not. Plenty of places where an out of work chef could doss down for the night and no one take any notice. I've left a sergeant there making enquiries, while we get on this end. I'm going to turn this place over from top to bottom, including all your guests' rooms again.'

A faint cry of protest from Auguste was cut off as he realised both its futility and its injustice.

'What are you looking for?' was all he managed to say with comparative calmness.

'Listen, Auguste, one of these guests of yours is probably a murderer and would-be assassin – unless we think Fancelli is operating on his own.'

'*Non*. He would not have worked here in that case, he would not have chosen the time he did to murder the girl since they were both sleeping on the premises, and most of all, Egbert, he would not have put the body in the chest!'

'Reasons,' Rose shot at him.

'It could not have been coincidence that that chest was chosen. It had to be someone who was present when the chest was used for the jest by the Misses Pembrey.'

'Right.' Rose fell silent, ruminating.

'Why otherwise would he take this job in the first place? And I do not understand why a job of such magnitude,' Auguste burst out, aggrieved, still shocked at such neglect of duty. 'Why not apply to be a footman, a dustman, anything, merely a delivery man, if assassination is his real trade. Wages, after all, cannot be material if Fancelli's mission is political.'

'We'll get him,' said Rose soothingly. 'And the villain behind him. My men are going to turn over every inch of this place, *now*.'

'What shall I tell the guests?'

'Tell them what you like,' said Rose impatiently.

'The truth,' said Auguste mournfully.

Those of the guests that had remained in the hotel for a quiet morning were gathered in the drawing room. They were not pleased at being herded unceremoniously out of their rooms or from billiard and smoking room to sit under the eagle eye of a nervous police constable while Rose and Twitch proceeded to examine their most intimate belongings once again.

'Damned odd ideas you have of Christmas games,' snarled Carruthers. 'Dalmaine and I were in the middle of most important discussions on Wellington's eighteen-pounders.'

Thérèse and Marie-Paul returned from a morning outing that had precluded the Baroness from kitchen duties and cast the fate of luncheon into the inexperienced hands of John. They, too, were far from amused to find themselves hustled into the drawing room.

'I must say,' said de Castillon, standing shoulder to shoulder over this with Sir John, 'that diplomatic status seems to count for extremely little nowadays. I demanded immunity from the Inspector and am told it has been refused after consultation with the Ambassador. I am not even permitted to leave to consult the Embassy.' He glared at Auguste.

'I am sure when you know the reason, sir, you will agree this is the only course. Today is the first of January. As you know, in two days' time precisely the Prince of Wales will greet Field Marshal Roberts at Paddington. We have every reason to believe it is there that the attempt will be made upon the Prince's life, an attempt,' he added amidst the sudden silence, 'orchestrated at least in part by one of yourselves.'

Auguste had had experience of making such speeches before in similar circumstances but rarely one that brought in its wake such an atmosphere of menace. He looked at the faces surrounding him, emotions varying from curiosity and bewilderment to anger and outrage.

Bowman was the first to speak.

'You think one of *us* has something to do with it?' His face bulged. 'Good God, I'm British. Why should I want to murder poor old Bertie?'

This, amid shrieking from Gladys, chattering excitement from the twins, Auguste adroitly managed to avoid answering as he slipped out to join Egbert Rose.

He found him in Bella's room gloomily regarding a display of lingerie that owed little to Dr Jaeger's adamant instructions for the wearing of sanitary wool next to the skin. The young constable with him was clearly overcome by the array of lace-trimmed garments and silk stockings. Auguste averted his eyes, for the perfume emanating from the drawer brought back all too vividly the events of two nights previously.

'Distasteful sort of job, eh?' said Rose at last. 'If you don't find something to make it worthwhile, you wonder what you're doing after a while, rifling through this sort of stuff.' He had a private and irreverent image of Edith in this lacy red corset, and hastily put it to one side.

Auguste accompanied Rose into Miss Guessings's room, whose spare Swanbill Bandalette definitely did not boast red lace.

The other rooms produced equally little of interest, save some fascinating sidelights on human nature: the Misses Pembrey's collection of objects destined to terrify, amuse and repulse their fellow beings; Marie-Paul's addiction to adorning her face with powders and cream; her mistress's almost total absence of anything save essentials; the Colonel's walking stick that turned out to be a sword stick, Dalmaine's surprisingly exciting choice of expensive sock suspenders and waistcoats, Bowman's supply of interesting literature, by anonymous writers.

'Anything strike you, Auguste?' Rose enquired.

'*Non*,' answered Auguste glumly.

'No guns. No bombs. How's our fellow proposing to kill the Prince?'

'Fancelli would have the gun,' Auguste pointed out.

'Twitch—' On cue the door was flung open and a self-important sergeant stood there.

'I think you'll be interested in something upstairs, sir,' he announced smugly in his moment of glory. He waved Auguste's master set of keys triumphantly.

They followed him up to the top attic floor where he proceeded to unlock the communicating door leading to the unused attic rooms on the east side. He grandiosely flung the door of one of them wide open. 'There, sir,' he announced.

Maisie's cleaners had not bothered with unneeded rooms. The dust of ten years adorned the cheap shabby wardrobe, the bedframe, an old chest, battered corded trunk, the single chair. All testimony to a room that had once been home for someone, thought Auguste.

Twitch had no time for sentimentality, eager to point out his finds. 'See this, sir? Now we know where Fancelli spent last night, don't we? A razor and strop. Shavo shaving cream, soap and bowl. Had this all planned, 'e did.'

'Nothing else, though,' observed August. 'No spare clothes. And how did he get in through the locked door?'

'There's his spare pair of braces,' Twitch pointed out defiantly. 'And it's easy enough to pick a lock.' He wasn't going to have the Frenchie doing him out of his hour of glory.

'Probably has the rest of his belongings tucked away somewhere. Left luggage store, perhaps,' he suggested grandly.

Rose was examining the mattress. 'Someone's slept on this all right. No dust. Well done, Sergeant Stitch.'

'Now we've found Fancelli's hiding place, we know his partner's right here – among *his* guests.' Twitch gave Auguste a smug and far from loving look, as though the guests had been personally selected by him.

'He's right,' said Rose. 'You best stay with them, Auguste, on all their visits. I suppose we can't keep them locked up here,' he added a little wistfully, 'but at least you can make sure none of them slips away. Sergeant Stitch and I will get back to the Factory.'

He might almost as well have added, 'Where the real work's done,' thought Auguste despondently, as he trailed down to luncheon. So much for Didier, the great detective. Always before, food had played a part in inspiring him to the heights of detection. Now he had been miraculously restored to his beloved kitchen, only to be snatched away again. He was bereft of all that made his mind work best – Egbert and food both gone. True, he should still be able to reason, but he needed the constant stimulation of the art of cuisine. Without it, he was as arid and dull as a pheasant without its casserole, a boiled fish without its sauce, a pudding without its crust. So convinced was he of his diagnosis that when he remembered that there had been no gun in the room Fancelli had been using, he dismissed it as unimportant. Which was a pity.

Auguste's announcement had somewhat dampened the frisson that the proposed afternoon's tour round the great private mansions of Hyde Park and St James's had previously caused. The prospect of viewing the valuable possessions of the richest in the land was definitely overshadowed by the news that one of their party was, according to the police, about to despatch the richest himself for ever. Nevertheless, the visit was well attended, with Thérèse joining the group after Auguste had told her, putting duty before dinner, that arrangements were well in hand. She had not in fact enquired after dinner, seeming far more interested in hearing graphically with many embellishments from the twins that they too were under suspicion of murder and would-be assassination.

'Bah!' she remarked in derision, casting a scornful look at the two police constables who stolidly accompanied them, making a brave pretence that they were as fascinated by Rubens's design for the coronation of Maria de Medici as their flock at least should be. Having privately applied to the Duke of Sutherland for admission to Stafford House, they were again the only party there, which was perhaps as well. Some of its members had matters on their minds more pressing than the charms of its Tintorettos.

'Who would want to murder the Prince?' asked Eva of Thomas in a high voice, intended to reach her neighbours.

'The Boers,' answered Gladys in hushed tones. Then, 'Oh, I forget, you are one, aren't you?' she added brightly. Then she went brick red: 'Not that anyone would think that you—'

'Eva is a very, *very* distant relation of ex-President Kruger,' answered Thomas hastily. 'And now she has the honour to be a Harbottle, I take it you don't feel the Harbottles have turned traitor?'

'Why not?' asked Bowman cheerfully, casting a passing glance at 'Lord Stafford on his way to the Scaffold'. 'The best heads in Britian used to land up in baskets. Or butts of wine. The British admire a chap with a spot of individuality.'

'I take it,' Harbottle's slight figure tried to bring centuries of British hauteur to this nouveau riche parvenu, 'you are not implying I am a traitor to Her Majesty, that I have plans to assassinate the Prince?'

The words fell into a sudden silence in the group as they turned to look at him. Harbottle flushed red: 'I wonder if you are aware,' he announced loudly, 'that this Correggio is said to have hung as an inn sign near Rome on the Via Flaminia?'

'Bella, I am disturbed.' The Marquis's announcement had all the weight of King Ahasuerus ordaining life or death for Esther. He cast an austere eye on the Earl of Ellesmere's fine collection of paintings in Bridgwater House. Paris, the eye seemed to suggest, could do better. The party had left Stafford House, leaving only as a record of their visit a false moustache attached (temporarily) to a naked Venus (fortunately it was only a 'School of') by two of the Honourable Misses Pembrey. Auguste did not notice. Major Dalmaine did, and wondered briefly whether, however desirable Rosanna might be, marriage into the Pembrey family would be entirely a wise move.

Bella was regarding through quite unnecessary lorgnettes that displayed her graceful white gloved hands to perfection, Titian's 'Venus of the Shell', fortunately as yet unadorned with moustaches. Her husband was compelled to make his point clearer.

'This foolish Inspector has got it into his head that this ridiculous notion of an attempt on the Prince of Wales is linked to Cranton's. Murder is objectionable enough when it disturbs one's Christmas, but assassination is too much when there are two diplomats of high importance in the party. It is, I consider, *libellous*.'

'Slanderous, actually,' his wife cheerfully corrected him. 'And just think, Gaston,' she gave him a rare and beatific smile, 'what stories you'll have to tell those stuffy old *ministres* when we return home. You will be a figure of importance, Gaston.'

'This is true,' he said, weighing her words with surprise.

'That's unless you're implicated,' she added laughing. 'Are you?'

The Marquis stiffened, his eyes going to Dalmaine who was bent on following Rosanna's progress round the gallery like Apollo stalking Daphne. 'Really, madame,' he replied formally to his wife, 'you go too far.'

Rosanna was quite aware of Frederick Dalmaine's pursuit. She had even slowed down a little so that it might be successful. She was more than a little annoyed with Danny who she had high suspicions was more enthusiastic about his career than about herself. She had commanded his presence outside Stafford House, in the hope that she would be able to absent herself from the rest of the afternoon 'by error', and he had not appeared. She was thus consigned to yet more Titians and Rembrandts, with all the more interesting-looking private rooms banned to them. Frederick Dalmaine was somewhat surprised at the warmth of her smile when at last she allowed him to catch up with her.

'I am so glad to see you, Fred—Major Dalmaine,' she dimpled prettily. 'I get so bored with these naval actions,' she dismissed Van de Velde with an airy wave of the hand. 'I do think the army is much more interesting. So active. So *dangerous*,' glancing quickly and effectively at his leg. She could never remember quite which one it was.

He flushed with pleasure. 'All in a day's work,' he

announced fatuously, patting the relevant limb.

'I want you to tell me about Africa again. Everything. And those Ashantis that your brother fought.'

Dalmaine turned bright red. 'How the deuce did you know about that?'

Rosanna looked nonplussed. Had it perhaps been Danny who had mentioned George Dalmaine? No matter. She had intended to please Frederick and please him she would. 'It must have been the Inspector or Mr Didier mentioned it,' she told him brightly, and proceeded to chatter on the delights of the social season. She was used to rapt attention but on this occasion failed to discover the difference between rapt and simulated.

Auguste was having a barren afternoon, and it was not made the more fruitful by his coming across Carruthers.

'No good under fire. Look at Quatre Bras.'

Auguste was at a loss, and seeing this, the Colonel said impatiently: 'The Dutch, man. Damned room's full of Dutch paintings.'

'But we are not at war—'

'*Not at war*? It was damned Frenchies like you Wellington went over to thrash. Waterloo, man. The Dutch-Belgian brigade. Supposed to be our allies. Might as well have been on your side, scared of a few Frenchies on horses.' He snorted, looking Auguste up and down. 'Surprised they let you into the country,' he informed his host, and marched stiffly away to inspect an 'Alpine Scene with Waterfall'.

After the exigencies of the afternoon, a nearby hostelry provided a refuge from the Cranton's party. It also, Rose thought cunningly, distanced Auguste from the preoccupation of worrying about how John might be faring with the provision of dinner. Looking rather wistfully at the fire, they retired to a more private corner, though there were few enough patrons on an early January night.

Rose watched Auguste drink a brandy and soda without enthusiasm, as he drank his own ale. No finesse, no subtlety in their drinks, the English. Their food, yes, it spelled infinite potential, but the drinks? *Non*. True, in the country he had tasted excellent fruit wines but how in London could one drink parsnip wine with coq au vin?

'You have to face it, Auguste,' Rose said at last. 'It's either Bowman or the Baroness we're after.'

'Bowman is the obvious choice,' said Auguste desperately. He pushed away the thought of a fellow chef (in which category he had not included Fancelli) being a murderer.

'Motive?'

'I have an idea about this,' said Auguste eagerly. 'Bowman is a dealer in iron, he travels to the Low Countries frequently. Too often for someone who merely deals in iron gates, for instance. Maisie observed at the Tower of London, as I did at the Wallace Collection, that he spends much time studying the collections of firearms. Suppose he is a dealer in guns, providing the Boers with their modern weapons, an intermediary between Krupp and the Boer government? At the moment they could not afford still to be seen supplying armaments to the Transvaal. Would Mr Bowman not have a motive for wishing the war to continue? Would he not wish to encourage guerrilla warfare among the Boer farmers resisting British rule? And what better way than assassinating the Prince of Wales so that it is assumed to be a plot by Kruger?'

'It's possible, Auguste.' High praise indeed from

Rose, whose face fell into its thinking lines. Then: 'Evidence?'

Auguste searched rapidly for ingredients, and laid them metaphorically on the table before Rose as they emerged from the storeroom of his mind.

'*Un*: the probability is that, as you say, the murder was committed by one of those on the second floor, of which only the Baroness and Bowman had tea. *Deux*: the murder was possibly done by a woman, but more probably by a man. *Trois*: the body was most certainly lifted by a man, for it would be too heavy for a woman once the girl was dead. It might have been Fancelli, but more likely, because of the fear of detection, it was a guest. *Quatre*: as the girl must have been killed in a guest's room, and Fancelli could not have come to assist until night-time, only Bowman, as a man, could have had the strength to lift the body to hide it until the hotel was quiet for the night. *Cinq* . . .' Auguste paused.

'*Cinq*, you don't like him and you do like the Baroness. You'll never make the CID, Auguste,' Rose informed him kindly. 'We have to suspect everyone, from the chimney sweep and chefs to our own mothers. *I'll* do the Baroness, then. *Motive*: her husband is German, at the Kaiser's court. Could be young Willie Kaiser having a go at underground politics, but unlikely. Royals don't go encouraging assassination. It could be a private argument between Kruger's supporters and the Baron. He goes off to Hungary to avoid suspicion, she comes here to arrange the dirty work.'

'Evidence?' asked Auguste mutinously.

'*One*: her room is conveniently placed, as you say. *Two*: she is strong for a woman. *Three*: she is an organiser. *Four*: no specific reason for her as a French-woman to choose to spend Christmas here. What's the matter?' he asked sharply at a slight exclamation from Auguste.

'*Mon ami*, I should confess I have reason to doubt . . .' Auguste looked unhappy.

'What?' Rose asked inexorably.

'That the Baroness *is* French, as she claims. I believe,' he continued unhappily, 'that she is Belgian.'

'Reasons?' Rose asked sharply.

'She uses the word *nonante* not *quatre-vingt-dix* for your ninety. This is the Belgian form. Either she *is* Belgian or has spent much time there. I believe, having observed her method of cooking, that it is the former. *Chicon gratiné* is much beloved in Belgium. And furthermore,' he added reluctantly, 'Maisie informs me that she referred to the "enemy's" view on Blenheim as though she herself were not French. But why,' he rushed on, 'if she knows Belgium well, did she come *here* to meet Fancelli? Why not come over with him just before the third of January?'

'We don't know what arrangements they have to make here,' said Rose deflatingly.

'And why bring a companion?' Auguste pressed on belligerently. 'Is Marie-Paul also in the plot? Perhaps she is the murderess? Perhaps she lied about ordering no tea? *Mon ami, that* is the answer.' He sat back, beaming happily.

'No tea tray,' Rose said dismissively.

'Why did she need one? She could have attacked Nancy after she left the Baroness's room, and she has strong hands,' Auguste pointed out eagerly.

Rose considered, then shook his head. 'Don't see our Miss Gonnet being strong enough to carry this out on her own, and if she were in league with Fancelli, how could she hope to get away with it unless the Baroness were involved too? The Baroness might go to her companion's adjoining room at any time; she couldn't be sure of being alone for the murder, but the companion would not go to her mistress unless summoned. She's been with the Baroness a fair time too; she didn't just take this job in order to bump off Bertie.' He coughed and looked round hastily in case anyone had overheard this lese-majesty from a senior detective of Scotland Yard. 'It's either the Baroness, both together,' he declared, 'or Bowm—What is it, Twitch?' he broke off impatiently, letting the nickname slip, which normally only happened under great provocation.

Sergeant Stitch had come through the door, and half the patrons of the pub hurriedly finished their beer and left at this unmistakable sign of the law.

'Thought you'd like to see this, sir.' He ignored Auguste. This was Yard business.

'It'd better be important.'

Rose glanced at the lengthy telegraphed message, whistled, and handed it to Auguste without a word.

The Prince of Wales settled back into his favourite armchair at Marlborough House and picked up the *Sporting Times*. There were, he supposed, compensations for being dragged back from decent shooting at Sandringham. Even if it did mean back to the grind of daily engagements in tight uniforms. He was reminded that one such engagement coming up on Thursday had a distinctly unpleasant variety to the routine planned. Tomorrow Mama would be meeting 'Bobs' at Cowes, and the next day it was his turn. He frowned. Not that he believed all this talk of a second Sipido. All the same, he'd make quite sure that Alexandra didn't come. Nor young George. Just in case. Not that there was a word of truth in the rumour.

It hadn't been a bad Christmas. Mama had been unusually quiet. For years he used to dread the sight of the telegraph room at Sandringham which always seemed to be clattering with messages from Osborne. Give him the days even before that when you could at least see the telegraph boy pedalling furiously up the path and have time to make yourself scarce. When they put the telephone instrument in, he'd had more than a few anxious moments, but fortunately Mama was a creature of habit. Dashing off a few furious words came more naturally than shouting through a round piece of metal. Why had she been so quiet? A sudden anxiety. Was there anything to Beattie's worries? No. The old girl would live for ever. They'd had these scares before and she'd always come through. Nothing would keep her from meeting her beloved Field Marshal tomorrow. Nevertheless he supposed he'd better go down to see her shortly. He viewed the prospect of visiting the Isle of Wight and its shrine to his late father, Osborne, without enthusiasm. It wasn't even the yachting season. Still, at least it meant that his beloved cousin, Kaiser Willie, wouldn't be there.

Breakfast at Cranton's was again unusually well-attended, now that news had got out of the improved menu under John, with the delights of smoked salmon and eggs, herring roes, truffled eggs, and kidneys. The pleasures of coddled eggs taken in solitary rooms paled beside this morning's menu. Auguste, at his post, flinched as Rose and Twitch entered, with two police constables guarding the door. For once he was entirely with the Colonel.

'I say,' shouted Carruthers, 'can't a fellow eat his kedgeree in peace?' Only the presence of ladies made his outburst so mild.

'My apologies, sir. I'm afraid it's necessary,' Twitch told him smugly.

'If we might have a word, madam.' Rose stopped at the Baroness's table.

'Certainly,' she told him.

'In private, madam.'

She raised her eyebrows. 'I am glad I can be of assistance, Inspector,' she said coolly, rising to follow him. 'Does Mr Didier require further assistance in the kitchens?'

'No, madam,' Rose told her woodenly, once outside. 'I'm here to arrest you in connection with the murder of Nancy Watkins.'

The Baroness said nothing. Her hands gripped her dorothy bag tightly.

'And,' Rose continued, 'in connection with a plot to murder the Prince of Wales.'

'*Quoi?* This is quite ridiculous, Inspector. Monsieur Didier, has not some mistake been made?'

Auguste shook his head mutely. In the face of the evidence what could he say?

Marie-Paul, descending the staircase for breakfast, took in the situation at a glance, flying to her mistress's side.

'What are you saying to Madame?' she demanded shrilly. 'Eh?'

A glance from the Baroness stilled her as Rose said: 'Do you deny, madam, that you are not the Baroness von Bechlein? There is indeed such a lady, but she is in Hungary at the moment with her husband. That you are in fact Thérèse Lepont, Belgian national, owner of the Hôtel Sud in Brussels?'

'No,' Thérèse said abruptly, as Marie-Paul clutched her arm. 'I do not deny it.'

'Madame?' Marie-Paul's hands gripped the more tightly, though the news was clearly no great shock to her.

Thérèse gently prised her arm away. 'All will be well, Marie-Paul,' she said firmly before turning to Rose: 'I do deny, however, that I have murdered anybody, or have any intention of doing so. Except perhaps Mr Didier,' she said lightly. 'I believed you were my friend,' reproachfully.

'Madame, if only it had been possible.' Now he knew how traitors felt.

'What about my poor Marie-Paul?' she asked briskly. 'Is she to be left here to see to my affairs or to be arrested as my accomplice?'

'Your accomplice will be caught soon enough, madam.'

'Caught?' she asked warily.

'We know where Fancelli's been sleeping, madam,' said Twitch, eager to join the festivities. 'You managed to warn him last night, because he didn't turn up, but we'll get him—'

'I think we'd better go, madam,' Rose interrupted quickly. The odds on Twitch's promotion lengthened.

'By all means,' Thérèse agreed cordially. 'By the way, do you have any evidence to charge me?'

'Enough to stop you and Fancelli murdering the Prince of Wales tomorrow.'

'If you can catch him,' she pointed out, amused.

Chapter Nine

'Madame? Ah non, *non*!' The hitherto subdued Mademoiselle Gonnet was promptly transformed into a fighting, spitting tigress on behalf of her maligned mistress. Having seen Madame escorted away, she had almost to be physically restrained from pursuit, her voice harsh as she imparted her views on the British police force to its members present. 'Tyrants', was the only word Rose could understand, which was just as well. Auguste, who understood a lot more, since they were in his native tongue, was shocked, unable to believe that for a few moments the other evening he had contemplated . . . Marie-Paul glanced at him, and subsided into a semblance of her normal self, eyes flashing, controlled fury in her tense figure. 'Murder *le Prince de Galles*? But how, monsieur?' She spread her ringless hands expressively. 'With what? And how could I not know if Madame intended such a thing?'

'How indeed?' commented Rose mildly.

She shot him a suspicious glance. 'Madame could not stab anybody, she has not the strength,' Marie-Paul declared.

'Together you might have,' observed Rose.

'You do not think that I—' She half rose from the chair in alarm.

'We'd like you to remain in the hotel, if you don't mind, miss. Just till this matter's settled. Just in case you have plans to meet Fancelli.'

'Who is this Fancelli?' she asked sullenly.

'He was employed here as a cook, until yesterday,' a graphic look at Auguste. He didn't see it, for his eyes were on Marie-Paul.

'I have never heard of this person,' was her defiant reply.

'Madame Lepont would hardly tell you. She could meet him without your knowledge.'

'How?' Marie-Paul answered. 'We arrive on Sunday, and she is with me always.'

'You visited friends some mornings,' observed Auguste. 'And there are the nights.'

She hesitated. 'This is true, but Madame would not descend to the kitchens during the night like a scullery-maid,' she added scornfully and triumphantly.

'You knew she was not a baroness, didn't you, Miss Gonnet?' Rose cut in.

She relaxed in her chair, and smirked. 'So if she pretends to be a baroness, is this a crime?'

'She carries false identity papers,' Rose pointed out.

'And so? For her it is real. To herself, she has been a baroness for many years.'

'And has she been French for many years too, to herself, and not Belgian?' Rose asked. 'Suppose you tell us a little more about your life with her?'

'Madame is Madame,' replied Marie-Paul indifferently. 'If Madame wishes you to know, she will tell you.'

'Madame is being held on a charge of two murders, and a suspected plotted assassination,' Rose pointed out.

The knuckles of the hands gripping the large black companion bag whitened, but it was Marie-Paul's only sign of concern. She merely remarked: *'C'est ridicule, ça.'*

'You told us you'd worked for Madame Lepont for five years. Do you want to change that statement?'

'No.'

'And you didn't know she was Belgian?'

'What does it matter, Belgian or French?'

Rose sighed. 'Tell her she's a *mur de pierre*, Auguste.'

The stone wall remained immovable.

'Very well,' said Rose. 'From now on, Miss Gonnet, you're going to have a companion of your own. A nice big English policeman. He'll be with you all day and one of his chums will be right outside your door tonight. And tomorrow, when we formally charge Madame with murder, yet another chum will be right with you when you come to the Yard to loosen a few boulders from that wall of yours.'

'They're waiting for something all right, our Madame and Mademoiselle,' Rose observed, after he had returned from the Yard. 'They both look as smug as a cat licking cream. Or don't they do that in France?'

'My mother used to say that in France the cat who stayed too long to lick the cream would find itself a cat *au vin en casserole*. She was, *naturellement*,' added Auguste hastily, 'jesting.' A memory flickered through his mind, and fled as swiftly as the taste of a rose-petal cream.

'And *my* mother used to say,' Rose told him, 'that the cat who licked the cream grew too fat to catch his mice. She wasn't joking, though. Albert Edward, Prince of Wales, could be in luck – provided we catch Fancelli.'

'No word?'

'We've got descriptions of him outside every police station, and on half the lampposts in London. Ma Bisley's runners ain't heard anything; the Leather Lane community swore he hadn't been there since before Christmas. Every Italian restaurant's been checked and every Italian we can lay our hands on has been stopped and questioned.'

'If he has slept here, it is not surprising he has not been found,' observed Auguste.

'He didn't sleep here last night, did he? Nor, incidentally, did young Nash. Somehow Fancelli must have been warned, because he didn't even show up. We've got the brains of this project safely tucked away, but we haven't got the brawn; and it's the brawn going to be carrying out the job tomorrow, unless we track him down.'

Brawn? Was there sufficient left for luncheon? And would John remember to add the zest and juice of an orange to the sauce? True, he had presented a creditable array of dishes yesterday, Auguste acknowledged, although there was undoubtedly too much juniper in the ptarmigan pie. It had been a wrench to leave this special seasonal pie to John, when in normal times he himself would have had the honour of creating every step of the delectable dish. And the port jelly too – a trifle too heavy. It required a touch of something – perhaps lemon? Orange? Jelly. How debased a word it was, rapidly becoming condemned to the nursery. Yet one of the lost great cooks of our time was called Jelly, he recalled. Or rather Gellée. But no, some foolish so-called cook had dismissed him, and he had been forced to take up painting instead. How great a chef Claude Lorraine Gellée might have become if he had put the delicacy, balance and order of his landscapes into cuisine!

'Which of them murdered the girl in the fog, do you think?' Rose was asking.

'A *Claude bavarois*,' replied Auguste dreamily, only drawn back to reality by the sight of Rose's blank face.

'I don't see our Thérèse wielding a stiletto in the fog

herself,' said Rose, having made nothing of Auguste's last utterance.

'I agree. We have no evidence she was even in England then. It is much more likely to have been Fancelli on his own, and for it to have been the reason he came here. Somehow this girl had found out about the threat to the Prince. Do you have any more information on her?' Auguste asked awkwardly. He took this corpse very personally. Every time he thought of that girl, he was transported back to the choking terrors of that November night. Had he moved more quickly, might he not have prevented it? Had he realised immediately that the speaker of those words '*At Cranton's? Christmas?*' and the murderer might not be the same, might he have found Fancelli lurking in a basement area, waiting, waiting for this intrusive stranger to depart?

'We've got a lead on her, but it will have to wait now till we've got tomorrow out of the way. Ma Bisley's runner in Hackney has found someone who thinks she recognises her. Girl who used to live in the same street in Shoreditch. She could be a fifteen-year-old called Mary White, who left home about a year ago.'

'She was on the streets?'

'Apparently not. Went into service, so her parents said. And they had not reported not hearing from her.'

Auguste was shocked.

Rose looked at him with kindly eye. 'Ever been out that way, Auguste? I'll take you some day. Worse than Soho for rabbit warrens of tenements. When you get families living eight to a room, they spend all their time trying to live themselves; no time for worrying about how one that's actually making some kind of living's getting on.'

'But it is Christmas.' Auguste had been long enough

in this country to know the ties that drew even to the poorest house.

'Christmas out there ain't changed since Scrooge and Bob Cratchit, without the goose or the happy ending. No,' said Rose regretfully, 'that's a dead end. We can only try to establish the link between the household she worked for and Thérèse Lepont.'

'But that is odd, is it not? A loose *fils* – the ingredient that does not fit. Another household—'

'Auguste,' Rose said sharply, 'tomorrow's the day. Start with the sure thing we've got – a suspect in custody. And Fancelli at large.'

'Do not forget Mademoiselle Gonnet,' Auguste said mutinously. Even now he could not believe the Baroness – for so he would always think of her – a political assassin.

'Marie-Paul's under guard,' said Rose grimly. 'Evidence or not.'

'It is true Thérèse Lepont could not have got the body into the lift alone, and Mademoiselle Gonnet was at hand. Fancelli was not,' Auguste said rather regretfully. The more iniquity he could believe that man capable of the better. 'Although,' he added, brightening, 'Egbert, it would be easy enough for Fancelli to come up after breakfast on some pretext – that floor is quite deserted. Ah yes, *mon ami*, I have it,' he crowed triumphantly. 'He came up *in the lift* pulled up by the murderer, put the corpse in it and walked down himself.'

'I don't like it,' said Rose at last, having considered. 'Smacks of one of your fancy solutions, Auguste.'

'My fancy solutions, as you call them,' replied Auguste with dignity, 'have proved correct in some instances in the past, Inspector.'

'Perhaps it takes hindsight to see them as not so fancy after all. Perhaps this will look the same, eh? I'll think about it. Maybe put it to the Baroness.'

'The Baroness?' asked Auguste, smiling.

'Our Madame Lepont, then.'

'What reason now does she give for being here?' Auguste asked curiously.

'She claims she wants her hotel to become more fashionable and thought she'd come here incognito, so to speak, to find out how an English hotel is run.'

'Perhaps, if she does so,' said Auguste sourly, 'she could inform *me*. I did not plan, Egbert,' he added sorrowfully, 'to open my career as a hotelier by accusing my guests of murder.'

The guests of Cranton's Hotel had just partaken of John's luncheon and showed no signs of dissatisfaction. Auguste relaxed, as far as he could, knowing that Egbert was about to address them. John was developing well, even though he had received no direct training from Auguste Didier. Only he could discern the very slight errors that had been made, but such was his relief that he was prepared to overlook the sharpness of the lemon sauce for the Hindle Wakes.

'I have to tell you,' Rose began, 'that at the moment we are questioning the Baroness von Bechlein, or Thérèse Lepont as is her real name, in connection with two murders and a plot to assassinate the Prince of Wales.'

Each member of his audience considered the implications of this announcement as regards themselves. Marie-Paul stared mutinously in front of her, a young constable hovering behind, anxious to be seen by the Inspector to be doing his duty by allowing her to mingle with no one, but wondering whether he stood any chance of a bite himself.

'She's not a baroness?' Gladys was the first to speak.

She had been looking forward to boasting of her new friends to Much Wallop.

'No. Madame Lepont runs a hotel in Belgium, and we believe she is a member of a group of Boer sympathisers, or if not a sympathiser herself, then a paid intermediary between the group and the assassin.'

'Who?' asked Frederick Dalmaine abruptly.

'Antonio Fancelli, who worked here.'

'How's a poor old cook going to assassinate Bertie?' shouted Bowman with a guffaw. 'Strangle him with spaghetti?'

'That we don't know yet. But he has vanished.'

'Perhaps he's in the chest,' offered Gladys brightly, then blushed as everyone stared at her.

The twins giggled and Auguste looked at Gladys disapprovingly. That chest was something he did not wish to be reminded of. All the same . . . He glanced at Rose who nodded slightly. Twitch slipped unobtrusively from the room, proud of his ability to divine Rose's intentions.

Carruthers had been thinking things over. 'You telling us that that little woman stabbed a girl to death and proposed to do the same to the Prince of Wales?'

'Yes, sir,' Rose replied patiently.

'Poppycock,' snorted Carruthers. 'How'd she manage it? We were all here. Got it wrong. It was one of the servants.'

'Perhaps, sir. But we think that the girl was killed in Madame Lepont's room when she brought tea, and that the body was then put into the service lift either temporarily or to be taken below by Fancelli and hidden in the basement area until it could be disposed of. In either event, something went wrong with their plans, and the body had to be put back in the bedroom after the room had been cleaned, and was disposed of later that night by being put into the chest, a safe

232

enough place since no one would use it again for Christmas games.'

Rose sensed a faint restlessness in his audience, but no one seemed disposed to comment, save Carruthers, who after thinking this over announced: This girl, Nancy Watkins, she was a servant. That right?'

'Yes, sir.'

'So was this Fancelli. Right?'

'Yes, sir.'

'There you are then. Lover's tiff,' said Carruthers conclusively.

'And what about the Prince of Wales, sir?'

Carruthers turned purple. 'If you fellows would stop chasing lifts at straightforward Christmas parties and get back in the outside world, you might stand a chance of finding this fellow, if there is such a plot – which I doubt.'

'We have one of the murderers, sir,' said Auguste. 'Madame Lepont.'

Carruthers eyed Auguste in disgust, then turned to Rose. 'If you'd apply a bit of English common sense, you'd see why Madame Lepont is where she is. It's because of him,' jerking his head at Auguste. 'You say she's Belgian?'

'Yes,' replied Rose, startled.

'There you are then. He's French – always disliked the Belgians. Ten to one, he's trumped this up. Vengeance, you know,' he said mysteriously.

'Vengeance,' said Rose, glad of a chance of a glimmer of amusement in an increasingly anxious time. 'You mean Madame Lepont rejected his advances?'

'That's correct, sir,' the Colonel said impatiently, slightly deaf. 'As I said, revenge for Waterloo, that's what's behind this.'

★ ★ ★

'Alfred,' said Gladys, gazing at a mummified Egyptian lady of 1,000 years BC without enthusiasm, 'do you think I should tell everybody about this murder – that's if I do go back to Much Wallop, of course,' she added, greatly daring.

'Why shouldn't you go back?' asked Bowman absently, caught off guard, moving away to a Coptic pall. Museums weren't his kind of thing, but they gave you a chance to think. And the British Museum was presenting plenty of such opportunities. Or had been, up to now. Thank heavens she hadn't arrived earlier. It had been hard enough to fade from the police guard's scrutiny. And if Gladys had seen—

'I thought I might be moving my abode,' Gladys said loudly.

'Go somewhere warm, that's my advice,' Bowman offered heartily.

'Could we?'

'Eh?' He began to pay attention.

'Could we?' she repeated, slightly pink. 'Together, that is.'

'Dear Gladys,' he replied quickly and easily. 'I have a factory to run, you know.'

'I could help you run it,' she told him, emboldened. He stared at her speechlessly, too late perceiving where this might conceivably lead.

'I don't take on female staff,' he answered, more cruelly than was wise.

'I did not intend to take paid employment,' she replied indignantly, too far in to draw back. 'I had more in mind a closer relationship.' There was, after all, nothing to lose, and so she plunged on recklessly. 'We could marry.'

'It's not a leap year, dear Gladys,' he tried to say fondly.

'I know that,' she said sharply.

'Dear lady, would that I could.' He sighed, thinking frantically.

'Why couldn't you?'

This was more than a joke, he thought feverishly, forgetting it was one he had fomented himself. 'I have a wife,' he announced baldly.

'But you said you were a widower,' Gladys cried piteously.

'Slight exaggeration. Invalid, you see. Don't see much of each other.'

'Oh.' Gladys was pink, down, but not out. 'You,' she said deliberately, 'are not all you seem to be, Alfred Bowman. And now I know, others will too.' She hurried away, leaving him staring after her in dismay, giving no thought at all to the mummy of Seshepsebhet.

'Don't believe in assassinating myself,' remarked Carruthers somewhat ambiguously, striding through the remains of one of the Seven Wonders of the World with scant appreciation of the Statue of Mausolus.

'Nor me,' agreed Dalmaine bleakly. Rosanna had slipped into the manuscript rooms and strictly forbidden him to follow her. And wherever he looked, he seemed to be surrounded by lumps of stone depicting gods chasing goddesses. It wasn't like that in real life, he thought gloomily. The best they could hope for was a good smoke with another god while the goddesses tripped around doing as they damn well pleased. Women! In the circumstances, Carruthers seemed a good choice of companion.

'Never works,' declared Carruthers judiciously, the old advising the young. 'Besides, we can't have foreign women coming here and killing off our royal family. You have anything to do with this?' he shot at Dalmaine unexpectedly.

'Me?' yelped Dalmaine in alarm.

'I've been watching you, young man. You've got something up your sleeve all right. Mind you, I know you're a West Kent but even the Royals choose their company. What's between you and that Frenchie?'

'Didier?' asked Dalmaine without hope.

Carruthers snorted. 'De Castillon.'

'You see, always you take what is not your own,' said Eva fiercely, gazing rapturously at the Elgin marbles.

'Come now, it was a legal agreement,' said Thomas soothingly.

'Like the annexation of the Transvaal?' asked Eva.

'Shh!' said Thomas, glancing round quickly in case they were overheard.

'The time is over for shushing, Thomas,' declared Eva forthrightly. 'Did you not hear the Inspector say that the Boers are rising?'

'No,' said Thomas firmly. 'I heard him say someone is going to try to assassinate the Prince of Wales. And they think it is a Boer plot.'

'Huh!' announced Eva fervently. 'This is but the beginning.'

'You are British now, beloved,' soothed her husband hopefully.

'England!' She turned on him and laughed. 'Since I arrived, there has been nothing but murder and policemen and talk of murder. And you tell me of England's green and pleasant land! Never, never, will I be English.'

'I wonder if you are aware,' observed Thomas desperately, 'that sixty-six years ago the man who smashed the priceless Portland Vase could not be accused of having committed a crime? He could only be accused of breaking the glass case in which it was placed.'

Eva Harbottle ignored this, a slight smile on her face. 'Tomorrow, Thomas, now that they have found the person who is planning to kill the Prince. . .'

'Yes, dearest?' he asked guardedly.

'I thought we might go to Paddington to see the royal procession,' said Eva firmly.

'What an excellent idea,' said Thomas unhappily.

Bella sidled up to Auguste. 'How delightful it is to be surrounded by such specimens of manhood,' she murmured innocently in the Graeco-Roman rooms.

Auguste, caught in front of a Young Satyr and quoit throwers, with Pan, Hermes and Cupid flanking him, turned red and Bella laughed.

'So modest, dear Auguste,' she murmured.

'I am not modest, madame,' he cried, wondering where his suavity had gone.

'In that case, dear Auguste, I will most certainly visit you again.'

He could not tell her no, his body told him to tell her yes, his common sense told him to run as fast as a nymph from a satyr. He played for time. 'Madame, until this case is over I must remain available for Inspector Rose to call me at any time. My personal feelings must not enter into it. I cannot allow . . .' He tried to look stricken, and it was not difficult. Part of him was. The scent from her hair wafted around him. 'I cannot see, madame, why you so desire my company,' he said plaintively and unusually modestly.

'Can't you, Auguste? We all have our secrets, do we not?' She smiled deliciously, and placed a kiss on her finger.

Her husband was meanwhile preoccupied with weighing up the consequences of Rose's announcement. If this woman was charged with the murder, the disruption in British political affairs might be almost as severe as if the attempt were carried out, if he played his cards carefully. The old Queen was indomitable, but a threat to the succession could keep the South African War warm, if not boiling, sufficiently to keep her attention from other parts of the new continent. France could move slowly forward unimpeded. He cleared his throat as he addressed his British counterpart.

'My dear Sir John, shall we proceed to the Room of Gold Ornaments and Gems? Would it not be amusing if the museum had acquired a certain stool?'

Sir John glared. He might look an old fogey, but looks could hide a shrewd mind. The fellow was fishing. At least – he suddenly had a doubt – he hoped he was. There'd be the devil's own rumpus if the museum bought that Stool, what with the murmurs over the Elgin marbles. No other collector would want it though. Except – a disagreeable thought struck him – the French. If a Frenchman appeared waving the Stool and promising liberty, fraternity and all that rubbish, it could be a damned difficult situation out on the Gold Coast. Visions of King Prempeh, bursting out of his chains and declaring himself French for ever, danced before his eyes. He mopped his forehead before speaking. His words were carefully chosen.

'You're right, de Castillon. They could do with a few more chairs in here. Damned tiring week, walking round museums.' What did the fellow want to celebrate Christmas in England for? Sir John thought irritably. Pity he couldn't be clapped inside too, but then if they started looking too closely at diplomats' lives, there was no telling where it might end up.

The twins were considering earnestly whether to add Rosanna's hatpin to the museum's collection of Anglo-Saxon antiquities, but on balance decided against such a move, on the grounds of their having more serious matters to discuss in their roles as private detectives.

Their sister, oblivious that the fate of her hatpin was under discussion, also had more important matters to discuss.

'Well, when *shall* I see you again, Danny?'

Danny looked confused. 'Naturally I have to follow up the story – for Nancy's sake.'

She stamped her foot. 'You mean a *story* is more important than me?' reducing the matter to essentials with womanly ease.

'Yes – well, no, but I have to put the newspaper first. You must see that.'

'No,' said Rosanna pettishly. 'As a matter of fact, I don't.' She turned on her heel and flounced out of the manuscript room, where the first person she met was Frederick Dalmaine, whom she had so forthrightly rejected not fifteen minutes since. 'Ah,' she said, giving him her prettiest smile, 'I am *so* glad to meet you, Major. Perhaps we shall be seated together at the theatre this evening? Would that not be delightful?'

Exotic and evocative words danced before his eyes. *Truffles, cailles, chanterelles.* What normally would have been a task absorbingly pleasant to anticipate was now a mocking distraction. For before tomorrow night's dinner must come tomorrow morning. How could he give due attention to a menu when the future of the world might have changed before its recipients could enjoy its delights? The unpleasant thought of Fancelli at large blotted out even the prospect of pheasant with brandy, truffles and *foie gras*. Perhaps a little rich . . . A delicate timbale of chicken, flavoured with precious *poivres de baie roses*, the delicacy from his own dear Provençal village. Pink pepper, not red. He thought of Mrs Marshall's coralline pepper almost with affection. Mrs Marshall was a strikingly handsome woman – perhaps she had Hungarian blood in her, so addicted she seemed to this unsubtle spice. Dear Mrs Marshall. How talented she really was, he was able to think in his less prejudiced moments, and what a good school she ran. It was not to be compared with the Didier School of Cuisine, of course, but nevertheless fulfilled a great need, if the craft of cookery, let alone the art, were not to die out at the unskilled hands of – he tried to push the traitorous thought away, but had not the integrity do so – such valiant souls as his friend Egbert's wife, dear Edith.

Names, names, names, all conjuring up untold delights of taste and sensation, let alone the pleasures of preparing them. He looked disconsolately at the menu so far: *velouté au curry et au paprika* – that would please Mrs Marshall; *oeufs Mireille, filets de sole* with mussel sauce, saddle of veal with paprika and truffles – impatiently he scored the latter out. What was he thinking of? He had Mrs Marshall and paprika on the brain. He substituted salmis of pheasant and roast wild duck, and added *poires Condé* and a Nesselrode pudding, and flung down his pen. A large blot landed in the middle of the wild duck as a result. Surveying his handiwork, Auguste thought moodily that something failed to satisfy. Something here, besides the ink blob, was out of place. There was one dish that did not fit. Like this afternoon. His thoughts jumped. The same feeling – something had been said that was completely wrong, for which there was no answer. It was flour in a bavarois, a scum in a stockpot, garlic with asparagus. But what it was he could not grasp, and stared at the menu as if by solving the one, the other too might clarify as an egg white a consommé.

Thursday, 3 January, did not begin well. There was a thick fog for a start. Nevertheless it had to be faced, a

240

conclusion shared by the Prince of Wales, by Auguste Didier, and Inspector Rose. The latter had been at Paddington since 4 a.m. So had Twitch. At Southampton the local police, not to be outdone, were swarming over the railway train that would later that morning be bearing Bobs to London on his triumphant way to Buckingham Palace.

Auguste, at Cranton's, had different concerns, but they did not include luncheon or dinner. He had given his word to Egbert that, the menus at last being selected, their execution would be left to John. At the moment his concerns were irritated by the arrival of the Honourable Pembrey twins glowing with self-importance.

'May we speak to you, Mr Didier?' one of them (he had no idea which) asked him meekly.

Auguste eyed them suspiciously. The twins were identified in his mind with trouble and today was too important to add gratuitous problems to his load. Nevertheless, he reminded himself conscientiously, they were guests at Cranton's.

'We have something to tell you. At least, Evelyn has.'

'It was you as much as me,' retorted Evelyn.

'It was your idea,' Ethel pointed out, this leading to further heated discussion.

'If this,' cut in Auguste at last, his tone indicating he had obviously forgotten all about their being guests, 'is another of your tricks—'

'Oh no, it isn't,' they assured him in unison, horror in their voices at the mere idea.

'It's about the service lift,' Ethel told him brightly. 'You remember you said the Baroness or Fancelli hid the body in the lift while the rooms were being cleaned – well, they couldn't have.'

'Why not?' asked Auguste, his heart sinking at the

241

mere idea of the one sure explanation of the case being thrown into doubt.

'Because we were using it that morning,' said Evelyn. 'We –' sidelong look at her twin – 'were going to play a trick on you, Mr Didier, and Ethel said—'

'No, that was you,' her twin informed her speedily.

'What was this trick?' Auguste demanded sternly.

'Evelyn got in,' said Ethel blithely, ignoring this, 'but the lift went down too quickly and jammed at a funny angle, so I had to call Danny—'

'Danny Nash? What was he doing inside the hotel on Christmas morning?' demanded Auguste.

Evelyn glanced at Ethel. 'He came in to see Rosanna,' she said vaguely. 'They were in the billiard room. Anyway, he managed to get the lift up again, and so Evelyn got out. Danny was rather cross, and jammed the lift where we couldn't reach it. That was about nine o'clock. Then very early next morning, he told us, he came in and unjammed it. It didn't matter because it isn't used during the day, so it didn't upset your staff, Mr Didier.'

Only my theory of how the murder was committed, thought Auguste savagely. 'Could the Baroness or Fancelli have freed it?'

'They might have done,' said Ethel helpfully, Sherlock Holmes to the fore, 'but Danny found it jammed just as he had left it, so it doesn't seem possible. The body couldn't have been in the lift, even for a little while.'

Auguste glared at them, most unfairly, he was aware. But revenge should be his. 'What was this trick?' he asked through gritted teeth.

The twins looked at each other, and Evelyn nodded.

'We were going to steal the boar's head,' Ethel told him, torn between terror and pride, 'and replace it with Guardian's bowler hat covered in icing. It did look nice,' she added regretfully. 'He had very nice eyes made out of your curtain rings.'

Auguste's fists were clenched, his chest puffed out in indignation. 'The art of cuisine is not a matter for jest.'

'Oh *no*,' said Evelyn fervently. 'Anyway we didn't do it, and we have made it up to you, Mr Didier, because we can tell you how it was done.'

'My boar's head?' asked Auguste, his mind still sidetracked to this enormity.

'No, the murder,' Ethel told him impatiently. 'If the lift wasn't used, there must have been another way.'

'And what was it?' Auguste asked grimly, arms folded, judgment suspended.

'Follow us, my man,' Evelyn announced importantly, in her best Holmes voice, 'for a reconstruction of the crime.'

Obediently Auguste followed the girls to the second floor, hoping that Marie-Paul and Alfred Bowman had decided not to spend the morning resting in their rooms.

'Watson and I have reason to believe,' Ethel began, gruffly waving aside Evelyn's protestations over her role, 'that the Baroness hid the body in one of the bathrooms opposite while the room was cleaned, staying in there herself with it. She avoided the risk of being seen by placing one of Miss Gonnet's shawls round the body so that it looked as if her companion were helping her to the bathroom to run the bath.'

'Dead bodies are heavy,' said Auguste firmly.

'It's only a few feet,' said Ethel crossly, 'and the risk of being seen was very small.'

'Have you asked the maids whether they saw the Baroness when they cleaned the room?' asked Evelyn.

'They did not,' answered Auguste unwillingly, 'but—'

'There you are then,' they chorused.

243

There was little point in an exposition on the difference between negative and positive evidence, so Auguste bowed to the inevitable. '*Très bien*,' he damned with faint praise. 'And what then?'

'With the corpse dressed in Miss Gonnet's clothes, she later walked her along the corridor, perhaps with Miss Gonnet's help or this man Fancelli who worked here, into one of the empty bedrooms along there. Look!' Ethel flung a door open. 'The maids wouldn't come in here, would they?'

'Suppose Mrs Pomfret decided to inspect the empty rooms?'

'It *was* Christmas morning,' they pointed out, as if this entitled servants to neglect their duty.

'And then?' asked Auguste resignedly. The number of holes in this theory made it resemble a colander of very little use, the largest being that on the morning in question these rooms were locked.

'Late that night,' Ethel informed him in hushed tones, 'the Baroness crept along to regain the corpse with Fancelli. Or Miss Gonnet. They intended to put it in the lift to take it downstairs, but finding it jammed, they were forced to take it down the service stairs at the end of this corridor. Come.'

With Auguste trailing behind, they ran down several flights of stairs, into the basement area, along the corridor and through the kitchens to John's great surprise and annoyance, clearly seeing this as an underhand way of checking up on him. Unable to explain, Auguste shrugged expressively, but John's subsequent blow on the meat for luncheon with the steak mallet did not suggest he was convinced.

'Here for some reason,' Evelyn told him gravely as they emerged into the basement corridors again, with the collection and delivery and boiler rooms in front, 'something went wrong. Perhaps it was Danny.'

'*Danny*?' repeated Auguste, bewildered.

'Yes,' said Ethel impatiently at his dull wits.

'He was sleeping down here in the cellars so he could see Rosanna and keep an eye on Nancy,' Evelyn added. 'Anyway, *something* frightened them, and they could not dispose of the body. So they think of the chest.' She led the way back into the kitchens, to John's fury. Ostentatiously not looking at the work in progress, Auguste followed them up the kitchen service stairs, emerging into the entrance hall.

'Here,' cried Ethel triumphantly, running across the hallway and into the drawing room. 'Here is this nice chest right by a side window. If they leave the body there for a day, the following night they can arrange to get it out of the window and smuggle it away. Can't you just picture the scene? Come, Evelyn, in with the body.' She flung the lid open, fortunately still with her eyes on Auguste and her twin. 'See?'

Auguste did see, and acting like lightning pushed between her and the chest, slamming it shut before Evelyn too could see. His face was very pale. 'Mesdemoiselles,' he said pleasantly, keeping his voice steady. 'Bravo. A most keenly observed theory. Kindly request the constable at the door to come here before you go. I – um – must pass on your suggestions quickly and confidentially. Inspector Rose must hear of this at the very first opportunity.'

Only the latter part of his speech was correct. Egbert Rose should indeed know, and very quickly, that in the chest was the smashed and battered corpse, identifiable with difficulty, of Alfred Bowman.

Splashes of bright colour emerging out of the swirling fog were transforming bleak Paddington. Red carpet, the brilliant uniforms of the Blue and Royals of the Household Cavalry, trumpets at the ready, flags almost canopying the railway station.

A telephone call had informed them that since the SS *Canada* had been delayed in its crossing, the Field Marshal's railway train would be late. Rose greeted this news with sinking heart. Another fifteen minutes in which that all too isolated figure could become a victim of a bullet. He tried to convince himself that everything that could be done had been done and that with so many pairs of eyes scanning every window and crevice for pointed guns, no assassin would stand a chance. Every constable in London was on the lookout for fat Italians with a furtive air and porkpie hat. A wide variety had thus been brought kicking and screaming into police stations all over the capital. Messages had flown back and forth, but all had been in vain. Of Fancelli there was no sign. Newspaper stalls, refreshment rooms and waiting rooms had been scanned and everyone on the station seemed to have a policeman by him – though many were not recognisable as such. Or indeed as anything, Rose thought glumly, remembering the motley assortment of 'disguises' he had seen early that morning: false beards, eye patches, farmers, fishermen, chestnut sellers, and a pièce de résistance by one ambitious lad, an Italian ice-cream vendor. 'In case Fancelli fancies an ice cream, Sarge,' he had told Twitch brightly. Their art of disguise would not make the stage of Her Majesty's, thought Rose. If he ever made Chief, he'd do something to remedy it.

All had been in vain. Fancelli had not been caught. All Rose had seen, an illusion he put down to the early hour of the morning, was a white-overalled chef with rounded figure and dark locks emerging from the first Inner Circle underground train. But he vanished from sight in the early morning work crowds and was not on the station now. Rose had personally inspected the kitchens of the station hotels with great care. Nothing and no one had been found.

Rose peered up at the vaulted roof, as though at any moment a long rope might descend with an assassin slithering down it. What method would an assassin use? A gun? Most likely. Dynamite? Possible. That's what the Boers had used to try to blow up Bobs in Johannesburg. But track and station had been scoured. How about the procession route to the palace? That was a danger. At least poison could be ruled out at Paddington Station, he thought wrily. Knife? Couldn't get close enough. A disagreeable thought struck him as memories of William Tell and bows and arrows came to him. Or how about one of those knife-throwing circus performers? True, Fancelli didn't look like a circus performer, but knife-throwing wouldn't need a lithe figure. Rose brushed the thought away. He was getting fanciful in his old age. All the same, he'd ask Twitch just to check circus lists for the future. After all, what about the Carlton and Pall Mall? Plenty of opportunities there for a man with a knife on his mind.

The band stopped playing stirring martial tunes at the sight of the train slowly puffing into the railway station.

On the red carpet, the Prince of Wales and Duke of Connaught stood to attention, behind them the Princess of Wales, who had as usual assumed deafness to Bertie's request for her absence. Nothing more to do now than pray, thought Rose grimly from his position ten yards away. Precisely opposite where the Prince and Duke waited on the red carpet, a carriage door was held open and the small figure of the Field Marshal responsible for apparent victory in South Africa, reliever of Kimberley, Mafeking and Ladysmith, stepped out. The trumpets of the Blues and Royals gave way to the national anthem. Salutes were given and acknowledged. No sound of guns, only of running footsteps. Rose whipped round, reflexes razor-sharp. Only a newsboy, determined to see his future monarch at closer quarters. Rose relaxed his taut muscles a fraction.

Five minutes later an open State carriage containing Bobs and Bertie drove away on its victory procession towards Buckingham Palace and luncheon. The ladies of the party and sundry other officials were packed into inferior hired carriages to take their back route to the palace, in order not to remove the limelight from Bobs himself. On this occasion the Yard had been gracious enough to grant expenditure for Rose and Stitch to follow this second procession, since they could hardly follow the Prince of Wales. Protection along the route was in the hands of Rose's men.

Rose was admiring the precision and competence of the British in such ceremonial, listening to the cheers of those lining Praed Street at the sight of the Prince of Wales's carriage turning in towards them, when he became aware of something wrong. The carriages in front of him were turning left, not right, and were following the Prince of Wales's carriage.

A sharp look at Twitch. What the hell was happening? Who was driving these hired carriages? Whom did they contain?

'Leave it to me, sir.' Twitch leapt from the carriage, in pursuit of promotion, power, and saving royalty from the plots of assassins. 'He must be in the front carriage.'

Rose, leaning from his window apprehensively, could see nothing in the blur of shouting, cheering faces, and the anonymous carriages of the second procession turning the corner to follow their leader. Then the crowd cleared, to reveal, as Rose's carriage came level, Sergeant Stitch picking himself up dustily and painfully from the ground. Rose grabbed him and pulled him up into the carriage.

'What's happening, man?' He shook him roughly.

Twitch was almost crying. 'It wasn't my fault, sir,' he babbled. 'I thought it was Fancelli in there for sure, going the wrong way like that. He wasn't driving, so I threw myself inside the carriage.' He looked at Rose beseechingly.

'Well?' Rose barked.

'It wasn't Fancelli, sir. It was the Princess of Wales, and Lady Roberts.'

Rose groaned.

'I fell over the Princess's feet, sir. She screamed. Then the door flew open the other side, and I sort of somersaulted straight out again.' Twitch sat before Rose penitent, waiting for the verdict that must surely come. Even if he escaped being clapped in irons for terrifying the Princess of Wales, promotion could never now be his.

He underestimated Rose, who was magnanimous in defeat. But not that magnanimous. He let him sweat a bit. Then: 'Tell you what, Stitch,' he remarked at last. 'Suppose I put in a report commending you for swift action in time of emergency, and preventing a dastardly attempt on the life of the Princess of Wales?'

Chapter Ten

Rose arrived at Cranton's, a docile and devoted Twitch in tow, at two o'clock. He was none too happy. Relief at the absence of calamity at Paddington had been completely obliterated on his return to the Yard by finding that there had been another murder at Cranton's. Furthermore he had had no time for luncheon, and for the first time in their acquaintance, Auguste let him down in this respect. So overcome was he at his macabre discovery that he omitted his usual summing up of a visitor's requirements in regard to food. The customary journey to the kitchen or restaurant was not offered. Auguste, not perceiving the reason for Rose's grumpiness, felt aggrieved. It was, he thought, as if Egbert considered he might be causing these crimes himself. Why? In order to ruin his first and probably his last opportunity to be a hotelier?

Sergeant Stitch was despatched to pacifying the guests who had been herded, to their annoyance, into the smoky billiard room after a luncheon served in a manner that could only be said to be perfunctory. The identity of the corpse had quickly become public knowledge if only through the absence of Mr Bowman from luncheon. Miss Guessings was missing from the billiard room, having swooned on hearing the news at luncheon.

In the drawing room, Rose stared down into the chest at the remains of Alfred Bowman. 'How did you recognise him?'

August hesitated. 'That lounge suit – and the brown boots.'

'Boots? Look quite standard to me.'

'But they are brown. No gentleman, except Mr Bowman, wears brown boots in London.'

Rose eyed him for a moment in none too friendly a fashion and decided to let it pass.

'Someone wanted to make quite sure he was dead all right. If it had been another knife killing, we'd know where to go.'

Auguste followed his thoughts. 'Marie-Paul Gonnet? But there cannot surely be *two* murderers at Cranton's?'

'Unlikely,' Rose grunted. 'But this don't fit our Marie-Paul. A woman wouldn't have the strength. Where in hell and Tommy's name is the doc?'

The latter obliged by bustling cheerily in.

'Blunt instrument, eh!' he remarked chattily, preparing for business. Having delivered himself of this only too obvious comment, he ceased to make comments, but Rose had no intention of waiting until the post-mortem was complete. Waiting in a mortuary while coroners formally requested PMs and doctors dictated their gruesome findings was never his favourite occupation.

'Time of death? Approximately.'

'Dead about twelve hours. Sometime during the night, I'd say – if I had to,' the doctor offered unwillingly.

'And what kind of instrument are we looking for, if that ain't a State secret too?'

The doctor looked at him in surprise. 'Why should it be?' he asked blankly. 'Heavy, weighted end, I'd say. Like a hammer, heavy mallet—'

'Steak mallet?' suggested Rose sharply.

'Possibly,' amended the doctor cautiously. 'The PM will tell you more.'

'Do you think he was killed in the chest?' Auguste asked the doctor.

'Why?' Rose demanded, his face turning dark.

'There is no – er – gore on the box, Inspector. And not much blood.'

'So Fancelli kills his victim somewhere else, and carries him down here to give us a good laugh, eh?'

'It was merely a deduction, Inspector. Where there is steak, there may be kidney,' Auguste murmured feebly.

'And what I'd give to see that,' muttered Rose grimly.

Auguste shot a sharp look at his friend, and the awful truth struck him. He had forgotten the first duty of a hotelier, the first of a chef, and the first of any human being. Has one's guest yet dined? Here he was clearly looking at a man who had not. True, the sight before them was not conducive to tempting the stomach, but *un peu de*. . .

'Inspector Rose,' he said formally, as the policeman began to remove the body, chest and all on this occasion, due to the problems of rigor mortis, 'I offer you my sympathy, my apologies, and *la bonne soupe.*'

His third mortuary this Christmas period, thought Rose, strengthened by soup but not inured to the sights before him. Usually he distanced himself; today it was difficult. This case was growing snake-like tentacles faster than Medusa.

He averted his eyes as the process seemed to be entering the final gruesome stages. He was going to have to go through all this again when Bowman's son came in for formal identification.

'Cause of death?' he asked automatically, as the doctor came over to him.

'No doubt about that,' the doctor replied informally. 'Hands.'

'Hands?' repeated Rose blankly.

'Oh yes, he was strangled. It wasn't obvious at first because of the state the head was in.'

'How much strength was used?' Rose shot at him. 'Could a woman have done it?'

'Impossible from the force used. She couldn't have rained down those blows, or carried out a manual strangulation on a man of that size.'

'Suppose she stunned him first?'

'Possible. But how's she going to carry him to the chest? Didn't you say there were no signs of blood in the room where the chest was?'

The last effects of the bonhomie created by the soup wore off remarkably suddenly, as Rose recalled that two of his male suspects, Fancelli and Nash, had escaped his control, an oversight which the Chief would undoubtedly view, in the manner of Lady Bracknell, not as unfortunate but as plain carelessness.

At Cranton's the effects of luncheon had long since worn off as the guests faced the disagreeable fact that not only were their rooms forbidden to them while the hotel was being searched yet again, but that their movements too were being curtailed. There would be no afternoon visit to Hampton Court. A different entertainment awaited them – that of explaining their movements in detail for the last twenty-four hours.

Twitch was in his element. Now was his chance to show that he too was capable of subtle interrogation of the swells. His chance to shine before his superiors, perhaps even to produce a master clue that would solve the case that had baffled the best minds of Scotland Yard (all except for his, that is). It didn't begin

254

auspiciously, as Gladys Guessings decided to rejoin the company, in order, apparently, to swoon again, where-after she had to be revived by sal volatile and Auguste's camomile tea.

At the end of an exhausting afternoon, interrogation of the servants, who were beginning to think that employment in Cranton's, however temporary, was by no means a wise career move, had revealed nothing. The search of the hotel, however, had been far more productive. There was no doubt as to where Bowman had been killed. His bed showed ample evidence of the results of the mallet attack, including a bloodstained towel.

'But it was the strangling killed him all right,' said Rose, surveying the bed closely. 'Not a patch on the amount of blood there'd have been if he had been alive at the time.'

There was quite sufficient for Auguste. He was, after all, merely an *amateur* detective, he reminded himself in expiation of his shame in seeking the nearest bath-room.

Stitch's interrogation of the guests had yielded little. No one had heard anything go bump in the night; they had all been asleep and only the twins showed any regret at this having been the case. Mr Bowman had appeared quite normal last evening, save that he was not as sociable as usual. Miss Guessings, weeping copiously, remained silent on this point. The Marquis de Castillon and Sir John Harnet debated their rights with themselves once again, and decided to conform, though disapproving of the mere sergeant status of their interviewer.

Late that afternoon Twitch had precious little to show for his efforts. But for the second time that day fortune was about to smile on Sergeant Stitch.

'What are you going to do about it, eh?' Carruthers

stood in front of him belligerently.

'The Yard's doing everything in its power, sir. No stone will remain unturned.'

Carruthers snorted. 'Won't find it under a stone. Too big.'

'What, sir?' Twitch asked, puzzled.

'The knobkerry that's missing from the smoking room, of course. What did you think I was talking about? Honour of the army at stake.'

Auguste regarded a row of uncleaned carp without enthusiasm. Their glazed eyes seemed to return his stare as if challenging him to invent a sauce to overcome their dull and muddy taste. This morning, however, he was in no mood to invent sauce, not even for . . . Perhaps anchovy? But no, it would not work. Not even the deliveries arriving for luncheon and dinner could raise him to his customary state of fraught tension as to whether Senn's had sent sufficient of their 'Hygienic Caviare (free from superfluous salt and oil)' and whether the widgeon had been hung precisely in accordance with his instructions. For once the sight of food dismayed, and did not cheer, for the events of the day before were all too vivid in his mind.

Gloom seemed to have descended in a cloud on the hotel, reflected Auguste unhappily as he entered the dining room, the Christmas decorations looking incongruous as policemen stalked the premises, outnumbering the guests, who appeared desperately to be attempting to maintain a façade that permitted them to ignore two murders and an arrest in the name of social convention.

'Slipping, are you, Didier?' said Carruthers, but there was no fire in his voice. 'Forgot the curry powder in the kedgeree this morning.' He stared disconsolately at his plate.

'Mr Didier,' said Eva Harbottle brightly. 'I am not used to kippers. I would like some Dutch cheese, if you please. Not English, *Dutch*!' She was a Kruger after all, even if only a distant relation of the former President.

Gladys was not present, having requested a tray in her room. That was one relief, thought Auguste, as he reassured the Harbottles that they would not be murdered in their beds, pacified de Castillon, soothed Sir John, and avoided Bella's eye. Running a hotel, he decided, was a job for a diplomatist. A chef could be free, independent, a law to himself; a hotelier was bound by the demands of his guests. He brooded darkly on his future.

Half an hour later, he was once more in his office with Egbert Rose.

'The only excitement yesterday,' Rose told him, 'was that the carriages with the women and staff officers in it went the wrong way, by sheer mistake, and followed the Prince of Wales along the procession route instead of going back to the Palace by a back way. And that was that. Another State banquet at the Palace, and they are all alive and kicking at the end of it.'

'So either your information was incorrect, or the attack on His Royal Highness will be made either at the Marlborough Club or the Carlton.'

'Albert Edward won't like that,' remarked Rose gloomily. 'It was hard enough convincing him when there was a definite time and place when he'd be at risk, but it's going to be even harder to persuade him he shouldn't drop in at his club or dine at the Carlton.'

'There is another possibility,' Auguste said thoughtfully, 'that Fancelli decided not to go ahead with the attack because you had his accomplice in custody. Have you charged her, Egbert?'

Rose shook his head. 'We're going to have to let her go. It was a gamble, but with this further murder, a murder I don't see how Fancelli could have carried out, I don't have the evidence.'

'Madame Lepont must be innocent,' said Auguste indignantly. 'The murderer of Monsieur Bowman is a man – and it could not be Fancelli. And *why* would Madame Lepont and Fancelli want Mr Bowman dead? There is no motive. If they are guilty and he knew it, his knowledge is superfluous even for blackmail now that Madame Lepont is arrested and Fancelli's description outside every police station.'

Marie-Paul Gonnet obviously agreed with them. With flashing eyes she was standing indignantly in the doorway, heavy shoes and thick stockings just visible beneath her plain dark serge dress, every inch the loyal retainer.

'You release her, heh?' she cried. 'You release her, *now*. There has been another murder. You say Madame do this one too? She is a magician?'

'We're considering it, miss,' Rose informed her kindly. 'Just as soon as we're further on in our investigations.'

'I help you,' she offered scornfully in marked contrast to her response to Sergeant Stitch's earlier interrogation. 'I 'ave the room next to this Bowman. And you ask *la dame* Guessings why she come to 'is room, eh? I hear someone outside. I am frightened. It is not nice this hotel. So I look very carefully. It is Miss Guessings who knocks on this Bowman's door.'

Rose had taken a distinct dislike to Madame's companion, and wasn't going to give a French centimetre to her.

'Most interesting. Now if you'll leave us.'

She was ejected with difficulty by the policeman.

They looked at each other, each knowing what the other was thinking.

'Crime passionnel, eh?' said Rose, breaking the silence.

'But she is a woman!' expostulated Auguste feebly.

'Hell hath no fury, as Edith sometimes tells me,' Rose commented. 'Lends strength, you know.'

'Only if Bowman lay there and wanted to be strangled.'

'Drugged him, perhaps,' said Rose.

Auguste sighed. 'I cannot believe it, my friend.'

'Let's see what she says.'

Gladys appeared half an hour later, it having taken some time to compose herself and remove her curlers. It had after all been a hard night.

'Poor, dear Alfred,' she offered as an opening gambit.

'When did you last see him, ma'am?'

'At dinner,' she announced promptly. Too promptly to Auguste's mind.

'We have a report that you went to see him in his room – about one o'clock.'

'Inspector! I am an unmarried woman. How dare you suggest—'

'You deny it, ma'am?'

'Certainly I do,' she said unhappily.

'We have a witness.'

'A mistaken one,' she gasped, then shut her lips primly together.

'No, ma'am,' said Rose inexorably.

Her face crumpled. 'I knocked and he came to the door. He unbolted it, but he wouldn't let me in. I told him I'd come to talk to him,' she stumbled, 'but he slammed the door shut and bolted it in my face.' She looked from one to the other. 'He was alive when I left. I didn't touch him.' The whisper became a wail.

'What did you go to see him about?' asked Rose. 'Was it, shall we say, intimate?'

Rose could say what he liked, but he would not get her, Gladys Guessings, to admit that it was exactly that hope that had spurred her there, convinced that Alfred could never resist such an opportunity. She had been wrong. And he had made it agonisingly, painfully clear. So clear she—

'We had business matters to discuss,' she replied with dignity.

'Crime passionnel, like I said?' asked Rose, once he had let her go, too easily in Auguste's opinion. 'He rejected her, and she gave him forty whacks like Lizzie Borden?'

'He was strangled first, *mon ami*,' said Auguste. 'And still it seems strange to me that, bad hotelier though I am, my small party could include two murderers. I see Bowman more as a murderer than Madame Lepont.'

'Someone could have gone in after her,' pointed out Rose. 'He must have let his murderer in.'

'By the state of the room, he did not put up much struggle, however. Almost as if,' Auguste paused, 'as if he'd been sleeping when attacked.'

'It's like that maze at Stockbery Towers,' grunted Rose.

'Every maze has a beginning, a pattern and a solution,' said Auguste. 'And in our case, assuming this is one maze not two, the beginning is not, surely, Mr Bowman's murder but that of Mary White.' Rose had told him the girl's identity had now been established. Whose household did she belong to? And how did she meet Nancy Watkins?

'Twitch has been on to the local police forces in your British guests' home towns. No one missing, except a flighty piece who ran away to Gretna with her follower.'

'And the knobkerry?'

'Disappeared,' said Rose succinctly. 'No one could have got in or out of the hotel except Father Christmas without being stopped. Yet it isn't anywhere to be found. Knobkerries,' Rose added disgustedly. 'Points to one of the army men, don't you think?'

'It would,' said Auguste, 'if he hadn't been strangled first. What was the reason he was battered after death?'

'To obscure identity.'

'But it did not.'

'The murderer couldn't have counted on you recognising his boots,' said Rose, but there was no conviction in his defence of his theory. 'Perhaps he wasn't sure he was dead then.'

Auguste looked at him. It was hardly necessary to point out no murderer came armed with a knobkerry just in case he was inefficient in his strangling. Rose blushed.

'Might as well begin with the army, at any rate.'

Major Dalmaine entered stiffly at the police summons, obviously about to salute them and thinking better of it. This wasn't Pretoria.

'Ever met Alfred Bowman before you came here?'

'No, sir,' came the cold reply.

'Had your brother?'

This shook him, but he made a visible attempt at recovery. 'My brother? I have no idea. I haven't seen him for eighteen months.'

'In Africa, isn't he?'

'I believe so.' Dalmaine hoped his air of finality would conclude the conversation. It did not.

'Had what they call a chequered career, your brother, so we're told.'

'We are not close,' was Dalmaine's only response.

261

'Seems to write to you often enough,' remarked Rose, 'judging by the letters we found in your room. One of them – a most interesting one – seemed to be missing a page or two.'

'Indeed?' said Dalmaine in a tone of indifference. 'I am a smoker, Inspector. I find writing paper makes excellent spills.'

Once again the constable was brushed aside in peremptory fashion as Carruthers burst through the door.

'What the devil do you think you're doing, accusing this chap of murder?'

'Not quite, sir. We were asking a few questions, that's all.'

'That knobkerry comes from the smoking room. Anyone could have used it. Even you, sir,' glaring at Auguste who blenched and looked to see whether Rose might be taking this seriously.

Dalmaine had the air of a Wellington saved by the arrival of the Prussians.

'I'll be wanting to talk to you again,' said Rose, submitting to military solidarity.

'Certainly, certainly,' cried Dalmaine, rapidly exiting with little sign of a limp. 'I'm indebted to you, Colonel,' he told his saviour outside.

'Think nothing of it,' grunted Carruthers gruffly. 'Even the Buffs and Dirty Half Hundreds can hold together in times of attack. Like Blücher and the Dutch, eh? All in a common cause.'

'Ah, that I dispute, Colonel,' said Dalmaine happily, back on familiar ground. Even the sight of Rosanna failed to distract him on this occasion, a fact she noted with great annoyance.

Back in the office, Rose sighed. 'I'm letting the Lepont woman go. And yet there was *something*. I was sure we had it in our grasp there, you know.'

Auguste shook his head. 'My friend, I knew you were wrong. Assassination, no. Murder perhaps, in extreme circumstances, but not assassination. Unlike salmon with fennel, the sauce did not fit. It irritated where it should soothe.'

'Who will be next?' enquired Gladys plaintively, secure in the knowledge that though the heart was broken, she was, thanks to her Hovenden's Easy Hair Curlers, looking her very best.

Eva Harbottle consulted her programme. 'The White-Eyed Kaffir,' she informed her.

'No, no,' Gladys said a little curtly at having been taken so literally. 'I mean, who will be next to be murdered, now poor dear Alfred—' She broke off.

'We're leaving Cranton's in two days,' Eva pointed out. 'Surely there won't be many more?'

Gladys eyed her crossly. Some sympathy might not come amiss. Really, Eva Harbottle was a very strange woman. Of course, she was a Boer, she remembered suddenly. The enemy, after all. She inched away, as the Great Chirgwin bounced onto the stage of the Alhambra Theatre, the famous white greasepainted eye hidden under the tall hat.

'Good evening, ladies and gempmums. . .'

Afterwards, Auguste walked eagerly at the head of his flock into the Carlton Hotel. Despite the troubles of the world, the *maître* could be relied upon to soothe even the dullest spirits. At first, however, the party was quiet, with the air of those surreptitiously wary of their neighbours, as if they expected them either to collapse, mortally wounded, or to leap up with a carving knife in their hands. However, the atmosphere grew less tense and good humour swelled once more at the arrival of the *velouté de champignons de Provence*. Ah, what memories that stirred, both of his native land and of his apprenticeship at the Faisan Doré. He recalled the enthusiasm the dear master inspired in him, that first dish approved by the *maître*, the little words of approval that meant so much. *Mousse de volaille au curry*. He picked up his fork now still in a reverie of long ago. One day he had created *le faisan Didier*. What excitement when he returned home to tell his parents. They hadn't believed him of course – he was so young to have achieved such heights. But he knew. Ah, how he rejoiced.

Tonight Egbert Rose would be dining *chez lui avec* Edith. And shortly the Prince of Wales would be dining here once more. This disagreeable thought almost drowned his appreciaton of the *émincé de truffes à la crème*. True, His Royal Highness was obstinately arguing that as nothing had happened at Paddington, nothing would happen thereafter. Clubs were clubs, and not to be invaded by policemen, and as for not dining at the Carlton, he was most certainly not going to miss one of Escoffier's dinners on the offchance Rose might be right. Escoffier understood his stomach and, like his tailor, fitted his creations to it – that was what cooks were for.

Lingering happily over his *mandarines glacées aux perles des Alpes*, Auguste was transported in his mind back to Cannes once more. It had been on a visit to his parents there that he had been discovered by the Duke of Stockbery and, parted from Tatiana, decided to bury his unhappiness in England. Maman, being half-English, had put a brave face on her son departing across the seas. But last year he had returned – only to take murder with him. Truly, tonight this food had transported him into the sun of Provence, the London January left far behind. He could see, too, the boulevards and *fiacres* of Paris, not the narrow streets and hansom cabs of London. A sudden nostalgia for his homeland stung him, before he could shake himself free. Did he not have good friends here? Did he not admire English food above all others, if not always its cooking? Did he not wish to present it as it should be cooked? He was, after all, half English; his food, *cuisine à la Didier*, should reflect the best of both nations. He would go to the kitchen now, to thank the *maître* for the honour of the dinner they had just eaten. He would arrange to meet, to discuss the philosophy of food, as Brillat-Savarin did with his friends, and most of all he would see his friend, his master Escoffier, once more.

A word to the *maître d'hôtel*, a word to the police constable solidly eating his way through food such as had never come his way before, in order not to appear too obtrusive in his guard-dog duties, and Auguste found his way to the kitchens. There he found engaged on the creating, garnish, presentation and faultless service of exquisite food, forty white overalled and -hatted kitchen assistants, and the *maître*.

Escoffier saw him, advanced with arms outstretched.

Auguste glowed. '*Mon ami*,' he said simply. It was the seal on a perfect evening.

As he was about to leave, the seal was ripped uncompromisingly off, however. The bang of a door, the sound of a familiar song, and footsteps hurrying up the basement area steps outside. That figure, that song. '*La donna è* . . .' Auguste raced out through the door and looked up, just as his quarry paused to look down. It was indeed Fancelli.

The thoughts tumbled through his head as Auguste pounded after him. Working in the kitchens at the Carlton – thank heavens he had scotched his plans by seeing him; he must be planning to kill the Prince on his visit to the Marlborough Suite; he had saved his master from the terrible fate of having the Prince killed at one of his banquets, perhaps even poisoned with the blame thrown onto him. How narrowly such disaster had been averted. Yet if he could not catch Fancelli now, he would be free to strike again.

His prey had taken fright, running up the Haymarket and crossing the road, weaving in between the endless streams of cabs, buses and motor vehicles, and already merging into the blue-grey mist of the crowd where the street lights failed to illuminate. Auguste threw himself after him, regretting his second *caille aux raisins*, yelling at a police constable to follow him. 'Fancelli,' he hurled at him in explanation.

'Cripes,' was the policeman's response. Like Twitch, he contemplated instant promotion as he hurtled across the road.

'Lost him,' panted Auguste.

'There he is!' shouted the constable, thus urging on Fancelli, now running down Panton Street, to new heights of achievement. Auguste, in front of the policeman, ran full tilt into three ladies of the night who plied their trade together, cheap perfumes and feathers vying with one another in ostentation. Auguste collided with an ostrich plume, apologised and endeavoured to move it and its owner to one side.

'I like you, darling,' she murmured, and as he ran on, 'Free?' she offered hopefully at his retreating back.

Auguste raised his hat as he ran, hurling back, '*Enchanté*.' She did not receive such respect from the police constable, whom she knew full well.

'Lost him, sir?' he cried, panting on towards Auguste, who was by now reaching the corner of Leicester Square and regretting the first *caille* as well. The Empire Theatre towards which Fancelli was headed was disgorging its evening clientele and hansom cabs were standing three deep, waiting for trade.

He'd lost him. Where was he? Auguste slithered to a

halt on the pavements sticky from rain, only to receive a violent push that sent him crashing to the pavement. His shout brought the constable to his side only to leap uncaringly over him to collar Fancelli who had been endeavouring to run back the way they had come. Meanwhile another lady of the night was bending solicitously over Auguste. 'Hope you haven't hurt yourself, dearie. You come with me. I'll look after you.'

He politely disengaged her. He *had* hurt himself. His face and hands were bleeding, his body was bruised. Nevertheless Fancelli was safely in the expert grip of the young police constable, who now that the danger was past was being assisted by several stalwart passersby. His flourish on the police whistle had gone unanswered.

'Let us take a hansom,' said Auguste faintly. 'I will pay for it,' he added, as the constable looked disconcerted. Hansoms weren't in the range of his salary. Auguste, however, was aching all over. A sitz bath seemed an exquisite idea. But before such pleasure came duty – and he wished to see the *maître* again. To warn him of what might yet be in store for the Prince of Wales.

'He's not saying anything,' grunted Rose three hours later to a weary Auguste, slumped in his uncomfortable office chair. 'Keeps saying he doesn't understand English.'

'He understood it very well in Cranton's.'

'Furthermore he insists that the only reason he's at the Carlton is that you dismissed him and he needed a job. The underchef hired him.'

'I did not think the *Maître* would have been so foolish,' announced Auguste.

'I told him we'd got his accomplice in prison – just to

test him out – and he got very alarmed indeed. Shifty geezer.'

'He is,' agreed Auguste fervently.

'Then I mentioned Bowman being dead. That was news to him. Very pale he looked at that. Do you know, Auguste, I reckon you're right, it was Bowman after all. Remember he referred to Fancelli as 'the cook', when all we said was that he worked at Cranton's? Your Madame Lepont is in the clear, and her companion. The Sûreté checked. Marie-Paul Gonnet, born Colmar 1868. Of course, Fancelli denies coming back to the hotel again after you dismissed him, but then he would. What's more, we're getting in information now from Brussels. Bowman did deal in arms. And for the Boers. So it looks to me very like the Prince of Wales may be able to sleep easy now, one way and another. Very grateful I am to you, Auguste. It hasn't been easy, I know. But now I hope we've seen the end of it.'

Auguste opened his sleepy eyes and tried to focus on the matter in hand. After much effort he did so: 'But Egbert, if Fancelli did not, then who *did* murder Bowman?'

Auguste almost tumbled down from the hansom cab, greeted as if in a dream the policeman on duty, the night porter, and the stray cat who had adopted Cranton's by night. Painfully he pulled himself up the front steps and through to his private rooms. At least, they should have been private.

In his tiny study-cum-lounge he started tearing off his clothes, his normal precision and orderliness forgotten. All he could think about was bed, the bliss of a comfortable bed in which the hot water jar might still conceivably be warm. After an ultimately successful battle with suspenders and socks, he fell thankfully at the last milepost and tumbled into what should have been paradise – on any other night but this. What he had assumed was a large hot water jar appeared to be a woman, a fragrant-smelling, soft and embraceable woman. With red hair.

'Auguste,' she murmured happily, 'how nice.'

One small cry of anguish escaped him before his battered body tried politely to cope with this emergency.

Tried, but ignominiously failed.

'I am delighted you have seen the error of your ways.' Madame Lepont swept through the doors of Cranton's Hotel on the morning of 5 January.

'Not all error, ma'am,' Rose pointed out. 'There's still the matter of the false identity.'

'My little ruse to investigate the running of a luxury hotel,' she smiled. 'Poor Marie-Paul. She did so enjoy being the companion of a baroness. You are very cruel, Inspector.' She paused. 'As for myself, I shall not complain. You had reason, I suppose. And the reason for my release?'

'The murder of Mr Alfred Bowman, ma'am.'

Shock flashed through her eyes. 'Another murder, Mr Didier? You provide your guests with very unexpected fare. Might I ask who has been arrested for this murder, and why he was murdered?'

'No arrests yet, ma'am.'

'But even Mr Didier cannot accuse me of it, I imagine,' she said lightly. 'I am, I confess, disappointed in you, Mr Didier. I had thought us friends, and to conspire to arrest me is hardly an amicable action.'

'I shall make it up to you this evening, madame,' Auguste told her fervently. 'For the grand banquet this evening, I shall create a *timbale Thérèse*. The Maître Escoffier sometimes claims he creates all his best dishes for women. And his former apprentice shall do the same. It will be an honour to name this dish for you.'

'I accept your peace offering, monsieur,' she said gravely. 'On condition you grant me the recipe in order that it may have pride of place in my own hotel.'

'Splendid,' said Albert Edward cordially to Inspector Rose. He meant it. One assassin probably dead, the other under lock and key, having now confessed, poor fellow. Couldn't be better. He waved aside all advice of caution in case this conclusion was premature. Rose took the hint and retired, wondering if this operation should be undertaken backwards as he was before his future monarch. Compromising on a half-shuffle sideways, he almost tripped up when royalty addressed him again.

'By the way,' asked the Prince of Wales, 'who caught the fellow?'

'Monsieur Auguste Didier.'

'That cook fellow?' Albert Edward was astounded. That fellow got everywhere. Name popped up all over the place. He thought of the letter in his writing desk still unanswered. He supposed he'd better agree. If Mama had no objection, that is.

Auguste looked round his regained kingdom and shuddered. John had clearly not been trained at the Didier School of Cuisine, judging by the disorder that had now crept into the kitchen. Creativity and inspiration must be ruled by order to be given full rein. What use to create a superb *pièce montée* if one ran out of almond paste? If the meringue were not yet baked? Tonight, Twelfth Night, was the last banquet. Tomorrow night the greenery and decorations would have vanished, and had not Inspector Rose requested their presence for another evening, so would the guests.

John in the midst of his own created chaos created his own order. On the blackboard he had duly listed the dishes still requiring his attention, but omitted those already prepared. Thus, Auguste frowned, one was unable to gain the whole picture, to carry in one's mind those last-minute garnishes still to be added. Perhaps he would have a word with John – after the banquet.

John saw him gazing at him and smiled happily, putting a thumb through a pie crust with a careless jerky movement, and covering it with an exquisitely executed pastry rose.

He must concentrate on the new dish to be created for Thérèse, Auguste remembered. Perhaps a *timbale Thérèse de caneton aux truffes*? Perhaps too rich. *Non!* This was after all the Twelfth Night banquet, signifying a glorious end to festivity. A strange festivity it had been. Tonight, however, he would do his best as host to give an evening of entertainment such as they would remember. Cranton's at Christmas would not be synonymous solely with murder. True, after the banquet, the entertainment was being organised by Maisie, but with the help of the twins. Rose had asked to be present, and was by no means pleased to be informed by Evelyn that he too must contribute. Auguste himself had reluctantly put aside his original intention of reading from the philosophical works of Monsieur Brillat-Savarin in favour of the gentleman who had committed the unforgivable at Monte Carlo.

'Ah, Auguste.' Maisie swept in. 'I hear you landed on your backside. Hurt yourself? What's this?' she swept on, sticking her finger in a bowl without too much concern for his backside.

'That is ginger syllabub,' said Auguste, 'for the Pall Mall Pudding *à la Guessings*, and I would prefer it to appear without the shape of your fingers in it, Maisie,' he added mildly.

'I'm your employer,' she told him serenely, 'I can do what I like.'

'Not after tomorrow,' Auguste told her with regret at how this opportunity had slipped by ungrasped.

'Come on now, Auguste,' she said sturdily. 'It's not your fault you've had three murders on your plate instead of stuffed oysters.'

'Three murders that I have not solved,' he pointed out bitterly. 'Maisie, *three* of them. What has happened to me, that I cannot see the solution?'

'You always used to say that the food would show you the way,' she said more cheerfully than she felt. Murder after all was no great inducement to join a 'Lady Gincrack's Tour for Gentlefolk'.

'But in this disorder?' he began until he saw John's reproachful face.

'Go back to the beginning, you always used to say,' she told him. 'Go back to the recipe and the ingredients.'

'The recipe is a plot to assassinate the Prince.'

'Or the girl in the fog.'

'True. We still have no explanation for poor Mary White. Where did she come from? She gave Nancy information about Cranton's. But how did she hear it?'

'From her master and mistress?' said Maisie valiantly, picking out an almond spike from the Hedgehog Pudding.

'We assumed she was a housemaid because of her print—Maisie, *please*,' he broke off anguished, as another spike followed the first.

Maisie hastily replaced her hands in her lap, and looked attentive.

'Now as to ingredients, clues, we have "Marlborough", we have—'

'The reference to the definite article, and—'

'We have Pall – *the* Pall Mall Pudding!' he shrieked.

'My custard.' He flew to the gas oven and removed the dish from its water jacket. Truly, some god of cuisine looked after him today. Well done, but not yet ruined. The delicate taste of honey, subtly blended with spice, would still shine through the custard. He set it to cool before moving it carefully onto its shortbread base. Then and then only could he add the syllabub, and the final garnish of fresh and crystallised fruit. Miss Guessings would remember this evening for ever.

'Pall Mall Pudding. Oh, Mr Didier.' Gladys so far forgot herself as to clasp her hands in excitement. The most delightful banquet and this to top it all. It was too much. She had reason to be gleeful, arguing that such favour shown by Mr Didier proved she was not under suspicion of Another's death. Everyone had professed enthusiasm for Auguste's creations; Dame Nellie herself was not more enthusiastic at the creation of her *pêches melba* by *le maître* Escoffier than were Madame Lepont and Miss Guessings at the honour done them, thought Auguste happily.

'It is Madame Emma Pryde's recipe, Miss Guessings. Naturally, it has been adapted by Auguste Didier specially for you,' as Gladys enthusiastically partook of his offering.

'What have you got in there, Auguste?' enquired Maisie gulping. 'Neat whisky?'

'*Mais non*,' said Auguste, hurt at the very idea that such crudeness could enter his creation. 'It is for Miss Guessings. Ginger wine, brandy—'

A shriek from Gladys. 'Mr Didier, you've done it on purpose, you know my secret,' and she relapsed into hysterics.

So startled was he, he was incapable of movement for a moment, then proceeded to act with commendable efficiency born of years of experience of such emergencies. It was not usual, it was true, for a hotelier to slap a paying guest round the face, but it was on occasion necessary – and effective. Edith Rose, dressed in her Christmas best, glided into position as second-in-command, bearing Gladys back to her room, leaving a bemused company to pick up their spoons and resume their attack on the Pall Mall Pudding.

Edith returned half an hour later, and took her place once more at the table, by which time the puddings had been replaced by savouries. She decorously concluded her meal, oblivious of all curious looks. Eventually she satisfied them. 'Mr Didier,' she began severely, 'had put alcohol in the pudding.'

'It is usual,' said Auguste defensively.

'Miss Guessings is a member of the Band of Hope,' said Edith, her look in the cause of feminine solidarity daring her husband to enquire further. But when the ladies withdrew to the drawing room, Rose followed her out.

'Edith,' he said meaningfully, preventing her escape into this temporary feminine sanctum, 'what's so secret about the Band of Hope?'

'Apparently, Egbert,' she replied with dignity, 'and I tell you this in case you suspect that dear lady of involvement in deeper doings, she has been known to break her vows and take a small sherry before luncheon on occasion. Nancy Watkins mocked her about it, it appears.'

Rose gave a guffaw. 'Fond of her tipple, is she?'

'Really, Egbert,' said his wife, shocked. 'Language, if you please.'

Auguste's rendering of 'The Man Who Broke the Bank at Monte Carlo' had been received well; he was gratified to remember just how well he could sing. True, his forte was to sing *de l'amour* and, better still, *to* a beloved. But music hall songs were amusing, and he had, Maisie informed him gravely, a natural flair for comedy. He looked at her suspiciously, but her face appeared guileless. Only one more performer now remained. A most reluctant one, but one prepared to do his duty by Twelfth Night.

Inspector Egbert Rose cleared his throat, donned spectacles and took up the leatherbound copy of Charles Dickens' *Christmas Stories* that had graced their bookshelves ever since Edith's uncle Cyril, who had been awarded it as a school prize, passed on.

'I'm going to be reading extracts from *Mugby Junction*,' he declared. A sigh of satisfaction from the English members of his audience, and resignation from the foreign members.

'Chapter IV. No. 1 Branch Line: The Signalman. "Halloa! Below there! . . ." '

Twenty minutes later Rose was working up to a tremendous peroration. 'I said, "Below there! Look out! Look out! For God's sake, clear the way!" '

'Very nice, Egbert!' beamed Edith approvingly, when at last he finished. 'I do like a nice piece of Dickens.'

But Auguste did not hear her comment. His mind was still racing rapidly through the awful possibilities that Egbert's reading had raised, coupled with his own offering. It all came together, suddenly, completely, like a *brandade de morue*.

Music hall songs, Dan Leno, the role of Alfred Bowman and now, all important, 'No. 1 Branch Line'. Perhaps the recipe from which they started had different interpretations, and he and Egbert had puffed and steamed their way down the Branch Line, and reached its terminus. They had hoped the matter over, trusting somehow that Fancelli could be proved to have carried out Bowman's murder. Yet the main line still awaited them – if only they could find the points.

Chapter Eleven

Auguste rose at 6 a.m. the following morning, to attend early Mass. One of the privileges of being a hotelier was that you did not necessarily have to be present at breakfast, let alone cook it. John, having been given now some guidance by a master chef, was perfectly capable of providing a breakfast of which even the Colonel would have no complaints. Auguste returned to the hotel, however, as the first glimpses of morning light illuminated the dark and misty streets. He sniffed at the dampness of English winter, so unlike the warm winds of Provence, or the penetrating biting cold of the Mistral. He pulled his overcoat more closely round him, as he approached the back door of the hotel. This was where it had all begun, only six weeks before, in the fog. Was this the junction of the branch line? He heard again Nancy's cry: 'At Cranton's? Christmas?' Saw again the girl lying dead at his feet; reconstructed carefully what they knew of her. Conclusion: could he have made false deductions? Like Miss Guessings and her big secret, exposed by a pudding. *The* pudding, the Pall Mall Pudding *à la Didier*.

A small boy delivering newspapers passed whistling on a bicycle. A familiar tune, given to the world by Signor Verdi, and adored by one of his countrymen, Fancelli. But suppose Fancelli, too, were merely a station on the branch line? The Pall Mall Pudding, the definite article, and the fact that Nancy was a lady journalist. He stopped suddenly, remembering that as a hotelier he should enter the front door of the hotel, not the back. He walked round slowly, so slowly that a crossing sweeper brightened, seeing trade at last. Absentmindedly Auguste tossed him a penny, then jubilantly threw another after it. For he knew now where the junction was.

He walked into a warm and welcoming hotel, full of Christmas decorations. It was the last day this cocoon of Christmas could hold them all. Later today the trappings of Christmas must go. The kissing bough taken down. The Father Christmas decoration on the tree removed. Ah, but his brain worked well now! Auguste Didier was himself again. Truly a *maître*, truly a great detective. Why had it taken so long?

Dickens should have called his amusing work *Muggins Junction*, not *Mugby*, for that is how he felt. A muggins. How could he have disappeared down that branch line so easily, lured by the garnish and not the essence of the dish?

At Highbury, Egbert Rose was enjoying a lie-in after their late night, luxuriating in his first Sunday off since Chesnais had summoned him in November. The royal welcome at Paddington having passed off without incident, and the villains being either dead or in custody, the Chief had given reluctant permission for a day off. Not that he would take it all. Tomorrow, Cranton's guests would disperse, unless he could get first-class evidence of why any or all should be detained. But that would be later. Now, Edith's appalling kippers were going to receive his full undivided attention for the first time in six weeks.

'I believe, Egbert,' said Edith blithely, as she placed a fragrant offering before him some half an hour later, 'that looks like Auguste descending from a hansom cab. And, oh Egbert,' her face suddenly fell, much as she liked Auguste, 'I do believe he's asking him to wait.' That boded ill.

The smell of the kipper wafted tantalisingly under Rose's nostrils, for not even Edith could entirely miscook a kipper. He picked up his silver fish knife and fork speedily as he heard 'the girl', as he always thought of her before breakfast restored him fully to the world, open the door. Two seconds later, Auguste entered, hat in hand. His face fell as he saw Egbert at table, belligerently clutching eating implements, but this was too important to wait.

'*Chère madame* Edith, my apologies,' he pleaded. 'My sympathy, Egbert –' Rose glared – 'but this is so important.'

'You can tell me while I eat this,' replied Rose firmly as Edith beamed at him approvingly. 'Kippers help me think.'

All the same, kipper progress grew slower as Auguste burst out excitedly: '*The Pall Mall Gazette*. Not Pall Mall the thoroughfare. Nancy was a journalist, but it was not *her* article to which she referred. But to the definite article "the" which made all the difference to the words Pall Mall.'

'Maybe,' said Rose grudgingly. 'But what about it? You mean, the assassination won't necessarily be at the Marlborough Club or the Carlton?'

'My friend, it means more perhaps. That the assassination plot was nothing to do with these murders. That we are, like Edith's good friend Mr Dickens, up a branch line.'

Rose took another mouthful of kipper. Auguste's ideas were good, but he was inclined to rise higher and quicker than one of his soufflés if he wasn't watched. He thought it over, crunching through cold burnt toast.

'That piece of paper Chesnais gave me was about the

279

assassination plot,' he announced, his tone brooking no denial.

'But how do we know that had any connection with Nancy? Suppose it did indeed indicate that Paddington, not Pall Mall, was the place where Alfred Bowman and Fancelli planned, as you tell me he has now confessed, to kill the Prince. How do we *know* this was Nancy's story? After all, *mon ami*, if she had wind of such a plot, she would surely inform the police?'

'She did say "It's all happening again", too, remember,' argued Egbert morosely, seeing Twelfth Day about to disappear after its eleven sisters. 'Just like Sipido, she meant.'

'Or something else,' said Auguste firmly. French terrier against English bulldog. The bulldog thought for a moment, then with another loving bite of tough kipper turned into a bloodhound.

'What about the *Gazette* anyway?' he asked sharply. 'An article? The management? Corruption?'

'We must seek out the issues for November. "It's all happening again" mean it connects with an old story,' said Auguste, trying to contain his excitement and think logically.

'How are we going to get at their files today?' muttered Rose.

'Babylon,' said Edith brightly, coming into the room with some of her special coffee for dear Auguste. She went slightly pink as both men stared at her.

'Modern Babylon,' she said firmly. 'I thought I heard you mention the *Pall Mall Gazette*. That poor editor, Mr Stead. Fancy being imprisoned after all he tried to do to help those poor girls.'

'Blow me down with a kipper,' said Rose slowly. 'I don't know about promoting Twitch. Seems to me you're the one with the brains, Edith.'

'Oh, Egbert,' said Edith, pleased.

'I do not understand,' said Auguste, bewildered.

''Course, you weren't here in the eighties,' Rose said kindly. '"A Maiden Tribute of Modern Babylon" was the *Gazette*'s finest hour. That article back in eighty-five by its editor, Stead, was all about how girls, many of them under fifteen, and quite a few under thirteen, were being bought out of overcrowded homes and sent under the pretence of being housemaids to the Continent for prostitution, complete with certificate, often fraudulent of course, to prove their virginity.'

Edith pursed her lips.

'Stead needed proof of its happening before he published, so he, with a Rebecca Jarrett, had bought a thirteen-year-old girl, Eliza Armstrong, from her parents for five pounds, had her put through the usual examination for another five pounds, lodged her with the Salvation Army, and took her to France, not to a brothel of course, but a respectable home. Then he exposed the story and as a result he, Jarrett and the Salvation Army all landed up in the dock.

'There'd been attempts for years to stop the trade, but the Committee for the Exposure and Suppression of the Traffic of English Girls for the Purpose of Prostitution could only get a hearing in Belgium, not here. Not even Lord Shaftesbury could get the courts or Parliament to move. Stead was going to have no better luck, it seemed. They were all found guilty of "Offence Against the Person", since the parents naturally enough swore blind that they thought Eliza was going to be a housemaid, and imprisoned. Luckily, there was such an outcry, specially since they wouldn't allow Stead to speak in his own defence at the trial, that even Parliament couldn't afford to overlook it. He went to prison, but he published his own defence in the *Gazette*, and although it took three goes, the Criminal Law Amendment Act went through later that year and

281

National Vigilance Committees were set up to make sure it was enforced. But the sentences passed on the real offenders were ludicrously light. Still, the Act has worked well enough.'

'Until now, perhaps,' said Auguste.

'Right. The National Vigilance Association had an international conference on the white slave traffic in London in ninety-nine. There were twelve countries officially represented, but not ours. Strange, when you think its own war had increased demand again. Touch of Nelson's blind eye, eh? But there was such a crackdown at the ports on both sides of the Channel after eighty-five that not much has been in evidence about any organised cross-Channel trade. You get the odd governess or dancer now, but nothing regular you can pin down.'

'It's all happening again,' observed Auguste. 'Not governesses, but housemaids again perhaps.'

Rose looked towards Auguste, but not at him, staring through him, with that feeling of satisfaction he always had as something dovetailed nicely, an instinctive feeling that the jigsaw was nearing completion.

'I'm sorry, my dear,' he said absently to Edith, the rest of the burnt toast disregarded with the kipper bones, 'your splendid roast will have to wait.'

'That's all right, Egbert,' said Edith bravely. 'I know Auguste wouldn't call you away unless it was really important. But it does seem a pity you'll miss Mr Pinpole's pork. I'd decided to try such a nice new sauce. From Mrs Marshall's cookery book, you know.' She beamed at Auguste, who managed a comradely smile, as one great chef to another.

'When this case is over,' she said diffidently, 'perhaps you'd join us one evening, Auguste?'

'That, madame, would be delightful,' he answered truthfully.

The hansom cab driver, gratified at this unusually long fare so early in the day, was all deference as they mounted, and this increased as Rose ordered 'Scotland Yard'. Under the impression that only time could prevent the avoidance of some unspeakable crime, the cab driver persuaded his horse to unusual feats of speed, a process that did not help the quiet digestion of kipper.

'If we're right, what connection could Cranton's have with the white slave traffic?'

'If it's organised, they need an organiser,' pointed out Auguste.

'Couriers,' grunted Rose. 'And where do the girls get so-called "trained" until they go across? There's a lot of ifs about this yet, Auguste. We've got to be sure this time. And we've only hours to do it with those guests leaving. I'm going to have trouble holding on to Harnet or de Castillon after tonight. I'd need some solid grounds. The Chief ain't going to be so impressed with Charles Dickens.'

'But we cannot surely seek out all this evidence today?' cried Auguste, appalled.

'We can try,' said Rose affably, setting his nose firmly forward, as if already baying after the scent. 'I'll start by trying to telephone Chesnais, if the lines aren't booked.' He paused, reflecting on the ways of the French. 'That'll put him off his Sunday dinner. And Twitch,' he added thoughtfully.

'Ah yes.' Auguste had not yet come to the second part of his new receipt for murder. 'Did you not say that you had asked the good Sergeant to make enquiries as to knife-throwing acts in circuses?'

'Fancy a fat lady, do you?'

'*Non*,' said Auguste, and explained why.

A grin spread over Rose's face. 'You and your ideas,' he said. 'Fanciful, that's what you are. Why

283

don't you produce a nice idea on how we can find out about fallen women at eleven a.m. on Sunday morning?'

'Maisie,' answered Auguste simply, 'Maisie is on the committee of a Society for Unfortunate Women.'

Rose rapped for the driver's attention. Had he but known, they had never lost it. It was as good as driving Sherlock Holmes. 'Eaton Square,' Rose told him. 'Then the Yard.'

The morning room of Maisie's town house, where Auguste impatiently waited for his erstwhile beloved, was a compromise between his lordship's and her ladyship's taste. Hunting prints and a somewhat inferior Reynolds jostled side by side with posters of the Galaxy Theatre and photographs of her former chorus girl friends. After half an hour Maisie appeared, none too pleased at his unexpected arrival on Sunday morning.

'But Maisie, I wish to talk to you about unfortunate women,' he told her eagerly.

'I feel rather unfortunate myself at the moment, thank you,' she replied tartly. 'I haven't had breakfast.'

'It is already eleven thirty,' said Auguste firmly, following her uninvited into the breakfast room, 'and moreover, how can you employ a cook – I will not say chef – who could present food such as this?' He peered into chafing dishes critically. 'Did I not teach you—'

'Firstly,' she replied, 'it is obvious you have no children, Auguste. You would be glad of any opportunity when they're away, as mine are this week, to sleep all day if you wish. Secondly,' she waggled her finger, 'one does not criticise cooks if you want them to stay. It is obvious you have never run a household, me old chum.'

'Ah, and will never do so,' he said wistfully.

'Oh, I don't know,' replied Maisie cheerfully. 'Never

give up hope. You never know who may come along.'

'You know very well there is only one for me – after you,' he added hastily, 'and Tatiana is beyond my reach for ever.'

'Have a muffin,' she suggested practically. 'And tell me all about unfortunate women instead.'

He explained briefly, for the background she knew.

'Sounds like one of your recipes, Auguste. A little rich on reading the ingredients, but best to reserve judgment till you taste it. So you think it may be all about white slaves, eh?'

'Sent abroad in groups, the real reason probably disguised by something else. And in this case, because of that print dress, probably as housemaids.'

'I wonder. It's possible, provided they were ostensibly being escorted from and to a respectable agency. France is our main stumbling block, of course, on white-slaving,' said Maisie scathingly. 'It's their insistence on regulated prostitution that opened a gateway again for it. You can see why. Lawful houses make illegal supply more difficult to spot. The French have agreed there's a link now, but too late. It's spread outside. France to Belgium and Amsterdam, and the organisation is too strong to break and too clever. Girls are being sent over to Hungary, and the rest of Eastern Europe, linking up with the Chinese trade. And Africa now of course.'

'All organised from Paris?'

'I'll try to find out.'

'Quickly, please, Maisie.'

'And where are they kept here, till they're taken abroad?' asked Maisie. 'Any ideas?'

'As you say, it must be somewhere so very respectable so that no one would think of questioning it,' said Auguste. He called forth the assistance of his wildest flights of imagination to illustrate his point. 'More respectable even than a school for housemaids. Like a school of cookery for instance.'

Maisie laughed. 'Mrs Marshall's perhaps?' she suggested mockingly. 'Or perhaps you prefer Mrs Crosby's Training School for Embassy Staff?'

'Embassy staff?' Auguste looked startled. 'What is that?'

'It's a school in Battersea. Haven't you heard of it? Does a lot of good work, training girls up from bad beginnings and fitting them for work in diplomatic households, according to capability. Housemaids to office workers and translators. They all learn languages. She takes girls from the slums, or from those who've been picked up soliciting outside the Empire or music halls. She finds many of her girls from Marlborough Street—'

'*Marlborough*?' croaked Auguste.

'Why are you sitting there with your mouth wide open like a carp *au Didier*?' she enquired rudely. 'Surely the Great Detective has heard of Great Marlborough Street? It's a police court,' she explained kindly.

Auguste sighed. 'Put on your hat, Maisie. I think there is work to do. Quickly.'

'Haven't you forgotten something?'

'Luncheon? *Ah, non*. Do not fear, we will eat—'

'Not that, Auguste,' she said patiently. 'The information you wanted. I've a friend in the *Union internationale des amies de la jeune fille*.'

'She too will be at luncheon,' murmured Auguste. Never had he resented that grand moment of the day more.

The hours of twelve o'clock to two o'clock were hardly in accordance with a day of rest for either of them. Maisie was the more fortunate since her role was merely to change her attire to one she deemed appropriate for the head of a committee for fallen women, travel to Scotland Yard and contact her friend via Egbert Rose, Inspecteur Chesnais and the London to Paris telephone link.

Sergeant Stitch, fervently agreeing with Rose's opinion of Mr Bell's annoying device of communication, reluctantly changed his Sunday attire for that of Scotland Yard approved garb, patted two small Stitches on the head, kissed Mrs Stitch on the cheek, and with the smell of the beef roasting in the oven lingering in his nostrils, left his Clapham abode in pursuit of promotion and the No.38 omnibus.

Egbert Rose had long forgotten the untasted delights of Mr Pinpole's pork. Telegraph and telephone wires were clicking and humming, and he sat, a thin and eager spider in the midst of its web waiting for sustenance to arrive. Great Marlborough Street proved as unco-operative as Paris, presented with the demand for quick action at the one sacrosanct time of day – Sunday luncheon – but eventually Twitch was despatched to their premises and granted access to their records. What he found there almost compensated for the loss of his roast beef. One Mary White, accused of vagrancy in London's Haymarket, was released into the custody of one Mrs Crosby for corrective training. As were several other girls, noted Twitch's eager eye.

It was Auguste who faced true disaster. Confident in the expectation that at twelve fifteen a wassail bowl would be flowing in the drawing room, the dining room prepared for luncheon, and his staff moving with precision into their service positions, he strolled into the entrance hall. Something was wrong! He knew it by the very atmosphere which held nothing of pleasant anticipation of joys to come; instead it held rancour, and the sound of testy voices. He flew to the door of the drawing room; guests but no staff, a few bowls of nuts, but no wassail bowl.

On winged feet he flew to the dining room. It was cold, cheerless – and staffless. True, the tables were laid after a fashion, but here he could see a mark on a glass, there a knife laid askew. His faced paled. A god of vengeance now, he rushed to the kitchens to find chaos. White-coated figures were rushing about aimlessly, bumping into one another; some ovens stood unattended, while others had three apiece fighting over the saucepans. On the tables, uncooked vegetables vied with half-eaten pies and cold fish for space. The remains of last evening's plum puddings seemed to look stolidly and reproachfully at him with their raisin eyes. Cheese yellowing at the edges like old newspaper tumbled in a heap with leftover fowl.

'Where is John?' he enquired faintly.

'Mumps, sir,' one of the underchefs informed him in quavering voice.

'Mumps?' Auguste repeated blankly.

'He's gone home, sir.'

It was for such emergencies every true chef must be prepared. First, he must not alarm his staff by pointing out the severity of the situation. Secondly, to forewarn was to disarm.

'Monsieur,' he addressed a young apprentice grandly, 'have the goodness to request the footmen to serve drinks immediately. You, you – and you, take up a wassail bowl. I take it we do have it prepared?'

A dozen voices assured him that John had the concoction of beer, ginger, yeast and sherry prepared some days ago and that it merely awaited its hot roasted apples.

'Add another bottle of sherry,' instructed Auguste grimly. Good humour would be restored the more quickly. 'And I will announce that luncheon will be

288

served at one, and not twelve thirty.'

A good general organises his army with the objective always in view. Aim: speedy luncheon. One-third of the staff were detailed to disguising leftovers, garnishing slices of half-eaten pie; another third to preparing side dishes and salads; and for himself and his own picked band: '*Alors, mes amis, la bataille commence.*'

Four pairs of hands promptly fell on every tomato that could be found. . .

One hour later, 'the kitchen' was receiving compliments channelled through the hotelier. The *fritot* of chicken *avec purée de tomates* was superb, his spaghetti *de Nice* (tomato sauce with *herbes de Provence*), the beef *à la Rose* (tomato sauce with horseradish), the devilled game (tomato sauce with mustard and Worcester Sauce) were exquisite. But highest praise was reserved for the lamb cutlets *à la* Twelfth Night. For here the tomatoes and meat were embellished with a very special spice – a spice no kitchen should be without, Auguste fervently decided. Mrs Marshall's coralline pepper.

'I still think you're barking up the wrong tree, picking on Mrs Crosby's school,' said Maisie crossly, as her coroneted carriage complete with Auguste and Egbert Rose made its way to Battersea.

'Maisie, it fits,' said Auguste firmly.

'You make her sound like a pie crust,' she muttered. 'What am I going to tell my girls?' she added belligerently. 'That instead of rescuing them, we've been sending them down the white slavers' road?'

'Anything is better than to risk the trade continuing,' Auguste pointed out, rather obviously, which earned him no thanks.

'What sort of woman are we dealing with?' asked Rose.

'Middle-aged, severe, spare the rod and spoil the child.'

'You do not like her?' observed Auguste.

Maisie glared at him. 'I don't suppose I'd have taken to St Paul much, but I wouldn't deny he did a good job.'

The Ferns was a large house, set in its own grounds, surrounded by greenery, though not ferns. It was shaded by pine trees, damp and depressing on this Sunday afternoon. In the street outside, families were out walking for their Sunday afternoon recreation; normal life passed by. It made their mission all the more incongruous, thought Auguste, an impression strengthened when they were shown in to meet Mrs Crosby. Severe-looking indeed, but plump with it; something about her denoted an impartial and kindly charity.

'It is odd, Inspector, that Scotland Yard should be involved in the hunt for one girl,' she observed as she took the only photograph they had of Mary White. She studied it carefully and returned it. 'I do not know her, or anyone of that name,' she told them.

'In the Great Marlborough Street records it says that you do.'

She frowned and took the picture once again. 'Possibly – if you say so. Some of our girls run away. We are not successful all the time, as Her Ladyship knows.' Deferential nod to the aristocracy.

'You have records yourself, ma'am, I'm sure. I'd like to see them. No doubt you keep them carefully, seeing as how you supply girls to embassies.'

'We do indeed.' She rang a bell. 'However, you will not find her listed if she left us as soon as she arrived.'

'Why would she do that, ma'am, if you're offering such a good opportunity here?'

'I fear,' she smiled thinly, after instructing the girl

who replied to her summons, 'that you have little acquaintance with young girls of that class.'

'Perhaps not, ma'am,' said the veteran of the Ratcliffe Highway beat humbly.

'Some, I regret to say, have no desire to be reformed. They prefer a life of immediate pleasure to storing up talents for the future. The courts may release them to us, but neither we nor they have any method of enforcing their wishes. Girls,' she informed the two men, 'are deceivers. They persuade the magistrates they wish to embrace a pure life, but have no intention of doing so.'

'Very reprehensible,' agreed Rose. 'I wonder if you'd mind showing us your school, Mrs Crosby. Her Ladyship here has told us a fair bit about it. Raised my interest, as you might say.'

His interest was gratified, as they were taken round sewing rooms, empty classrooms and dormitories. 'This is Sunday, of course, Inspector. The girls have leisure now.' It didn't look much like it to Rose, with girls employed sewing heavy coarse sheets, working in the kitchens and cleaning dormitories.

'And where do your girls go, Mrs Crosby, when they're trained up to your high standard?' Rose asked blandly.

'Mostly to the Continent. We have connections all over Europe.'

'There can't be that many British embassies.'

Another thin smile. 'We supply chiefly foreign embassies, Inspector, particularly those of the smaller countries, who are eager to have English staff to gain a prestige that otherwise they could not aspire to.'

'How do your girls get to their destinations? Singly, or in groups?'

'It varies, Inspector. Sometimes I or one of my assistants take a group. Occasionally they are collected.

Now, you wished to inspect my records.' She led the way back into her office. 'My dear Inspector,' she exclaimed, 'I owe you an apology. White, Mary. She was here. You were quite right. But then, so am I.'

In the column under comments was the terse sentence: Left after two days, 18th September 1900.

'Does this mean anything to you, ma'am?' Rose exhibited a piece of the dead girl's dress.

She stared at it. 'It is an ordinary print, like the print dresses my girls wear, only this is a different design, is it not?'

'It is indeed, ma'am, and I'm most grateful for your help.'

'Not a thing I can get an arrest on,' Rose said disgustedly, as the carriage made its way back to the Yard.

'Did you notice nothing strange?' asked Auguste smugly.

'What?' Rose looked at him sharply.

'I fear that you have little acquaintance with young girls of that class,' Auguste repeated, smiling. 'Especially housemaids and the like. Every single one of those print dresses was new.'

'Once upon a time I'd have had to have gone there to get all this.' Unlike his sergeant, Rose had changed his opinion of Mr Bell as he looked with satisfaction at the record of Stitch's telephone conversation with Chesnais. Not so much a conversation, in fact, more like sheaves and sheaves of information.

'It boils down to this, Auguste. They've been doing their best in France to cut down on regulated prostitution ever since the London conference, and as a result the illegal trade is tending to move.'

'To where?'

'Brussels.'

'Ah.'

'Where,' Rose went on, 'a particularly efficient network has sprung up linking not only to East Europe, but to Africa. The Belgian police can't pin the headquarters down precisely, but they know the man that's running it. It's an East Europe-run venture, by a man called Hajo. Hungarian. There's a woman in it too, though there are no details.'

Cranton's at Christmas. Auguste began to think rapidly, as he left to return to the hotel. Hungarian? A woman? Had he once again been so easily deceived?

''E's come to give himself up, but 'e won't talk to me, sir!' Twitch was indignant.

'I want to see *you*,' Danny Nash said belligerently, his arm comfortingly round a young, shabbily-dressed girl. 'And I haven't come to give myself up. I haven't done anything.'

Rose sighed. 'It's a bad afternoon, Nash. Make it quick before I hand you over to the Sergeant. What's this about?'

'Solving your crime,' said Danny grandly. 'This is Elsie Tree. Come along, Elsie. He won't bite you.'

The girl looked unconvinced and retired behind his stalwart back.

'Elsie was a friend of Mary White. She met her at a place called The Ferns. I don't think Nancy was murdered because of the Prince of Wales at all, sir,' he said importantly. 'I know this will surprise you, but—'

'Oh no it won't,' said Rose grimly. 'Got your notebook, Sergeant?'

'Best day of the lot,' Carruthers grunted. He was in his element. This Christmas idea wasn't so bad after all, and the benefits of its being organised by a woman, particularly a Lady, were now apparent. The Shrine was only open by personal introduction to the Duke and she had obtained permission to tour No 1 London for them. True, Apsley House showed more relics of the present Duke than the one he was interested in, but nevertheless it was something to be here at all. Even if there were only a few pictures to see. He thus dismissed Velasquez, Correggio, Breughel, Reubens and Murillo among others. Yet Wellington had lived here, that was the main thing. He too had stared at that repulsive naked object by the stairway, the huge Canova statue of Napoleon. He wouldn't have liked to live with it, but if the Duke had chosen to dwell with his old enemy so close, it was all right as far as he was concerned. He contemplated Allan's painting of the Battle of Waterloo for some time.

'Of course,' he cleared his throat, taking it for granted that Dalmaine would be at his side, 'I don't suppose you're down in the West Country much?' he said offhandedly. 'Pity, otherwise you could come and see my reconstruction of Quatre Bras.'

'As a matter of fact,' said Dalmaine, his eyes carefully on the painting, 'as soon as this damned war is over, I thought of retiring there. Get married . . .' His eyes strained hopefully to Rosanna, who had not yet forgiven him. That's if he could afford it, he thought desperately. De Castillon was still hovering, quite sure he'd succumb in the end. Well, he *wasn't* so sure.

Gladys trotted happily up the staircase, chatting to the twins. She found it very strange. No one appeared to mind that she took, well, just the occasional strong liquid refreshment. Indeed, it was almost as if they approved, she thought, quite shocked.

Thomas Harbottle squeezed his wife's hand, as bored with Wellington as with Rorke's Drift, Marlborough, the Battle of Hastings and every other army manoeuvre he'd had rammed down him, all his life.

The reason he'd chosen to go into banking. Half of Eva's attraction had been that she didn't want to talk about South Africa. All the same, he wondered uneasily what was going to happen about these murders. Surely they couldn't be going to let the guests all leave, just like that?

Bella, walking sedately by her husband, was wondering much the same thing. It would be pleasant to travel without a police escort again, she thought ruefully. What a strange Christmas this had been. Most unexpected in all directions. She was not used to failure. But it was not yet too late. There was yet one more night. Should she? No, on the whole she knew what she had set out to discover, albeit unasked. Her friend would be horrified, had she known.

Marie-Paul and Thérèse Lepont were beaming, as though no such thing as murder had marred their Christmas. After all, they reasoned, with suspicion of plotting the murder of the Prince of Wales removed, what a tale they would have to tell.

And thus, on the whole well satisfied with their various lots, Lady Gincrack's Christmas party returned to Cranton's for tea.

'We cannot arrest anyone at tea time. Not in England,' Auguste pleaded feebly, arranging the walnut bread on a plate. 'And surely he will suspect?'

'Perhaps. What's he going to do about it? Can hardly go skipping out, can he?'

Tea. It was as much a ritual here as in Japan or China, thought Auguste, as one by one the guests entered the drawing room to partake in its mysteries. He remembered the pleasures of afternoon tea at Stockbery Towers, the women in their delightful tea gowns or, if gentlemen were present, in elegant dresses. The corsets would have to struggle all the harder after *his* tea. Auguste eyed the array with satisfaction. Wafer-thin sandwiches, seed cake, victoria cake, chocolate cake – how his mother would approve. She had tried in vain to make him appreciate the proper importance of tea in a day's diet.

Auguste surveyed his guests. The Harbottles, talking earnestly to themselves, wrapped in young love; Miss Guessings, clearly recovered from her indisposition; the Marquis de Castillon *and* Bella, with all the charms of maturity, and the Pembrey girls with those of youth. Madame Lepont, Mademoiselle Gonnet, Sir John Harnet, Carruthers, Dalmaine – how could one believe that murder had touched their lives so recently and so nearly?

And into this peaceful scene marched Egbert Rose and Sergeant Stitch. 'Ladies and gentlemen, if I might have your attention.'

The company looked decidedly more interested in seed cake than this pronouncement.

'Are you still in pursuit of this terrible person who wishes to have the Prince of Wales's blood?' enquired Bella interestedly.

'No, madam,' replied Rose evenly. 'That little matter is concluded now. We have Signor Fancelli in custody and he's confessed to planning to kill the Prince, and with being in conspiracy with Alfred Bowman. Nothing happened, of course, so he'll be on a light charge, fortunately for him.'

'This cake is stale,' remarked Carruthers critically.

'Dry, monsieur, it is meant to be so.'

'Yesterday's,' Carruthers maintained.

'The chef is not here,' explained Auguste, while Rose waited patiently.

'Not too good at keeping your chefs, are you, Didier? You employ a damn sight too many murderers.'

Rose maintained a straight face at Auguste's impotent fury. 'The murders had nothing to do with the plot to kill the Prince,' he explained patiently, 'except by mistake, in a way. Alfred Bowman, Fancelli's contact, was killed. Fancelli got scared when Bowman didn't turn up as arranged at Paddington early that morning, so he gave the plan up and decided he might as well take a nice safe job at the Carlton out of the way. Then Mr Didier here came along and spoiled that plan for him too.' He averted his eyes from Auguste's indignation.

'Fancelli and Bowman had a very simple plan and an effective one. The Field Marshal's train carried cooks for light refreshments. Fancelli had in mind to catch a train for Southampton early that morning, work his way on to the train, wearing his uniform so to speak, then shoot the Prince from the train. We were all looking for someone *outside* the train; we never thought of anyone on the train itself. And it might have worked, too. Fancelli could have got away in the confusion.'

'But who did the murders then?' asked Evelyn, a note of disappointment in her voice.

'And why?' added her twin querulously, annoyed that they, the two Sherlocks, should have to enquire of others.

'The murders had a quite different motive behind them,' said Rose. 'Organised crime, you might say.' His tact employed for the purpose of not upsetting young ladies was wasted.

'White slavery. Opium,' the twins offered in unison.

'Not opium, miss, so far as we know. This pair stuck to the white slaves.'

'Pair?' asked Bella sharply.

'Yes, ma'am, a man and a woman. Thérèse Lepont, I must ask you to come with me to answer questions regarding the murder of Miss Nancy Watkins.'

Her face was quite unmoved as she shrugged. 'You have proof, I presume?' she asked coldly.

'We have, madam.'

'And my male accomplice is who, Inspector?' she asked scornfully, dismissively.

'Paul-Marie Gonnet, I must ask you to accompany us to answer questions regarding the murders of Miss Mary White and Mr Alfred Bowman.'

By common consent the wassail bowl was left untouched. These traditions were all very well in their place, but enough was enough, especially of what was essentially cooked beer. Sunday or not, the vote was unanimously taken in favour of champagne. Secure in the knowledge that one more Didier-supervised meal awaited them, Cranton's guests waited for the seal to be set on their unusual Christmas. Lady Gincrack, resplendent in pink velvet, was present, as well as Edith Rose, once again in her best blue.

A curious contentment reigned, perhaps born of the knowledge that the party would soon disperse to face their own worlds again. Safe in the armchairs and sofas of Cranton's they listened to Rose's explanation of the white slave traffic of Europe and the darker side of Christmas at Cranton's.

After he'd finished, Dalmaine nodded gravely. 'I have heard of such matters,' he pontificated, with a glance at Rosanna. Before dinner, in the billiard room, Rosanna had done him the honour of accepting his proposal of marriage, and all the might of family responsibility now devolved on him. But it had settled one thing: Rosanna had declared she'd be happy to starve in a garret with him (though looking at her ornate dress, he had doubts) and so he had decided against revealing the whereabouts of a certain golden object to de Castillon. After all, he was British, and had no desire to go sailing through a metaphorical traitor's gate.

'I still don't see the Baroness running a business in fallen women,' said Bella defiantly.

'Alas, she is ruthless,' said Auguste sadly. 'Charming, but only superficially. Her husband was behind the organisation, and she ran the hotel and the staff agency as a cover with her so-called companion's help. We soon discovered that her adoption of the name Baroness von Bechlein was false – as she intended us to do, should she come under suspicion. What took us longer to realise was that the name Lepont was also false. She is by birth Thérèse Karol, born of Hungarian parents living in Belgium, hence her expertise in French, and married to a notorious trafficker in women, called Hajo. His speciality is English girls – or rather was, for now he will operate no more. The girls would arrive in Brussels assuming they were to be embassy staff and were then sent all over Europe, as would be natural, to embassies. By the time they discovered embassies had nothing to do with it, some of them sank back into their old way of life, and those that were, er, new to it, had no possibility of escape.'

'I don't think this is fit for young ladies' ears,' declared Sir John angrily.

'Oh, Guardian, I'm so glad you think murder is,' said Evelyn. 'And the Baroness, or whatever we call her now, was a murderess, wasn't she, Inspector?'

'Oh yes. She killed Nancy Watkins. But the other two, the young lady killed last November, and Alfred Bowman, were killed by her companion.'

'Poor Nancy,' observed Gladys. She had assuaged her conscience now. Those harsh unladylike words she had flung at the girl when she teased her about her little weakness could be forgiven in the light of what she,

Gladys, had suffered this Christmas.

'When did you first suspect, Mr Didier?' breathed Evelyn.

'The Baroness called him *chat*, not *chatte*, on one occasion, referring to him as her cat that scratched, your worm that turns. In France we notice such matters. It was little indeed, but later I wondered why. Either the Baroness had insufficient command of French or there was some other reason. Moreover, there was a distinct Hungarian influence in her cooking, as well as Belgian – she was particularly fond of paprika,' he announced severely. 'Or coralline pepper. And it fitted. Madame needed a "companion" for protection. The girls needed a courier.

'In November Paul-Marie Gonnet came here to take a group of girls to Belgium, one of whom was Elsie Tree. But Elsie escaped and made her way back to England and contacted a newspaper – a woman reporter, thinking she would probably take up the case more vigorously than a man. Elsie told Nancy to contact her friend Mary, to try to find out more, which she duly did. And Mary obliged, thus sealing both their fates. For Paul-Marie was on Elsie's track; she managed to escape by leaving London and going to Maidstone where she had an aunt. When she saw Mary's picture in the newspapers, she wrote to the *Examiner*, too scared to go to the London police. They sent young Master Nash to see her. It was Paul-Marie who killed Mary and of course Alfred Bowman, as well as helping Thérèse Hajo with Nancy's body – a murder they had come here prepared to commit.'

'But why kill Bowman?' asked Thomas Harbottle, bewildered, suddenly glad of the quiet life of a banker.

'To establish both his own and Madame's innocence. It could have been anyone. He chanced on Bowman simply because the room was conveniently next door.

300

His death demonstrated that his employer, to whom he is devoted, was in all likelihood innocent of murder, being in police custody at the time.'

'And where,' asked Ethel wistfully, 'did the first body go, if not into the lift?'

'You were nearly right, Miss Pembrey,' Rose told her kindly. 'Only we did not listen to you carefully enough. The body of Nancy Watkins *was* taken into the bathroom opposite, but not brought back. It was taken through the window into the empty attic room above. They are sash windows, and not very far apart for even a moderate gymnast. Into the same room he later put personal articles that would cause comment if a search was made, such as razor and strop. With his fair hair, he did not have a big problem over his beard, but it nevertheless required attention with a razor and the application of concealing creams. And of course he wore a concealing wig.'

'Just a minute,' said Carruthers, who had been puzzling over something. 'How could he lift a body out of a window?' he snorted. 'Ever tried to lift a body? Tried it in Zululand. Couldn't shift it two yards, let alone dance around in a window frame.'

'But if you had been a trapeze artist, you could have done, Colonel,' said Auguste. 'The good Sergeant Stitch checked further and found that there was indeed a Marie-Paul Gonnet, but she had died when she was three. Paul-Marie Gonnet was her twin, and survived. They came of a famous circus family, so Sergeant Stitch discovered, well known for their work on the high wire and the flying trapeze as the Flying Brothers. Paul-Marie had an accident six years ago, which left him with a permanent weakness in his foot, and no use for the high wire any more. Embittered, he went to work for Madame. He made a useful guardian and courier, for the strength in his arms remained, for all his slight figure. He was well able to shift that body, bringing it down again that night, where something very much as you suspected, Miss Pembrey, happened. They planned to move the body out but were prevented by the unfortunate presence of Danny Nash. So, thinking the chest, having been used in the game, would never be so used again as a hiding place, in went Nancy's body. Roughly the opposite reasoning applied to Alfred Bowman. It was necessary to make clear he was dead, and to demonstrate that a man had killed him. Hence the blows to his head, and later transporting his body to the chest – something no woman could do alone, certainly not slender Miss Gonnet.'

De Castillon was intrigued for once. 'How, if I may enquire, did this enterprising young man manage to climb dressed as a woman? Did his skirts not hamper him?'

'Those thick black stockings, sir. Not stockings, but a leotard. He had no masculine clothes other than that, and a pair of braces we found upstairs. He may have used those round his body, or used the rope round the trunk up there. Either way, the stiletto dagger had to be taken out of the body.'

'Why wasn't he seen, Holmes?' asked Evelyn brightly. 'It was light by the time he was shifting the body.'

'My dear Miss Watson,' Auguste could not resist addressing her, 'the windows overlook a mews. True, there is a public house and one or two commercial premises there, as well as stables, but I feel that early on Christmas morning, when Father Christmas had departed, no one would be present to wonder why gymnastics were in progress high above them.' He hummed: 'From two storeys high, he had lowered her down to the ground on his flying trapeze!'

302

'Do you recall Mr Bowman singing that song one evening? It remained in my mind, as did also the inestimable Dan Leno as a pantomime dame. When it came to Mr Bowman's murder, I suspect Gonnet approached through the window also to avoid raising suspicions if Bowman had to come to the door to unbolt it.'

'I *said* only Father Christmas could have committed this crime. We found the knobkerry up on the roof, another feat by our daring young man,' said Rose a little smugly, then noticing Auguste's crestfallen face, added hastily, 'and it was Mr Didier here cleverly worked out who it was.'

Auguste brightened. 'And the Hungarian link also. At first I thought—' He stopped abruptly.

'You thought it was *me*?' cried Bella in horror, while de Castillon stiffened. 'Oh Auguste, how could you?' she said reproachfully.

'It had to be considered, ma'am, especially with the embassy link,' Rose confessed.

Bella looked at her husband ruefully. For the first time the Marquis laughed. 'I shall have great pleasure, Inspector, in informing Monsieur le Président de la République that I am not only a murderer three times over, but a white slave trafficker.' And all he'd wanted to do was disrupt the British Empire, he thought to himself. How strange.

His wife smiled happily at him. They could return to Paris, her mission was accomplished, and Auguste had suspected nothing. It had been all her idea, and she was glad he hadn't yielded – almost glad, she amended, looking at his dark eyes and slim figure.

'I still don't understand,' said Sir John querulously, 'why the fellow kept his leotard.'

'He'd come prepared for murder,' pointed out Rose. 'Didn't come prepared to lug bodies up and down buildings, I'll be bound,' Sir John commented triumphantly.

'Then perhaps, sir,' said Auguste quietly, 'an acrobat can no more give up the accoutrements of his trade than a cook his. Can a chef be separated from his knife?'

Auguste sadly considered the results of his Christmas party. He had helped solve the murders, but at what cost? He had let Maisie down as a hotelier, his life's ambition was in ruins. He glanced at her. Dear, dear Maisie. Would she ever forgive him? She winked at him.

'Are you putting a party on next Christmas, Lady Gincrack?' asked Gladys brightly.

'Oh yes, *do*,' breathed the twins in unison, moving to the piano.

'We might spend our honeymoon here, darling,' Dalmaine cast a fond look at his bride-to-be.

'Not a bad Christmas, all in all,' ruminated Carruthers. 'You be here next Christmas, Miss Guessings?'

She grew pink with pleasure. 'I'm sure I shall, Colonel,' she declared.

'Oh the mistletoe bough, the mistletoe bough,' struck up the twins at the piano.

By eleven thirty the room was empty of all save Auguste and the footmen, busy clearing the greenery and decorations lest ill luck fall upon this place. Why bother? thought Auguste wearily. What worse could happen? The kissing bough fell to the ground with a crash. Christmas was over.

Epilogue

It was February. It was damp and cheerless. No snow-drop had dared yet flower. Auguste stood shivering on Charing Cross railway station, wondering why this twentieth century seemed even bleaker than the nine-teenth. Christmas was past, his one and only opportunity to be a hotelier was ruined. And perhaps wisely so. Never would he forsake his kitchens again.

He and Egbert had received their due reward for thwarting an attempt on the Prince of Wales's life by being summoned to Marlborough House to receive his personal thanks – and a signed photograph. Ironic. They had done nothing, a murderer had done it for them, but they could hardly tell Albert Edward this. And that was why he was here now.

'By the way,' HRH had remarked, 'you speak French, don't you?' Auguste admitted to royalty that he did.

'I thought so. You're just the fellow then. Maisie,' he told them informally, 'is meeting this relative of mine. Distant relative of course,' he said hastily. 'You can go with her.'

Since then, only three weeks ago, much had happened. The old Queen was dead, along with the nineteenth century. An era had passed, and a new era supposedly dawned. It had seemed she was immortal, but now the Prince of Wales was King; it seemed on this bleak day as if the Empire were rudderless, rushing towards an unknown future, until Edward VII could gather the reins in his hands. Dear Egbert was now Chief Inspector. Even Twitch had become Inspector Stitch at last. It seemed everything was changing, save for him, Auguste Didier. For him it was back to the school of cuisine, a procession of faces passing in and then out of his life. Would it ever be thus?

Now here he was at Charing Cross. Naturally Maisie had not yet arrived, he thought annoyed. This royal relative, however distant, was also the owner of Cranton's, she had told him casually only yesterday as she hurried back to greet her returning husband. So much for the importance she attached to Cranton's that she had not even mentioned this earlier, he thought viciously, watching young lovers kiss under the clock.

The Channel train puffed its way into the railway station, and he walked towards it helplessly. Still no sign of Her Ladyship. Whom was he looking for? How would he recognise this person whose sex he did not even know?

Doors opened, porters rushed up to first class compartments, baggage attendants and passengers milled round customs officials. He looked feverishly for signs of important passengers. They were everywhere. Where was Maisie? Whom did he seek?

A brilliant idea occurred to him. He would cry out in French for 'the visitor for Windsor Castle'.

But there was no need. Glowing even in the February chill, surrounded by swarming, jostling people, he glimpsed a face he recognised. Someone coming towards him. Hurrying. Arms outstretched. It was the Princess Maniovskaya. It was Tatiana.

MURDER AT PLUM'S
A Victorian Whodunnit
Amy Myers

Plum's in St James's Square in London, with its worn
leather armchairs and cocoon of inviting warmth providing
a refuge from the world, is the very acme of respectability.
In short, everything an English gentleman's club should be.
With one exception: excellent cuisine provided by master
chef Auguste Didier. For food is the very reason the club
first came into being – its founder believing that if men can
enjoy food together they can get on and rule the world
together. But the late Captain Plum was an incurable optimist.

The trouble really starts the day women are allowed, for the
first time, within the hallowed portals to watch the time-
honoured ceremony of Plum's Passing. A series of bizarre
incidents has already plagued the club – a rat left upon a
dining table, newspapers wantonly mutilated, death threats
made to a member, even obscene letters sent to the
doorman. And Auguste, having always maintained that
cooking and sleuthing go naturally hand in hand, is
persuaded by his friend and rival Emma Pryde to delve
once more into the realms of mystery. But murder at
Plum's? Impossible!

Abruptly, inevitably, however, Auguste's investigations with
his friend Inspector Egbert Rose of Scotland Yard turn into
a hunt for a demonically clever and ruthless killer . . .

'Reading like a cross between Hercule Poirot and Mrs
Beeton, *Murder at Plum's* provides a third outing for one of
fiction's most unusual detectives . . . This feast of
entertainment is packed with splendid late-Victorian
detail' *Evening Standard*

FICTION/CRIME   0 7472 3397 7

More Crime Fiction from Headline:

AN ECCLESIASTICAL WHODUNNIT

CLERICAL ERRORS

D. M. GREENWOOD

In the shadow of honey-coloured Medewich
Cathedral, amidst the perfect lawns of the Cathedral
Close, the diocesan office of St Manicus should have
been a peaceful if not an especially exciting place for
nineteen-year-old Julia Smith to start her first job.
Yet she has been in its precincts for less than an hour
when she stumbles on a horror of Biblical
proportions - a severed head in the Cathedral font.

And she has worked for the suave Canon Wheeler
for less than a day when she realises that the Dean
and Chapter is as riven by rivalry, ambition and
petty jealousy as the court of any Renaissance
prelate. In this jungle of intrigue a young deaconess,
Theodora Braithwaite, stands out as a lone pillar of
common sense. Taciturn but kindly, she takes Julia
under her wing, and with the assistance of Ian
Caretaker - a young man who hates Canon Wheeler
as much as he loves the Church - they attempt to
unravel the truth behind the death of a well-
meaning man, the Reverend Paul Gray, late
incumbent of Markham cum Cumbermound.

FICTION/CRIME   0 7472 3582 1

JANET LAURENCE
A DEEPE
COFFYN

A DELICIOUS CONCOCTION OF CRIME
AND CUISINE

The Society of Historical Gastronomes is
gathering for a weekend symposium on food
from the past. Darina Lisle has been asked to
cater for the occasion and has prepared a
multitude of exquisite dishes – from
salmagundis to a deepe coffyn – culled from
ancient recipe books.

But when the chairman is found stabbed to
death with a boning knife, the professional
pique of the attendant foodies takes on a more
sinister meaning. Discarded lovers, jealous
colleagues and a plagiarised author have
good reason to resent the victim's success.
Darina, too, is under suspicion and
determines to clear her name by revealing the
murderer's true identity.

'Darina's debut performance is immediately
appealing; she should return soon'
Financial Times

Don t miss Janet Laurence's A TASTY WAY
TO DIE and HOTEL MORGUE, featuring
Darina Lisle and available from Headline:
'Filled with mouth-watering recipes as well as
mystery' *Sunday Express*

FICTION/CRIME   0 7472 3772 7

A selection of bestsellers from Headline

MONSIEUR PAMPLEMOUSSE STANDS FIRM	Michael Bond	£4.50 ☐
THE CAT WHO MOVED A MOUNTAIN	Lilian Jackson Braun	£4.50 ☐
BURY HIM KINDLY	Pat Burden	£3.99 ☐
A DRINK OF DEADLY WINE	Kate Charles	£4.99 ☐
THE PRINCE OF DARKNESS	P C Doherty	£4.50 ☐
DEATH OF A DUCHESS	Elizabeth Eyre	£4.50 ☐
A SEASON FOR MURDER	Ann Granger	£4.50 ☐
UNHOLY GHOSTS	D M Greenwood	£4.50 ☐
THE OLD CONTEMPTIBLES	Martha Grimes	£4.99 ☐
THE HOUSE OF THE RED SLAYER	Paul Harding	£4.50 ☐
HOTEL MORGUE	Janet Laurence	£4.99 ☐
HOLIDAY WITH VIOLENCE	Ellis Peters	£4.99 ☐

All Headline books are available at your local bookshop or newsagent, or can be ordered direct from the publisher. Just tick the titles you want and fill in the form below. Prices and availability subject to change without notice.

Headline Book Publishing PLC, Cash Sales Department, Bookpoint, 3 Milton Park, Abingdon, OXON, OX14 4TD, UK. If you have a credit card you may order by telephone — 0235 831700.

Please enclose a cheque or postal order made payable to Bookpoint Ltd to the value of the cover price and allow the following for postage and packing:

UK & BFPO: £1.00 for the first book, 50p for the second book and 30p for each additional book ordered up to a maximum charge of £3.00.

OVERSEAS & EIRE: £2.00 for the first book, £1.00 for the second book and 50p for each additional book.

Name ....

Address ....

....

....

If you would prefer to pay by credit card, please complete:
Please debit my Visa/Access/Diner's Card/American Express (delete as applicable) card no:

Signature ....Expiry Date .....